Deborah Morgan se[...] slinger to pick up her son's body in ''Mrs. Crawford's Odyssey'' . . .

Luke Short questions the relationship between law and justice in ''Pull Your Freight!'' . . .

Two men named Hickok and Cody meet on a railroad car—and share philosophical musings—in **Joe R. Lansdale**'s ''Trains Not Taken'' . . .

. . . plus 15 more outstanding stories of the American West in . . .

The Best of the American West

THE BEST OF THE AMERICAN WEST

—

Outstanding Frontier Fiction by
Louis L'Amour, Loren D. Estleman,
Richard Matheson, Luke Short
and many others

EDITED BY
Ed Gorman
and Martin H. Greenberg

BERKLEY BOOKS, NEW YORK

THE BEST OF THE AMERICAN WEST

A Berkley Book / published by arrangement with
Tekno Books and Ed Gorman

PRINTING HISTORY
Berkley edition / September 1998

The Penguin Putnam Inc. World Wide Web site address is
http://www.penguinputnam.com

ISBN: 0-425-16508-6

BERKLEY®
Berkley Books are published by The Berkley Publishing Group,
a member of Penguin Putnam Inc.,
375 Hudson Street, New York, New York 10014.
BERKLEY and the "B" design
are trademarks belonging to Berkley Publishing Corporation.

PRINTED IN THE UNITED STATES OF AMERICA

10 9 8 7 6 5 4 3 2 1

CONTENTS

—

AUTHOR NOTES

—

In the last few years, **Joe R. Lansdale** has won a wide following for his Hap Collin and Leonard Pine novels which, while serio-comic contemporary crime tales, also have a flavor of the Western about them. The story in this collection is one of the best ever written in the Western genre, a melancholy tale that offers us an entirely different look at a famous Western icon.

Loren Estleman is generally acknowledged to be the leading Western writer of his generation. "The Alchemist" is a title that might fit its creator, for Estleman is able to turn the dross of history into dazzling fiction. His crime novels, especially those featuring Amos Walker, are just as good as his Westerns.

Marcia Muller's name is invariably followed with the phrase "the mother of the female private eye novel." And while that's true, Marcia has written various kinds of fiction, both criminal and Western, and has excelled at her chosen form virtually every time out. "Sisters" is a particularly good story, and shows off both Marcia's stylist gifts and her great good heart.

Bill Pronzini has created a number of memorable crime series protagonists; the longest-lived is his deservedly famous "Nameless Detective." Yet he has always been slighted as a Western writer, despite his book *The Hangings* being one of the most unique and memorable novels of the past decade. Here is another example of Pronzini's finesse with the Western form.

L. J. Washburn has distinguished herself in both the Western and the crime genres. Her Hallam series, in fact, has fused the two genres neatly and ably. They detailed the life of movie-making back in the silent days, and the sub-culture of real-life cowboys who came to Hollywood to make a living after the wide-open prairie became fenced in.

James Reasoner is the pro's pro. He has worked in virtually every field of popular fiction and done exceedingly well in all of them. His private-eye novel *Texas Wind* is a true cult classic, and he has authored at least a dozen short stories that will stand any test time (or taste) cares to put up to them.

W. W. Lee is another writer who works in both the Western and crime fields. Wendi has a light, graceful touch with her prose and a sure feel for her characters. She always tries to bring something different to each piece she writes, whether that's a little-known historical fact, or a character you've never seen before.

Arthur Winfield Knight has chronicled the Beat generation, written poetry, crime fiction, Western fiction, and literary fiction. He brings his own sensibility and style to whatever the piece is. He seems especially at home with Western fiction, where he is fond of exploding some of our most cherished myths about frontier life.

Deborah Morgan is just beginning a career that looks to be long and notable. She is exceptionally good with characters, and has a real feel for historical settings, giving them a truth that makes them come alive for readers. One looks forward to her first novel.

Michael Stotter is a young Englishman who has written a number of Western novels, including the powerful *Mc-Kimmey's Revenge*, that have earned favorable notice on both sides of the Atlantic. To date, though, " 'Til Death" is his most accomplished piece of work, a quiet but powerful piece about immigrant America. He's an author who just gets better every time out.

Spur-award winner **Judy Alter** is one of the leading Western writers in contemporary America. Her prose is subtle and supple and her ideas fresh and first-rate. She brings not only a Western elegance but also a Western honesty to her material, producing a number of stories that would please literary as well as genre readers. Here's one of her best.

Brian Garfield is probably best known for his novel *Death Wish*, through he has written first-rate novels in a number of fields, most notably in the Western genre. His work is not only historically authentic but emotionally authentic as well. His characters are frequently offbeat, not the stereotypes you find in a lot of Western fiction. Here is a good example of his work.

Robert J. Randisi is one of those writers who gets better with each book. Recently, he has concentrated on dark suspense novels that have been received enthusiastically by readers and critics alike. But he has not forsaken the Western field, as this very polished tale indicates.

Luke Short was one of the true originals, and true masters, of the Western novel and short story. His books are filled with the details of everyday life on the American frontier, and his characters are made all the more real for these details. While there are gunslingers and lawmen in his stories, to be sure, there are also dentists, blacksmiths, and grocery store owners. His is a true portrait of the true West.

Richard Matheson, author of such classics as "Duel" and *I Am Legend*, has had not only a legendary career but a legendary influence on the next generations of writers who grew up reading his books and stories. Stephen King has said that Matheson was his primary early influence. As this is being written, Ridley Scott will direct the third version of *I Am Legend*.

John Lee Gray is a writer with a powerful voice that deserves to be heard. His Western stories are direct slices-of-life of the

West, so accurate and detailed that you just seem to fall right into them, and straight into the past.

Louis L'Amour was the all-time bestselling champion of Western fiction. At one time, his books outsold virtually every other author on the planet. He worked the traditional vein of Western fiction, the kind that proved so popular at Saturday matinees and on early television. He also wrote some exceptional and memorable short stories, of which the piece included here is a prime example.

Wolf Moon was nominated as best paperback original when it was first published. One European critic said, "If Humphrey Bogart had ever made a Western, this would have been it. **Ed Gorman** has created a perfect fusion of authentic Western story and hard-boiled *film noir*. Bogie would have loved it."

INTRODUCTION

—

Elmore Leonard once noted that he grew up watching Western movies, and they were his inspiration to write Western stories and novels.

Just about everybody in this treasury grew up watching Western movies and it's interesting to note the influences of film on the writing found in this collection. Some writers prefer the bold strokes of the action movie, while others are more comfortable with the subtler shades of the psychological Western that came into vogue in the movies of the 1950s, and dominated television well into the mid-1960s.

The other major difference among these stories is the way the different writers treat the myth of the West. Some writers want to disabuse you of certain accepted but untrue "truths" about the old West; other writers are happy to leave those myths intact for the sake of drama.

The death of the Western story has been announced many times in this half of the century. Fortunately, for those of us who love Western fiction, those announcements proved premature.

What follows is proof positive that the Western story is alive and well in the capable hands of men and women authors alike.

—Martin H. Greenberg

TRAINS NOT TAKEN

——

Joe R. Lansdale

Dappled sunlight danced on the Eastern side of the train. The boughs of the great cherry trees reached out along the tracks and almost touched the cars, but not quite; they had purposefully been trimmed to fall short of that.

James Butler Hickok wondered how far the rows of cherry trees went. He leaned against the window of the Pullman Car and tried to look down the track. The speed of the train, the shadows of the trees and the illness of his eyesight did not make the attempt very successful. But the dark line that filled his vision went on and on and on.

Leaning back, he felt more than just a bit awed. He was actually seeing the famous Japanese cherry trees of the Western Plains; one of the Great Cherry Roads that stretched along the tracks from mid-continent to the Black Hills of the Dakotas.

Turning, he glanced at his wife. She was sleeping, her attractive, sharp-boned face marred by the pout of her mouth and the tight lines around her eyes. That look was a perpetual item she had cultivated in the last few years, and it stayed in place both awake or asleep. Once her face held nothing but laughter, vision and hope, but now it hurt him to look at her.

For a while he turned his attention back to the trees, allowing the rhythmic beat of the tracks, the overhead hiss of the fire line and the shadows of the limbs to pleasantly massage his mind into white oblivion.

1

After a while, he opened his eyes, noted that his wife had left her seat. Gone back to the sleeping car, most likely. He did not hasten to join her. He took out his pocket watch and looked at it. He had been asleep just under an hour. Both he and Mary Jane had had their breakfast early, and had decided to sit in the parlor car and watch the people pass. But they had proved disinterested in their fellow passengers and in each other, and had both fallen asleep.

Well, he did not blame her for going back to bed, though she spent a lot of time there these days. He was, and had been all morning, sorry company.

A big man with blonde goatee and mustache came down the aisle, spotted the empty seat next to Hickok and sat down. He produced a pipe and a leather pouch of tobacco, held it hopefully. "Could I trouble you for a light, sir?"

Hickok found a lucifer and lit the pipe while the man puffed.

"Thank you," the man said. "Name's Cody. Bill Cody."

"Jim Hickok."

They shook hands.

"Your first trip to the Dakotas?" Cody asked.

Hickok nodded.

"Beautiful country, Jim, beautiful. The Japanese may have been a pain in the neck in their time, but they sure know how to make a garden spot of the world. White men couldn't have grown sagebrush or tree moss in the places they've beautified."

"Quite true," Hickok said. He got out the makings and rolled himself a smoke. He did this slowly, with precision, as if the anticipation and preparation were greater than the final event. When he had rolled the cigarette to his satisfaction, he put a lucifer to it and glanced out the window. A small, attractive stone shrine, nestled among the cherry trees, whizzed past his vision.

Glancing back at Cody, Hickok said, "I take it this is not your first trip?"

"Oh no, no. I'm in politics. Something of an ambassador, guess you'd say. Necessary that I make a lot of trips this way. Cementing relationships with the Japanese, you know. To pat myself on the back a bit, friend, I'm responsible for the cherry

road being expanded into the area of the U.S. Sort of a dip-
lomatic gesture I arranged with the Japanese.''

"Do you believe there will be more war?"

"Uncertain. But with the Sioux and the Cheyenne forming
up again, I figure the yellows and the whites are going to be
pretty busy with the reds. Especially after last week.''

"Last week?"

"You haven't heard?''

Hickok shook his head.

"The Sioux and some Cheyenne under Crazy Horse and
Sitting Bull wiped out General Custer and the Japanese General Miyamoto Yoshii.''

"The whole command?"

"To the man. U.S. Cavalry and Samurai alike.''

"My God!"

"Terrible. But I think it's the last rise for the red man, and
not to sound ghoulish, friend, but I believe this will further
cement Japanese and American relationships. A good thing,
considering a number of miners in Cherrywood, both white
and yellow have found gold. In a case like that, it's good to
have a common enemy.''

"I didn't know that either.''

"Soon the whole continent will know, and there will be a
scrambling to Cherrywood the likes you've never seen.''

Hickok rubbed his eyes. Blast the things. His sight was good
in the dark or in shadowed areas, but direct sunlight stabbed
them like needles.

At the moment Hickok uncovered his eyes and glanced toward the shadowed comfort of the aisle, a slightly overweight
woman came down it tugging on the ear of a little boy in short
pants. "John Luther Jones," she said, "I've told you time and
again to leave the Engineer alone. Not to ask so many questions." She pulled the boy on.

Cody looked at Hickok, said softly: "I've never seen a little
boy that loves trains as much as that one. He's always trying
to go up front and his mother is on him all the time. She must
have whipped his little butt three times yesterday. Actually, I
don't think the Engineer minds the boy.''

Hickok started to smile, but his attention was drawn to an

attractive woman who was following not far behind mother
and son. In Dime Novels she would have been classified "a
vision." Health lived on her heart-shaped face as surely as ill-
content lived on that of his wife. Her hair was wheat-ripe yellow and her eyes were as green as the leaves of a spring-fresh
tree. She was sleek in blue and white calico with a thick, black
Japanese cloth belt gathered about her slim waist. All the joy
of the world was in her motion, and Hickok did not want to
look at her and compare her to his wife, but he did not want
to lose sight of her either, and it was with near embarrassment
that he turned his head and watched her pass until the joyful
swing of her hips waved him goodbye, passing out of sight
into the next car of the train.

When Hickok settled back in his seat, feeling somewhat
worn under the collar, he noted that Cody was smiling at him.

"Kind of catches the eye, does she not?" Cody said. "My
wife, Louisa, noticed me noticing the young thing yesterday,
and she has since developed the irritating habit of waving her
new Japanese fan in front of my face 'accidently', when she
passes."

"You've seen her a lot?"

"Believe she has a sleeping car above the next parlor car.
I think about that sleeping car a bunch. Every man on this
train that's seen her, probably thinks about that sleeping car a
bunch."

"Probably so."

"You single?"

"No."

"Ah, something of a pain sometimes, is it not? Well, friend,
must get back to the wife, least she think I'm chasing the
sweet, young thing. And if the Old Woman were not on this
trip, I just might be."

Cody got up, and with a handshake and a politician wave,
strode up the aisle and was gone.

Hickok turned to look out the window again, squinting
somewhat to comfort his eyes. He actually saw little. His vision was turned inward. He thought about the girl. He had
been more than a bit infatuated with her looks. For the first
time in his life, infidelity truly crossed his mind.

Not since he had married Mary Jane and become a clerk, had he actually thought of trespassing on their marriage agreement. But as of late the mere sight of her was like a wound with salt in it.

After rolling and smoking another cigarette, Hickok rose and walked back toward his sleeping car, imagining that it was not his pinch-faced wife he was returning to, but the blonde girl and her sexual heaven. He imagined that she was a young girl on her first solo outing. Going out West to meet the man of her dreams. Probably had a father who worked as a military officer at the fort outside of Cherrywood, and now that Japanese and American relations had solidified considerably, she had been called to join him. Perhaps the woman with the child was her mother and the boy her brother.

He carried on this pretty fantasy until he reached the sleeping car and found his cabin. When he went inside, he found that Mary Jane was still sleeping.

She lay tossed out on the bunk with her arm thrown across her eyes. Her sour, puckering lips had not lost their bitterness. They projected upwards like the mouth of an active volcano about to spew. She had taken off her clothes and laid them neatly over the back of a chair, and her somewhat angular body was visible because the sheet she had pulled over herself had fallen half off and lay draped only over her right leg and the edge of the bunk. Hickok noted that the glass decanter of whiskey on the little table was less than half full. As of this morning only a drink or two had been missing. She had taken more than enough to fall comfortably back to sleep again, another habit of near recent vintage.

He let his eyes roam over her, looking for something that would stir old feelings—not sexual but loving. Her dark hair curled around her neck. Her shoulders, sharp as Army sabres, were her next most obvious feature. The light through the windows made the little freckles on her alabaster skin look like some sort of pox. The waist and hips that used to excite him still looked wasp-thin, but the sensuality and lividness of her flesh had disappeared. She was just thin from not eating enough. Whisky was now often her breakfast, lunch and supper.

A tinge of sadness crept into Hickok as he looked at this angry, alcoholic lady with a life and a husband that had not lived up to her romantic and wealthy dreams. In the last two years she had lost her hope and her heart, and the bottle had become her lifeblood. Her faith in him had died, along with the little girl look in her once-bright eyes.

Well, he had had his dreams too. Some of them a bit wild perhaps, but they had dreamed him through the dullness of a Kansas clerkery that had paid the dues of the flesh but not of the mind.

Pouring himself a shot from the decanter, he sat on the wall bench and looked at his wife some more. When he got tired of that, he put his hand on the bench, but found a book instead of wood. He picked it up and looked at it. It was titled: *Down the Whiskey River Blue*, by Edward Zane Carroll Judson.

Hickok placed his drink beside him and thumbed through the book. It did not do much for him. As were all of Judson's novels, it was a sensitive and overly poetic portrayal of life in our times. It was in a word, boring. Or perhaps he did not like it because his wife liked it so much. Or because she made certain that he knew the Dime Novels he read by Sam Clemens and the verse by Walt Whitman were trash and doggerel. She was the sensitive one, she said. She stuck to Judson and poets like John Wallace Crawford and Cincinnatus Hiner.

Well, she could have them.

Hickok put the book down and glanced at his wife. This trip had not worked out. They had designed it to remold what had been lost, but no effort had been expended on her part that he could see. He tried to feel guilty, conclude that he too had not pushed the matter, but that simply was not true. She had turned him into bad company with her sourness. When they had started out he had mined for their old love like a frantic prospector looking for color in a vein he knew was long mined out.

Finishing his drink, and placing the book behind his head for a pillow, Hickok threw his feet up on the long bench and stretched out, long fingered hands meshed over his eyes. He found the weight of his discontent was more able than Morpheus to bring sleep.

• • •

When he awoke, it was because his wife was running a finger along the edge of his cheek, tracing his jawbone with it. He looked up into her smiling face, and for a moment he thought he had dreamed all the bad times and that things were fine and as they should be; imagined that time had not put a weight on their marriage and that it was shortly after their wedding when they were very much on fire with each other. But the rumble of the train assured him that this was not the case, and that time had indeed passed. The moment of their marriage was far behind.

Mary Jane smiled at him, and for a moment the smile held all of her lost hopes and dreams. He smiled back at her. At that moment he wished deeply that they had had children. But it had never worked. One of them had a flaw and no children came from their couplings.

She bent to kiss him and it was a warm kiss that tingled him all over. In that moment he wanted nothing but their marriage and for it to be good. He even forgot the young girl he had seen while talking to Cody.

They did not make love, though he hoped they would. But she kissed him deeply several times and said that after bath and dinner they would go to bed. It would be like old times. When they often performed the ceremony of pleasure.

After the Cherokee porter had filled their tub with water, and after she had bathed and he had bathed in the dregs of her bath and they had toweled themselves dry, they laughed while they dressed. He kissed her and she kissed him back, their bodies pushed together in familiar ritual, but the ritual was not consummated. Mary Jane would have nothing of that. ''After dinner,'' she said. ''Like old times.''

''Like old times,'' he said.

Arm in arm they went to the dining car, dressed to the hilt and smiling. They paid their dollar and were conducted to their table where they were offered a drink to begin the meal. As if to suggest hope for later, he denied one, but Mary Jane did not follow his lead. She had one, then another.

When she was on her third drink and dinner was in the

process of being served, the blonde girl with the sunshine smile came in and sat not three tables down from them. She sat with the matronly woman and the little boy who loved trains. He found he could not take his eyes off the young lovely.

"Are you thinking about something?" Mary Jane asked.

"No, not really. Mind was wandering," he said. He smiled at her and saw that her eyes were a trifle shiny with drunkenness.

They ate in near silence and Mary Jane drank two more whiskies.

When they went back to the cabin, she was leaning on him and his heart had fallen. He knew the signs.

They went into their cabin and he hoped she was not as far along in drunkenness as he thought. She kissed him and made movements against his body with hers. He felt desire.

She went to the bed and undressed, and he undressed by the bench seat and placed his clothes there. He turned down the lamp and climbed into bed with her.

She had fallen asleep. Her breath came out in alcoholic snores. There would be no lovemaking tonight.

He lay there for a while and thought of nothing. Then he got up, dressed, went into the cars to look for some diversion, a poker game perhaps.

No poker game was to be found and no face offered any friendly summons to him. He found a place to sit in the parlor car where the overhead lamp was turned down and there was no one sitting nearby. He got out the makings, rolled himself a smoke, and was putting a lucifer to it when Cody fell into the seat across from him. Cody had his pipe like before. "You'd think I'd have found some lucifers of my own by now, wouldn't you?"

Hickok thought just that, but he offered his still burning light to Cody. Cody bent forward and puffed flame into his packed pipe. When it was lit he sat back and said, "I thought you had turned in early. I saw you leave the dining car."

"I didn't see you."

"You were not looking in my direction. I was nearby."

Hickok understood what Cody was implying, but he did not acknowledge. He smoked his cigarette furiously.

"She is quite lovely," Cody said.

"I guess I made a fool out of myself looking at her. She is half my age."

"I meant your wife, but yes, the girl is a beauty. And she has a way with her eyes, don't you think?"

Hickok grunted agreement. He felt like a school boy who had been caught looking up the teacher's dress.

"I was looking too," Cody said cheerfully. "You see, I don't care for my wife much. You?"

"I want to, but she is not making it easy. We're like two trains on different tracks. We pass close enough to wave, but never close enough to touch."

"My God, friend, but you are a poet."

"I didn't mean to be."

"Well, mean to. I could use a bit of color and poetry in my life."

"An ambassador is more colorful than a clerk."

"An ambassador is little more than a clerk who travels. Maybe it's not so bad, but I just don't feel tailored to it."

"Then we are both cut from the wrong cloth, Cody."

Hickok finished his cigarette and looked out into the night. The shapes of the cherry trees flew by, looked like multi-armed men waving gentle goodbyes.

"It seems I have done nothing with my life," Hickok said after a while, and he did not look at Cody when he said it. He continued to watch the night and the trees. "Today when you told me about Custer and Yoshii, I did not feel sadness. Surprise, but not sadness. Now I know why. I envy them. Not their death, but their glory. A hundred years from now, probably more, they will be remembered. I will be forgotten a month after my passing—if it takes that long."

Cody reached over and opened a window. The wind felt cool and comfortable. He tapped his pipe on the outside of the train. Sparks flew from it and blew down the length of the cars like fireflies in a blizzard. Cody left the window open, returned his pipe to his pocket.

"You know," Cody said, "I wanted to go out West during the Japanese Wars: the time the Japanese were trying to push down into Colorado on account of the gold we'd found there, and on account of we'd taken the place away from them back when it was part of New Japan. I was young then and I should have gone. I wanted to be a soldier. I might have been a great scout, or a buffalo hunter had my life gone different then."

"Do you sometimes wonder that your dreams are your real life, Cody? That if you hope for them enough they become solid? Maybe our dreams are our trains not taken."

"Come again."

"Our possible futures. The things we might have done had we just edged our lives another way."

"I hadn't thought much about it actually, but I like the sound of it."

"Will you laugh if I tell you my dream?"

"How could I? I've just told you mine."

"I dream that I'm a gunman—and with these light-sensitive eyes that's a joke. But that's what I am. One of those long haired shootists like in the Dime Novels, or that real life fellow Wild Jack McCall. I even dream of lying facedown on a card table, my pistol career ended by some skulking knave who didn't have the guts to face me and so shot me from behind. It's a good dream, even with the death, because I am remembered, like those soldiers who died at The Little Big Horn. It's such a strong dream I like to believe that it is actually happening somewhere, and that I am that man that I would rather be."

"I think I understand you, friend. I even envy Morse and these damn trains; him and his telegraph and '*pulsating energy*.' Those discoveries will make him live forever. Every time a message is flashed across the country or a train bullets along on the crackling power of its fire line, it's like thousands of people crying his name."

"Sometimes—a lot of the time—I just wish that for once I could live a dream."

They sat in silence. The night and the shadowed limbs of the cherry trees fled by, occasionally mixed with the staggered light of the moon and the stars.

Finally Cody said, "To bed. Cherrywood is an early stop."
He opened his pocket watch and looked at it. "Less than four
hours. The wife will awake and call out the Cavalry if I'm not
there."

As Cody stood, Hickok said, "I have something for you."
He handed Cody a handful of lucifers.

Cody smiled. "Next time we meet, friend, perhaps I will
have my own." As he stepped into the aisle he said, "I've
enjoyed our little talk."

"So have I," Hickok said. "I don't feel any happier, but I
feel less lonesome."

"Maybe that's the best we can do."

Hickok went back to his cabin but did not try to be overly
quiet. There was no need. Mary Jane, when drunk, slept like
an anvil.

He slipped out of his clothes and crawled into bed. Lay there
feeling the warmth of his wife's shoulder and hip; smelling
the alcoholic aroma of her breath. He could remember a
time when they could not crawl into bed together without touching
and expressing their love. Now he did not want to touch her
and he did not want to be touched by her. He could not remember the last time she had bothered to tell him she loved
him, and he could not remember the last time he had said it
and it was not partly a lie.

Earlier, before dinner, the old good times had been recalled
and for a few moments he adored her. Now he lay beside her
feeling anger. Anger because she would not try. Or could not
try. Anger because he was always the one to try, the one to
apologize, even when he felt he was not wrong. Trains on a
different track going opposite directions, passing fast in the
night, going nowhere really. That was them.

Closing his eyes, he fell asleep instantly and dreamed of the
blonde lovely in blue and white calico with a thick, black
Japanese belt. He dreamed of her without the calico, lying here
beside him white-skinned and soft and passionate and all the
things his wife was not.

Goodbye, Little Pretty, he thought. I will think and dream
of you often.

Suddenly he realized that his cheeks were wet with tears.

God, but he was unhappy and lonely. He wondered if behind her smiles the young girl might be lonely too.

He stood and walked toward the light even as the porter reached to turn it out.

"Excuse me," Hickok said to the man. "I'd like to get off here."

The porter blinked. "Yes sir, but the schedule only calls for three."

"I have a ticket for Cherrywood, but I've changed my mind, I'd like to get off here."

"As you wish, sir." The porter turned up the lamp. "Best hurry, the train's starting. Watch your step. Uh, any luggage?"

"None."

Briskly, Hickok stepped down the steps and into the night. The three he had followed were gone. He strained his eyes and saw between a path of cherry trees that they were walking toward the lights of the rail station.

He turned back to the train. The porter had turned out the light and was no longer visible. The train sang its song. On the roof he saw a ripple of blue-white fulmination jump along the metal fire line. Then the train made a sound like a boiling tea pot and began to move.

For a moment he thought of his wife lying there in their cabin. He thought of her waking in Cherrywood and not finding him there. He did not know what she would do, nor did he know what he would do.

Perhaps the blonde girl would have nothing to do with him. Or maybe, he thought suddenly, she is married or has a sweetheart already.

No matter. It was the ambition of her that had lifted him out of the old funeral pyre, and like a phoenix fresh from the flames, he intended to stretch his wings and soar.

The train gained momentum, lashed shadows by him. He turned his back on it and looked through the cherrywood path. The three had reached the rail station and had gone inside.

Straightening his collar and buttoning his jacket, he walked toward the station and the pretty blonde girl with a face like a hopeful heart.

THE ALCHEMIST

— ◆ —

Loren D. Estleman

Part 1
The Visit of the Long Man

The long man smelled like a French king.

The scent, heavy with crushed violets and lime water and
oil of oleander, was his principal distinguishing feature after
his great height, which compelled him to bow his head to clear
the lintel and afterward stand with shoulders rounded and his
hat off to avoid colliding with the objects that hung from the
beams. The hat was a new Stetson, blocked into the Texas
pinch, with a brown leather sweatband to which clung a number of cut hairs. He had been to see Juan Morales then, and
after his haircut and shave had visited the Aztec Baths and
had his brown wool suit brushed and his white shirt boiled in
corn water and pressed with a flatiron while he soaked away
the hard crust of sweat and sand that had formed like a salt
rind during the long ride from the border. His plastered hair
was black and glossy, he wore a gringo moustache with ends
that trailed, and his thinker's face was long with sorrow. To
his vest was pinned a five-pointed star in a shield, nickel-
plated, without engraving.

He was perhaps thirty, but his soul was older than even
mine.

For a time, as I sat on my tall stool grinding yellow beetles
in a mortar, he did not speak or look in my direction, but

wandered the dim room, examining with a browser's interest
the globes, astrolabes, flaking books, and apothecary jars
crowding the plane table and shelves, the stuffed crow perched
on the lintel over the doorway, the hard varnished shell of the
armadillo suspended by rawhide from the center beam of the
ceiling. He squinted at the calligraphy on the labels attached
to the jars, trying to make out the foreign words, picked up
the skull of a prairie dog, registering surprise that it weighed
little more than air, smelled the unfamiliar odors that I myself
had ceased to smell, of dessicated herbs and she-wolf urine
and the exhalations of the athanor. He would know from instinct that these odors were as old as the building itself, per-
meating the adobe when the clay was yet damp, in the time
of the trouble with the Indians up in New Mexico two hundred
years ago. Such things cannot be manufactured.

At last he came up to where I sat before the chimney, the
table in front of me littered with retorts, iron tongs, wooden
scoops, clumps of borax, and my grandfather's bellows,
spliced and patched all over so that scarcely a square inch of
the original apparatus survived; cleared his throat loudly, and
shouted, in dreadful Spanish:

"You are the one the villagers call El Viejo?"

"I am," said I in English, without looking up from my
pestle. "It is not necessary to raise your voice. I am not deaf.
Merely old."

He blinked, but he dropped his tone. "You speak good
American for a Mexican."

"I speak good English for an Englishman. And I am not
Mexican. I am Spanish."

"I don't see the difference."

"You would if you came here from Castile with my great-
grandfather in fifteen fifty-six."

"Sorry to give offense," he said. "I'm a stranger here. They
told me in Socorro you're the man to see when things need
fixing that a doctor can't fix. I expected you'd be Indian."

His accent was not Southwestern, nor was it the high honk-
ing bray of the Yankee. He was a Southerner, and he was
genuinely apologetic; this too cannot be manufactured. I laid
aside my chore.

"I am not a shaman," I said, "although I have learned much from their society that has helped me to subsist in this country. You saw my herb garden on your way to my door. Does it impress you that I have succeeded in making things grow on this bare rock where the rain comes once in three years?"

"I know a piece about growing things. I was raised on a plantation."

"For ten years I employed Yaquis to carry soil by the basket up the naked face of the rock. Nothing grew the first five years. During the next four, the plants reached a height of a sixteenth of an inch, then turned white and died. It was then that I sought out a shaman one third my age and acquired the secret that has allowed me to harvest my own herbs for seventy-three years. I continue to employ a boy to bring water each day, and once each month to carry and spread horse manure and some other substance that he refuses to identify for anyone but another Yaqui. To know some things it is not enough even to be born in a place to generations born there. You must also share blood."

"What do you pay him with?"

"Instruction works two ways."

He nodded, as if he understood. "You've lived here better than eighty years?"

"I was born here one hundred and three years ago."

He said nothing, too polite to express disbelief.

"It is no great personal feat to live a long time," I said.

"It is for me."

I saw then that the sorrow in his face came from behind it, and that his eyes were but the surface of a subterranean pool whose depth was impossible to sound. They were the eyes of my grandfather in a painting made by my father from memory at my request upon the one hundred fourteenth anniversary of his own birth. My grandfather was slain in his ninety-eighth year by the Pueblo Indians in Santa Fe. They pierced his eyes with the lancet he used to bleed lizards and poured molten silver from his own athanor into the sockets, then threw him off a cliff. His third wife fled to this place with my father, who was then in swaddles. He was an alchemist, like his father and grandfather, who left Castile to avoid the inquisitors. We have all sought the secret of the Philosopher's Stone. What we have learned from our failures has been of greater value than what most seekers learn from their successes.

I asked the long man what had brought him so many days from Socorro.

"I ain't from Socorro. I was just riding through. I'm sheriff up in Lincoln County."

I had heard of this place, and of its troubles. I said, "I cannot help you to apprehend fugitives from your justice. It is not the kind of knowledge I possess or pursue."

"I ain't looking to find anyone. I'm looking to get rid of something."

"A sickness?"

"Dreams," he said, circling the brim of his hat through his long fingers. "I want you to stop the dreams."

Part 2
The Phantasms of the Night

The long man's name was Pat Garrett. After leaving his birthplace in Alabama he had worked as a cowhand, hunted buffalo, and tended bar in Fort Sumner in the Territory of New Mexico, where he became friendly with a young man named Billy Bonney. Bonney was small-boned and garrulous and spoke incessantly of his plans to take up ranching with a friend named Charlie Bowdre in the Staked Plains of Texas, for which enterprise they were energetically rounding up stray cattle from the big ranches in the County of Lincoln. Bonney carried a big Colt pistol and wore a wide-brimmed sombrero with an Irish-green band.

While in Fort Sumner, Bonney shot and killed a drunk named Joe Grant. A rancher named Chisum then endorsed Pat Garrett's candidacy for the post of Lincoln County sheriff with orders to arrest Bonney, but many people believed Chisum's motives had less to do with Grant than with Bonney's cattle stealing. In a December fight at a place called Stinking Springs, Pat Garrett and his posse killed Charlie Bowdre and took Bonney prisoner, but he later escaped, killing two deputies, and his recapture became a condition of Garrett's continued employment as sheriff.

Finally, in July of that year, Pat Garrett put in at Fort Sumner to ask Pete Maxwell, a mutual friend, if he had heard from Bonney. There, crouched in the dark bedroom of Maxwell's adobe house, Garrett observed a slight figure, naked to the waist and carrying a knife, enter from the next room. Maxwell grasped Garrett's thigh, whispering, "That's him!" Whereupon Pat Garrett produced his Colt pistol and fired twice at close range.

All this had taken place a year ago. In the time between, Bonney's fame had spread like black Spanish moss beyond the boundaries of Lincoln County. He was written of as far east as New York City, where newspaper accounts of his youthful exploits (he was said to be but twenty-one at the time of his death) had inspired a number of fabulists to embellish upon them between the bright paper covers of nickel novels. These found their way into the libraries of civilized homes on the Hudson River and the saddle pockets of cowboys not much older than Bonney, who mouthed the unfamiliar words by the light of campfires and lanterns from the grasslands of Nebraska, as flat as a scraping stone, to those same fluted canyons into which Bonney had fled in New Mexico to elude Pat Garrett. In death Billy Bonney had acquired both a legend and a *nombre de guerra* that he had not known in life. As Billy the Kid, his name was spoken in places whose very existence he himself had not suspected.

Pat Garrett acquired notoriety in equal measure. The body had scarcely begun to stiffen when he published a narrative bearing the daunting title *The Authentic Life of Billy the Kid: The Noted Desperado of the Southwest, Whose Deeds of Daring and Blood Made his Name a Terror in New Mexico, Arizona, and Northern Mexico*; and there made public the details of his triumph over this force of lawlessness, if not of his former friendship with it. Although the book did not sell well, Garrett's standing as Bonney's killer increased, and when two vacancies appeared on the New Mexico Territorial Council, Garrett announced his candidacy.

It was at about this time that the dreams began.

One night, arriving home weary and stinking of horse from ten days of riding in search of votes, Pat Garrett poured himself a tall whiskey and stretched his long legs toward the fire. His wife had retired hours before, and not having left home on the best of marital terms he was unwilling to wake her. The big, shabby, leather armchair was suited uniquely to his own physical irregularities, the piñon flames in the kiva fireplace were warm and danced mesmerically, and very soon he dozed. A light sleeper by trade as well as natural inclination, he started awake at the creak of a light footstep on the pine floor, or so he was certain at the time, so vivid were the details of the room and what he heard there.

"Apolinaria?" said he, raising his chin from his chest; for he thought that his wife had entered the room.

"Well, Big Casino," came a voice in response.

Pat Garrett was on his feet in an instant, clawing at his belt for a pistol scabbard that hung there no longer. Only one person in this world had ever addressed him by that name, and in his state of exhaustion Pat Garrett had forgotten that person was dead.

"Billy?"

But this time there was no response. The room was filled with shadows, much like another room he remembered in another house, and though they stirred in the crawling light from the hearth they were empty.

He knew then he had dreamt. He did not suffer physical hardship so well in his maturity as he had when he was a young man in *chaparejos*, and the quest for political support in the bunkhouses and barrios of that vast territory had proven every bit as frustrating as the hunt for Billy Bonney, with the tracks less tangible. Dissipation and strong spirits had made fissures in the walls that enclosed the present, allowing a shade from the past to slip through. He undressed and went to bed, sliding carefully between the crisp linen sheets to avoid waking Apolinaria.

"*¿Quien es?*"

Now he sat up rifle straight, and again reached for a phantom weapon. An exclamation escaped him, startling his wife awake, her hair in her eyes.

And for an instant he saw.

Saw a pale, half-naked figure, translucent in the moonlight shining through the window upon the whitewashed wall facing the bed, approaching in leather breeches only; saw the hairless cylinder of his torso and the slack jaw beneath the band of shadow covering the top half of his face; saw the prominent front teeth, as large as dove's eggs, in the mouth that opened to repeat the question:

"*¿Quien es?*"

Who is it?

Saw the blade in the intruder's hand, shining like cold fire. . . .

And then the figure was gone, evaporated in mid-stride as completely as the stain of breath upon glass.

Pat Garrett did not tell his wife about the apparition. He explained merely that he had been awakened by a nightmare whose details he could not remember. Apolinaria was Mexican and superstitious. If he told her he had seen Billy Bonney she would insist upon bringing the local padre to the house to make the sign of the cross and pronounce three long and tiresome exorcisms, and Garrett could not abide this particular padre, who considered him an infidel. He turned over, but he did not sleep for hours. Bonney had looked exactly as he had that night in Fort Sumner, and asked the very question he had had upon his lips when he died. The scene had not been so real even when Garrett had set it down for publication.

Since then, Pat Garrett had dreamt of Billy dozens of times: at home, in the gaudy and flyblown hotel rooms along the electioneering circuit, lying on the ground beside a fire, sitting upright in a day coach on the A. T. & S. F.; wherever bone-weariness overcame his fear of the phantasms of the night. Sometimes his tormentor was fully dressed in the Spanish costumes he favored, complete with the sombrero with the green band; more often he appeared as he had died, fresh from bed and holding the knife with which he intended to carve himself a piece of beef from Pete Maxwell's storeroom, unaware that soon he would be as cold as the beef. On occasion he recog-

nized Garrett, addressing him as Big Casino. Other times he
did not know him. Pat Garrett could not say which Bonney he
found more frightening, the swaggering dandy or the sleep-
fuddled lamb trotting all unknowing to slaughter. He only
knew that if the dreams continued he would soon be as mad
as those excursionists from Rhode Island who struck out across
La Journada del Muerta with heads uncovered, jet their brains
frying in the sun like tortillas.

Part 3
The Nostrum

I listened without interruption to the narrative of the long man.
He was a man on the cusp: When his account touched upon
his public life, he spoke in elongated, windy phrases, invoking
politicians' fustian; only when it became personal did he sub-
side into the broken, shambling speech of the plantation youth,
the western drifter, the laconic lawman. At these times I rather
liked him. Insofar as a man of my cloth could ever enjoy the
person of an Anglo-Saxon.

"No other words pass between you?" I asked when he fell
silent.

He shook his head. "Just them. He calls to me, or he wants
to know who I am. That's it."

"I don't suppose you've tried talking back."

"No. Maybe I'm loco, but I ain't so loco as to try talking
to a dead man."

"And yet who among us possesses the wisdom of the
dead?" I stepped down from the stool and crossed the room,
conscious that with each step I eradicated a measure of whatever belief he held that I had passed the century mark; for it
was only since my ninetieth year that I paid heed to the final
two rungs on the ladder that led from my rock to the desert
floor. From a high shelf I brought down an apothecary jar,
removed its glass lid to sniff at its contents, and replaced the
lid.

"Do you know grams?" said I.

"I sure don't."

"A teaspoon will suffice, or a quarter of a jigger if you haven't a spoon. Heat that amount over a low flame until it liquefies, then swallow it, just before retiring. The dreams should stop."

He peered at the label. "That Mexican?"

"Latin. You wouldn't understand it even if you could translate it. My people have used it as a nostrum against phantasms since before Christ."

"It smells it." He wrinkled his nose and clamped down the lid.

"Come back if the dreams continue."

"Ain't you got any more faith in your medicine than that?"

"One day it will be gone. The same is not always true of a ghost's patience."

"I don't believe in ghosts any more than I believe in God or the Devil," he said.

"Perhaps if you live to be as old as I you will not be so certain about the Devil."

"How much?" He produced a drawstring pouch from the pocket of his trousers.

"I have no need of money. The villagers provide me with food and I have no reason to leave my rock."

"What, then?"

"Bring me wisdom."

He bounced the pouch on his palm. The coins shifted and clanked. He smiled then, as slowly as shadows lengthening. "That's a stiff bargain, seeing as I got so little to spare."

"It is the only medium of exchange I honor."

"Just what kind of wisdom are you wanting?"

"You will recognize it," I said. "When the dreams stop."

He put away the pouch and tugged on his big hat. At the door he stopped and looked back. The long solemn face clouded with thought. "I'm kind of a long time paying my debts. It's a failing."

"I will be here. I am always here."

He left my shop. He remained in my thoughts.

The nostrum is but a sleeping draught, distilled of poppies and wormwood, with oil of creosote to bind. It was first composed by my great-great-grandfather, alchemical master to

King Philip II, to send that ruler to the black depths below the level where dwelt the demons that gnawed at him in the dark. In return, my clever ancestor was granted the whole of Chihuahua, of which the rock upon which stands my simple workshop is all that remains. My great-great grandfather was a quack, a mere puffer who worked his bellows to no good purpose but his own exalted station. He was drawn and quartered when his crystal failed to reveal the Armada's destruction. But his nostrum has its uses.

Part 4
The Return of the Long Man

These things I heard; for a lone village in a naked desert draws travelers as spring water draws the creatures that fly and the beasts that crawl, and wisdom is the coin of my tiny realm.

Membership in the New Mexico Territorial Council did not come to Pat Garrett. He lost in a close election after he accosted the author of a spurious letter to the *Rio Grande Republican* on the subject of his character and battered him about the head with the Colt he had used to kill Billy Bonney. (Whether this incident cost him votes or attracted them was a matter of lively discussion in certain quarters.) Disenchanted with public life, he retired to his thousand-acre ranch on the Rio Hondo, but that existence only made him restless, and in rapid succession he served as a captain with the Texas Rangers, managed a detective agency in the Panhandle, and formed the Pecos Valley Irrigation Company, tapping the liquid wealth of the artesian springs that lay beneath Roswell, New Mexico. When that palled, he ran for sheriff of Chavez County, but lost, then accepted a governor-appointed post as sheriff in Doña Ana County. He was by every account a hard man behind a star, short in his dealings with citizens and brutal with prisoners; a driven man, many said, running roughshod over his office as if something were flogging him from deep inside.

I thought that it would not be long before the long man returned to my door.

In this I was wrong. The years passed, slowly in the desert,

like gilas on their pale bellies, and for many of them I heard
nothing of Pat Garrett. Villagers and strangers came to me with
their complaints, shouting them at the top of their lungs as my
eardrums thickened. I slept at a level close to waking, I shrank
in stature, my joints swelled and pained me when the mon-
soons came. But my eyes were keen, and my mind was as a
thing honed by the wisdom that came my way in small quan-
tities, like grit on a grindstone. I felt an urgency to unlock the
key to the transmutation of base metal, an urgency unique in
my long line. I had no grandchildren, no children. The thick
and braided vine with roots in the court of Carolus Magnus
ended with me. There would be none to work the bellows
when I relinquished the handles; no hand would take up my
pestle when I set it down at last. I who now had lived in three
centuries would close a way of life that was already ancient
when the pyramids of Egypt rose from the quarries.

Clay to iron, iron to steel. The son of the boy who carried
water to my garden when first the long man came, a father
now himself, assisted me when I could not apprentice myself,
recording the long list of failures in the yellow leaves of my
notebook when I was unable to hold a pen and gathering the
coals to feed the athanor when my back would not bend. Tin
to bronze, bronze to brass. The books I had read rotted on the
shelves, like oranges that had surrendered their juices and
whose seeds were barren. Quicksilver to silver; elusive. Silver
to gold; unlikely. But if clay to iron and clay to gold, why not
iron to gold? Not for personal wealth, never that, but for the
benefit of knowledge, and of man's mastery of the natural
world. Iron to rust, rust to clay. Gold to gold. Gold did not
oxidize; of all the metals it was the only one to break the circle.
There was the lock that fit the key.

In a seizure of pique I threw my grains of ore into the fire.
They ignited, sending sparks up the flue.

"Well, you ain't no ghost, that's a fact. You told me once't
there's no end to a ghost's patience."

I started; for age and command had brought an edge to the
long man's tone that overcame my deafness. I turned my head.
Gaunt he was now, his hair and moustaches white, and the
years of stooping to hear and to be heard had rounded his

back. The long face was as brown and cracked as a dry lake-bed. His suit of clothes was smarter than the one he had worn on his first visit, and now that the railroads had come it had no need of brushing. He no longer smelled like a French king, but like harnesses that had been left in the weather. Where the nickel-plated star had been depended a platinum chain with a staghorn fob. The hat in his hand was a slouch with a four-inch brim and a wide silk band. The sorrow he wore was the same.

"The nostrum has run out," said I.

"Years and years ago. It never did stop even one dream."

"Did you follow the instructions I gave you?"

"A quarter of a jigger a night for two years. After that I switched to whiskey. That didn't stop them neither, though it did sunny up my disposition. We had us some fine talks, Billy and me."

After a time, so Pat Garrett told it, the half-naked Bonney of Fort Sumner came less often. Mostly it was Billy in his Spanish costume and green-banded sombrero, although some-times he appeared in the same caved-in black hat and heavy cable sweater he had posed in for the photograph that still circulated on cigarette cards throughout the Southwestern United States. He spoke of old times with Chisum and John Tunstall, the English rancher for whom Bonney once worked, and whose death in the Lincoln County range war had trig-gered the events that led eventually to that bedroom crawling with shadows in Fort Sumner. He spoke of dealing monte in Garrett's saloon. On occasion he brought cards, and the pair played poker until dawn, or until Pat Garrett awoke. Often the visits were quite ordinary. The thing Garrett dreaded—and be-cause he could not predict when it would happen even the ordinary visits were torturous—was the times when Bonney's amiable, slack-jawed expression would change suddenly in the middle of some folksy anecdote or while he was drawing from the deck; when his skin would grow ashen and a black band of shadow would fall across the top half of his visage, and he would shout: "*¿Quien es?*" Then there would be an explo-sion, very loud, well beyond the volume entrusted to a mere dream, and Garrett would wake up, bathed in icy sweat, his nostrils burning with the stench of sulfur and cordite. It required half of a bottle of whiskey to help him back to sleep; whereupon another dream would come, or it would not. When it came there was no determining whether it would play itself out peacefully or end in the same disturbing way.

He did not always dream. When he did not, and when the dreams were peaceful, his life the next day would go one way or the other, as do all our days. In time, however, he came to see that the death-dream, in which he killed his friend, invariably preceded a black day in his passage. He had slain Billy Bonney the night before he pistol-whipped the writer of the letter to the *Rio Grande Republican*, and subsequently lost the Territorial Council election. He was defeated for sheriff in Chavez County on a day following a night during which he had slain Billy Bonney. He had not dreamt at all before making the acquaintance of President Theodore Roosevelt, who appointed Pat Garrett a collector of customs at El Paso. During Roosevelt's second term, Garrett one night relived in ghastly detail the circumstances of Bonney's death; the next day he allowed the president to be photographed with himself and a notorious saloon-keeper, and when the matter was brought to the abstemious Roosevelt's attention, Pat Garrett lost his appointment. There were other such episodes, but the above serves to establish the pattern.

"Is it your belief that Bonney is responsible for all your misfortunes?" I asked.

"Not all. No man's lucky all the time. But the ones I brung up suit Billy's damn sense of humor down to the ground. Take that time he kilt Olinger and Bell and jumped jail. He done it to vex me as much as to keep from getting hung."

"Ghosts enjoy a joke as well as the next man."

He made no response, but shifted his weight on his big mirrored boots.

I turned up a palm. "What is it you ask of me?"

"I come down here thinking you'd have some nostrum that works where the other didn't. It's been better than twenty-five years. I reckon that makes you a hunnert and twenty-eight."

"Twenty-nine; I was born on Twelfth Night. The one I gave

you was three hundred years old. There have been no developments.''

"That tears it then. Last time I kilt Billy I got into a fight next day with one of my tenant ranchers over some goats he ran on my property. I can't abide a goat. I'm meeting him tomorrow to iron it all out, but I wanted to make sure I didn't dream about killing Billy tonight.''

"I am sorry.''

He tugged on his slouch hat with the same gesture he had used a quarter-century before. Perhaps it was this similarity that brought to his mind our words of parting on that occasion. The same gradual grin deepened the cracks in his face.

"I clean forgot to bring any of that wisdom you asked for,'' he said. "I told you I'm slow settling debts.''

"I am confident that you pay the ones that matter.''

The next day—I learned of it many months later, from a New Mexico taxidermist who tried to purchase my armadillo—Pat Garrett argued on the Las Cruces road with a tenant over goats. The long man was shot twice with a Colt pistol while sitting on his buckboard and died before he struck the earth. I do not know if the night before the encounter he dreamed of killing Billy Bonney. All things that come from clay go back to it in the end. Save gold.

SISTERS

—

Marcia Muller

The first time Lydia Whitesides saw Curious Cat looking through her kitchen window, she was more startled than frightened. She was sifting flour preparatory to making the day's bread, and had turned to see where she'd set her big wooden spoon when a face appeared above the sill. It was deeply tanned, framed by shiny black braids. The dark eyes regarded Lydia solemnly for a moment, and then the face disappeared.

Well, that's quite something, she thought. The Indians in this part of central Kansas were well known for their curiosity about the white man's ways, and Lydia had heard tell of squaws and braves who would enter settlers' homes unbidden and snoop about, but none had ever paid the Whitesides a visit. Until now.

"Thank the Lord it was a timid squaw," she murmured, and went on with her baking.

Lydia was not unfamiliar with Indians. She and her husband, Ben, operated a general store on the main street of Salina, and when she clerked there in the afternoons she traded bolts of cloth, sacks of flour and sugar, and dried fruit (but never firearms or whiskey; the Whitesides' stood firm on that point) for the pelts and furs that the Kaw tribesmen brought in. The members of this friendly tribe spent hours examining the many wares, and the women in particular displayed a fascination with white babies. Their demeanor, however, was restrained,

27

and previously Lydia had seen no evidence of the Indians' legendary boldness.

In the remaining few days of that month of April, 1866, the squaw's face appeared frequently at the kitchen window. At first she would merely stare at Lydia; then her gaze became more lively, moving about the room, stopping here and there at objects of interest. Lydia watched and waited, in much the same way she would were she attempting to tame a bird or squirrel. Finally, a week after her initial visit, the woman climbed up on the sill and dropped lightly to the kitchen floor. Lydia smiled, but made no move that would frighten her.

The squaw returned the smile tentatively and glanced about. Then she went to the nearby stove and put out a hand to touch it. Its black iron was hot, since Lydia had just finished her baking, and the woman quickly drew back her hand. She regarded the stove for a moment, then went on to the dish cupboard, drawing aside its curtain and examining the crockery. As she proceeded through the room, looking into drawers and cupboards, she barely acknowledged Lydia's presence. After some ten minutes of this, she climbed through the window and was gone.

Curious, Lydia thought, like a cat. And at that moment, in her mind, Curious Cat was named.

The next day Curious Cat returned and reexamined the kitchen. The day after that she moved boldly through the rest of the house. Lydia followed, not attempting to stop her. She had heard from other settlers that an Indian intent on snooping could not be reasoned with; to them, their behavior was not rude and intrusive, but merely friendly. Besides, Lydia was as interested in the squaw as the squaw was in the house.

Curious Cat seemed fascinated by the mantel clock; she stood before it, her head swaying, as if mesmerized by its ticking. The spinning wheel likewise enchanted her; she touched the wheel and, when it moved, pulled her hand away in surprise. She gazed for a long moment at the bed with its patchwork quilt and lace pillow covers. When she turned her eyes to Lydia, they were clouded by bewilderment. Lydia placed her hands together and tilted her head against them, eyes closed. Curious Cat nodded, the universal symbol for sleep having explained all. Before she left that morning she placed her hand on Lydia's stomach, rounded in her fourth month of pregnancy.

"You papoose?" she asked.

"Yes. Papoose in five moons."

Curious Cat beamed with pleasure and departed her usual way.

Thus began the friendship between the two women—so different that they could barely converse. Lydia did not mention Curious Cat's morning visits to her husband. Ben had spent a year in Dodge City before he had met Lydia and settled in Salina. He had arrived there in 1864, shortly after the government massacre of the Cheyenne at Sand Creek, Colorado, and had seen the dreadful Indian retaliation against the plains settlers. Murder, plundering, and destruction had been the fruits of the white man's arrogance, and on the frontier no settler was safe.

Although Ben was fully aware of the differences between the peaceable Kaw and the hostile Comanche, Cheyenne, Arapaho, and Kiowa, he had been badly scarred by his frontier experiences—so much so that he preferred Lydia or his hired clerk to wait on the Indians who came to the store. He would have been most alarmed had he known that a Kaw woman regularly visited his pregnant wife at home. Although Lydia was not afraid of her husband's anger, she held her tongue about the squaw. After all, she did not wish Ben to be troubled, nor did she intend to bar the door—or in this case, the window—to Curious Cat.

During her afternoons at the store, Lydia made discreet inquiries about Curious Cat among the squaws whose English she knew to be better than average. The woman was easy to describe because of an odd buffalo horn necklace she habitually wore. When Lydia did so, the women exchanged glances that she could only interpret as disapproving.

Finally a tall, rawboned woman who seemed to be leader of the group spoke scornfully. "That one. Cheyenne squaw of White Tail."

That explained the disapproving looks. White Tail was a

local chieftain who at times in the past had allied himself with the hostile tribes to the west. That he had taken a Cheyenne wife had further proven his renegade leanings to his people. Curious Cat undoubtedly lived a lonely existence among the Kaw—as lonely, for sure, as that which Lydia herself lived among the ladies of Salina.

It was not that the townswomen shunned her. If anything, they were exceptionally polite in their dealings, particularly when they came to trade at the Whitesides' store. But between them and Lydia there was a distance as tangible as the pane of glass that would stand between her and Curious Cat should she close the window to her. The townswomen did not mean to ostracize or hurt Lydia; they simply had no way of engaging in social intercourse with one of her background.

She had been born nearly eighteen years before to parents who traveled with a medicine show—one of the first small ragtag bands to roam the frontier, hawking their nostrums to the settlers. Her parents had performed a magic act—The Sultan and Princess Fatima—and Lydia's earliest recollections were of the swaying motion of the wagons as they moved from outpost to outpost. Even now she could close her eyes and easily conjure up the creak of their wheels, the murmur and roar of the crowds. She could see the flickering of torchlight on the canvas tent. And she could smell the sweat and greasepaint and kerosene and—after her mother died when she was only five—the whiskey.

After his wife's death, her father had taken to drink, and to gambling. After the shows he went to the saloons in the strange towns, looking for a game of faro. Often he took his young daughter with him. Lydia learned to sleep on his lap, under poker tables, anywhere—oblivious to the talk and occasional shouts and tinny piano music that went on around her. When she was nine he put her to work as Princess Fatima. She hated the whistles and catcalls and often-evil attention from the men in the crowd. Many was the time that she stumbled with weariness. But in her world one did what one had to, even a nine-year-old. And she was effective as Princess Fatima. She knew that.

Ben Whitesides had realized it, too, the first time he saw

her in Wichita, where he had drifted after leaving Dodge City. But, as he confided to her later, he had seen more than her prettiness and easy charm, had seen the goodness she hid deep inside her. In spite of the unwholesome reputation of the show people, he had courted her: for three weeks he had followed the caravan as it made its way from Wichita to Montgomery Country; at night his clean, shining face would be the first she would spy in the crowd. Lydia had her doubts about this gentle, soft-spoken young man: his fascination with her, she thought, bespoke a lack of good sense. And much as she hated her nomadic existence, it was all she had known. Much as her increasingly besotted father angered her, she loved him. But Ben persisted, and in one month more he made her his wife.

Ben Whitesides had given her a home, a respectable livelihood, the promise of a child. But he could not eradicate the loneliness of her life here in Salina. No one had been able to do that. Until now. Now there were the eagerly awaited visits from the Indian woman she had named Curious Cat.

At first the two could converse very little. Curious Cat knew some English—as most of the members of the local tribe did—but she seemed reluctant to speak it. Lydia knew a few Indian words, so one day she gave Curious Cat a piece of fresh-baked cornbread and said the word for it in Kaw. She was rewarded by an immediate softening in the other woman's eyes. The next day Curious Cat pointed questioningly at the stove. Lydia named it in English. Curious Cat repeated the word. Their mutual language lessons had begun.

In the weeks that followed, Curious Cat learned the English for every object in the house. Lydia learned words, too—whether they were Kaw or Cheyenne she wasn't certain. Curious Cat told her her name—Silent Bird—and Lydia called her by it, but since the woman was neither birdlike nor silent, she remained Curious Cat in Lydia's mind. In a short time she and her Indian friend were able to communicate simple thoughts and stories, to give one another some idea of their lives before the day Curious Cat had decided to look into the white woman's world through Lydia's kitchen window.

The first of these exchanges came about on the day after

Lydia's birthday, when she wore for the first time a soapstone brooch etched with the shape of a graceful, leafless tree—her gift from Ben. The tree, her husband said, reminded him of those he had seen on the far western plains, before fortune had brought him to her.

Curious Cat noticed the brooch immediately upon her arrival. She approached Lydia and fingered it hesitantly. The intensity of emotion in her liquid brown eyes startled Lydia; the squaw seldom betrayed her feelings. Now she seemed in pain, as if the brooch called forth some unwanted memory.

After a moment she moved away and went to see what Lydia was baking—her ritual upon arriving. Her movements were listless, however, her curiosity about what was in the oven obviously forced. Lydia motioned for her to come into the parlor and sit beside her on the settee. Curious Cat did so, placing her hands together in the lap of her faded calico skirt.

Lydia touched the brooch with her forefinger. "What is it? What is wrong?"

Curious Cat looked away, feigning interest in the spinning wheel.

"No, you must tell me."

The anguished brown eyes returned to Lydia's. "The tree . . . my home. . . ."

"The tree reminds you of where you were born, on the plains?"

Hesitation. Then a nod.

"Tell me about it."

Curious Cat's face became a battleground where emotions warred: sadness, yearning, and anger. For a moment Lydia feared that what she wanted to say would be too much for their shared rudimentary language, but then Curious Cat began to tell her story in a patchwork of broken phrases, gestures, and facial expressions that conveyed far more than the most eloquent speech.

She had been born on the far western reaches of the Great Plains, to a chieftain of one of the Cheyenne's most powerful clans. When she reached womanhood, a match had been arranged with the son of another powerful chieftain—a union that would ally the two great clans. The young man, Curious

Cat indicated, was more than agreeable. She had watched him from afar, and found him brave as well as handsome.

But then came the massacre of the Cheyenne at Sand Creek. Curious Cat's father was killed, and her brother disappeared after subsequent hostilities near Wichita. It was said among his tribesmen that he had fled, a coward. Now Curious Cat and her mother found themselves ostracized as family of a traitor, with no man to protect and provide for them. The young brave to whom Curious Cat had been promised would no longer look upon her face.

Within months Curious Cat's mother had died, broken and weakened by the struggle to survive. Curious Cat lived off the meager kindnesses people showed her. When White Tail of the Kaw traveled west hoping to strike an alliance between his tribe and the warlike Cheyenne, his eye was caught by the ragged outcast; he spoke of his interest to the chief of her clan, and it was deemed suitable that she leave as White Tail's squaw. With her departure, a shameful reminder would be removed.

Now, Curious Cat told Lydia, she lived among the Kaw much as she had among her own people. True, she had White Tail to protect her, and life was not such a struggle. But his warlike ways had made him and his family suspect, and the women kept their distance from his squaw. She was to be forever a stranger in the Kaw village.

So this, Lydia thought when Curious Cat was still, was the root of the bond she had sensed between them. They were both strangers condemned to loneliness. After a moment she told her own story to the Cheyenne woman, and when she was finished they sat silent yet at ease. The bond between them was welded strong.

The trouble began when customers at the store told Ben they had seen a squaw entering and leaving his property on a number of occasions. Ben was concerned and questioned Lydia about it. She readily admitted as much.

"The Kaw are a curious people, Ben. The squaw comes to spy. But she is harmless."

"She may very well be, but what of her tribesmen?"

"No one has come here but her."

"Still . . . they say she is a strange one. An outcast."

"And how do they know this is the woman of whom they speak?"

"The buffalo horn necklace she wears makes her recognizable. It is Cheyenne, and they *are* warlike."

Lydia pictured the necklace, which Curious Cat fingered often, as if to preserve her last link to the people who had sent her into exile. "But if she is with the Kaw, she is Cheyenne no longer."

"You cannot be sure of that. The Indians are a peculiar race; who knows what they may be thinking, or where their loyalties lie?"

Lydia was quite sure that Curious Cat's loyalties lay with no tribe, but she knew she could not explain that to Ben. She fell silent, seeking a way out of the dilemma.

Ben said, "I am only thinking of you and our child. The next time this squaw comes around, you must bar her the door."

The way out was in his words. "That I will," she agreed. Ben was unaware that Curious Cat entered and left by the window. By saying she would bar her the door, she was not actually lying to her husband.

As spring turned to summer Lydia continued to enjoy the Indian woman's companionship. Curious Cat came most mornings, cautiously so as not to come to the further attention of the townspeople. Together they baked bread, and Lydia demonstrated the uses of the spinning wheel, which was still an object of fascination for the squaw. They conversed with greater ease, and sometimes Curious Cat would sing—songs with strange words and odd melodies that somehow conveyed their meaning. Lydia reciprocated with the lullabies that she would soon sing to her child. The child quickened within her, and the days passed swiftly.

The weather turned hot and arid. No breeze cooled the flat land. From the west the news was bad: prairie fires swept out of control near Wilson and Lincoln; a sudden fierce gale had caused fire to jump the Saline River and destroy the tiny settlement of Greenport. The Indians were on the rampage again, too. Enraged by the wholesale slaughter of buffalo, the Cheyenne and Comanche attacked railroad crews and frontier settlements, plundering and murdering. Nearby Mitchell County was in a constant state of siege, and the people of Salina began to fear that the raids would soon extend east to their own territory. Of the prairie fires Lydia and Curious Cat spoke often. About the Indian raids they remained silent.

As the news from the beleaguered settlements worsened, the populace of Salina grew fearful. The Kaw, always welcomed before, were looked at askance when they came to trade at the Whitesides' store. Peaceable merchants such as Ben, who seldom handled guns, armed themselves. Women kept doors locked and rifles close to hand. The heat intensified the undercurrent of panic. Tempers grew raw; brawls and shootings in the saloons increased. During the first week in August the distant glow of prairie fire intruded on slumber.

Ben Whitesides took to returning home for his midday meal, to reassure himself of Lydia's safety now that the days of her confinement approached and she was no longer able to come to the store. She was agreeable to the arrangement, but it meant taking care that Curious Cat departed before the time Ben customarily arrived. On a stifling day in mid-August, however, she let awareness of the hour slip away from her. She and Curious Cat were taking cornbread from the oven when Ben came through the kitchen door.

Ben saw the squaw immediately. He stopped, suddenly pale, his hand on the doorknob. Curious Cat seemed frozen. Lydia herself could not move or breathe. The sweat that beaded her forehead and upper lip felt oddly cold. The hush was so great that she could hear the mantel clock ticking in the parlor.

Ben's eyes were jumpy, wild. Lydia knew he did not comprehend that he had walked in on a peaceable scene. She put out a hand to him, opened her mouth to explain.

The motion freed Curious Cat; she slipped over toward the window. Ben's glazed eyes jerked after her, and his hand moved under his coat, to where he had taken to carrying his pistol.

Curious Cat gave a guttural cry and began scrambling onto

the sill. Lydia's gaze was transfixed as Ben took out the gun. Then she heard a tearing sound and whirled. Curious Cat's skirt has caught on a nail, and she was struggling to free it. Lydia swung back toward Ben. He was leveling the pistol at the squaw.

"No, Ben!" she cried.

He paid her no mind.

"No!" Lydia flung herself at him.

Ben jerked the gun up. A shot boomed, deafeningly. The room seemed to shake, and plaster showered down from the ceiling.

Lydia crumpled to the floor and cowered there, her ears ringing. The plaster continued to rain down, stinging the skin of her arms and face. When she looked up, she saw Ben standing over her. He was staring at the gun, his whole body shaking.

"Dear God," he said in a choked voice. "Dear God, what I might have done!"

Lydia turned her head toward the window. It was empty. Curious Cat had gone.

After that day Curious Cat came no more, and a silence descended upon the Whitesides' home. A familiar but unaccustomed silence during the days as Lydia went about her household tasks alone. An unnatural silence at night, between herself and Ben.

Once his shock had abated, Ben had become angry and remained angry for days. When the anger faded, he was left with a deep sense of betrayal at Lydia's months-long deception, a hurt that shone in his eyes every time he looked at her. Lydia's pain was twofold: by lying to Ben she had put distance between them just before the birth of their child, when they should have been drawing closer than ever. And she had exposed Curious Cat, her only friend, to danger and humiliation.

During the stifling late-summer nights she lay huge and restless in the double bed, listening to Ben's deep breathing and thinking of how she had wronged him. Then her thoughts would turn to Curious Cat, and she would wonder how her friend was faring. She feared that, like Ben, the squaw thought

she had betrayed her, somehow held her responsible for the
near-shooting. But mostly she pictured Curious Cat as lonely,
exiled once again to her life among the unaccepting Kaw.

Even the now-strong movements of her unborn child failed
to cheer Lydia. She felt incapable of facing the momentous
event ahead. Not the birth itself; that was painful and dangerous, but physical ordeals had never daunted her. What she
feared was that she might not be wise enough to guide the
small and helpless life that would soon be placed in her hands.
After all, if she had so wronged her husband and her only
friend, how could she expect to do the right things for her
child?

On a brilliant September morning Curious Cat came again. She
slipped through the kitchen window and dropped to the floor
as Lydia was shelling a bushel of peas. When she saw her
Indian friend, Lydia felt her face flush with delight. But Curious Cat did not smile. She did not check the baking bread
or peer into the larder. Instead she stared at Lydia, her face
intense.

"What is it?" Lydia asked, starting to rise.

Curious Cat came to her, placed her hands on her shoulders,
and pushed her gently into the chair. She squatted on the floor
in front of her, eyes burning with determination.

"You help," she said.

"Help? Yes. of course. What . . . ?"

"You tell. Save people."

"Tell what? Who?"

Curious Cat's gaze wavered. For a moment Lydia thought
she might run off. Then she said, "Cheyenne. Many. Come
White Tail, talk war."

"War? Where?"

"Now near Shady Bend. Be here two sleeps."

Shady Bend was in Lincoln County, on the other side of the
Saline River. Two sleeps—two days—was what it would take
a war party, traveling fast, to reach Salina. "They plan to
attack *here*?"

Curious Cat nodded.

"Will White Tail join them?"

She shook her head in the negative. "White Tail grows old. Tired of war. I come tell you make ready. Save people."

"Why are you telling me? The Cheyenne are *your* people. They will be slaughtered."

Curious Cat fingered her buffalo horn necklace. Then she rose and was gone through the window.

At first Ben was skeptical of what Lydia told him.

"Why would this squaw betray her people in order to save our town?" he asked. "I fear this is a false story—some sort of retaliation for my nearly shooting her."

"I think not. Curious Cat was badly used by the Cheyenne; her loyalty is no longer with them. She is Kaw now, and her husband White Tail wants no part of this war."

Ben was watching Lydia's face, frowning. "How do you know so much about the squaw?"

"She told me."

"How could she tell you? Indians can barely speak English. And surely you cannot speak Kaw or Cheyenne."

"Curious Cat speaks English well, and I know a fair amount of her language as well. We taught one another, and we used to talk often."

Ben's face darkened. He did not like to be reminded of how the squaw had visited his house. "Perhaps you talked, but not of such important things as those. Of baking and spinning, yes. But of the squaw's loyalty to her people, or White Tail's feelings about a Cheyenne war? I think not."

Lydia felt her anger rise at his patronizing dismissal. "One does not need important-sounding words to discuss important things, Ben."

"I am only saying that it seems improbable—"

"Curious Cat and I may share a limited language, but we talked about anything we wished. And we did not hide our feelings within a cloak of silence."

Her husband looked as if he were about to make a sharp retort. Then he bit his lip, obviously understanding her reference to his recent silence. After a moment he said, "Do you really believe the squaw is telling the truth?"

"I do."

"And you are certain her loyalty no longer lies with the Cheyenne?"

"Nor with the Kaw. She feels alone in the world."

Lydia could see that Ben did not want to believe her, did not want to give up his conviction that all Indians were devious and sly. But he was a reasonable man, and after thinking for a moment he shook his head, looking ashamed. "I have placed little value on your friendship with the squaw, merely because she is of another race. Now I see what it means to you—and to her. Your Curious Cat does have loyalties, but they lie not with her people, but with you." He reached out to stroke her cheek—something he had not done since he had found Curious Cat in their kitchen.

Lydia touched his hand, knowing all was mended between them.

Of course the men of Salina were equally skeptical of the threat of Indian attack. But Ben Whitesides had the forceful qualities of a leader, and once he had assembled them, his newfound conviction in the truth of Curious Cat's story gave strength to his words. When the attack came, the town was prepared, and the Cheyenne were driven off.

In the days that followed, many of the townswomen paid stiff formal calls on Lydia, to thank her for her part in the victory. The awkwardness was dispelled, however, when talk turned to her expected child, and several of the women returned bearing small gifts for the baby. Lydia knew Salina had finally taken her in on the day when Mrs. Ellerbee, wife of the bank president, hesitantly asked if she would consider joining a new musical society the ladies were thinking of forming. And while she realized she would never take as much pleasure in the ladies' refined company as she had in the mornings she'd spent with Curious Cat, she assented readily.

Curious Cat came one last time, on a day when wintry clouds lowered overhead. Lydia was tending to her newborn son in his cradle next to the stove, and she had to raise the window, which had been shut against the chill, to admit her friend.

The squaw went immediately to the cradle. She stared at

Ben Junior for a long moment, then said, "Fine papoose.
Strong." Quickly she moved on to the stove and inspected the
bread that was browning there.

Lydia said, "I'm so glad you've come. I've wanted to thank
you—"

Curious Cat cut her short with a gesture of dismissal. She
looked around the kitchen, as if to fix it in her mind. Then she
said, "Come for goodbye."

"But there's no need! You are welcome here anytime."

The Indian woman shook her head sorrowfully. "White Tail
go north. I go with. One sleep, then go."

Lydia was overcome with a sharp sense of loss. She moved
forward, taking the other woman's hands. "But there is so
much I must say to you—"

Curious Cat shook her head again. "One sleep, then go.
Come for goodbye." Gently she disentwined her fingers from
Lydia's. Lydia knew Curious Cat was not one for touching,
so she let her go.

The Indian woman glanced at the cradle once more. "Fine
papoose. You raise him strong Brave."

"Yes, I promise I will."

Curious Cat nodded in satisfaction. Then she put her hands
to the buffalo horn necklace she still wore and lifted it over
her head. She lowered it over Lydia's curls and placed it
around her neck, smoothing the collar of her dress over it.

"White sister," she said.

Tears rose to Lydia's eyes. She blinked them away, unable
to speak. She had no parting gift, nothing so fine. . . . And then
she looked down at her bodice, secured by the soapstone
brooch etched with the tree of the prairie, Ben's birthday gift
to her. He would approve, think it fitting, too.

With fumbling fingers Lydia undid the brooch and pinned
it to the faded calico at Curious Cat's throat. "Not white sister," she said. "True sister."

McIntosh's Chute

—

Bill Pronzini

It was right after supper and we were all settled around the cookfire, smoking, none of us saying much because it was well along in the roundup and we were all dog-tired from the long days of riding and chousing cows out of brush-clogged coulees. I wasn't doing anything except taking in the night—warm Montana fall night, sky all hazed with stars, no moon to speak of. Then, of a sudden, something come streaking across all that velvet-black and silver from east to west: a ball of smoky red-orange with a long fiery tail. Everybody stirred around and commenced to gawping and pointing. But not for long. Quick as it had come, the thing was gone beyond the broken sawteeth of the Rockies.

There was a hush. Then young Poley said, "What in hell was *that*?" He was just eighteen and big for his britches in more ways than one. But that heavenly fireball had taken him down to an awed whisper.

"Comet," Cass Buckram said.

"That fire-tail . . . whooee!" Poley said. "I never seen nothing like it. Comet, eh? Well, it's the damnedest sight a man ever set eyes on."

"Damnedest sight a *button* ever set eyes on, maybe."

"I ain't a button!"

"You are from where I sit," Cass said. "Big shiny man-sized button with your threads still dangling."

Everybody laughed except Poley. Being as he was the youngest on the roundup crew, he'd taken his share of ragging since we'd left the Box 8 and he was about fed up with it. He said, "Well, what do *you* know about it, old-timer?"

That didn't faze Cass. He was close to sixty, though you'd never know it to look at him or watch him when he worked cattle or at anything else, but age didn't mean much to him. He was of a philosophical turn of mind. You were what you were and no sense in pretending otherwise—that was how he looked at it.

In his younger days he'd been an adventuresome gent. Worked at jobs most of us wouldn't have tried in places we'd never even hoped to visit. Oil rigger in Texas and Oklahoma, logger in Oregon, fur trapper in the Canadian Barrens, prospector in the Yukon during the '98 Rush, cowhand in half a dozen states and territories. He'd packed more living into the past forty-odd years than a whole regiment of men, and he didn't mind talking about his experiences. No, he sure didn't mind. First time I met him, I'd taken him for a blowhard. Plenty took him that way in the beginning, on account of his windy nature. But the stories he told were true, or at least every one had a core of truth in it. He had too many facts and a whole warbag full of mementoes and photographs and such to back 'em up.

All you had to do was prime him a little—and without knowing it, young Poley had primed him just now. But that was all right with the rest of us. Cass had honed his storytelling skills over the years; one of his yarns was always worthwhile entertainment.

He said to the kid, "I saw more strange things before I was twenty than you'll ever see."

"Cowflop."

"Correct word is 'bullshit,' " Cass said, solemn, and everybody laughed again. "But neither one is accurate."

"I suppose you seen something stranger and more spectacular than that there comet."

"Twice as strange and three times as spectacular."

"Cowflop."

"Fact. Ninth wonder of the world, in its way."

"Well? What was it?"

"McIntosh and his chute."

"Chute? What chute? Who was McIntosh?"

"Keep our lip buttoned, button, and I'll tell you. I'll tell you about *the* damnedest sight I or any other man ever laid eyes on."

Happened more than twenty years ago [Cass went on], in southern Oregon in the early nineties. I'd had my fill of fur trapping in the Barrens and developed a hankering to see what timber work was like, so I'd come on down into Oregon and hooked on with a logging outfit near Coos Bay. But for the first six months I was just a bullcook, not a timberjack. Low-down work, bullcooking—cleaning up after the jacks, making up their bunks, cutting firewood, helping out in the kitchen. Without experience, that's the only kind of job you can get in a decent logging camp. Boss finally put me on one of the yarding crews, but even then there was no thrill in the work and the wages were low. So I was ready for a change of venue when word filtered in that a man named Saginaw Tom McIntosh was hiring for his camp on Black Mountain.

McIntosh was from Michigan and had made a pile logging in the North Woods. What had brought him west to Oregon was the opportunity to buy better than 25,000 acres of virgin timberland on Black Mountain. He'd rebuilt an old dam on the Klamath River nearby that had been washed out by high water, built a sawmill and a millpond below the dam, and then started a settlement there that he named after himself. And once he had a camp operating on the mountain, first thing he did was construct a chute, or skidway, down to the river.

Word of McIntosh's chute spread just as fast and far as word that he was hiring timber beasts at princely wages. It was supposed to be an engineering marvel, unlike any other logging chute ever built. Some scoffed when they were told about it; claimed it was just one of those tall stories that get flung around among Northwest loggers, like the one about Paul Bunyan and Babe the blue ox. Me, I was willing to give Saginaw Tom McIntosh the benefit of the doubt. I figured that if he was half the man he was talked of being, he could accomplish just about anything he set his mind to.

He had two kinds of reputation. First, as a demon logger—a man who could get timber cut faster and turned into board lumber quicker than any other boss jack. And second, as a ruthless cold-hearted son of a bitch who bullied his men, worked them like animals, and wasn't above using fists, peaveys, calks, and any other handy weapon if the need arose. Rumor had it that he—

What's that, boy? No, I ain't going to say any more about that chute just yet. I'll get to it in good time. You just keep your pants on and let me tell this my own way.

Well, rumor had it that McIntosh was offering top dollar because it was the only way he could get jacks to work steady for him. That and his reputation didn't bother me one way or another. I'd dealt with hard cases before, and have since. So I determined to see what Saginaw Tom and his chute and Black Mountain were all about.

I quit the Coos Bay outfit and traveled down to McIntosh's settlement on the Klamath. Turned out to be bigger than I'd expected. The sawmill was twice the size of the one up at Coos Bay, and there was a blacksmith shop, a box factory, a hotel and half a dozen boarding-houses, two big stores, a school, two churches, and a lodge hall. McIntosh may have been a son of a bitch, but he sure did know how to get maximum production and how to provide for his men and their families.

I hired on at the mill, and the next day a crew chief named Lars Nilson drove me and another new man, a youngster called Johnny Cline, upriver to the Black Mountain camp. Long, hot trip in the back of a buckboard, up steep grades and past gold-mining claims strung along the rough-water river. Nilson told us there was bad blood between McIntosh and those miners. They got gold out of the sand by trapping silt in wing dams, and they didn't like it when McIntosh's river drivers built holding cribs along the banks or herded long chains of logs downstream to the cribs and then on to the mill. There hadn't been any trouble yet, but it could erupt at any time; feelings were running high on both sides.

Heat and flies and hornets deviled us all the way up into scrub timber: lodgepole, jack, and yellow pine. The bigger trees—white sugar pine—grew higher up, and what fine old trees they were. Clean-growing, hardly any underbrush. Huge trunks that rose up straight from brace roots close to four feet broad, and no branches on 'em until thirty to forty feet above the ground. Every lumberman's dream, the cutlog timber on that mountain.

McIntosh was taking full advantage of it too. His camp was twice the size of most—two enormous bunkhouses, a cook-shack, a barn and blacksmith shop, clusters of sheds and shan-ties and heavy wagons, corrals full of work horses and oxen. Close to a hundred men, altogether. And better than two dozen big wheels, stinger-tongue and slip-tongue both—

What's a big wheel? Just that, boy—wheels ten and twelve feet high, some made of wood and some of iron, each pair connected by an axle that had a chain and a long tongue pok-ing back from the middle. Four-horse team drew each one. Man on the wheel crew dug a shallow trench under one or two logs, depending on their size; loader pushed the chain through it under the logs and secured it to the axle; driver lunged his team ahead and the tongue slid forward and yanked on the chain to lift the front end of the logs off the ground. Harder the horses pulled, the higher the logs hung. When the team came to a stop, the logs dropped and dragged. Only trou-ble was, sometimes they didn't drop and drag just right— didn't act as a brake like they were supposed to—and the wheel horses got their hind legs smashed. Much safer and fas-ter to use a steam lokey to get cut logs out of the woods, but laying narrow-gauge track takes time and so does ordering a lokey and having it packed in sections up the side of a wil-derness mountain. McIntosh figured to have his track laid and a lokey operating by the following spring. Meanwhile, it was the big wheels and the teams of horses and oxen and men that had to do the heavy work.

Now then. The chute—McIntosh's chute.

First I seen of it was across the breadth of the camp, at the edge of a steep drop-off: the chute head, a big two-level plat-form built of logs. Cut logs were stacked on the top level as they came off the big wheels, by jacks crowhopping over the deck with cant hooks. On the lower level other jacks looped a cable around the foremost log, and a donkey engine wound up the cable and hauled the log forward into a trough built at the outer edge of the platform. You follow me so far?

Well, that was all I could see until Nilson took Johnny Cline and me over close to the chute head. From the edge of the drop-off you had a miles-wide view—long snaky stretches of the Klamath, timberland all the way south to the California border. But it wasn't the vista that had my attention; it was the chute itself. An engineering marvel, all right, that near took my breath away.

McIntosh and his crew had cut a channel in the rocky hill-side straight on down to the riverbank, and lined the sides and bottom with flat-hewn logs—big ones at the sides and smaller ones on the bottom, all worn glass-smooth. Midway along was a short trestle that spanned an outcrop and acted as a kind of speed-brake. Nothing legendary about that chute: it was the longest built up to that time, maybe the longest ever. More than twenty-six hundred feet of timber had gone into the con-struction, top to bottom.

While I was gawking down at it, somebody shouted, "Clear back!" and right away Nilson herded Johnny Cline and me onto a hummock to one side. At the chute head a chain of logs was lined and ready, held back by an iron bar wedged into the rock. Far down below one of the river crew showed a white flag, and as soon as he did the chute tender yanked the iron bar aside and the first log shuddered through and down.

After a hundred feet or so, it began to pick up speed. You could hear it squealing against the sides and bottom of the trough. By the time it went over the trestle and into the lower part of the chute, it was a blur. Took just eighteen seconds for it to drop more than eight hundred feet to the river, and when it hit the splash was bigger than a barn and the fan of water drenched trees on both banks—

"Hell!" young Poley interrupted. "I don't believe none of that. You're funning us, Cass."

"Be damned if I am. What don't you believe?"

"None of it. Chute twenty-six hundred feet long, logs shooting down over eight hundred feet in less than twenty seconds, splashes bigger than a barn . . .''

"Well, it's the gospel truth. So's the rest of it. Sides and bottom a third of the way down were burned black from the friction—black as coal. On cold mornings you could see smoke from the logs going down: that's how fast they traveled. Went even faster when there was frost, so the river crew had to drive spikes in the chute's bottom end to slow 'em up. Even so, sometimes a log would hit the river with enough force to split it in half, clean, like it'd gone through a buzz saw. But I expect you don't believe none of that, either.''

Poley grunted. "Not hardly.''

I said, "Well, *I* believe it, Cass. Man can do just about anything he sets his mind to, like you said, if he wants it bad enough. That chute must of been something. I can sure see why it was the damnedest thing you ever saw.''

"No, it wasn't,'' Cass said.

"What? But you said—''

"No, I didn't. McIntosh's chute was a wonder but not the damnedest thing I ever saw.''

"Then what *is*?'' Poley demanded.

"If I wasn't interrupted every few minutes, you'd of found out by now.'' Cass glared at him. "You going to be quiet and let me get to it or you intend to keep flapping your gums so this here story takes all night?''

Poley wasn't cowed, but he did button his lip. And surprised us all—maybe even himself—by keeping it buttoned for the time being.

I thought I might get put on one of the wheel crews [Cass resumed], but I'd made the mistake of telling Nilson I'd worked a yarding crew up at Coos Bay, so a yarding crew was where I got put on Black Mountain. Working as a chokesetter in the slash out back of the camp—man that sets heavy cable chokers around the end of a log that's fallen down a hillside or into a ravine so the log can be hauled out by means of a donkey engine. Hard, sweaty, dangerous work in the best of camps, and McIntosh's was anything but the best. The rumors had been right about that too. We worked long hours for our pay, seven days a week. And if a man dropped from sheer exhaustion, he was expected to get up under his own power—and docked for the time he spent lying down.

Johnny Cline got put on the same crew, as a whistle-punk on the donkey, and him and me took up friendly. He was a Californian, from down near San Francisco; young and feisty and too smart-ass for his own good . . . some like you, Poley. But decent enough, underneath. His brother was a logger somewhere in Canada, and he'd determined to try his hand too. He was about as green as me, but you could see that logging was in his blood in a way that it wasn't in mine. I knew I'd be moving on to other things one day; he knew he'd be a logger till the day he died.

I got along with Nilson and most of the other timber beasts, but Saginaw Tom McIntosh was another matter. If anything, he was worse than his reputation—mean clear through, with about as much decency as a vulture on a fence post waiting for something to die. Giant of a man, face weathered the color of heartwood, droopy yellow mustache stained with juice from the quids of Spearhead tobacco he always kept stowed in one cheek, eyes like pale fire that gave you the feeling you'd been burned whenever they touched you. Stalked around camp in worn cruisers, stagged corduroy pants, and steel-calked boots, yelling out orders, knocking men down with his fists if they didn't ask how high when he hollered jump. Ran that camp the way a hardass warden runs a prison. Everybody hated him, including me and Johnny Cline before long. But most of the jacks feared him, too, which was how he kept them in line.

He drove all his crews hard, demanding that a dozen turns of logs go down his chute every day to feed the saws working twenty-four hours at the mill. Cut lumber was fetching more than a hundred dollars per thousand feet at the time and he wanted to keep production at a fever pitch before the heavy winter rains set in. There was plenty of grumbling among the men, and tempers were short, but nobody quit the camp. Pay was too good, even with all the abuse that went along with it.

I'd been at the Black Mountain camp three weeks when the real trouble started. One of the gold miners down on the Klamath, man named Coogan, got drunk and decided to tear up a holding crib because he blamed McIntosh for ruining his claim. McIntosh flew into a rage when he heard about it. He ranted and raved for half a day about how he'd had enough of those goddamn miners. Then, when he'd worked himself up enough, he ordered a dozen jacks down on a night raid to bust up Coogan's wing dam and raise some hell with the other miners' claims. The jacks didn't want to do it but he bullied them into it with threats and promises of bonus money.

But the miners were expecting retaliation; had joined forces and were waiting when the jacks showed up. There was a riverbank brawl, mostly with fists and ax handles, but with a few shots fired too. Three timber stiffs were hurt bad enough so that they had to be carried back to camp and would be laid up for a while.

The county law came next day and threatened to close McIntosh down if there was any more trouble. That threw him into another fit. Kind of man he was, he took it out on the men in the raiding party.

"What kind of jack lets a gold-grubber beat him down?" he yelled at them. "You buggers ain't worth the name timberjack. If I didn't need your hands and backs, I'd send the lot of you packing. As is, I'm cutting your pay. And you three that can't work—you get no pay at all until you can hoist your peaveys and swing your axes."

One of the jacks challenged him. McIntosh kicked the man in the crotch, knocked him down, and then gave him a case of logger's smallpox: pinned his right arm to the ground with those steel calks of his. There were no other challenges. But in all those bearded faces you could see the hate that was building for McIntosh. You could feel it too; it was in the air, crackles of it like electricity in a storm.

Another week went by. There was no more trouble with the miners, but McIntosh drove his crews with a vengeance. Up to fifteen turns of logs down the chute each day. The big-wheel crews hauling until their horses were ready to drop; and two did drop dead in harness, while another two had to be destroyed when logs crushed their hind legs on the drag. Buckers and fallers working the slash from dawn to dark, so that the skirl of crosscuts and bucksaws and the thud of axes rolled like constant thunder across the face of Black Mountain.

Some men can stand that kind of killing pace without busting down one way or another, and some men can't. Johnny Cline was one of those who couldn't. He was hotheaded, like I said before, and ten times every day and twenty times every night he cursed McIntosh and damned his black soul. Then, one day when he'd had all he could swallow, he made the mistake of cursing and damning McIntosh to the boss logger's face.

The yarding crew we were on was deep in the slash, struggling to get logs out of a small valley. It was coming on dusk and we'd been at it for hours; we were all bone-tired. I set the choker around the end of yet another log, and the hook-tender signaled Johnny Cline, who stood behind him with one hand on the wire running to the whistle on the donkey engine. When Johnny pulled the wire and the short blast sounded, the cable snapped tight and the big log started to move, its nose plowing up dirt and crushing saplings in its path. But as it came up the slope it struck a sunken log, as sometimes happens, and shied off. The hook-tender signaled for slack, but Johnny didn't give it fast enough to keep the log from burying its nose in the roots of a fir stump.

McIntosh saw it. He'd come catfooting up and was ten feet from the donkey engine. He ran up to Johnny yelling, "You stupid goddamn green-horn!" and gave him a shove that knocked the kid halfway down to where the log was stumped.

Johnny caught himself and scrambled back up the incline. I could see the hate afire in his eyes and I tried to get between him and McIntosh, but he brushed me aside. He put his face up close to the boss logger's, spat out a string of cuss words, and finished up with, "I've had all I'm gonna take from you, you son of a bitch." And then he swung with his right hand.

But all he hit was air. McIntosh had seen it coming; he stepped inside the punch and spat tobacco juice into Johnny's face. The squirt and spatter threw the kid off balance and blinded him at the same time—left him wide open for McIntosh to wade in with fists and knees.

McIntosh seemed to go berserk, as if all the rage and meanness had built to an explosion point inside him and Johnny's words had triggered it. Johnny Cline never had a chance. McIntosh beat him to the ground, kept on beating him even though me and some of the others fought to pull him off. And when he saw his chance he raised up one leg and he stomped the kid's face with his calks—drove those sharp steel spikes down into Johnny's face as if he was grinding a bug under his heel.

Johnny screamed once, went stiff, then lay still. Nilson and some others had come running up by then and it took six of us to drag McIntosh away before he could stomp Johnny Cline a second time. He battled us for a few seconds, like a crazy man; then, all at once, the wildness went out of him. But he was no more human when it did. He tore himself loose, and without a word, without any concern for the boy he'd stomped, he stalked off through the slash.

Johnny Cline's face was a red ruin, pitted and torn by half a hundred steel points. I thought he was dead at first, but when I got down beside him I found a weak pulse. Four of us picked him up and carried him to our bunkhouse.

The bullcook and me cleaned the blood off him and doctored his wounds as best we could. But he was in a bad way. His right eye was gone, pierced by one of McIntosh's calks, and he was hurt inside, too, for he kept coughing up red foam. There just wasn't much we could do for him. The nearest doctor was thirty miles away; by the time somebody went and fetched him back, it would be too late. I reckon we all knew from the first that Johnny Cline would be dead by morning.

There was no more work for any of us that day. None of the jacks in our bunkhouse took any grub, either, nor slept much as the night wore on. We all just sat around in little groups with our lamps lit, talking low, smoking and drinking coffee or tea. Checking on Johnny now and then. Waiting.

He never regained consciousness. An hour before dawn the bullcook went to look at him and announced, "He's gone." The waiting was done. Yes, and so were Saginaw Tom McIntosh and the Black Mountain camp.

Nilson and the other crew chiefs had a meeting outside, between the two bunkhouses. The rest of us kept our places. When Nilson and the two others who bunked in our building came back in, it was plain enough from their expressions what had been decided. And plainer still when the three of them shouldered their peaveys. Loggers will take so much from a boss like Saginaw Tom McIntosh—only so much and no more. What he'd done to Johnne Cline was the next to last straw; Johnny dying was the final one.

At the door Nilson said, "We're on our way to cut down a rotted tree. Rest of you can stay or join us, as you see fit. But you'll all keep your mouths shut either way. Clear?"

Nobody had any objections. Nilson turned and went out with the other two chiefs.

Well, none of the men in our bunkhouse stayed, nor did anybody in the other one. We were all of the same mind. I thought I knew what would happen to McIntosh, but I was wrong. The crew heads weren't fixing to give him the same as he gave Johnny Cline. No, they had other plans. When a logging crew turns, it turns hard—and it gives no quarter.

The near-dawn dark was chill and damp, and I don't mind saying it put a shiver on my back. We all walked quiet through it to McIntosh's shanty—close to a hundred of us, so he heard us coming anyway. But not in time to get up a weapon. He fought with the same wildness he had earlier but he didn't have any more chance than he gave Johnny Cline. Nilson stunned him with his peavey. Then half a dozen men stuffed him into his clothes and his blood-stained boots and took him out.

Straight across the camp we went, with four of the crew heads carrying McIntosh by the arms and legs. He came around just before they got him to the edge of the drop-off. Realized what was going to happen to him, looked like, at about the same time I did.

He was struggling fierce, bellowing curses, when Nilson and the others pitched him into the chute.

He went down slow at first, the way one of the big logs always did. Clawing at the flat-hewn sides, trying to dig his calks into the glass-smooth bottom logs. Then he commenced to pick up speed, and his yells turned to banshee screams. Two hundred feet down the screaming stopped; he was just a blur by then. His clothes started to smoke from the friction, then burst into flame. When he went sailing over the trestle he was a lump of fire that lit up the dark ... then a streak of fire as he shot down into the lower section ... then a fireball with a tail longer and brighter than the one on that comet a while ago, so bright the river and the woods on both banks showed plain as day for two or three seconds before he smacked the river—smacked it and went out in a splash and steamy sizzle you could see and hear all the way up at the chute head.

"And that," Cass Buckram finished, "*that*, by God, was the damnedest sight I or any other man ever set eyes on—McIntosh going down McIntosh's chute, eight hundred feet straight into hell."

None of us argued with him. Not even Poley the button.

BETWEEN THE MOUNTAINS AND THE SKY

—

L. J. Washburn

Hallam slapped the horse on the rump as he turned it into the corral. For anyone who knew men and horses, the gesture said a lot.

The young man known as Pecos stood nearby, leaning on the fence and watching the animals. He flinched as an automobile horn blasted from the road behind him. Glancing angrily over his shoulder at the busy boulevard less than a hundred yards away, he muttered, "Damned machines."

Hallam took off his hat and mopped sweat from his forehead. The day's shooting had been on location out in the Valley, and there had been plenty of hard riding before the cameras. Seemed like Hallam got tired more quickly these days.

"Nothin' beats a good horse," Hallam said, joining Pecos next to the fence of the Hollywood Corral, "but there ain't nothin' wrong with progress, son."

Pecos squinted suspiciously at him. "I'm surprised to hear you say something like that, Lucas. Hell, you saw the West the way it really was, back in the good old days. How can you say this is better?" He waved a hand to indicate the hustle and bustle of Hollywood that surrounded them.

Hallam grinned. He'd been doing riding extra work in the moving pictures ever since arriving in Hollywood back in '16. For the last couple of years, Pecos had seemed to attach himself to the craggy-faced old-timer. The youngster loved the West, loved horses, wanted nothing more than to be a cowboy. The movies had given him that chance.

But there was a hell of a lot that Pecos still didn't know about the way things had really been back then.

As he watched the horses milling around the corral, Hallam said softly, "I remember some things my granddaddy told me once about progress and lookin' back. You talk about a man who'd been to see the elephant . . . Esau'd been there and back a few times."

Hallam leaned on the fence and kept talking in a quiet voice, remembering the last time he had seen his grandfather.

As far as Lucas Hallam was concerned, Esau Sloane was a legend. One of the last of the mountain men, Esau had seen the country when it was new, gone out into territory where few white men had ever been . . . and fewer still had come back.

And now, as Hallam rode up to his grandfather's house in south Texas in this year of our Lord 1890, he knew he was coming to see Esau for probably the last time. The old man had never been sure just how many years he had seen.

Hallam was a big young man in dusty range clothes, wearing a battered hat. There was a Colt on his hip, riding easy in a well-oiled holster. It hadn't been that many years since he left home, but already folks had begun to talk about Lucas Hallam and his speed with a gun. He worked as a cowboy whenever he could, but it seemed like his employers were usually more interested in his other talents.

So far he'd never shot anybody who wasn't shooting at him.

As he swung down from the saddle, the front door of the whitewashed clapboard house opened, and a tall old man came out onto the porch. He had to use a cane, but he still stood straight and proud. His head was nearly bald, but his flowing moustaches were full and snowy white. He gazed at Hallam with clear blue eyes.

"Hello, Lucas," Esau Sloane said, nodding.

"Howdy, Grandpa." Hallam stepped up on the porch and stuck out his hand. "Been a long time."

Esau's grip was firm. "Too long. Come on in out of the sun. Reckon you got my letter."

"Caught up to me in El Paso. I rode on over as soon as I could. What kind of trouble is this friend of yours in?"

Esau shook his head. "Time for that after we eat," he said. "I can still fix up a fine mess of beans and bacon and corn-bread."

Hallam had to grin. "Sounds good to me, Grandpa."

While they talked, Esau prepared the food, refusing any help from Hallam. He lived alone there and seemed to be doing quite well. Underneath his self-sufficient exterior was an air of fragility, and Hallam knew Esau couldn't have too many more years left. The old man knew it, too, but he wasn't going to let the knowledge slow him down.

The meal was good. They kept talking as they ate, Esau casting his memory back over the years and recalling the glory days of the fur trade, the uproarious rendezvouses of the trappers, the wonder of a crisp clear mountain morning when you knew you might be the only living soul in a hundred miles.

Esau spoke too of Hallam's Uncle Tom and Aunt Siobhan and the great brood of cousins who were now scattered all over the Great Plains. Hallam's mother had been born late in Esau's life, born to he and his second wife. Hallam's grandmother was long dead now, in fact, Esau had outlived quite a few younger members of his family. The mountains bred tough men.

Esau poured corn whiskey from a jug into glasses, and he and Hallam sipped it appreciatively. Hallam glanced out the window of the house at the setting sun and said, "Don't you ever want to go back, Grandpa?"

"Back to what?" Esau asked.

"To the old days, when things were better. When the West was really a frontier."

Esau snorted and shook his head. "Let me tell you, boy, them days weren't better. They was different, right enough. But not better."

"You don't miss the wild times?"

Again, Esau slowly shook his head. "I saw the way it was then, Lucas, and I see the way it is now. Hell, I've seen near all there is to see between the mountains and the sky. And I go on. Ain't no point in lookin' back." He sighed. "Wish Truman'd understand that, him and Logan both."

Hallam leaned forward. "Truman's the friend you wrote me about, the one who's got the trouble."

"That's right," Esau nodded. He glanced sharply at Hallam. "I ain't said much 'bout the things I've heard folks say when your name comes up, Lucas. But I know you're gettin' quite a reputation with that gun of your'n."

Hallam grimaced and shrugged. "Never set out to get any kind of reputation," he said.

"Maybe not, but once people know you're fast on the draw, you get it whether you want it or not." Esau tossed back the rest of his drink. "Here it is. Truman and Logan been feudin' for years over this and that. Reckon it probably started over a woman; them things usually do. I wouldn't know, since I wasn't around these parts then. But Truman's been a good friend to me, and I don't want to see him hurt."

"Has it got to the point where this here Logan fella is gunning for him?"

"It's worse'n that," Esau said grimly. "Logan's gone out and hired him a gunfighter. You ever heard tell of a man named Stitch Macklin?"

Hallam nodded slowly. He had heard of Macklin, all right. "He's young, but he's good, from what I know of him."

"Hell, you're young, too, Lucas. Is this Macklin feller faster'n you?"

Hallam stood up from the table and walked to the window, standing slightly to one side out of habit so he wouldn't be as good a target. "Don't reckon I know which one of us is faster," he said. "Only one way to find that out, Grandpa."

Esau sighed. "Yeah, I reckon I knew you'd say that." He looked up as Hallam turned away from the window, met the younger man's eyes. "Would it do any good to talk to this Macklin?"

"And tell him what?"

"That he's got no business mixin' in a fight between two crazy old coots."

"From what I know about Macklin, he won't care about that, long as one of the old coots is willing to meet his price."

"Logan's got one of the biggest spreads around here," Esau said. "He can meet Macklin's price." The old man's face set in grim lines. "What about you, Lucas? What's your price?"

Hallam stared at his grandfather. "You want me to hire out to Truman?"

"I can't stand by and watch him be killed by that gunfighter. What'll it cost, Lucas?"

Hallam nodded toward the empty plates. "Reckon I've already been paid."

"No, boy, I mean it—"

"So do I," Hallam cut in. He was thinking rapidly. "There's no reason anybody has to get killed. I'll talk to Macklin."

"You'll have to do it quick. I know Truman's goin' into town tomorrow to pick up some supplies for his farm. And from what I've heard, Logan's plannin' to be there, too, with this Macklin feller."

"Tomorrow, then," Hallam nodded. "We'll be there, Grandpa. Don't worry."

Hallam didn't sleep as well as he had expected to in Esau's spare bedroom. He kept thinking about the yarns the old man had spun over supper. It was obvious from the enthusiasm with which Esau told the stories that he had enjoyed that time in his life. And yet he had no desire to go back to those days, even if he could have. Hallam was having a hard time understanding that.

He could see the West changing around him all the time, and even though he was young, he already missed the way it used to be. Civilization was pressing in on all sides; the frontier was still alive, but it was steadily shrinking. Hallam felt it like a personal loss. He had grown up with stories of the Wild West, and now he was watching firsthand as it died. He couldn't help but be saddened.

Morning came, and it was hot and clear. Esau had biscuits

on the table when Hallam came into the kitchen. "Don't dawdle over your food," the old man warned. "I reckon Truman and Logan will be gettin' to town early, 'fore it gets too hot."

Hallam nodded and poured himself a cup of coffee from the pot that was simmering on the stove.

"You ain't got your gun on," Esau said as he joined Hallam at the table.

"Don't need it here, do I?" Hallam asked.

"Reckon not."

They ate in silence for the most part. Hallam spread butter and preserves on the biscuits and wished he could cook as well as Esau.

When they were done with breakfast, Esau slipped on a black jacket over his white shirt. He buttoned the top button of the shirt, then took a wide-brimmed, flat-crowned hat from a hook on the wall and settled it on his head. He looked almost like a church deacon until you looked in his eyes and saw the hint of something wild there that no amount of time could take away.

"Get your gun, boy," he said to Hallam. "Let's go stop those old fools from killing themselves."

Hallam got his holster and shell belt from the bedroom and strapped them on. He checked the loads in the gun and left the hammer resting on the empty sixth chamber. He and the long-barreled Colt were old friends; the feel of its walnut grips against his palm was second nature by now.

Esau was waiting on the porch. Hallam joined him, put on his own hat, and then went down the two steps beside his grandfather. The two of them walked east, along the road that led into the settlement a couple of hundred yards away. Esau didn't move very fast, but his step was sure.

The place was a typical little crossroads town, Hallam saw. One main street with businesses on both sides, a few cross streets with houses scattered along them. The biggest building was the general store. It had a high porch and two stories. Even this early in the day, Hallam noted as they approached, there were quite a few horses and wagons tied up in front of the building.

"There's Truman's buckboard," Esau said as they went up

the steps at one end of the covered porch. "Don't see Logan's outfit, so maybe we got here in time."

Hallam nodded. He had been thinking about what he was going to say to Stitch Macklin, and he still wasn't sure what tack to use. Probably the best thing would be to appeal to the man's vanity.

Esau led the way into the store. He nodded and said hello to several of the men inside who were picking up their week's supplies. Hallam felt eyes on him and knew that the townspeople had guessed he was Esau's gunslinging grandson, but no one said anything to him.

A short, wide man was standing in front of the counter at the rear of the store. He turned and nodded curtly to Esau. "Mr. Sloane," he said stiffly. "Good morning to you."

Esau blew air disgustedly through his moustaches. "Dammit, Truman, you still got your back up 'cause I tried to talk you out of this foolishness?"

"It's not foolishness for a man to stand up for himself. Logan's run roughshod over this whole country for twenty years. It's time somebody stopped him."

Hallam wondered what had prompted the feud to flare up again. There was no telling, and it really didn't matter. A couple of proddy old-timers like Truman and Logan would probably see offenses where none really existed.

"You know Logan's takin' this serious," Esau went on. "You've heard the talk, Truman. He's hired him a gunfighter."

"Nothing Logan does scares me, Esau," Truman replied. "He's trying to buffalo me off my land. Nobody's going to do that and get away with it." Truman looked past Esau at Hallam. His mouth tightened, but he said nothing else.

Esau sighed wearily. "You're a damn fool, Truman, you know that. Well, I ain't goin' to let you go up against no shootist and get yourself killed. I brung my grandson along to put a stop to this."

Truman looked at Hallam again. "You'd be Lucas Hallam," he said flatly.

"That's right," Hallam admitted.

"I didn't ask your grandpa to send for you, but since you're here . . . How does five hundred sound to you?"

"For what?" Hallam asked, already knowing the answer to the question but wanting to make Truman say it.

"Why, to kill that bastard and his hired gun, of course. Why else would I want to hire you?"

Hallam took a deep breath, then nodded. "All right," he said.

Esau jerked his head around and stared at Hallam. "What the hell's got into you, boy? This ain't the way I wanted it."

"That's the way it is."

"I thought you was goin' to talk to Macklin."

Hallam looked back at Truman. "You've got the money?"

"Not with me. I'm good for it, though," the man blustered. "Just ask anybody."

"I'll take your word for it." Hallam heard the excited murmur that was spreading through the store. Within moments, the word would be out on the street that Truman had hired Lucas Hallam, the infamous gunfighter from Flat Rock.

Esau was still staring. "Reckon I knew this would happen," he said under his breath. "Thought from the way you talked last night that you wanted it different."

Hallam made no reply. He heard booted footsteps on the planks of the porch, heard the sudden silence that fell as the door was opened.

He turned slowly, not wanting to spook anybody. Two men were coming into the store, and Hallam knew without asking that they were Logan and Stitch Macklin.

Logan was a small man with a bristly gray moustache. His clothes were plain, nothing fancy, and to look at him nobody would guess that he was one of the richest men in this part of the state. The man with him was a different story.

Stitch Macklin wore high black boots with his corduroy pants stuffed down into their tops. His shirt was white, and over it he wore a dark leather vest. There was a string tie with a silver clasp around his throat. His cream-colored Stetson was pushed back from thick sandy hair.

The broad shell belt he wore was ornamented with silver conchos. The holster was tied down, and riding inside it was a pearl-handled revolver. The grips of the gun shone brightly in the morning sunlight coming through the doorway.

Hallam thought he looked like something right out of a dime novel illustration. A figure from a Wild West fable come to life, right enough.

But none of that mattered one damn bit. No matter how fancy Macklin looked, all that was really important was what he could do with that pearl-handled gun.

Logan stopped and faced Truman at the other end of the aisle that cut through the center of the store. "I thought I told you not to be here in town today, Truman," Logan snapped.

"I don't take orders from you, you son of a bitch," Truman shot back.

Logan cursed. Hallam paid little attention to the little banty rooster of a man. He kept his eye on Macklin. A lazy smile stretched across Macklin's face as he met Hallam's gaze. Neither of them said anything as the two old enemies traded harsh words. There was nothing being said that Hallam and Macklin had not heard before.

"You ain't the only one who can hired a goddamn gunfighter," Truman finally sputtered. He jerked a thumb at Hallam, who was standing nearby, legs spread, arms hanging loose at his sides.

"Well, then, let's settle this, you old goat," Logan replied hotly. "Macklin!"

Macklin sauntered forward a couple of steps. "Don't reckon we've been introduced," he said. "I'm Stitch Macklin. You've probably heard of me."

"Lucas Hallam. I've heard some stories, all right."

Macklin shook his head. "They weren't stories, Hallam. They were all true. You care to step out into the street?"

Hallam felt his grandfather's bony fingers clutch his arm. He ignored Esau's grip and nodded. "Reckon that's what we're here for." He pulled away from the old mountain man and started toward the door.

Still grinning, Macklin turned his back and went out onto the porch. Hallam followed. The general store suddenly emptied as the citizens of the town scurried either for cover or a good vantage point to watch the gunfight.

Hallam glanced inside. Esau still stood in front of the

counter, a lonely figure, his age beginning to show more now.

Macklin was leaning against the rail along the front of the porch. "How much you getting paid for this, Hallam?" he asked.

"Five hundred," Hallam answered honestly.

Macklin laughed. "Hell, that ain't much to die for. Logan's paying me a thousand."

Hallam looked at him for a long moment, then said, "Heard tell you got five thousand up in Wyoming during that trouble last summer."

Macklin nodded. "And sixty-five hundred last fall over in Nevada. Of course, the odds were pretty steep there."

"Seems like we've both come down in the world then, risking our necks for a couple of penny-ante old-timers." Hallam glanced along the sidewalk and saw Logan standing at the end of the porch. He knew that Truman had gone to the other end, as far away from his hated enemy as he could get.

Macklin shrugged as he considered Hallam's words. "Could be, but a man takes what he can get. Seems like there's not as much work as there used to be."

Hallam nodded thoughtfully. Their voices were pitched low enough that only the two of them could hear this conversation. "I don't much want to die for a lousy five hundred bucks," he said flatly. "And I don't reckon you want to risk it for a thousand, either."

Macklin narrowed his eyes and regarded him suspiciously. "You trying to talk me out of this, Hallam?"

"'Just tryin' to make some sense of it. Seems like you and me both ought to have something better to do."

The sun was bright in the street. Hallam could feel all the eyes watching them, waiting for the violence that would surely come. Waiting for a good, old-fashioned Wild West shoot-out.

And Hallam knew now what Esau had been talking about the night before. Times changed. This was all wrong now. There had been a time when a showdown like this might've made sense, but not now. Truman and Logan were hanging on to old hatreds and old solutions . . . and either Hallam or Macklin would die today because of them.

Unless Hallam could get through to the other man.

Slowly, Macklin nodded. "Does seem like a mighty piddling fight for a couple of men like us to be mixed up in, Hallam. How about it? You want to say the hell with it?"

Hallam let a smile of relief tug at his mouth. "Seems like the smart thing to do. 'Course, we'll disappoint all these folks who're watchin'."

Macklin laughed. "Let 'em fight their own fights." He turned away abruptly and walked over to Logan. Hallam heard the rancher's amazed anger as Macklin told him that there wouldn't be any shoot-out today.

Truman appeared at Hallam's side and grabbed his arm. "What the hell are you doing?" he demanded. "I promised you five hundred dollars to kill that bastard!"

"Reckon I need a better reason than that," Hallam said shortly. "You don't owe me a damn thing, Mr. Truman. Let's keep it that way."

He glanced over his shoulder and saw Esau smiling now. Hallam nodded to him, and felt damned good right now. Esau came out of the store and fell in beside him as Hallam walked down the porch to the steps.

"Let's go home, Lucas," the old man said. "Nothin' wrong with talkin' about old times, I reckon, as long as you don't try to live 'em over again."

Hallam nodded and started to agree.

"Hallam!"

The voice cracked through the air behind him. Hallam stopped and looked back to see Stitch Macklin slowly strolling into the center of the street.

A lump of coldness suddenly settled in the bottom of Hallam's stomach.

"Wait here, Grandpa," he said quietly. Esau started to reply, then closed his mouth and shook his head. Hallam had done his best. There was nothing else to say.

Hallam eased into the street, facing Macklin with about twenty feet between them. "Thought we agreed this was foolishness, Macklin," he said.

"Going up against you for a measly grand would be, Hallam," the young man answered with that cocky smile. "I'm not doing this for Logan. Oh, I'll collect from him when we're done, but I got to thinking. If I put you down now, maybe the jobs will start coming again. The real jobs, the ones that pay what a man's worth." He laughed. "I'm doing this for myself, Hallam, for my future."

"Don't," Hallam said.

Macklin shook his head. "There's nothing else out there for either one of us, Hallam."

His hand flashed toward the pearl-handled revolver.

Hallam barely felt the butt of his own gun, was only distantly aware of the crash as it bucked back against his palm. But Hallam saw all too clearly the puff of dust from Macklin's shirt as the bullet smacked into his chest. Hallam saw the sudden crimson stain, saw Macklin stagger back a step as he involuntarily fired the gun in his hand. Macklin's slug plowed into the dust of the street, nowhere near Hallam.

The gunfighter crumpled.

Hallam kept his gun out as he walked slowly toward Macklin's body. He didn't return the weapon to his holster until he was sure that the other man was dead. Then he turned and walked back to Esau.

"I didn't want this," Hallam said to his grandfather.

Esau nodded. "I know. The boy didn't have much of a past, but he couldn't let go of what he did have."

Hallam felt Truman tugging at his arm excitedly. He shrugged the man off, ignored his promises of payment. Logan was staring bleakly at Macklin's body as he stood over it, Hallam saw. The rancher's shoulders slumped in defeat. This would blunt the feud, at least for a while.

And if it started up again, Hallam intended to be a long ways off when it did.

He and Esau walked down to the house. Hallam said his goodbyes quickly, and the old man seemed to understand. As Hallam swung into the saddle, Esau reached up to shake his hand. "You come see an old mountain man, you hear?" he said.

Hallam nodded. "I will," he promised.

"But I never did get back to see him," Hallam told Pecos. "Always wished that I could have. But I joined up with the Rangers not long after that, and it seemed like there was always too much work to do. I owe that old man a lot. Reckon it was because of him that I wound up on the right side of the law.''

Pecos grinned. ''Nope. You're just a natural-born do-gooder, Lucas. Reckon I see what you mean about hangin' on to the past, though.''

Hallam rubbed his jaw and gazed down the street toward the Waterhole. The speakeasy where the riding extras and stuntmen spent most of their free time would be getting busy about now. The drinks would be flowing, and the air would be blue with cigarette smoke, and there would probably be a poker game getting underway any time now.

''Reckon there's some things about the past worth keepin','' he said with a smile. He slapped Pecos on the shoulder. ''Come on, boy. This here reminiscin's thirsty work.''

THE WISH BOOK

—

James Reasoner

Someone was screaming in the fog.

Cobb reined in his horse and listened to the sound, keeping his Winchester lined on Spivey's back just ahead of him. The outlaw was riding about five feet in front of Cobb, and that was the edge of visibility in this cottony mess.

"Hold it," Cobb growled. "You hear that?"

Spivey glanced over his shoulder. Night was closing in, and Cobb had a hard time seeing his features. From experience, though, he knew that Spivey was sneering.

"I hear it. Sounds like somebody ain't happy, Ranger."

Cobb nodded. The scream was one of rage and frustration, rather than pain, and it was coming from a man's throat. It cut off abruptly. Off to the left, a gun cracked, the sound strangely muffled by the shrouding mist.

Cobb rubbed the beard stubble on his face. He was a big man and looked even bigger on the back of a horse. Reaching a decision, he said to Spivey, "Ride on, but take it slow. I want to find a place to get in out of this. I don't like not being able to see where I'm going."

Spivey laughed. "So you send me out in front, in case there's a cliff or something."

"Now you're catchin' on," Cobb said. He allowed himself a tiny smile for a moment. He didn't like Harland Spivey, not even a little bit, and he'd be damned glad when he got the man back to the Ranger post at Veal Station. From there

Spivey would be taken on to Fort Worth by stage, and then he'd be hung, no doubt, for killing a settler and the man's wife and child during a robbery at their isolated farm.

More words came floating to them out of the gloom. "You damn son of a bitch!" a man shouted. There were hoofbeats, another shot.

Spivey looked over his shoulder again as he walked his horse forward. Cobb thought he looked a little more worried now. "I don't like this, Cobb," he said. "There's crazy folks out there, and one of them stray bullets might come through here."

"All the more reason to find a place to hole up for the night," Cobb grunted.

They were riding through a rugged, hilly country dotted by thickets of oak and elm. Gullies wound between sandstone bluffs and made the two men detour from time to time. Since the fog had closed in during the late afternoon, bringing with it a damp chill, Cobb had had trouble following the trail and had eventually given up.

Now Spivey glanced back again and said, "Where you reckon we are, Cobb?"

The big Ranger shook his head. "Don't rightly know. Weatherford ought to be over there south of us someplace. I'm pretty sure we're going in the right direction. Thought we might run onto Peaster before now, but we could've rode right past it in this stuff and never known."

"I'm gettin' kinda nervous, and I don't mind admittin' it."

Your nerves didn't bother you when you were slaughtering that family, Cobb thought, but he didn't say it. Talking to a man like Spivey about his crimes didn't accomplish a damn thing.

Something loomed out of the fog. Spivey saw it first and reined in abruptly. "It's a cabin!" he exclaimed as Cobb brought his horse to a stop.

"Line shack," Cobb said. "Good a place as any to spend the night, I suppose. This fog'll burn off in the morning, and we can get on to Veal Station."

"I don't reckon I'm looking forward to that."

"Don't reckon you are, either. Sit still." Cobb swung down

out of the saddle, then said, "Now get down from that horse."

Spivey dismounted. At Cobb's command, he went over to the door of the line shack and pulled it open. The hinges gave a long, loud squeal as he did so.

A rifle blasted somewhere, and the slug knocked splinters from the door jamb.

Cobb lunged forward. He was so disoriented that he couldn't tell where the shot had come from, but he was sure that it wasn't from inside the cabin. His free hand hit Spivey in the center of the back and shoved him through the opening. As the outlaw sprawled on the rough plank floor of the shack, Cobb darted through the door and kicked it shut behind him.

Light flared, blinding him. He moved back instinctively, putting his back against the cabin wall and lifting the Winchester. He was braced for the shock of a bullet, but it didn't come.

"Hold it!" a strange voice said. "I mean you no harm, mister."

Cobb blinked rapidly, some of his sight coming back. He saw Spivey still lying on the floor, somewhat stunned by his fall, and on the other side of the shack's one room, a man stood holding a lucifer that was burning perilously close to his fingers. The man turned slowly to one side and put the match to the wick of a lantern. The wick caught, guttered for a moment, then grew and cast a soft glow through the cabin.

"I don't know who you men are, but I got no quarrel with you," the man said. He was short and thin, in his forties, and his skin was leathery. A cowhand, Cobb decided.

He kept the Winchester pointing in Spivey's general direction and asked the stranger, "This your cabin?"

"It's one of the Turkey Track line shacks," the man said, "and that's the brand I ride for. So I reckon it's mine for the time being."

Cobb nodded. With his left hand, he moved aside his coat so that the man could see the badge on his flannel shirt. The silver star in a silver circle was recognizable all over the state, so there was no real reason for Cobb to say, "I'm a Texas Ranger." He said it anyway, then went on, "This man's my prisoner. We're on our way back to Veal Station. All right with you if we spend the night here and wait out this fog?"

The puncher shrugged. "Don't make no never mind to me. 'Course, you're liable to get shot at if you stay around here tonight." A smile creased his face. "There's a couple of crazy men out there tryin' to kill each other."

Cobb watched while Spivey got up and brushed himself off. "We heard the shooting. What's it all about?"

The cowboy gave a cackling laugh. "Each of 'em thinks the other has got something he wants. But they're both wrong, the damn fools. I got it." He reached behind him to a wobbly table and picked up something. "I got it right here, and they ain't ever goin' to get their grubby hands on it!"

Cobb's eyes narrowed. This waddy sounded a little touched in the head himself. The thing he was waving around was a book of some sort, Cobb saw, and as the cowboy took a step forward, Cobb recognized it as a mail-order catalog.

"It's *my* wish book," the man said, then laughed again. "All mine . . ."

Spivey looked at Cobb, and the outlaw's eyes were uneasy. Cobb grimaced and nodded slightly to let Spivey know that he understood and agreed. The puncher was some sort of loon, and spending the night here might not be such a good idea after all.

The cowboy sat down at the table and spread the book out in front of him, seeming to forget the other two men in the room. "Goin' to order me the best damn suit of clothes you ever did see," he muttered to himself. "I'll make all them other fellers look silly." He looked up, suddenly aware again that he was not alone. Stabbing a finger at the catalog, he said, "Look at that, mister. You ever see such a dandy suit of clothes?"

Cobb thought it might be best to humor the man. He moved slightly so that he could see the illustration in the catalog. It showed an eastern gentleman in a fancy tweed suit, complete with spats and a bowler hat. Cobb thought an outfit like that would look pretty damned strange on a ranch, but he kept his mouth shut.

"Shorty, he wants to order some sort of damned cuckoo clock for the shack here," the cowboy went on. "Foolishness, if you ask me. And Doug, he's got hisself a gal friend over at Flat Rock, and he wants to get her one of them whalebone corsets. What kind of present is that for a gal, I ask you?''

"Royal? You in there, you durned old fool?''

The shout came from outside, somewhere close by. The cowboy lunged up from the table and snatched a pistol from a holster that was lying on one of the bunks. He threw back the shutter on the shack's single window and emptied the gun into the foggy night.

Cobb tensed and kept the rifle on Spivey. "Don't try anything," he growled.

As the echoes of the ear-numbing gunshots faded, the cowboy shouted out the window, "You boys stay away! I'll kill you dead, Shorty!''

The voice from outside answered, "Me an' Doug figgered out you got the book, Royal! You ain't goin' to get away with it! We want it back!''

"It's mine now!" Royal declared. He took fresh cartridges from a box on the table and began shoving them into the Colt's cylinder. "You ain't gettin' it!" He turned to Cobb and Spivey, grinned, and continued, "I told you they was crazy.''

Something thudded on the roof. A second later, a shotgun roared, blasting its charge through the flimsy shingles and leaving a gaping hole behind.

Cobb reached out and grabbed Spivey's collar, jerking the man out of the center of the room. He slammed Spivey against the wall to stun him for a moment, then tipped the barrel of the Winchester toward the roof.

The old cowboy called Royal had his pistol reloaded now. He ducked into a corner and began shooting toward the roof. A pained yelp came through the hole along with some fog.

The door of the shack slammed open. A man tumbled through, awkwardly rolling over on the floor and trying to bring the gun in his hand to bear on Royal. "Drop it!" he screamed.

Royal whirled around as the man on the floor fired. The slug smacked into the wall beside Royal's head. Instead of returning the fire, he lashed out with an arm and sent the lantern crashing off the table. It shattered when it hit the floor, the spilled oil igniting with a whoosh. In the harsh glare, Cobb saw Royal snatch up the catalog.

That was all he had time to notice. Cobb grabbed Spivey's shoulder and hauled him toward the door. The outlaw was eight inches shorter and ninety pounds lighter than the big Ranger, and his boots barely touched the floor as Cobb hustled him out of the shack.

Guns boomed right behind them. Cobb dove forward, hugging dirt and taking Spivey with him. He rolled over and saw shadows darting around inside the blazing line shack. More shots sounded, then there were running footsteps audible over the crackling of the fire.

The flames lit up the fog, making it look like billows of bloody cotton.

Cobb got to his knees. A figure appeared in front of him, running full-tilt toward him. There was no time to get out of the way. The man ran into Cobb's shoulder, sending him spinning to the ground again. The Winchester slipped out of Cobb's hand as he landed heavily. For a second, he couldn't get his breath, and then he realized that the man had tripped and fallen right on top of him.

Cobb got his hands on the man and shoved him off. "You bastard!" the man snarled, and Cobb knew it wasn't the one called Royal. It had to be one of the others, either Shorty or Doug. Whoever it was punched him in the belly. Cobb saw the man's other hand lifting a knife.

The Ranger drove his left arm out, crashing his elbow into the man's breastbone. Cobb brought his right fist across his body, smashed it into the man's face. The man fell away from him with a groan.

Where the hell was Spivey? Where was the Winchester?

Cobb's big hand felt around on the ground. He didn't find the rifle, but his fingers fell on something else, something smooth and slick. The pages of the catalog—

He picked it up and shoved it inside his coat without thinking. Then he rolled over a couple of times and surged to his feet, looking around.

The line shack was still blazing, its dry wood burning fiercely even in this dampness. The night and the fog seemed to swallow up the light from the fire, leaving only a small circle of illumination. The man Cobb had fought with seconds before had disappeared now, but he could be out there anywhere, only a few yards away.

Somebody ran behind Cobb. Somebody else fired a gun.

"It's my wish book!" Royal screamed from yet another direction.

Cobb's head swiveled. Spivey was nowhere to be seen, and neither was the Winchester.

The outlaw was out there somewhere in the fog, too, and Cobb figured he had the rifle now.

Cobb's hat had been knocked off in the scuffle. He didn't bother looking for it. The big Colt was still in the holster on his hip, and he was thankful for that. Stooping, he felt the hilt of the Bowie that was sheathed on his right calf. The Winchester might be gone, but as long as he had the Colt and the Bowie, he was more than a match for a little snake like Harland Spivey.

Of course, a man like Spivey wouldn't think anything of backshooting out of the dark.

Cobb trotted away from the burning shack, letting instinct guide him. He found one of the gullies and slid down its bank, crouching for a moment under the overhanging sandstone. He took a deep breath, dragging the cold damp air into his lungs.

More shooting, somewhere close.

Cobb reached inside his coat and felt the mail-order catalog. He had a pretty good idea what had happened. The three punchers had been stuck out here at the line shack for so long that something had gone wrong in their heads. The little things got to be awfully important in a situation like that. Even a damned wish book was worth killing over—

The man who ran into him must have taken it from Royal in the fight at the cabin, then dropped it when he fell. Now Cobb had it, for all the good it would do him. He had something more important to worry about.

Spivey would know that his only real hope of escape was to kill Cobb. If he ran, Cobb would just track him down again. If he put Cobb under, the Rangers would send out somebody else, but at least there would be time to get a head start on them.

Cobb leaned his head against the bank and closed his eyes. He could wait here. Spivey—or some of the others—would show up sooner or later, and he could deal with them then.

But he didn't like being hunted. It had always been the other way around.

The decision made, Cobb stood up and moved away down the gulley, keeping his left hand brushing the bank. He walked quietly, his boots softly crunching the sand underfoot.

He'd gone maybe fifty yards when somebody jumped on his back.

A grunt had warned him a split-second before that someone was about to leap off the bank at him. Cobb was trying to twist away when the man hit him. The attacker tried to grab Cobb around the neck, but instead he glanced off, rolling off Cobb's shoulder and falling to the floor of the wash. As he tried to get up, Cobb met him with a looping right hand.

The blow knocked the man backwards. Cobb lunged after him, slipping the Colt from his holster. He didn't want to kill the man, whoever it was. If it was one of the crazed cowboys, then Cobb would be satisfied to put him out of action for a while.

And if it was Spivey, Cobb wanted him alive to hang.

Cobb landed on top of the man and slashed at him with the gun. The barrel thudded into his head, and the shadowy figure went limp under Cobb. Cobb rolled off and knelt beside the man, reaching out to feel his face in the darkness.

A beard. Not Spivey, then, and not Royal, either. It was either Shorty or Doug. Whoever, he was still alive, his breath raspy.

Cobb holstered his gun, stripped the man's belt from his pants, rolled him over, tied his hands tightly behind his back. That would hold him for a while. He felt the man's head, found the bump from the blow with the Colt. The wound wasn't bleeding.

Cobb stood up. He went a little farther down the gulley, then climbed out. The fire had died down now, but it was still bright enough for Cobb to see off to the left. The fog seemed to be tearing in shreds now. Maybe it was breaking up and would blow away. Cobb thought he felt the faint touch of a breeze against his face, but that could have been his imagination.

He wondered where the horses had gone. They were probably close by.

The click of a hammer being eased back behind him made him freeze.

"Stand still, you bastard!" Royal grated. "And give me back my damned wish book!"

How did he know . . . ? Cobb gave a shake of his head. Royal couldn't know. He probably didn't even know who he was pointing his gun at. Cobb started to open his mouth to identify himself, then stopped short.

What if Spivey was close by? If he heard Cobb's voice, and if he had the Winchester, he would start blasting.

There was a step as Royal came closer. "Which one are you, dammit? That you, Shorty? Where's my book?"

The gun barrel suddenly prodded Cobb in the back. That was a mistake on Royal's part. Cobb had been waiting for him to get that close.

Spinning around, Cobb flung one arm toward Royal and knocked the gun aside as it thundered. The explosion was deafening at this range and Cobb felt a stinging on his wrist from the muzzle blast. He bulled into Royal with his shoulder, driving the cowboy back. Before Royal could bring the gun back into line, Cobb kicked him in the groin. Royal shrieked thinly.

Cobb hit him with a short uppercut that clicked his teeth together. He sagged bonelessly against Cobb. Cobb caught his shirt and let him down gently on the ground. Royal wasn't a threat any longer. But just to make sure, Cobb repeated his actions with the other man and tied Royal's hands with his belt.

Straightening, Cobb took a deep breath and looked around. The cabin was just a heap of embers now, invisible more than a few feet away. Instead of breaking up, as he had hoped, the fog seemed to be thickening again. It brought a heavy silence with it.

Cobb remembered how quiet a night could be when it was

lit by a Comanche moon and the savages were closing in. That had been bad, damned bad.

This silence was worse.

Cobb couldn't stand still. He started moving again. He knew now that he was drawing the attackers to him, but he didn't care. He wondered for a second if he was getting as crazy as Royal and Shorty and Doug.

The scrape of a boot in front of him, the shocking blast of a gun—Cobb was diving forward as the slug whistled over his head. Instinct made him palm out the Colt as he fell, and when he landed, he squeezed off a shot, the heavy gun bucking in his fist.

There was a strangled yell up ahead, a thump as someone fell. Cobb scrambled up, ran forward, then paused. He heard a sound he'd heard too many times before—a death rattle.

"Damn," Cobb breathed. He moved forward slowly, and then his foot hit the body. Kneeling, he put his hand on the man's chest. It touched a warm, sticky mess, and Cobb grimaced as he moved it to a new location. No breath, no pulse. The man was dead, all right.

And he wasn't Harland Spivey, because Spivey stepped out of the fog and pointed the Winchester at Cobb and said, "Drop the gun, Ranger."

Cobb hesitated, aware that the last wave of fog was moving on again. A silvery glow filtered through from the moon, enough light for him to faintly see the face of the young puncher he had just been forced to kill. And to see Spivey, standing ten feet away. Too far away to jump, too close to miss with the rifle.

Cobb put the Colt on the ground.

Spivey jerked the barrel of the Winchester. "That Bowie on your leg, too."

Cobb drew out the big blade and placed it next to the Colt.

"Stand up," Spivey said. "I want you on your feet when I kill you, Ranger."

Slowly, Cobb straightened. "The Rangers will send another man after you," he pointed out.

"Hell, I know that. But they'll wait a while first, to see if you're coming back. And I'll be long gone."

Cobb's left hand was under the tail of his coat. He had never been one to carry a hide-out gun. He believed in a man putting his weapons in plain sight. But as he took a deep breath, expanding his chest as far as he could, the mail-order catalog slipped down from its position inside his coat and dropped into his hand.

Spivey grinned over the rifle. The fog was definitely breaking up. Stars were starting to be visible overhead.

"I told you you'd never get me back there to hang," Spivey said.

Cobb threw the wish book at him.

Pages fluttering, it spun through the air like some misshapen bird. Spivey jerked the rifle toward it and fired, reacting without thinking.

Cobb crossed the space between them as the Winchester blasted. His shoulder drove into Spivey. Both men staggered. Cobb got his hand on the barrel of the rifle and twisted.

The Winchester came free. Cobb thrust out with it, slamming the butt into Spivey's middle. As the outlaw doubled over, Cobb brought his other hand across. The punch caught Spivey on the jaw. It would have knocked most men down and out, but Spivey found the strength in desperation to keep his feet.

Cobb hit him twice in the head with the butt of the rifle. Spivey stayed down after that.

The Winchester dangling from his hand, Cobb threw his head back and gulped down air. All the tension of the last few hours caught up with him, and a shiver ran through him.

He laughed abruptly. Hours? Now that he thought about it, it had probably only been fifteen minutes or so since he and Spivey had ridden up to the line shack in the fog.

Morning would be soon enough to hunt up the horses, Cobb decided. And to bury the man he had killed. The other two he'd have to take with him, get some help for them. He tied up Spivey and then sat down to wait. The ground was cold and wet, but Cobb didn't care.

By dawn, the fog was gone, and it was one of the prettiest sunrises Cobb had ever seen. As he stood up, unkinking his muscles, he spotted the catalog lying on the ground nearby. As he picked it up, he had to grin. Spivey was a good shot, give him that much.

The wish book was drilled, plumb center.

RED FEATHER'S DAUGHTER

—

W. W. Lee

Jefferson Birch had to admit it—this was the strangest meeting place his employer, Arthur Tisdale, had ever arranged. Birch shifted in his saddle and his horse, Cactus, shook his head nervously as they left Nez Percé territory. His horse seemed be less nervous now that they were heading for the town of Coeur d'Alene. Birch reached down and patted Cactus's neck to reassure him.

A few hours earlier, Birch had entered the Nez Percé camp with a guide and encountered his employer, Arthur Tisdale, who ran a detective agency out of San Francisco called Tisdale Investigations. An ex-army man, Tisdale was short and always neatly dressed in a suit, even on the hottest summer day. He had shaved off his mustache recently, and his upper lip shone like a beacon in contrast to the rest of his tanned face.

They shook hands and Tisdale led the way to the main lodge, obviously the village head's home.

"His name is Red Feather, and his daughter is missing," Tisdale had explained.

"I don't mean to sound ungrateful, Tisdale, but we are in Indian territory. I didn't know you hired out to Indians."

Tisdale turned around, making Birch stop short to avoid bumping into him. "Do you have a problem with this assignment?"

Birch blinked. He'd never really thought about it. His only
encounters with Indians up until now had been when he was
a Ranger back in Texas. Town Apaches and Navahos had pop-
ulated El Paso, and he had the occasional run-in with groups
of drunken Apaches that had destroyed some homesteader's
ranch.

He'd met some men who hated Indians, all Indians. Birch
never thought of himself that way—Indians were just like
white men in some ways—you could like some of them, and
hate some of them. It all depended on his mood and the Indian's mood.

Birch found himself inside the village head's lodge, being
introduced to Red Feather, the man whose daughter was missing, and Bear Who Touched the Sky, who turned out to be the
daughter's betrothed.

Red Feather was a squat, sad-looking elderly Indian who
didn't speak English. Bear Who Touched the Sky was a tall,
handsome Nez Percé whose attitude toward Birch and Tisdale
was just a small sign of the bitterness that was beginning to
seep into the relations between white men and Indians.

Birch understood, having read the accounts of what was
happening to the Nez Percé. Greedy miners had come into
their territory, the land that had been set aside for the Nez
Percé, and found gold. The miners had been putting pressure
on the government to make the Nez Percé abandon the land
so they could stake claims. Until now, the Nez Percé had always welcomed the white man, always willing to share the
land. But bitterness was setting in as talk between government
officials and Indian representatives continued, and the officials
were trying to pressure the Nez Percé chief, Joseph, into moving his people onto a much smaller reservation to be shared
with other tribes. So far, Chief Joseph was resisting the efforts,
and Birch had a feeling that this time, his government would
push the agreeable Nez Percé too far.

Through Tisdale, who served as interpreter, Birch found out
that Red Feather's daughter, Morning Star, had been missing
over a week, and that she had last been seen walking by a
stream that ran half a mile beyond the Nez Percé village.

Birch also learned that Morning Star had been educated by

a local missionary, and had been sent back East to finish up her education, courtesy of a local rich family, the Prouxs. She had been christened Marie Christine by the missionary, a Reverend Joseph Kirk.

Birch turned to Bear. "Were you looking forward to Morning Star becoming your wife?"

Bear, after Tisdale translated Birch's question, showed no emotion, no elation, no grief. Birch didn't need Tisdale to translate Bear's answer. He said, "Yes," in Nez Percé.

Birch wondered how it must feel for a proud, fierce warrior like Bear Who Touched the Sky to be marrying a woman from the same tribe who had been brought up partially in the white man's world.

For that matter, Birch wondered how Morning Star felt about the impending union. He asked Red Feather. "How did your daughter feel about marrying Bear Who Touched the Sky?"

"She was looking forward to her duties as a good wife to Bear Who Touched the Sky," was Red Feather's answer, but Birch caught a troubled look on his face. There was more to it, but Birch had a feeling that Red Feather wouldn't tell the entire truth.

He thought of another line of questioning. He addressed Red Feather. "Have you talked to this reverend, the one who helped send your daughter back East to complete her education?"

Red Feather and Bear Who Touched the Sky glanced at each other before answering. "Yes, we have talked to him. He is the first person we thought to talk to when Morning Star disappeared."

"And what was his reaction to her disappearance?" Birch asked.

"He did not seem very concerned," Bear said in a fierce tone. Birch noticed that his fists were clenched tightly at his sides.

Tisdale took out his Waltham pocket watch. "Well, Mr. Birch, there seems to be nothing more to be known here. I must be in Lewiston within the week." He gave no explanation beyond that, and Birch had no reason to stay beyond the time he had already spent.

Through Tisdale, Red Feather gave Birch several names of people Morning Star had known in Coeur d'Alene where she had been educated.

"I expect," came Tisdale's short reply, "I'll be in contact soon."

With that, Tisdale headed southwest, Birch due south.

It took several hours for Birch to ride to the town of Coeur d'Alene. He found Reverend Joseph Kirk's house easily. It was a modest dwelling, but it looked comfortable, as if the reverend was satisfied with his life. Birch knocked on the door, and a few moments later, a plump, red-cheeked man with a perpetual smile on his face and a shock of thick, white hair came to the door.

"Am I speaking to the Reverend Joseph Kirk?" Birch had taken his hat off in deference to this man of authority.

"That's me," the man said with a chuckle. "What can I do for you, young fellow?"

He hadn't called Birch "stranger," the common greeting for anyone who wasn't known to the general populace of a small town, he had used the term "young man." Very friendly. Birch wondered how friendly he would be when he was questioned about Morning Star. He explained why he was there.

The reverend surprised him by opening the door wider and stepping back. "Come in, come in."

They sat in the front room and were waited upon by Reverend Kirk's wife, a woman as spare as the reverend was round.

"Come here, wife. This is Jefferson Birch. He has come for some information about Morning Star, known to us now as Marie Christine," Reverend Kirk said, gesturing to his wife. She sidled over to him and he put his arm around her. "Mr. Birch, this is my wife, Anna. Morning Star took her first name when she was being tutored by us."

"Pleased to meet you, Mr. Birch," Anna Kirk replied, bobbing her head. Her eyes darted toward the back of the house.

"Let me put some water on for tea." She slipped out of her husband's hold and left the room.

The reverend lowered his voice. "Anna will be back in a few minutes with a tray of breads and jams as well as tea. I hope that you haven't eaten yet."

As a matter of fact, Birch hadn't eaten since early morning, and the promise of something to eat would be most welcome. "Reverend, I'll come straight to the point. I have just come from the Nez Percé village, and Red Feather is very concerned about the fate of his daughter. He thinks you have some knowledge of her whereabouts and would be grateful if you would cooperate."

The reverend frowned and took a pair of bifocals from a side table by the chair he sat in. He rubbed them absently with a large handkerchief. "I am sorry if I left him with that impression, but I do not know where Marie Christine is." He didn't look all that concerned. Birch was getting the same feeling that Red Feather and Bear Who Touched the Sky had gotten.

He decided to get the information from another angle. "Did she have any friends here in Coeur d'Alene?"

"Oh, yes," the reverend said, obviously pleased to get off the subject of Morning Star's disappearance, but just as pleased to talk about her. "She didn't look very Indian, which was one of the reasons I had chosen her to tutor. She fit very well into Coeur d'Alene society, and she has several friends who live here in town."

"Can you give me their names?"

Reverend Kirk hesitated for a fraction of a second, then smiled. "Of course. If you think it would help." He got up and went over to his desk, took a sheet of paper and dipped his pen in the inkwell. He then wrote down a couple of names with a flourish, blotted the paper, and handed it to Birch just as Mrs. Kirk brought in a tea tray.

The reverend rubbed his hands together as his wife poured tea. "Now, Mr. Birch, shall we partake of this repast?"

Birch wasn't sure how the reverend's wife had come up with such an elaborate tray in such a short time. There were thick slices of fresh-baked bread, homemade gooseberry jam and sweet churned butter, molasses cookies, some kind of sweet cake with brown sugar topping, and tea with cream and sugar.

While they ate, Mrs. Kirk withdrew again to the kitchen. The reverend didn't seem to notice this time, his hand reaching greedily for another cookie, his tea sloshing over his cup. Birch decided that while the reverend's guard was down, this was a good time to talk to him.

"Why did you offer to send Marie Christine back East?" Birch asked.

Reverend Kirk swallowed a bite of cookie and slurped some of his milky tea. "Marie was a quick learner, and I could see that she enjoyed our world. As I said earlier, Marie fit nicely into Coeur d'Alene society. Sometimes I think her mother might have been a white woman."

"What about her father, Red Feather, and the man she is betrothed to, Bear Who Touched the Sky?"

The reverend stopped sipping tea and looked at Birch curiously. "What about them?"

"You don't seem very concerned about Marie's well-being, so I'm assuming you know where she is. Don't you think her father has the right to know that she's well?"

The reverend frowned. "Mr. Birch, I don't think you understand Red Feather's concern very well." His cup clattered onto its saucer and he started.

"Enlighten me."

"Red Feather wanted, well, the whole Nez Percé nation wanted, Marie Christine to become a symbol of their new nation. They wanted her to be," here, Reverence Kirk seemed to be searching for a word or description, "they wanted her to be another Sarah Winnemucca."

Birch was aware of who Sarah Winnemucca was, a Paiute woman who had been taught by Christian missionaries. She had become a negotiator and a spokeswoman for the Indian nation. Still, she was a controversial figure—her own people did not always trust her. She had been married twice, to date, and from what Birch had read about her, he did not imagine that she felt comfortable in either the white man's world, or in her own tribe. Without telling him anything of use, the reverend was filling in the picture of Morning Star/Marie Christine for Birch. The only thing Birch needed to do now was to figure out where Marie Christine was staying, and go to speak to her.

"Reverend," he began, "I think I understand part of the reason why Marie Christine left her tribe. But it will do no good to keep her in hiding." Birch finished off his tea and stood up, taking his hat up, ready to leave. "Please tell me where she is, and let me go speak to her. Her father needs to know where she is, needs to know that she wasn't taken away against her will. And if she is unhappy with the plans her father and Chief Joseph have for her, she should confront her father."

The reverend looked up at Birch with sad eyes and shook his head. He put his tea cup down and stood up to shake Birch's hand. "I'm sorry, Mr. Birch, but you know how women are treated. I don't think the girl would have much of a choice. Besides," he smiled regretfully here, "I gave Marie Christine my word and I can't go back on it. Please convey my sympathies to her Indian family." He turned and called to his wife, who appeared quickly enough. "Please show Mr. Birch to the door, dear. I have a sermon to write."

Mrs. Kirk walked Birch to the door and went outside with him.

"If I don't bring news back to her father," Birch told Mrs. Kirk, "there could be trouble for the reverend and yourself, possibly the entire town." He wasn't sure if that would happen, but Bear Who Touched the Sky seemed to be the sort of man who would take things into his own hands if he didn't see results soon. Birch looked the reverend's wife straight in the eye. "You could avert a tragedy, Mrs. Kirk."

She hesitated, turning away for a moment and catching her breath, and when she turned back, there was determination in her eye. "My husband gave his word, but no one asked me to give mine. I love Marie Christine as I would love my own daughter, but I've been against her decision to leave her father and tribe since the beginning. But I cannot, in good faith, tell you where Marie Christine is living. However, I can tell you a name of someone who might help you." She told him, then Birch thanked her and left.

It was ninety miles to Lewiston, through the Coeur d'Alene Mountains, and it took Birch three days to get there. The Proux name was well known in Lewiston, hanging above a general store, a hotel, and a saloon. Even a street was named after the Proux family. In one of the saloons in Lewiston, he learned more about the Proux family. Jean Proux had been a merchant who had made his money by moving West and opening up a trading post near Fort Hall during the early days of the Emigrant Trail. When he had amassed his fortune, he moved his family to Lewiston and they had been there for ten years. Jason, the youngest, had recently returned from back East, where he had attended Harvard College.

It was early in the evening when Birch left the saloon to pay a visit to Jean Proux. He had just entered the stable and was getting ready to saddle up Cactus when he heard two men approaching. Birch thought little of it since this was a boarding stable. The first man caught Birch off guard with a blow to the head. The second man pinned his arms back and let the first man throw a few more punches to Birch's gut. Through all of this, Birch could hear Cactus prancing around, nervously eyeing Birch's attackers. When the men stopped beating him up, Birch fell to his knees on the hay-strewn floor, his arms clutching his middle as he tried to catch his breath.

"We hear you been asking questions about the Prouxs," one of the men said. Birch couldn't have identified either of them—he had been too busy taking blows to notice what they looked like. "Stay away from the Prouxs. In fact, it would be better for your health to leave town tonight." When Birch finally recovered enough to look up, they were gone.

Nothing made Birch more determined to find out the truth than someone who told him he couldn't investigate. He rode out to Jean Proux's house, his hand near his gun, all the time wary of possible ambushes.

When he got to the house, a large handsome mansion befitting a man of Proux's status, Birch dismounted and climbed the steps to the imposing front door. A stiff butler with a British accent answered and, looking down his nose at Birch, left him outside while he went in search of his employer. Ten minutes later, a barrel of a man, thick graying mustache, monocle in his left eye, cigar clenched between his teeth, came to the door.

"I'm Jean Proux. Who are you?" He eyed Birch warily. "Are you a messenger?"

Birch didn't feel much like playing games. He came straight to the point. "Yes. I've been hired to give you a message from Red Feather and Bear Who Touched the Sky. Red Feather wants to see his daughter."

Proux went stone-faced. "I don't know what you're talking about, mister, but I'm calling my guards to throw you out."

"The way you called the other men who sucker-punched me back at the stable in Coeur d'Alene?"

A strange expression crossed Proux's face. "What are you talking about? I sent no men to come after you. I don't even know you."

Birch was getting tired of facing hostility and secrecy. "Well, someone in the Proux family knows me, knew that I was coming here. Reverend Kirk had three days to send a wire to someone, and I can go down to the telegraph office to find out who it was, then I can bring in the marshal." Birch had checked earlier on the Coeur d'Alene marshal and discovered that he was an honest lawman, not bought and paid for by powerful men like some lawmen.

Jean Proux went pale, then took a few moments to think about it. He seemed to make up his mind quickly as to who had sent the men and why. "We'd better settle this right now." He ordered a horse saddled up, and led Birch to his son's house, about a mile away.

"My son has recently returned from Harvard in Boston, and was just married the other day," was all Jean Proux would say on the ride over.

No expense has been spared on this house either. Birch wondered if it had been a wedding gift to the young couple. Ornate wrought ironwork and gingerbread cutouts decorated the house. Proux knocked on the massive carved mahogany door, hat already in his hand. A maid opened the door, and looked curiously at him.

"Mr. Proux, your son is indisposed at the moment. Would you like to come in and wait while I tell him you're here?" She opened the door wider to usher him in, then seemed to catch sight of Birch.

"He's with me, Martha," Proux said. "Is the lady of the house at home as well?"

"Yes, Mr. Proux. I'll tell her you're here." She threw another interested look at Birch before withdrawing from the parlor.

A few moments later, a young woman with dark good looks came into the room. She was beautiful in an exotic way, her black hair held back with diamond and ruby combs, her ebony eyes sparkling brighter than the jewels that graced her hair. She had that special glow that only newlywed women can wear and Birch hated to bring up her past. She glanced at Birch, then went over to Jean Proux. He took her hands as she lightly kissed him on the cheek.

"You must be Morning Star," Birch said.

She withdrew her hands from her father-in-law and took a few steps back. Her dusky complexion turned pale and she put a hand to her mouth.

"I-I'm sorry, sir, there is no one by that name here," came a voice from behind her. A handsome young man, outfitted in the latest fashion from back East, put his hands on her shoulders and tried to draw her away from the door. He noticed Birch's companion. "Father, what are you doing here?"

Jean Proux gazed steadily at his son. "And I might ask you what you meant by hiring two men to beat up this man for asking questions."

Jason Proux paled. "I-I don't know what you mean."

His father's brow darkened. "Don't lie to me, my son. You've never been very good at it."

Morning Star stepped between the two men. "Please, Father, don't be angry with him. He did it for me. For us."

All the anger drained out of Jean Proux. He looked kindly at her and put a hand to her cheek. "I know, dear. I know." He looked tired. "But it's time to tell the truth. No more deception."

She nodded and turned to Birch. "I am sorry about what

happened to you, Mr. Birch." She glanced at her new husband, who stared at Birch in a hateful, protective manner.

"I've been hired by your father to find you."

"Well you can tell him that there is no Morning Star here." Jason had shouldered his way past his father, and threw a weak punch at Birch, who easily avoided it. "Come on, step outside and show me you're a man."

Birch studied him, then said, "Son, one thing your father obviously hasn't taught you. Never pick a fight with an armed man." He pulled back the edge of his duster and showed Jason his gun. Jason deflated and stepped back.

"Jason, it's time." Morning Star, now Marie Christine, turned back to Birch and ushered him inside. "I'll be happy to talk to you, Mr. Birch."

Marie Christine sat on the settee and indicated that everyone else should sit. Birch liked the fact that she had taken charge of the situation. Her husband sat next to her.

"Mr. . . . . Birch, is it?" He nodded and waited. Marie Christine continued. "Mr. Birch, please convey my apologies to my father for any worries that I may have caused him." She glanced at her husband. "As you can see, I am well taken care of." Jason Proux put a hand over her hand and smiled. It was clear to Birch that he loved her, and that he would do anything to protect her.

"Mrs. Proux, may I ask one thing?"

She turned her bright smile to him and said, "Of course. Ask anything."

"Why?"

Her smile dimmed a bit, as if a stiff wind had blown through her heart and she looked down. "Mr. Birch, I met Jason when I was being tutored by the reverend and his wife." She paused here and laughed a bit. "You went to see the reverend, didn't you? That's how you found out I was here."

Birch felt the reverend and his wife needed defending, but he didn't have to say a word. The question was rhetorical. Marie Christine shook her head. "The reverend probably didn't give up my whereabouts. It was Mrs. Kirk, wasn't it?"

Birch shrugged, wanting to remain noncommittal. She continued. "I bear her no ill will. Mrs. Kirk has always counseled me to face my father, and she knew it was just a matter of time.'' The maid came in with a tea tray—it would be the first time today that Birch had eaten. As the maid poured tea, Marie Christine said, ''You must have given Mrs. Kirk a pressing reason why she should violate my confidence. Even though she didn't approve of the way I left, she would not have told you unless there was some threat.'' She looked up as if an unpleasant thought had just occurred to her. ''You didn't scare her badly, did you?''

Birch smiled and shook his head. ''I just told her what might happen if your father and his tribe didn't find you. The Kirks are not good liars, and both your father and your betrothed knew that the reverend was lying to them.''

Her husband had remained quiet until now, but it was clear that he was getting restless. ''Marie, you don't have to talk to him.''

She eyed Birch speculatively. ''Is that right, Mr. Birch? I don't have to talk to you?''

Birch shook his head. ''No, I can't make you talk to me.''

''But my father will hear only what I have told you so far.'' She looked at her husband, who met her gaze, then reluctantly nodded his understanding that things had progressed too far for her to stop now.

She stood up abruptly, her arms crossed, and paced languidly, as if she had been born to this life. ''As I said before, I had grown up partly in the Reverend and Mrs. Kirk's house, and I knew Jason and his family. We didn't fall in love until we were both in Boston. We saw each other more frequently there, going for Sunday buggy rides in the countryside, walks in the Boston Common, and to the opera and theater. All with a chaperone, of course.''

Birch nodded and sipped his tea. He was getting tired of tea and wished for something stronger. As if reading his mind, Jean Proux stood up and went over to a table on which a cut glass brandy decanter and four snifters stood. He poured three healthy shots and offered one to Birch, and one to his son.

Marie Christine turned to look fondly at her husband. ''We fell in love, and decided that nothing would keep us apart.''

"Not even Bear Who Touched the Sky?" Birch could feel Jason Proux's tension.

"Not even my father's plans for me, for the future of our tribe," Marie Christine replied pointedly.

"So you were running away from expectations," Birch suggested.

Marie Christine gave him a warm smile. "No, I was running to my future." She looked out the window, then turned back to Birch. "Come for a walk with me in my garden." It was not a suggestion, it was a command. Birch complied.

It was a hot spring day and rows of daffodils, irises, and crocuses were springing up. Even a peony bush had buds on it, ready to burst at the end of May.

"You have heard something of my father's expectations for me, haven't you?" Marie Christine asked.

"Yes, it seemed that he was trying to do some good for your people by getting you an education in the white man's world."

She smiled bitterly. "He got the idea after meeting Sarah Winnemucca many years ago when she was first becoming known to Indians and white men alike. When Reverend and Mrs. Kirk offered to take me in, he saw it as an opportunity to do some good for the people, he saw me as destined to become just like her."

"That had to be hard to live up to," Birch said.

She nodded. "I had the opportunity to meet Miss Winnemucca at a lecture at Harvard. Jason escorted me, and afterwards, we were introduced. I found myself telling her about my dilemma. She seemed to understand, my vacillation between doing what was expected of me, and what I really wanted. She saw the love between Jason and me." Marie Christine stopped and faced me. "And do you know what she told me?"

"I have a pretty good idea," he said.

She started to walk again, slower this time. "She told me that some people were born to a destiny, and others were pressed into it against their will. I felt as if she could see right through me. Then she encouraged me to do what was right for me."

"She sounds like a wise woman," Birch replied.

Marie Christine nodded decisively. "She is. But it's been hard, not knowing how to tell my father, and eventually Chief Joseph, not wanting to dash their hopes and dreams of a better day for our people. But I don't think I'm their answer." She paused, then said in a sad voice, "I don't think there is an answer."

"It must be hard to live with someone else's expectations, and not be able to live your own life."

She nodded. "You understand." She sighed. "But I suppose that I have to face my father. It has been a little over two weeks since I left, and it's time to make things right."

She held out her hand. "Thank you, Mr. Birch."

He stood up to shake her hand. She had a firm, dry handshake. She would have made a fine translator, but she would have been unhappy. In the background, Jason was coming toward them. Jean Proux stayed in the background. "I'll have to consult with my husband."

"I think he will support you, Mrs. Proux," Birch said. The Prouxs escorted him to the front of their house, where he swung up in the saddle. "I'll be riding back to your father's village, Mrs. Proux. When should I tell him to expect you?"

She looked at her husband, talked softly for a few moments, then replied, "We will be packing today, and should be there a day behind you, Mr. Birch."

He tipped his hat to them, wheeled Cactus around, and headed back north. Although it was not the ending Red Feather or Bear Who Touched the Sky would have wanted, at least he could assure them that Morning Star was safe and happy. But Birch had to wonder if she had bought her own happiness at the expense of her nation's future.

THE DEATH(S) OF BILLY THE KID

—

Arthur Winfield Knight

Billy: Home

Friends tell me I ought to leave the territory. But what would I do in Mexico with no money? I can stay here awhile and get some money, then go to Mexico.

Fort Sumner's home. I love this country: the Valley of Fires, the Pecos River.

I'm not going to let Garrett scare me away.

Friends think I don't know what I'm doing when I ride around the country in circles, tracking myself; I know where I'm going because I've been there. I've been to Alamogordo, Tularosa, too.

I like the purple light on the mountains at twilight and the sound of guitars coming from the cantinas along with the laughter of the señoritas. Once, I fucked the earth, I loved it so.

I want *this* soil in my face when I die.

I know times are changing. There's a new law each day of the week. Men like Pat call it progress. I call it loss.

This is my home. Nobody's going to make me go.

Garrett: Apples

The Kid was eating an apple minutes before I shot him.

He and Paulita were in bed together, naked. She'd take a bite of the apple, then give it to Billy. They were laughing in the moonlight, passing the apple back and forth, the moon in their eyes, licking each other's lips. Some of the juice dribbled onto Paulita's dark breasts.

Billy kissed them and said, "I love apples," then he went into the kitchen. He was silhouetted against the light when I pulled the trigger. The juice was still running down his chin when he fell.

Billy: The Premonition

"Can you feel the baby moving?" Paulita asks, placing my hand on her stomach. I hold it there a long time, too tired to move, too tired to talk. But I feel the life within her.

We lie on the double bed. The windows are open, but it's July. The heat is trapped like a fly in the barrel of a pistol, and the moon seems blue.

"The baby should be here by the first frost," she says. "I know it will be a boy."

Sometimes my groin is numb, as if a cold wind blew across my body, but there is no wind.

When I shiver, Paulita puts her arms around me. "What are you thinking?" she asks.

I think Garrett must be getting close by now; I can almost imagine him coming through the peach orchard with some men, coming to kill me, but I don't tell Paulita that.

The baby kicks like a .45 beneath my hand. "See, see," she says, laughing.

Suddenly, I'm sad.

I won't be here to see our son.

Paulita Maxwell: Peaches

He brought me a peach the first time he came. It was the Fourth of July, dusk, and some children were playing with fireworks.

Billy and I sat on my father's porch, sharing the peach he'd plucked from the orchard behind our house. He seemed embarrassed when I put his left hand on my breast, holding it there. The juice from the peach ran between my breasts and my breath came faster.

A rocket exploded, showering us with blue and green sparks, and Billy's eyes were blue and green.

I was surprised at how thin his wrist was. I looked at his right palm in the light from the doorway and knew he was going to die soon.

I said, "A dark woman will love you."

Pete Maxwell: Apple Brandy

I come into the house and find them—Billy and Paulita—naked. I tell her she's disgraced herself, but she just laughs. "You're my brother, not my keeper."

(When we were small, I played with Paulita in the tub.)

It's tornado weather, hot and still, and the sky's electric.

Paulita grabs Billy's black sombrero, covering her breasts, her eyes huge in the soft light.

Billy's pud's tumescent.

Paulita says, "Billy brought me brandy so the afternoon wouldn't seem so long," and I can smell apples on her breath and death on his.

Billy: Hymns

I'm tired of singing. It seems like that's all we ever do on Sundays.

I want to dance, want to get drunk, and I'm tired of dressing like a country Jake. But Mr. Tunstall says it's good to get some religion, so we go to McSween's house every Sunday afternoon. When we're not singing, we listen to Dr. Ealy preach about Paul and Silas at Philippi, but I'd rather be at the Wortley Hotel. They have a nice bar and the beer's cold.

I don't even know where Philippi is and I don't want to know if I can't get there on my horse. Do they serve beer?

I want to sing "Turkey in the Straw" or "Sewanee River," something I can stomp my foot to.

Why do I have to listen to all these damn hymns?

I'm not going to heaven.

Celsa Gutierrez: Adulteress

Sometimes Billy comes to me when my husband's gone.

I know Billy has another woman and it hurts when I see Paulita. She's younger. Prettier.

I know what they call women like me: Whore. *Puta.* Adulteress. They are just words. When Billy touches me, they have no meaning.

Now I hear distant fiddles as I lie next to my sleeping husband. I imagine Billy whirling around and around, dizzy, in Paulita's arms, imagine his lips touching her cheek.

I know the things he says: Oh my love.

I touch the inside of my husband's thigh, touch his sex, rubbing it, until he awakens, hard. I keep my eyes shut. I say, "Make love to me."

Garrett: Marriage

When my wife died, I married her sister. I needed someone and she always cared for me. Even the priest approved. It was a church wedding. Most of my friends came for the reception.

When Billy arrived he asked, "How does it feel to fuck your dead wife's sister?" He was holding a bottle, drunk, but that didn't make it right. I hated him all that hot afternoon.

My wife asked, "How come you sweat so much?" My white suit turned dark under the arms.

A lot of people wondered how I could shoot Billy. We'd ridden together. We'd been friends. How could I do it? They thought I must have needed the money or that I was ambitious, but it's simple: Billy ruined my wedding.

Zaval Gutierrez: Cuckold

The men in Fort Sumner make clucking sounds when I walk past them, and I no longer go to the cantina. I drink alone.

I watch my wife hang the laundry, watch her breasts stretch against her blouse, and I want her even though I know she has a lover.

Once, I watched from a window as Billy and Celsa undressed each other. They were laughing and did not know I was there with a pistol. I aimed at Billy, my finger tightening on the trigger at the moment he came. I wanted to say, "I hope that fuck was worth dying for," but I ran clucking into the apple orchard.

I'm not even man enough to kill my wife's lover.

Billy: The Wasp

One of the boys caught a wasp and brought it inside, trapped in a bottle. He said, "It's going to die anyway."

It was almost fall, but the days were still hot.

The boys began to bet how long the wasp would last.

It made it through the morning and the afternoon. By dusk it was barely moving, but it was still alive when we blew out the lantern. I thought I could hear it hitting the sides of the bottle.

The heat seemed suffocating.

There was a five-hundred-dollar reward for me, dead or alive.

In the moonlight I could see beads of sweat on my arm, could see the bottle with the wasp in it on the table.

As I got up, I felt my lungs constrict. By the time I got to the table, I was panting.

Outside, I let the wasp go.

Garrett: The Job

They say I never gave the Kid a chance that night in Fort Sumner. They say he came toward me naked, unarmed, and they wonder how I could shoot a friend.

Let me tell you, Billy had a six-shooter in his right hand and a butcher knife in his left. I was just defending myself, doing a job; I had a warrant for his arrest, dead or alive.

I let the Mexican women carry his body across the yard to the carpenter shop, where they laid him out on a work-bench and lit candles around his body, conducting a wake. You'd have thought he was Jesus the way they were all crying when I went to look at his body.

Some of the women spit at me and swore although I told them, "He was a dangerous man, a killer. I shot him mercifully through the heart, a clean shot. Look! I'm the sheriff. I was just doing my job." But they still spit at me and called me names.

Billy: Whores

They're always glad to see me when I go to the Doll House. Becky and Soap Suds Sal run toward me, Sal with her hands wet; she used to be a laundress and still loves hot water.

They both ask, "What did you bring us?" and I give them dried flowers and chocolate hearts because it's nice to be wanted for something besides the price on my head.

They tug at me, both wanting me to go upstairs.

Here, I'm not a killer. I'm kind. I give them money and they say, "Billy, you're such a man." Here, things are simple. There's no bickering. No jealousy. Just an exchange: love for money.

I shiver when Sal puts a wet hand into my pants. She says,
"Come with me."

Garrett: Piss-pot

They butchered a yearling the morning they knew Billy would
be back because he'd want beefsteak and beer and Billy always got what Billy wanted.

When I saw the Kid, he was silhouetted against the light
from Maxwell's kitchen, licking his fingers. I wondered why
so many women loved him, then I pulled the trigger.

I heard his body hitting the table, heard dishes breaking as
I ran outside. An Indian woman cursed me: "Sonofabitch.
Piss-pot."

I think she'd imagined Billy a prodigal son come home.
After he ate the fatted calf, he wasn't supposed to die.

Billy: Shackled

They bring me in chains to the house of my girlfriend so we
can say goodbye.

"It's a hell of a Christmas," I say, trying to smile.

It must be ten below outside and the snow's deep enough
to hide the chains on my legs.

Paulita's mother asks my guard if he'll unlock the irons so
Paulita and I can go into the bedroom for an "affectionate
farewell," but he tells her, "I ain't Santa Claus," and laughs
when I stumble toward Paulita, my chains clanking. They put
them on me when I was captured at Stinking Springs yesterday.

Paulita's face is soft in the light from the candles.

She cries, hugging me, and says, "Merry Christmas."

Bob Olinger: Deputy

"You little bastard. You twerp. I'm goin' to enjoy watchin'
you hang. The great Billy the Kid will kick his feet and crap

in his pants just like anyone else at the end of a rope.

"You better get straight with Jesus, boy. Get straight now.

"One prisoner they hung had his head ripped off. It was bruised, kind of purple lookin'. Someone put it in a bottle of alcohol and charged people to see it.

"Maybe I could pickle your head if it rips off. Huh? Or if it don't, maybe some other part.

"They say you get a hell of a hard-on when that rope tightens around your neck. It sends all your blood rushin' down below, boy. You'll have the biggest boner of your life."

Billy: Revenge

They hung me by my thumbs when I tried to escape from the jail in Santa Fe. The jailer would jab me in the stomach with his shotgun and hum, "Rock-a-bye, Billy," as he watched me swing.

"This'll prepare you for the hangin'," he said, and laughed until he shook.

I spit in his face, but he put his weight on me, hard, and I thought my thumbs would rip off.

When they cut me down, I couldn't move my hands or legs for hours. All I could think was, I'll get you, I'll get you.

Later, I stuck my pistol into his mouth and said, "Suck on this, you bastard." I could hear his teeth chattering on the barrel and his eyes were bloodshot between my sights.

I pulled the hammer back and asked, "How come you're not laughing now?"

Sister Blandina: Nails

When I heard they brought Billy to town, I went to see him.

The shackles around his hands and feet were nailed to the floor so he couldn't sit or stand.

He said, "I wish I could offer you a chair, Sister." That was all.

I wanted to say, "Forgive us," but I just stood there. He must have thought I was dumb.

Then I ran out of the room into the dark streets. A March wind blew.

In my dreams that night I kept seeing our Lord, His hands and feet bloody, nailed to the Cross, but He had the Kid's face and He kept saying, "I'll kill them before I let them take me again."

Billy: Snow Birds

"Suppose Pat Garrett was a pretty little bird and suppose that pretty little bird in the street was him," I say, pointing at a snow bird in front of the saloon. "If I was to shoot that little bird and hit him anywhere except in the head, it would be murder."

We've been drinking all morning.

I shoot from the hip and a headless snow bird floats in the bloody air.

I say, "No murder," then fire again and another bird runs in a bloody circle, its head missing.

Acquitted again.

The boys laugh and cheer.

The third time I fire feathers fly and the bird has a red bib where its breast used to be.

"Boys," I say, "I've murdered Pat."

Garrett: New Year's Eve 1900

Men shy away from me since I shot the Kid. I even had to hire an attorney to get the five hundred dollars I'd been promised for killing him.

I had a wife and seven kids to support, but no one cared about that.

When I go into a bar, the conversation stops and, these days, I always drink alone.

When the Kid was alive, we'd ride out into the country

together, playing cards, drinking, dancing. Even my kids ask why I did it. I've tried to explain; I even wrote a book about me and the Kid.

Since I shot him, I've tried ranching in Roswell and Fort Stanton. Tried breeding horses in Uvalde.

I failed.

Then I rode with the Home Rangers. Worked as a cattle boss.

Failed again.

Ran for sheriff in Chaves County.

Failed.

Now it's a new century, but everything ended the night I shot the Kid.

Billy: Last Words

In the other room, the girl I made love to is sleeping now.

I love these hot nights in New Mexico, love the desert air on my naked body. I'll never leave Fort Sumner.

Paulita says I can't stop laughing when I start. It's true I like to laugh and I've done it while I'm dancing or drinking or whoring, even when I've killed men. (They all deserved it.)

After I shot Deputy Olinger with his own shotgun, I danced on the balcony of the Lincoln jail for an hour, laughing.

Some of the boys asked why I didn't just ride away, but you don't get many moments like that.

Somebody's coming toward me, silhouetted against the moon. He has a familiar walk, but it's so dark I can't focus my eyes.

"*¿Quién es?* Garrett?"

I ask again, louder: "Who's that?"

Sallie Chisum: Candy Hearts

They say he was a bad man, that it was a good thing Garrett shot him, but that's a lie.

Billy brought me two candy hearts one hot afternoon in

August. I remember how soft his hands seemed. It was like being touched by a cloud.

I was new at my uncle's ranch, lonely. Billy smiled and said, "Don't believe everything you hear about me."

I was thirteen and had never been kissed and the chocolate melted on my lips.

Garrett: Pals

We drank double shots of bourbon back-to-back with beer. I told Billy's older brother it had to be the way it was, the Kid would never surrender, and Joe said he understood. Billy was always wild.

I told Joe that the Kid and I rode together, played cards together, drank together, slept with the same women; we were pals.

Joe said, "Now we're pals," slurring his words, his arm on my unsteady shoulder, but it wasn't the same as when Billy touched me.

MRS. CRAWFORD'S ODYSSEY

Deborah Morgan

They tried to keep him another day.

The woman had arrived the night before to fetch him, take him home to the little farm in Colorado. She stepped off the Union Pacific and onto the platform of a whistle-stop of a town in Nebraska that appeared to be unusually lively.

The porter handed down her tapestry carpetbag. Effortlessly, she took the weight of it in one hand and with the other stayed her hat against the autumn winds. A glance westward told her that only a few hours of daylight remained.

A colored boy, about eleven years old and favoring his right leg came toward her, hand outstretched. Was he a beggar? she wondered. Did he wish to secure a few coins in exchange for carrying her bag?

As he approached, the woman saw that his hand was cupped around something and in a blink, she saw her own son and a "bird's nest" hand cradling two tiny robin's eggs he had brought her one Easter a dozen years ago. The memory warmed her and she smiled slightly.

Her smile gave way to a look of confusion when she saw that in this boy's hand, secured with a bit of blue ribbon, rested a small scrap of hair. It looked white as lye soap against his black skin.

"Wanna buy a piece of history, lady? This here's the real thing, lifted straight off a outlaw corpse."

She frowned. "I am afraid I do not understand."

"They's been a slew of folks comin' in for a souvenir. I can save you a passel of time waitin' in line."

"I am not here for souvenirs, so, if you will excuse me."

He called out to her as she walked away. "Ever'one think it gotta be fake 'cause I'm a color, but I axe you, where else would I get dis?"

"Marshal Drew?"

The marshal struggled to hoist his plump body from the oak armchair behind a desk strewn with wanted posters and official-looking reports. Without the slope-creased hat, she figured him to be about four inches shorter than her own five feet ten inches. "Afternoon, ma'am," he said finally, after catching his breath. "Is there something I can help you with?"

She extended her hand, shook his with a firm grip. "I am here to claim the body of my son, Matthew." She slipped a flimsy from its secure place in the palm of her gloved right hand and passed it to him. "I believe you sent this. I was not sure whether I should check with you first or go directly to the undertaker."

He looked at the telegram, then at her. "You're Mrs. Crawford. My apologies, ma'am. I weren't expectin' you so soon. And," he added, shaking his head, "I just can't get used to his Christian name." He shuffled through the papers on his desk, retrieved a wanted poster and handed it to her along with the flimsy. "This is all I knew about him until a few days ago. Seems to've picked up the name 'Talent' right fast. Had the peculiar habit, they say, of giving a tithe to the church out of every job he pulled. Now Margaret—that's my missus—Margaret, she holds all the Bible learnin' in the family. She says that a talent was Biblical money, sorta like our silver dollars of today."

She skimmed the poster. A nickname. Why hadn't she known? The sketch held a remarkable likeness to Matthew, but the words? Robberies and depredations. Reward. Arrest and Conviction. She could not bear to read more, yet she recognized the part of her that would later require answers. "May I keep this?"

"Well, I suppose there'd be no harm in it. As you can see, I was lucky I found a letter from you in that little Bible he carried, or he'd be up on the hill in a corner marked off for leftovers."

Matthew's Bible. A prize he had won as a child in Sunday School for reciting the most verses from memory. It was brown leather, what they called a traveling edition, with his initials stamped in gold on the cover and his favorite verse written out by his teacher across from a picture of Jesus in a meadow with children and lambs: "Be ye, therefore, ready also; for the Son of man cometh at an hour when ye think not. Luke 12:40."

"Would you take me to see him?"

Marshal Drew could not match the woman's quick, long strides and was trotting alongside her. "Maybe I should go on ahead of you, make sure everything's ready." The words came out in short puffs.

"That will not be necessary."

"Then, wait a minute, please." He took her arm, guided her into the vacant entryway of the barbershop. "I should warn you first, Mrs. Crawford. People are drawn to this sort of thing. Curiosity seekers and the sort. Undertakers have quite a chore of overseeing, so it's customary for them to charge a fee. You know, for crowd control and such."

"Are you saying that I have to *pay*—"

"No, ma'am! Lands, no! I just want you to be prepared for what you're about to see. We—I mean Barnes, the undertaker—figured the mourners would be thinned out before you got here. Like I said, nobody was expectin' you this soon." He was out of breath, his face sweaty and flushed.

She resumed walking, heard him behind her trying to keep up.

The sight of the crowd around the entrance to the funeral parlor sickened her. Where was their respect for family? Did they have nothing better to do with their money than spend it to look at the body of someone they did not even know? She elbowed her way into the well-appointed foyer, ignoring the demands that she wait her turn.

A young man in a suit too small for his bulky frame was leaning against the door facing of a side parlor, handing out leaflets and collecting money. Printed on the cover of the leaflet in embossed letters were the words: *Barnes and Son Funeral Emporium. Always here for you in your time of need.*

She looked at him, resisted the urge to brush his scruffy bangs from his eyes. "Are you Barnes or Son?"

"Neither." It was Marshal Drew. "This is my boy. Billy, this is Talent's mother. Now clear out this room and give her some time alone with him."

"Old man Barnes ain't gonna—"

"Billy," the marshal gave him a stern look, "shut up and do what I tell you."

She gasped when she saw the body, and the candles flanking the polished mahogany casket fluttered as though the woman had sucked away their last breath.

This could not be her twenty-two-year-old son. Matthew had golden features, sunlit hair, a strong, square-set jaw. Laid out before her was an old man, bald, with flesh of a blue-white translucency, like watered-down milk. The heavily rouged cheekbones emphasized vast, dark hollows that should have been a jawline.

Someone had made a terrible mistake, she was sure of it. She grabbed at that thread of hope, caught it, held it taut. This eased her and she approached the deceased like any slight acquaintance might—respectfully, but thankful it's not one of your own. Only when she was leaning over the body did she discover death's ruse and see, unmistakably, her child.

She clasped her hand over her mouth, a futile attempt to contain her emotions. Tears flowed until she believed that she would never be able to cry again.

"My dear, precious boy," she said at last, "what have they done to you?"

Presently, she came to terms with the condition of his body. But his hair? She looked more closely at the scalp. It appeared to have been shaved, but there were also gouges, gashes, as if someone had carelessly chopped at his beautiful golden locks.

While she puzzled over this a tall man, lean and stoop-shouldered, entered the parlor. "Mrs. Crawford, I am your funeral director, Josiah Barnes. Let me offer my sincere condolences upon the demise of your son."

"Who did this to his hair?"

"You should not be here alone, Mrs. Crawford. You are obviously distraught."

"I asked you a question."

"We can take care of that, Mrs. Crawford, I assure you. I am afraid some of the mourners get carried away, want some kind of memento of those departed souls who have gained a reputation. And, I must say, your son did make quite a name for himself."

Before she could respond, the marshal came in. "That Pinkerton fella wasn't on the train."

She stiffened. "What does that have to do with me?"

"Sorry, ma'am, I thought you knew. We're required to keep your boy longer for the Pinkertons. They have to review the case, gather statistics, determine if this really is the outlaw called Talent."

"Is my word as his mother not good enough for you?"

"Of course it is, ma'am, of course it is. The thing is, procedure's the name of the game nowadays." The marshal frowned. "You look awful spent, Mrs. Crawford. You should get a room before there ain't any left to be got."

She started to tell him that she didn't plan to stay the night, then thought better of it. For some reason, they were stalling. "I suppose I am tired." She smiled as convincingly as she could. "Would you point out the nearest hotel with a restaurant?"

"That'll be easy," said the marshal. "There's only one."

The dining room was large, but deserted. She was just ahead of the supper crowd and for this the woman was thankful. She glanced at the blackboard menu, then chose a table near one of the windows.

A hefty woman in a crisp, white apron walked over with a coffee tray. "Evenin', dear. You look like you might be needing this."

"You're right. And the chicken and noodles, please."

The waitress jotted down the order. "Come in on the train?"

Mrs. Crawford nodded. "My first time here. Could you tell me how long the businesses stay open?"

"Well, today's Friday and that's the busiest as far as the train schedule goes. Most of 'em will close up soon, but the mercantile will be open late to accomodate the travelers."

As Mrs. Crawford ate her supper, the things Marshal Drew and the undertaker, Barnes, had said gnawed at her. *You should get a room. We're required to keep him longer for the Pink-ertons. Procedure. Required to keep him longer.*

Across the street, she could see that the crowd was thinning out around the funeral parlor. She still could not grasp the idea of paying to see a stranger's remains.

Then it came to her. She had been thinking more about *why* these people paid, and not giving enough attention to who was on the profitable end.

Slowly she realized that there was no Pinkerton agent on his way. Under the guise of profession and some mysterious loyalty to one another, the marshal and the undertaker must have believed they could get away with this excuse to buy time. They were no better than the outlaws from which they benefited.

After a few moments, she had a plan. She would need to make one purchase before returning to the funeral parlor.

"Lady! Hey, lady!"

Mrs. Crawford jumped. Night was settling in and she didn't like the idea of being out alone.

The colored boy from the depot hobbled up to her and held out the ribboned lock of hair. "You can have dis. I heard you was his mammy."

"Thank you." She held it, studied it for a few moments. "What is your name, boy?"

He told her it was Eli.

"I could use your help, Eli. Would you like to earn some money?"

"Yes'm." His broad grin revealed a crooked row of chalk-white teeth.

Mr. Barnes was in the foyer of his funeral parlor. After instructing the boy to stay behind her, the woman knocked on the etched glass door.

"Mrs. Crawford, I am surprised to see you back so soon." He noticed her carpetbag and frowned slightly. "Was there no lodging available?"

"I just need to make sure I have room in here for Matthew's things."

"Smart thinking, Mrs. Crawford. Frankly, I was just tallying your account. We can complete our business transactions this evening."

She followed the undertaker, motioned for Eli to wait just outside the office door.

"Your son's belongings are over there, in the corner. I do not think, however, you will manage to make that rifle fit." He chuckled.

She packed Matthew's belongings, then picked up the gun, held the familiar weight of it. "I remember when my husband—God rest him—brought this home for Matthew." She smiled, spoke gently, as she would at a tea social. "Actually, he bought two of them. He was so proud, you would have thought he had a matched set of thoroughbreds." She watched Mr. Barnes as he busily rechecked the figures of a ledger sheet with the heading: Matthew Crawford, alias TALENT.

"There," he proclaimed, rising from the black tufted leather chair. "Let me explain how I have arrived at the amount for my services."

He was standing beside her, holding the ledger, when she pressed the release lever and quietly broke open the gun.

"I took care of that little problem with your son's hair," he was saying.

From the pocket of her skirt, she slipped two of the slugs she had purchased and slid them into the twin barrels.

"I believe you will approve." He was pointing to a price. "The wig is of good quality and looks quite natural."

She slammed the gun shut.

Startled, the undertaker retreated several feet.

She rolled back the hammers. "This is not a rifle, Mr. Barnes. This is a Stevens ten-gauge double barrel breech-loading shotgun. It will take either buckshot or slugs. I have chosen slugs. A slug, Mr. Barnes, can carve a hole in you the size of a dinner plate.

"The Stevens ten-gauge offers another choice. I can move to this double trigger back here," she paused, pointed out the difference, "and give *you* a matched set. I believe, however, that one will do just fine." She placed her finger back on the single trigger.

She told Eli to run on ahead with her carpetbag and get the baggage car ready. She turned to the trembling undertaker. "Start walking. We're going to get Matthew."

Mr. Barnes spoke, his voice weak and shaky. "I've moved him to the back for the night. Billy's back there, too, watching over things while we're closed."

The marshal's son was snoring loudly when the pair walked in. He leaped off the couch when Mrs. Crawford banged the door shut. "I have no time to waste, Billy. Close the lid on that coffin. You and your boss are going to carry it out the back door and to the station. Quick and quiet, you hear me?"

He looked at Barnes. "Are you gonna let her get away with this?"

"Shut up, Billy."

The Union Pacific engine was faunching at the bit, coughing little bursts of smoke toward the moonlit sky in order to maintain a steady pressure.

The procession had reached the baggage car when the marshal came trotting up.

"Now looka here, ma'am . . ." He held up a hand.

"Do not underestimate my ability to send your son to glory, Marshal."

Eli had a couple of lanterns burning in the car near Mrs. Crawford's carpetbag and some rolled up canvas awnings. "They's so you can sleep."

"Thank you, Eli, that is just what I need." She paid the boy handsomely.

"Marshal, help Mr. Barnes load the coffin while I keep Billy attached to this shotgun."

After the railroad hands secured the ramp, the woman

backed up the steps of the car and through the door as the train pulled out of the station.

"You would be proud, Matthew," she said, settling herself on the canvas next to the boy's coffin. "We are on our way home. The worst is behind us and, truth be told, I am looking forward to a boring trip."

Maybe, she thought, *if I just keep talking to him I can somehow keep him with me.*

She reached out, touched the coffin. How would she ever learn to accept the slaughter of her son? She had heard some people say that you get used to it. Others disagreed, said that you never get over losing a child; you just try to deal with it from one day to the next.

Maybe they could tell her how to deal with Christmas. His birthday. What would the summers be like without his "surprise" visit to help her and Reuben, the hired hand, bring in the crops?

Did she raise him proper? She believed she had. Feelings of guilt, doubt, had surfaced lately, gained momentum with the news of his death. Still, when she asked herself if she had made some dire mistake in his upbringing, she couldn't pin one down.

Every Bible verse that he may have needed to call upon in time of trouble had been taught to him by her. Only one verse she kept for herself, held it fast in her heart, claimed its promise night after night. It was in Proverbs, Chapter 22, Verse 6. It said, "Train up a child in the way he should go and, when he is old, he will not depart from it."

God had promised it and she had believed it, taken it personally. God had promised *her*. And God had let her down. "How old do they have to be, God?" she shouted. "How old?"

She had suspected that Matthew was hanging around the pits of vipers, but when she confronted him, he always convinced her otherwise. So, she gave him the benefit of the doubt. She told herself that he was only keeping the truth from her to protect her. She knew he had loved her. Did he ever realize that she loved him *unconditionally*? He was, after all, her firstborn son—and there were no words strong enough to describe that special bond.

She wondered about the mothers of other outlaws. Were they like her? Did they struggle with the same doubts, the same feelings? What were *their* sons like?

She had just experienced, firsthand, the behavior of so-called "decent" people. Maybe her son had seen this too, decided that anything was better than being a hypocrite. Embracing this new thought, she justified her son's actions, began to understand his way of life.

The train moved along at a steady clip and the cadence relaxed the woman, gave her a sense of security. Exhaustion overtook her and she slept.

Dreams visited her, fitful dreams where Matthew and Reuben were in the fields, running and playing like children, ignoring her screaming, her warnings of the tornado moving in on them. "It's just rain, Mamma," Matthew called, laughing. "It's just rain."

A flash of lightning, a muffled clap of thunder woke her. As she lay there, sorting through the strange dream, she again saw the lightning, heard the thunder.

In an instant, she bolted upright, the 10-gauge aimed at a box-shaped apparatus on a tripod in front of a slight man with thick spectacles that distorted the size and shape of his eyes.

"Who are you?"

"Don't be hasty with that thing, madam. I'm with the *Omaha Standard*. Now, if I can get some facts from you—"

"Get out."

"You don't understand. Your photograph will be in all the papers. You'll be famous."

"I will be more famous if I shoot you now."

The little man reached for his camera, started toward the door.

"Leave it."

"You can't keep this! I'll lose my job if—"

She cocked the hammers. "I said leave it." She stood, walked toward him.

"All right, all right. I'm going." As he stepped out the door, he yelled, "You'll be hearing from my boss!"

She looked at the camera. She had never seen one in action, didn't know how to get the photographs out that the reporter had taken. With no other recourse, she released the hammers of the shotgun and with the butt of it, knocked the equipment to the floor and smashed it until all her strength was gone.

Breathless, she collapsed onto the canvas. She must find a way to stay awake, alert. She took Matthew's saddlebags from her own bag and, one by one, brought out each item and laid it on top of the coffin.

One side held the typical things: a shirt, needle and thread, a well-worn deck of cards. The other side contained more personal things: a comb she had given him several years before, the little Bible and the letter Marshal Drew had mentioned earlier. The last item was a strangely shaped envelope, with a receipt written on the front. It was dated three days before Matthew's death. She opened the flap and peered inside. She gasped, clutched it to her chest for a brief moment, skeptical of this stroke of good fortune. Then, gathering her strength, she pulled the tintype from the envelope. Suddenly, the primitive sketch on the wanted poster was as nothing. Here was an actual photograph! In it, her tall, handsome Matthew stood on a deserted railroad track, his Stevens beside him.

Was he waiting to rob the next train that came through?

She looked at the back. There, in her son's handwriting, was scrawled: *To Mamma, so's you won't ever forget what your son looks like.*

Something caught in her throat. It was difficult to look at the image but, in its own way, it was a reassurance. She would come to rely upon it, to superimpose it over the one burned in her mind of the exploited shell that used to be her child.

The saddlebags were repacked when Mrs. Crawford heard the deafening screech of metal against metal. Everything in the baggage car skidded forward.

Seconds later, a portly figure stepped into the car. He was dressed in a black suit of clothes and a starched white shirt. Strung across his ample waist was a bulky gold watch chain that winked in the lantern light. "I heard you were back here. We've got a robbery going on, and I have no doubt that you and that heathen son of yours brought it down on us."

"My son is not a heathen." She located the shotgun beside her.

"Apologize to the lady, you corn-fed hog." From the shadows stepped a man in cowboy garb, his words toned down by a bandana tied over his nose and mouth. A Colt's pistol was in his hand.

"I will do no such thing! I have sizable investments in this railroad line, and—"

"Explain it to Lucifer." The cowboy's bullet found its mark well and the man pitched forward, his dead weight jarring the car when he hit the plank floor.

Mrs. Crawford stared at the corpse.

"Sorry, ma'am. I will not abide rudeness to a lady." The cowboy removed his hat, pulled the bandana from his face. "That would be Talent in the box, wouldn't it." It was stated as fact.

"You know him?"

"He rode with us for awhile. That was somethin', how he cut ten percent out of his share and gave it to the churches and orphanages."

Someone knocked on the door. The cowboy said to enter.

"Heard Talent was back here." Another outlaw stepped into the car, removed his hat. "You must be his ma. My name's Andy. I'm a desperado." He grinned and shook her hand. "Your boy spoke mighty highly of you, ma'am."

He didn't even look old enough to shave.

"I left Roberts in charge," Andy addressed the cowboy, then turned to the woman. "Not that he's bein' disrespectful or nothin', ma'am. It's just that he never got to meet Talent and, well, somebody's gotta mind the store."

"If it's not imposin'," said the cowboy, "could we see him?"

Mrs. Crawford hesitated. "Have you boys ever seen what they do to a body that's considered famous?"

Andy spoke up. "You mean that rouge that makes you look like an embarrassed girl and the hair all slicked up with massacre oil?"

"That's *Macassar* oil, you fool." The cowboy walloped Andy with his hat, then apologized to the woman.

Mrs. Crawford slowly lifted the lid of the coffin and slipped the wig off Matthew's head. She wanted the boys to get the full impact.

They held up a lantern, leaned over the body. Andy let out a yell. The cowboy turned away.

At length, Andy said, "I can't hardly tell it's him. How did you know?"

"I didn't at first, but when I got beyond the things they did to his body, I could see my son. When he was little, he would climb up in my lap and I would brush his thick, golden hair." She choked back tears. "You see what they did. Why are such things allowed?"

She closed the coffin. Suddenly, she struck it with her fists. "There is nothing left of him to take and still I've had to fight off the people on this train! I can't even leave this baggage car!"

The cowboy stooped, held her shoulders. "You mean you've been in here since you boarded?"

"They won't give me a moment's peace," she cried.

"Why don't you go take care of business. I'll send Andy to fetch you some food from the dining car."

Andy turned red. "You shouldn't talk like that in front of a lady. *Take care of business*," he muttered.

"I've got sisters. I know how things are."

When Mrs. Crawford returned, the man that the cowboy had shot was gone and all the blood had been cleaned up.

"Andy, we best be gettin'."

"Here's your food, ma'am." Andy set the tray on a trunk.

The cowboy shook Mrs. Crawford's hand. "My grandma always said that the young are taken because there's some tragedy up ahead for 'em that they ain't gonna be able to handle. That's the Almighty's way of protectin' them from a fate worse than death."

She managed a smile. "Thank you for everything."

Mrs. Crawford watched Andy squeeze his eyes shut. Tears ran down his face and he brushed at them with his shirtsleeve. She hugged him and he held on tight.

"Go home, son."

He nodded.

Once more, she was alone with her son. The train started moving, resumed its pace, and fell into its soothing cadence.

'TIL DEATH

—

Mike Stotter

Cornelius Hallisey's wake was held in the back room of the Big Nugget saloon, Gold Creek, California. It was a simple frame structure with starched calico walls and blue drill stretched across all four walls. As with all Irish wakes the coffin lid had not been secured, allowing those present to pay their last respects to the deceased. The undertaker had used the best of his limited capabilities to restore Hallisey's features. The broken cheekbones had been re-set and where a piece of the right forehead was missing he had filled it with baker's dough but doused too much baking flour over the skin. The final result was a touch comical rather than respectful.

Mary Ann Hallisey, spouse of the deceased, sat in a cane chair next to the barrel of Irish ale that she had paid ten dollars for. A table was set up to one side carrying the food, mainly sandwiches and a side of baked ham, covered with dampened towels. More than twenty-five miners had arrived to say fare-well to one of their fellow countrymen. The Emerald Isle diggings had attracted attention since Patrick Andersen discovered a rich vein in September 1850. There had been a rush to stake claims from fortune seekers but Andersen had gathered a small army of Irishmen and they fought off any other races. The diggings now boasted forty-eight Irish gold miners and no other immigrants dared venture onto the claim for fear of having their skulls cracked by the bad-tempered Irishmen.

Mary Ann, attired in a black dress borrowed from Dorothy

Berry, the wife of Charlie Berry, who owned the Big Nugget, kept an eye on the miners and sipped her cup of ale. She didn't want it to turn into a drunken party. Well, not until they had put Cornelius into the ground.

A broad-shouldered miner who went by the name of Uncle Taylor left the group of men he had been drinking with and stood in front of the coffin. He was truly saddened by the death of his second cousin. They had left their homeland together and journeyed across the Atlantic with nothing more than the clothes on their backs and the gleam of fortunes in their eyes. Uncle Taylor bent and softly kissed Cornelius Hallisey's forehead. Turning to Mary Ann he said, "Do you know what you'll be doing next, Mary Ann?"

"I can't rightly say, Uncle Taylor."

"Our Connie, did he leave you . . . provided for?"

"I only got what is left in the shack," she replied.

"If it's money you need."

She ignored his embarrassment. "No, no. I'm sure that Connie had something put to one side."

Uncle Taylor had taken a fancy to Mary Ann ever since she arrived at the diggings. Her creamy complexion, dark hair, laughing eyes and fiery temper reminded him so much of the women he had left behind in Southern Ireland. Until she had arrived he hadn't thought he had missed his home, his family and loved ones. Her appearance had stirred up a homesickness that had stayed with him for weeks.

He laid a hand gently on her forearm. "Well, you know where to come if things don't work out. If you know what I mean."

Mary Ann looked him in the eyes and slowly nodded.

A quick smile from Uncle Taylor and he was gone. For the next fifteen minutes there was a procession of similar offers from all the miners attending the wake. Mary Ann Hallisey spoke to everyone courteously, thanking them for their time and their respects for Cornelius. The usual platitudes were given and received in a matter-of-fact manner.

Their marriage had been a short one. Just a little over twelve weeks. In that time other miners considered Cornelius the luckiest man at the diggings. He was the first to capture the young

Irish lass when she arrived at Gold Creek riding a mule like a man. What he had that others didn't was beyond their comprehension but Mary Ann took just three days to accept his proposal. They married and moved into the Irish camp.

The ceremony lasted no more than one minute but the celebrations went on for three days. Their shack was up in the hills with the rest of the Irish miners, and already the community had made its presence felt amongst the Mexicans, Chinese and Negroes. Cornelius called his shack The Irish Lady in Mary Ann's honor and spent eighteen hours a day, seven days a week panning for gold. Mary Ann brought him food and soon found that her cooking skills were in demand from the other miners. Never one to turn down an opportunity she began cooking for the miners, charging a dollar or gold per meal. She took whatever the miner was happy to part with. She was quickly on her way to becoming rich.

Outside the wind had picked up, slapping at the calico like it was a ship's sail. By the time the rain started Charlie Berry had brought in the barrel from the back room and set it in the main bar. Dorothy had likewise brought in the food and lit the potbellied stove and arranged a scattering of chairs around it. Several miners had shrugged off their jackets, draping them over the backs of the chairs with the serious intentions of getting their insides wet. A miner had fetched his fiddle and began scratching out a tune.

Uncle Taylor made sure that Mary Ann had been given a chair near the stove and a cup of ale in her hands before he saw to himself. Dorothy Berry came over to Mary Ann and gently touched her on the shoulder. Mary Ann looked up at the older woman and smiled weakly.

"It'll pass, dearie," Dorothy said.

"Thank you, Dorothy," Mary Ann replied. "I suppose it will."

"Give it time."

"Time heals all wounds, so they say."

Dorothy gave Mary Ann a glass of brandy. "Real French stuff. Been saving it for . . ."

"Oh don't go worrying yourself, girl. Connie's gone now and I'm sure he appreciates this fine do you've put on for him.

And I appreciate it, too.'' She rubbed the back of Dorothy's hand reassuringly.

"You're a strong woman so you are, Mary Ann Hallisey.''

"And don't let anyone tell you otherwise,'' Uncle Taylor said rejoining the woman. He carried a mug of ale and a sandwich.

"And thanks to you, Uncle Taylor.''

"Aach, think nothing of it. Family's family, and we got to stick together in this heathen land.''

Someone produced a second fiddle and soon the place was filled with music and laughter. Outside the rain continued to lash the hard-packed earth. The thunderheads rolled in from the sea bringing more rain. The last threads of daylight disappeared as the black clouds blocked out the sun. There'd be more drinking and laughter before Cornelius Hallisey was buried and forgotten.

Uncle Taylor said, "You know, I still can't get over the way he died.''

"Aye, it was a shock.''

"That too. But I meant the accident.''

"Ah, yes.''

Uncle Taylor said, "I've never seen such injuries Connie suffered in such a small fall.''

Mary Ann nodded. "Sure enough, I thought he was fooling me. The hole couldn't have been no more than six feet deep.''

"Strange.'' Uncle Taylor shook his head. "Strange. But there you are. Who knows what lays around the next corner?''

"Absolutely.''

It was Michael Anderson who started the fight. He was talking with Joseph and William Desmond, brothers from County Cork who had come over to California in the fall of 1848 just one step in front of the law. Anderson came from Kerry himself and as a Kerry man thought he was the better for it.

"I tell you I heard it from the ship's doctor hisself,'' Anderson said.

"Away with you!'' William said.

"It's true. He said that they picked her up in New York.''

Joseph said, "Now what would she be doing in New York?''

Anderson glanced over his shoulder at Uncle Taylor. He didn't want him to overhear any of this. He turned back to the brothers. "She arrived there from Dublin just after Easter last year. The doctor said she wanted to get to California the quickest and cheapest way possible. Now the captain quickly looked her over and between them agreed a price."

"You saying she's an Irish Queen?" William demanded.

Anderson smiled. "I ain't saying that but I heard that it cost her no more than twenty dollars for the trip."

Joseph said, "You're lying!"

Anderson ignored him and said, "During the journey the doctor learned that Mary Ann had heard that women were a rarity at the mines. She wanted to marry real quick. And she did." He looked over his shoulder again before continuing. "She married the captain!"

"Away with you!" The brothers said in unison.

"It's true as I'm standing here. The doctor married 'em on board ship."

Joseph said, "Then how come she married Cornelius if she was already married? Answer me that?"

"She was a widow by the time they docked," Anderson said smugly.

"That's got to be one big lie," William said.

"And what reason would I have to lie?"

Joseph said. "You know that I would have married her first."

"Ah but you didn't," Anderson laughed. "Connie got to her first."

Joseph knocked back his drink. "I still say you're lying. You're trying to start trouble like you always do. Look at her, man. Just look at her. That soft round face, those dark eyes and that lovely long hair."

"Would you listen to him?" Anderson shook his head in amazement. "Listen to him. He's in love with her, so he is."

Joseph threw a short right jab that ended between Anderson's eyes. The miner staggered back and fell into a group of seated mourners. They pushed him back up onto his feet. Joseph followed the jab with a crushing haymaker to Anderson's right ear which laid him on the dirt floor.

Anderson bled from both strikes and lay on the floor panting for breath. His ears rang and the blood stung his eyes. The fierce blows had weakened him, and knew he wouldn't be able to take many more like them. He pushed himself up onto his knees, then climbed unsteadily to his feet. Anderson swayed a little waiting for his vision to clear.

"Look out!"

Joseph Desmond didn't know who shouted the warning but he turned his body away from Anderson. Just enough that the Green River blade sliced open his forearm instead of his guts. William Desmond took one long stride and lashed out with a heavy work boot. The kick struck Anderson under the chin and jerked his head back. The Kerry man collapsed to the floor, his body going into violent spasms.

Although the miners had made a circle around the fighters, no one stepped forward to help Anderson whose body continued to jerk uncontrollably for a full minute before it ceased. Uncle Taylor stepped forward and put his callused hand over Anderson's heart.

"He's dead," he said standing up. "I saw it all and say it was self-defense. Does anyone argue with that?"

There was a chorus of "No"s and a shaking of heads. Uncle Taylor pointed to three men and ordered, "Get that scum out of here." He turned to Marry Ann and said, "I'm sorry it has to finish this way, Mary Ann."

"Pay it no mind," she said lightly. "Connie would have enjoyed it."

Cornelius Hallisey's funeral took place in bright sunshine the next morning. Many of the mourners were nursing sore heads. Uncle Taylor had seen to Anderson's body, there wouldn't be anyone mourning over him nor a wake. Joseph Desmond's forearm had been taken care of by one of the miners who used to be a vet. By mid-morning everyone was back working on their claims. Come nightfall Uncle Taylor decided to pay Mary Ann a visit. He considered that a whole day was a respectful enough time to elapse before he put himself forward as a suitor. He arrived at the shack to find it padlocked shut. The plaque Connie had painted in his wife's honor had

been ripped down and thrown on the floor. Of Mary Ann—
there was no sign.

There was something familiar about the man standing up at
the bar drinking beer. His hair was long, face partially hidden
beneath a red scraggly beard but the hard eyes were disturb-
ingly familiar. Sitting at the Monte table Annie O'Neil
watched him as she smoked her cigar. The dealer waited for
her bet. Casually she dropped her counters on the table and
watched the dealer draw the two cards. They didn't match up
and she was fifty dollars down. The loss didn't bother her. She
thanked the dealer gracefully and vacated her seat. The loss
of fifty dollars would be recouped because, after all, she did
own the Shamrock Gambling House, said to be one of the
finest in Sacramento City.

Walking to the bottom of the stairs she stopped a young
Creole girl dressed in a sequinned basque, with her hair hanging loose around her shoulders. "That red-bearded man at the
bar," Annie said. "Have you seen him before?"

The Creole looked at him. "Non, never Madame Annie."

"I'd like to find out his name and where he comes from.
Would you do that for me, Marie?"

"Oui, Madame Annie."

Annie nodded. "Come to my room and report to me straight
afterwards." She lifted her skirts and walked up the stairs. At
the head of the balcony she watched Marie and the man
exchange a few words, then they headed for a private room.
Just as they were about to open the door he stopped. The man
slowly looked around the room as though looking for someone. Marie tugged at his arm and pulled him through the doorway. Annie sensed that he was looking for her.

Sitting in a soft-padded armchair and drinking brandy Annie
looked at the framed daguerreotype of her and her husband
posing in their finest clothes. She was seated and Henri stood
to one side of her with one hand on her shoulder, face grimly
set for the photographer. She could count the times that they
were together after the daguerreotype was taken on the side
table on the fingers of one hand. A soft knocking on the door
disrupted her reverie.

Crossing the room to open the door she stopped to check her hair in the mirror on the way. She ushered Marie into the room and for some unknown reason Annie was nervous.

"What did you find out, girl?"

"The man, he is not from here."

"Not a California?"

Marie said, "Not American."

Annie knew what was coming next. She asked, "Did he tell you where he was from?"

"Non," Marie said softly, her French accent only more noticeable when she became excited. "He comes from your land."

"Irish?"

"*Oui*, Irishland."

She nodded.

Marie continued. "He ask many questions about this house. Who own it, how long and such things."

"And what did you tell him?"

"The truth."

Annie picked up her drink and rolled the glass in between the palms of her hands, thinking. *It has to be one of them*, she thought.

"His name. Did he tell you his name?"

"*Oui*, madame. Very strange name. He calls himself Kerry."

Annie's heart missed a beat. She knew from the very first time she laid eyes on him that she knew him. Now he had given his name, though obviously not his real name, it was confirmed. She thought that moving away, changing her name and stepping up the social ladder would change the past. What a foolish thought.

What a very stupid mistake.

"Marie, this is what I want you to do." She put her arm around the prostitute's shoulder and pulled her closer.

The man who called himself Kerry had taken a seat by the monte table. He watched the card players and from time to time the stairs leading up to the owner's private quarters. After the quick union with the prostitute Kerry had quickly dressed and was only a minute behind her in leaving the room. He spied on her taking the stairs. He then settled at a table where he could watch the stairs without drawing attention to himself. The jug of Irish ale was half-full or half-empty, depending which way you looked at it. Kerry, being of good drinking stock, considered it the latter, and bellied up to the bar to order a fresh jug.

It was mid-week and the gambling house was quieter than usual. It depended on a passing trade, mainly travelling salesmen and miners who had hit pay dirt and didn't mind letting off a little bit of steam. In fact, if it wasn't for them, Henri Charbonieu would not have started the venture. His own luck came in a card game where he won the deeds to a mine on a pair of kings against a pair of queens. In the first week he struck a rich vein and was able to extract over two thousand dollars worth of gold. The second week only six hundred. The very next week he sold the mine to a Russian immigrant who parted with ten thousand dollars for the deeds. Charbonieu did mislead him slightly by hinting that the deed included four adjacent mines. By the time the Russian found out, Charbonieu had gone.

The original Shamrock Gambling House was nothing more than a tent with a bar running along its length. Charbonieu's eye for a deal was sharp and he bought into the partnership. It's strange how some partnerships are destined to be short-lived. T. C. Walters, the original partner, was found facedown in a ditch one early morning, his throat slit from ear to ear. A victim of a robbery, so the law announced. Charbonieu became sole owner. Within two months the Shamrock grew into a wooden, two-storey structure with a large gambling floor, three back rooms for entertainment and the upstairs was set aside as Charbonieu's quarters. No expense was spared bringing in French champagne, barrels of Irish ale and even English whisky. The Shamrock was Charbonieu's pride and joy. Then Annie O'Neil came into his life.

The bartender finished this particular version of how the Shamrock got its start and poured Kerry a shot of grain whisky.

"Here you go. To the home country!" He threw his shot down in one go. Kerry followed suit.

"You can tell a good tale, my friend."

"It's the God's honest truth, I swear."

"Sshhh. Not so loud." Kerry pointed up to the ceiling. "He might hear you."

"Uh! Charbonieu's been dead and buried this last month!"

The news was nothing more than Kerry expected. He leaned over the counter, looking over both shoulders like a melodramatic villain about to confide in his co-conspirator. "And I be supposing the little lady won the pot?"

"Yessiree."

"And what would she be named?"

"Annie Charbonieu . . . well she's gone back to her maiden name now."

"Yes?" Kerry sighed. It was like extracting teeth, getting information from him.

"Annie O'Neil."

"And why should I be of so much interest to you?"

Kerry and the bartender had been so engrossed in their conversation that neither of them noticed Annie walk down the length of the bar, arriving to catch the end of their discussion of her. He turned around slowly to face her. He leaned one elbow casually on the counter top. A lazy smile creased his weather-beaten features.

He asked, "Are you the famous Annie O'Neil?"

"You have the advantage of me . . . Mister . . . ?"

"Kerry."

"Your name or where you come from?"

"Ah, now that would be telling now, wouldn't it?"

"Wouldn't it just?" A smile played on her lips but her eyes were cool as mountain ice.

He said, "Can I buy you a drink?"

She shook her head. "Sorry, a house rule. I never drink with customers."

"C'mon, Miss Annie Surely a drink with someone from the old country . . ."

"If I had a drink with every Irishman in Sacramento I'd be drunk from dawn til dusk."

The put-down was final.

Annie turned her back to Kerry. He caught her upper arm

in a tight grip, pulling her back against his body.

"You'll turn your back once too often on the wrong man," he whispered.

Annie pulled away from his grip. She spun around fast and slapped him hard across the face with an open-palmed swipe.

"You'll be a disgrace to all decent Irish folk!" she snapped and immediately held up her hand.

Kerry quickly looked over his shoulder. A large man, about six feet six and a hundred and ninety pounds halted in his tracks. The single-barrel shotgun was pointing at Kerry's midriff. The Irishman saw the mildly vacant look in the giant's eyes, the dribble slowly worming its way out of the corner of his mouth and silently thanked the Lord that Annie had intervened.

He turned back to her. "My apologies Miss Annie . . . the drink."

"Uh! It's a piss poor Irishman who blames all his ills on the drink!" She waved the shotgun bearer away with a casual flick of her hand. Her eyes fixed on Kerry. "Now if it's information you want, then it's best to ask me. But first I want to ask you some questions."

Kerry shrugged his shoulders.

"Come with me," she ordered and let him trail behind her up to her room.

Once inside she dropped into her seat with a heavy sigh. Her previous drink had not been finished and she took a sip before asking, "How did you find me, Joseph?"

"No more pretending then, Mary Ann?"

"Not with you, Joseph Desmond."

"That's fine. All this skulking around doesn't do a man's health any good."

Mary Ann smiled genuinely. "You've been tracking me down, have you Joseph?"

He nodded sheepishly. He took a deep breath before saying, "I couldn't get you out of my mind. Every night I went to sleep the last image I could see was you. When I awoke your face was the first I saw. Then the images faded after a while. I just knew I had to find you."

"Why, Joseph! It sounds as though you are in love!"

In three steps he was kneeling by Mary Ann, not menacingly but a forlorn pillar of love. "I knew that I just had to find you. Uncle Taylor said that you was nothing but a cheap wh ... harlot and that I should get you out of my mind and have nothing more to do with you. But it was no good. Even though you had gone you was still with me."

Mary Ann put her drink down and taking his hand in hers, squeezed it gently.

"Joseph, I don't think that I've ever heard anyone speak such lovely words as those. But Uncle Taylor's right—you should have nothing to do with me. I can never keep a man I love."

Joseph said, "Mary Ann, if I asked you to leave this place with me and start a new life, what would you answer?"

"Leave? Don't be ... Joseph, all my money is tied up here. I can't leave, I'll have nothing."

"You'll have me."

"And what have you got to offer?"

Joseph reached into his jacket and brought out a large bundle. Slowly he unwrapped the neckerchief to finally reveal a solid lump of gold.

"It's one of the last pieces of gold William dug out before the cave-in."

Mary Ann put a hand to her mouth in shock. She waited a second or two before asking, "Is William dead, then?"

"Aye, these last three months."

She dropped her hand to his forearm, patting it gently. "I'm so sorry, Joseph."

"There was nothing anyone could do for him. I was away down the stream and the roof collapsed. He never stood a chance. God rest his soul."

Mary Ann stood up, pulling Joseph up onto his feet and looked into his face. "*If* I sold this place, and *you* cashed in the gold, *then* we'd have enough to go away."

"Then you'd marry me?"

Her smile was big and wide. "Oh, Joseph, of course I would!"

●   ●   ●

The marriage was held in the small Catholic church of St Mary's. The staff of the Shamrock Gambling House had turned out dressed in their finery. Marie was the maid of honor and Patsy, the barman, the best man. The sky was cobalt blue without a trace of clouds and carriages lined the street to take the wedding party back to the Shamrock for the reception. They wed using their assumed names and no one seemed to care about the speed of their courtship.

Mary Ann had spent a busy three weeks organizing the joyous occasion. Arranging flowers and wines from New Orleans, her dress had been made by the local seamstress of ivory lace and a feast awaited the guests that would have befitted a medieval king. The Shamrock was decorated in bunting and had been given a fresh lick of paint. Sacramento had never seen the like of it before.

The festivities began as Joseph carried his bride over the threshold. Scores of people filled the room, champagne corks popped and the cheers of congratulations could have lifted the rafters. Mary Ann turned to her husband and kissed him.

"This is the happiest day of my life!" she declared.

"Aye, and mine too."

They danced to the accompaniment of three fiddle players and a banjo player. Others joined in and quickly the room was filled with people dancing. One or two miners were happy to get to grips with the house girls without having to part with a dollar. Others got a slapped face for dare bringing up business on such an occasion. Mary Ann and Joseph whirled across the floor until they had to stop through Mary Ann's dizziness.

As she was gathering her breath she looked around the room. Her smile slipped as she realized that there was something missing.

"Bejezus Joseph, there's no cake! Where's the cake?"

"Steady there, me darling. There's got to be one surprise for the bride."

"What a curious thing to say. But I ordered it, so I did."

"Hush now and come here."

Mary Ann moved over to her husband. He pulled out a neckerchief from his pocket.

"If you'll allow me," he said.

She was puzzled but he insisted about the surprise and that she should allow him to blindfold her.

Joseph said, "Now take my hand and let me lead you away."

"I feel foolish, Joseph."

"Oh don't fret so. Trust in me."

So she let Joseph lead her across the room and out into the backyard. Here there were other guests waiting, their smiles plastered thickly on their faces. They were silent and Mary Ann was totally unaware of their presence. A horse whinnied in its stable, breaking the silence. She asked Joseph questions all the time but he told her to hush—in the nicest terms, of course. He led her up some steps onto a platform made of bails of hay. He turned her around a couple of times then held her by the shoulders.

He bent to her ear and whispered, "Are you ready, my love?"

"Yes, yes."

He ripped away the blindfold and she blinked against the bright sunlight. She looked around for the cake, the surprise or whatever Joseph had arranged but only her guests looked back at her.

"Joseph, what? I mean where is it?"

"Look around the faces. Do you not recognize them?"

Mary Ann slowly looked at the faces. As she moved from one to another her joy turned to lead inside her. Uncle Taylor tipped his hat to her. William Desmond smiled back. Yvette Charbonieu, her ex-husband's sister, merely stared with hatred.

The panic rose to the surface and she struggled against Joseph's grip but he held her fast.

"And my present to you," he said. His eyes indicating that she should look up.

The hemp noose dropped over her head and was quickly tightened.

"No! Joseph! I thought you loved me!"

He dismissed her claim of love with a wave. "You loved only yourself and money. Enough men have died because of it. Now no more."

"Joseph, dear Lord. Please no!"

He was deaf to her entreaties and gave her one good shove in the back, launching her into the air. There was a satisfying crack as her neck was broken. Now the crowd broke their silence with cheers.

" 'Til death do us part," muttered Joseph.

SWEET REVENGE

Judy Alter

The woman in the bed next to me lies curled in a ball all day, moaning for her lost baby. The child, as I understand it, died at birth, and the mother went mad with grief. On the other side of me is a woman who calls out stridently, "Release me this minute! I do not belong here! If my daughter knew how you were treating me . . ." In truth, it was her daughter, unable to care for her any longer, who put her here, saw to it that she was tied each day in a rocking chair, untied only to take care of personal needs and, sometimes, for a brief walk around.

I've been here six months, and during that long, tedious time, I have made it a point to be very quiet, so I am neither tied nor confined. Not that I am free to come and go. No, indeed. I sit here each day, staring out the window at the Kansas prairie, plotting my quiet revenge against the husband who put me in the county poor farm, the only place able to care for the "dangerously insane."

That was what the judge said of me at the hearing, "dangerously insane." Howard Smith stood there with all his might and influence—the town's banker who holds the mortgages on every home and business for ten counties—and swore that I'd come after him with a butcher knife when he was sleeping. "Only the grace of God that I'm alive today, your honor," he said humbly. "The woman's dangerous. I tried, Lord knows, I tried to care for her, keep her at home"—here his voice

137

broke a little with emotion—"keep the world from knowing my shame. . . ."

In spite of good old Brother Bacon, the preacher who protested strongly and who is still my champion, the judge ruled that I should be confined in the poor farm where, as he put it, "they have the facilities to care for someone like her."

I did take after him with a butcher knife once, but the story was different than he told it. I never wanted to marry Howard Smith. When I was seventeen, he was a widower of forty, wealthy beyond measure because he was mean as sin to those that owed his bank money. He approached my parents with a marriage proposal which they leapt to accept without consulting me.

Father was a farmer in southwestern Kansas and, it pains me to admit, a weak man, bent on doing the Lord's work but never sure which way the Lord wanted him to jump. He was a great deal surer which way my mother wanted him to jump, for she made it perfectly clear. She also made it perfectly clear that the Lord had not meant her to live the poverty-stricken life of a sod farmer's wife, and she blamed my father for not providing for her in a more fitting manner. That he was a farmer when she married him never seemed to occur to her.

"A perfect marriage," she had crowed, when she told me of Howard's proposal. "You will live a life of comfort, and perhaps your poor dear father and I will not have to scrimp so—"

"Did he offer a marriage settlement?" I asked coldly.

"Oh, now, dear Callie . . . how can you think such . . ." She was off in a flutter of denials, but I had my answer.

I never pleaded nor cried hysterically, neither being my style, but I made it plain that I did not want to go through with this marriage, that I would do almost anything to avoid it. I considered, seriously, running away but reasoned that Mr. Smith, with his wealth and connections, would no doubt find me, even in Topeka. My logical arguments to him had met with bland confidence, "Once we are married, it will all work out."

Work out, my foot! We were married in the church at Liberal, with Brother Bacon performing the ceremony and me a reluctant bride in white, Howard a beaming groom in his best black suit, though I thought the knees and seat shiny from wear. For me, a kind of hell began with that ceremony. Howard was a randy old man, always pawing at me, sometimes waking me in the middle of the night with his insatiable passion. I learned to lie perfectly still, close my eyes, and take my mind to a faraway place during his rutting. When he rolled over, sated, and began to snore, I rose to clean myself, praying each time that no child had been conceived, for I don't know what I would have done to avoid bringing a child into that household.

Days, I was a servant, though he could well have afforded household help for me. He preferred, he said, to think that his own little wife was taking care of him. So I ran the house, fed him the hearty meals he expected three times a day, made my own clothes and most of his, and worked like a dog from dawn to dark. Howard was as demanding upright as he was in bed, expecting meals on time, whisky when he called for it, my undivided attention when he wanted to recount his latest triumph.

His temper, when aroused, was fearful, and he had his hates and his dislikes. In spite of the fact they had made him wealthy, he hated farmers, swore that they were out to cheat him, that the only honest men he'd ever met were those who refused to toil on the land—just the opposite of what most men believed. And he hated schools, thought young people should be put to work at the age of twelve instead of filling their heads with the foolishness called "higher education." When he'd yell and carry on about how the universities were ruining people, I cringed, for I wanted nothing more than to attend the state university in Wichita and become a teacher. "No school will ever get a penny of my money," he would rage, shaking his mighty fist in the air. He was the epitome of the man who would, as they say, take his fortune with him to the grave if he could.

By the time I'd been married five years, I was twenty-two years old, thin and gaunt, with dark circles under my eyes and, occasionally, a bruise on my cheekbone, a black eye, and once or twice, cracked ribs. Good Brother Bacon asked often how

I was feeling, but I brushed his concern aside. What could he do?

I began to refuse Howard in the night, and then I took to sleeping in a separate bedroom. Twice, he kicked open a locked door to drag me back to his bed, and on those occasions he was rougher than usual. "I'll teach you," he'd mutter between clenched teeth.

The night I took the butcher knife after him, he was drunker than usual and more violent. He'd throttled me until I nearly lost consciousness, and then had forced me to the parlor floor, where he raped me and then fell asleep. I left him on the floor and would have left him all night, but he roused, and I could see from the murderous look in his eye that he was coming for me again. Hoarse and unable to cry out—as though anyone would have helped me—I ran for the kitchen and grabbed the first thing handy, the butcher knife.

He thought I was bluffing, that I was too soft to cut someone, even him, but when he got close enough I sliced at his ribs, opening a long, wide cut that bled so hard I was reminded of the proverbial stuck pig, an analogy that fit in more ways than one. Scared, he retreated to his bedroom, and I went to mine, building a barricade of furniture and sleeping with my hand on the knife handle.

Next morning, he was gone. Curious but unconcerned, I set about straightening the house and, unfortunately, had it all tidy and repaired—no sign of a struggle—by the time Howard arrived with the sheriff.

That was how I ended up in the poor farm. Howard said only one thing to me in private and that was, "A lot of women would love to have your chances. I'll find one won't come after me with a knife."

My only revenge is that it is against state law to divorce an insane person. Howard is saddled with me, and the next ladies in his life are condemned to illegitimacy. But that's cold comfort as I sit here, rocking away the endless days.

"Brother Bacon!" I fight the impulse to grin, to let my eyes light with happiness—bland is safer in this place—but I am glad beyond belief to see the old man.

"Callie, dear," he says, leaning to touch me on the shoulder, "come with me. You're leaving here."

It is almost too much to believe, too much to bear. "Leaving?" I echo.

"Take me away from here this instant!" the woman next to me demands. "I know you came to get me!"

Brother Bacon ignores her, speaking softly to me. "You're leaving. I've just gotten a court order."

"How . . ." I am almost unable to speak, and when I rise, my knees threaten to buckle under me.

"Finally had a traveling judge come through," he says, "one that didn't know Howard. I convinced him you weren't dangerous . . . said I'd take responsibility for you myself. Now we must go."

"Howard?"

"He doesn't know."

We go through the formalities, with a disapproving matron frowning all the while she signs the necessary papers, but Brother Bacon is his usual kind and patient self. I stifle the urge to scream at the woman. When we finally are in the buggy and driving away, I demand, "Take me to Howard."

"Now, Callie . . ."

"I want to see Howard," I say with steel in my voice, though I am not sure what I will say once I am in front of the devil who has engineered my misery.

He protests but finally agrees, and we ride in silence for a long time.

"You can't just go in there," he warns as we approach the house. "It . . . well, it might be dangerous for you."

"It might be dangerous for Howard," I reply, and see in his face the first sign of doubt. Maybe, he is thinking, she did go after him with a butcher knife for no reason, and maybe I've done the wrong thing. By then we are in front of the house, and he has stopped the horse.

"It will be all right," I tell him, heading boldly up the steps of the front stoop.

The door is locked, but I knock loudly, wait a minute, and then knock again. There is no answer, no sound within. After a long wait, I return down the steps, march around the house, and enter through the kitchen door. The kitchen is a mess—dirty dishes, food crumbs, all the signs that no one has been taking care. Howard has been too cheap to hire someone to replace me.

I walk through the dining room, parlor, up the stairs to the bedroom, and there is Howard, dead in his bed, his face beginning to mottle. For a moment, I am furious enough with him to go again for the butcher knife, furious that he has had the final laugh, robbed me of whatever revenge I sought. His empty eyes stare glassily at me, and I turn slowly and with deliberate, measured tread return to Brother Bacon.

"You best come," I say. "He's dead."

"Dead?" He is alarmed. How, he wonders, could I have killed him so soon.

"I didn't do it," I assure him. "I think his own cooking killed him. You should see the kitchen."

When Brother Bacon examines Howard, he suggests it was probably a heart attack. I long instead to see a butcher knife sticking out of his chest, but it's a longing I don't even whisper.

Brother Bacon goes for the sheriff, and I wait. To pass the time, I clean the kitchen, remembering ruefully that cleaning has once before gotten me into trouble. But this is now my house, I reason, and I cannot bear for anyone to see it so ill-kept.

The sheriff is not kind. "I won't offer you sympathy, Mrs. Smith," he says. "I 'spect you're rejoicin'."

"Not quite, Sheriff," I say, "I've been robbed."

He is puzzled but won't admit it. "If I could prove you did this. . . ." His threat dangles.

"Sheriff!" Brother Bacon is angry. "Mrs. Smith was at the home and then with me. There is no way she could have any involvement in her husband's death. Ate and drank himself to death, if you ask me."

"I didn't ask," the sheriff says rudely. He used to drink with Howard of a night, and they were friends, which means he has always been my enemy.

I am the nearest relation and so in charge of arrangements. Howard is buried in the town cemetery, with bank employees

and a few townspeople in attendance—he was not popular—
and Brother Bacon says a few words over the grave. The good
man speaks nervously as he commends Howard's soul to God,
and I throw a handful of dirt on the coffin and turn away. The
sheriff, who has come uninvited, opines that it's a crime not
to give a man a proper church burial.

"Not," I say, "a crime for which one can be tried."

Within a week, I have made the house my own, given away
every trace of Howard's clothing and personal effects, opened
the windows to sunshine and air, beaten the old dust out of
the rugs, and put flowers in every room, even the cubicle Howard called his office. His papers have been packed and sent to
the lawyer.

Said lawyer comes to call a week later. "Mrs. Smith, you're
a wealthy woman," he says and proceeds to outline my wealth.

My instructions are direct: a certain amount to my parents,
not generous but enough to ensure that I won't have to worry
with them daily; another, larger amount to the county poor
farm, with the stipulation that it be used for treatment of the
"dangerously insane."

"That barely makes a dent," the lawyer says. "Any further
plans?"

"Yes. I plan to attend the university in Wichita and get an
education. And I'll build them . . . let's see, a library. Yes, a
library. Howard hated books. We'll call it the Howard Smith
Memorial Library." I envision Howard, spinning in frustration
for all eternity.

The lawyer's face is blank.

After he leaves, I go to the kitchen for the butcher knife.
Now it hangs framed, in a place of honor, over my desk in
the private library I have built for myself. No one ever asks
about the knife, but I find it a great comfort.

PEACE OFFICER

—

Brian Garfield

It was hot. A gauze of tan dust hung low over the street.

Matt Paradise rode his horse into Aztec, coming off the coach road at four in the afternoon, and when he passed a dry goods store at the western end of the street a lady under a parasol smiled at him. Matt Paradise tipped his hat, rode on by, and muttered *sotto voce*, "A friendly face, a sleepy town. Don't I wish."

He was a big-boned young man. He took off his hat to scrape a flannel sleeve across his forehead, and exposed to view a wild, thick crop of bright red hair. He had a bold face, vividly scarred down the right cheek. His eyes were gold-flecked, hard as jacketed bullets. There was the touch of isolation about him. He carried a badge, pinned to the front of his shirt.

An intense layer of heat lay along the earth. He found the county sheriff's office, midway down a block between the hardware store and the barbershop; he dismounted there and climbed onto the dusty boardwalk with legs stiffened from a long day's hot ride.

He rested his shoulder against the frame of the open door and waited for his eyes to accustom themselves to the gloom inside. A voice reached forward from the dimness: "Something I can do for you?"

"Sun's pretty strong this time of year," Matt Paradise said. "I can't make you out yet. Sheriff Morgan?"

"I am."

Matt Paradise took three paces into the office. As his pupils began to dilate he took in the office—not very much different from a dozen other sheriffs' offices in Arizona Territory—and its occupant:

Sheriff John Morgan was stripped down to a faded pink undershirt. The empty right sleeve was pinned up at the shoulder.

Morgan was middle-aged. His shoulders were heavy, and his belly was beginning to swell out over his belt line. His face was craggy and weathered, topped by a sidewise slash of hair that was going thin and of salt-and-pepper color.

And so this—*this*—was the legendary Morgan, the peace officer who had cleaned up Coyotero County single-handed. This tired man, getting older, with his chin softening up. Morgan's eyes were pouched. His left hand drummed nervously on the desk. Matt Paradise masked his shock behind squinted eyes. The years had reduced John Morgan to a kind of bookmark, which only marked the place where a great lawman had been. The disappointment of it made Paradise guard his voice:

"Name's Paradise. Arizona Rangers."

Morgan touched his stiff mustache. He seemed to notice Paradise's badge for the first time. He tried to make his voice sound friendly: "Glad to see you."

Paradise wanted to turn around and ride out of town and not look back.

Morgan said, "Business or just traveling through?"

Just traveling through, Paradise wanted to say. But he fastened his will around him. "Business, I'm afraid."

"Afraid, Ranger?"

Matt Paradise inhaled deeply. *Better get it over with. Why beat around the bush? You poor, tired old man.* He said, almost harshly, "Your house isn't in order, Sheriff. I've been sent down here to help you clean it out."

He saw color rise in Morgan's cheeks, and he wanted to look away, but he held the sheriff's sad glance.

"You're just a kid," Sheriff Morgan said. "I don't want any amateur help, Ranger."

"Afraid you've got it, Sheriff, whether you want it or not."

He saw an abrupt touch of sullenness in Morgan's glance, and he thought, *I pity you, Morgan, but I've got to lay it on the line so there's no mistake.* He said: "You're getting fat—where you sit and where you think."

Instantly, Morgan's eyes showed cruel hatred. Paradise walked forward to the desk and spoke flatly. "Doc Wargo has been in this town for two weeks and you haven't done anything about it."

"That's right," Morgan said evenly. "Wargo's broken no laws in this county. I can't touch him." His eyes gleamed brutally.

"The Territory wants him for murder, Sheriff, and you know it. You've received two wires from our headquarters, to arrest Wargo and deliver him to Prescott for trial."

Morgan sighed out a long breath. "Ranger, you're young and impatient and there are certain things you've got to learn. This country isn't easy on anybody, young fellow, and if you want to survive very long, you learn that certain stones are better left unturned. There's a difference between making a stand and rocking the boat. Now, with this business, I'm alone in this office, no deputies, and I had my right arm shot off a year ago in a fight. What kind of chance do you think I'd stand if I went after Wargo and his gang?"

"Gang?" Matt Paradise murmured. "He's got one man with him, the way I hear it."

"Ernie Crouch isn't one man, Ranger. He's a crowd."

"So you're not lifting a finger."

"I am not," Morgan told him. "You can do whatever you like, Ranger, but I hate to see you come so far just to get killed. Those two haven't made any trouble in my county. And until they do, I leave them alone. That's my policy." He shook his head. "Go on home, son. You can't fight Wargo and Crouch."

"How do you know, Sheriff?" Paradise said softly. "You've never tried."

He expected Morgan to explode, but Morgan just sat and looked at him as if he were slightly crazy. Then Morgan said, "The only times lawmen have tried to close Doc Wargo down, he's closed them down. Do you understand what I'm telling you, boy? You ever handled anything like this before?''

"Maybe."

"And you think you can handle Wargo and Crouch, do
you?"

"If I didn't," said Matt Paradise, "I wouldn't be here."

Morgan scrutinized the hang of Paradise's twin revolvers.
"How good do you think you are with those things?"

"Good enough. Nobody's killed me yet."

"Suit yourself, then."

It made Paradise lean forward and plant both palms on the
desk. He brought his face near the level of Morgan's. "Don't
you care, Sheriff? Don't you care at all? All the legends about
John Morgan—are they all lies?"

Morgan's left hand reached the desk and gripped its edge.
"Legends are for the far past, boy. That was a lot of miles
ago. Let me tell you what a smart man does. When the likes
of Doc Wargo takes over your town, you just hunker down
and take it like a jackrabbit in a hailstorm. Because sooner or
later the hailstorm moves on. Wargo will move on too, and if
he's not prodded, he won't hurt anybody in the meantime."

"And you're willing to take the chance on that, are you?"

Morgan sat back and studied him. "Tell me something.
What do you do with all your time, Ranger? Just ride around
hunting up trouble for yourself?"

"Trouble and I are old friends," Paradise said. "We understand each other."

"Sure."

"I'm arresting Doc Wargo," Paradise told him. "Do I get
your help or not?"

"I'll think about it," the sheriff said, and turned away in
his chair to reach for a newspaper.

"You've got five seconds." Paradise said flatly.

The sheriff looked up angrily, but before he could reply, a
figure barred the door, blocking out the light. Paradise turned
and his eyes fixed themselves on the girl.

She had long eyes. Smooth dark hair gracefully surrounded
her face. Looking at the rich warm tone of her flesh, Paradise
knew she was the most stunning human creature he had ever
seen.

He stared at her until she blushed. Suddenly she gave him a blinding smile. Her smile was as good as a kiss.

Morgan said in a cranky tone, "You want something, Terry?"

She had a smoky voice. Her eyes did not stray from Paradise when she answered the sheriff. "Nothing important, Dad. I didn't know you were busy. I'll see you later."

Her body turned away before her head did. She gave Paradise a last, level glance, and was gone.

"My daughter," Morgan said unnecessarily. He grunted getting out of his chair. "I'll go down to the Occidental with you. That's where Wargo's putting up."

"You'll back my play?"

"I don't know," the sheriff said. He put on a severe, flat-crowned hat. "Come on."

When they reached the street, the girl Terry was a block away, just turning a corner. She wore riding trousers and a cotton blouse that hugged her at waist and breasts. She went out of sight and around the corner. Morgan said, "That your horse?"

"Yes."

"Nice-looking animal. What'll I do with it if you get dead?"

"Give it to your daughter," Paradise said, and walked away.

Morgan caught up and they went down the street together. The merciless orange sun burned wherever it struck. Heat clung to the street like melted tar.

The Occidental was the biggest building in town. The sign on the tall front was painted in a crescent shape: GAMING TABLES—SALOON—DANCING. It looked as though there were hotel bedrooms on the second floor.

It was four-thirty. The sun burst through the west-facing windows upon an almost deserted, long, low-ceilinged room. An aproned bartender polished glasses at the backbar. Three men sat playing cards at a table. That was all.

Paradise recognized Wargo right away, from the reward flyer portraits. Wargo was a neat, slight, lizard of a man; his

hair was Indian black. He wore sleeve garters and celluloi
collar and cuffs; no coat, no hat. Cigar smoke trailed from
Wargo's mouth and nostrils. He watched the two newcomer
come forward.

At Wargo's right sat a slope-chinned card player, evidentl
a house gambler. At Wargo's left sat an enormous shape, th
biggest man Paradise had ever seen. That would be Erni
Crouch. *Ernie Crouch isn't one man, Ranger. He's a crowa
All Crouch's fat looked hard; hard as granite. He had a placi
bovine face, but his deep-slit eyes were shrewd and he wa
festooned like a gun collector after an auction: knives and gun
bristled all over—at his boottops; at his waist; in sheaths sew
to his butternut trousers. Paradise could have walked aroune
inside one leg of Crouch's trousers.

Crouch was sitting on two chairs, side by side, one unde
each buttock.

He looked like a puppeteer, with Doc Wargo his marionette
But actually, Paradise knew, it was the other way around.

Doc Wargo spoke, in a voice surprisingly deep for his smal
body. "Hello, Sheriff. Where've you been keeping yourself?"
His face was amused. When Morgan made no answer, Warge
murmured, "I hear you're getting old."

Morgan's eyes flickered when they touched Wargo's. Par
adise took a pace forward, and seeing the look on Paradise'
face, Wargo started to rise.

"Keep your seat," Paradise said coolly.

Wargo's eyes, triangular like a snake's, became wicked. A
mustache drooped past the edges of his mouth. "What's this—
what's this?"

Sheriff Morgan had stepped back, and suddenly Paradise fe
the cold muzzle of a revolver against his back ribs. Morgar
said gently, "I changed my mind. I'm sworn to keep the peace
It wouldn't be peaceful if you let these two men kill you
would it?"

Paradise's jaw muscles rippled. "You're all though, Sheriff
as of right now."

"Maybe."

Wargo was smiling gently. "What's this all about?"

Paradise ignored the gun in his back. He spoke to Wargo: "What happened to Carlos Ramirez?"

"I killed him."

"Why?"

"I forget," Wargo murmured. He halved his smile. "You'd better beg your pardon and get out of here."

Ernie Crouch spoke without stirring on his chairs. "He's one of them Rangers, Doc."

"I can see that for myself," Wargo snapped. "Ramirez was a Ranger, wasn't he?"

"He was," Paradise said bleakly.

"Go on," Wargo told him. "Clear out of here before you do something that'll make me have to kill you."

Paradise glanced over his shoulder at Morgan. The sheriff had backed away, but his gun was leveled on Paradise. Paradise said, "This badge of mine won't die, Wargo, any more than Ramirez's died. It will get up and come after you, on another man's shirt."

While he was talking, he took a pace back, and whipped his elbow around behind him. It jarred against the gun in Morgan's fist, turning the gun away. Paradise whipped his left hand around and down, yanked the gun out of Morgan's grip, and pushed the surprised sheriff back. Morgan windmilled his single arm and almost lost his footing.

Paradise wheeled, starting to talk: "You're under arrest—"

But Crouch, as soundless as he was enormous, was on top of him. Crouch batted the gun away as if it were paper; he swatted Paradise contemptuously across the cheek and Paradise caromed back against the edge of the bar. The scar on his face went ghostly white. A half-full tumbler of whisky stood on the bar. He made a grab for it. Crouch was shifting forward; Paradise could hear Wargo's husky chuckling in the background. Crouch began to swing.

Paradise flung the whisky in Crouch's fleshy face.

Crouch yelled and clawed at his stung eyes. Paradise stepped in and brought the heel of his left hand up under Crouch's pointed nose. The blow smashed in: he heard the crush of cartilege, felt the spurt of blood on his palm. Agony exploded in his wrist—it was like pounding a concrete wall— but Crouch backpedaled in pain.

Paradise still had the empty tumbler in his right hand. He smashed it, edge-first, down on top of Crouch's head— smashed it down once and again. Crouch sagged against the bar and began to slip to the floor.

Paradise didn't wait. He turned, dropping the glass, reaching for his gun.

But Doc Wargo had him covered with a nickel-plated revolver. Wargo was still in his chair; he looked slightly amused. "Nice job," he remarked.

Paradise's hands became still. He glanced at Morgan. Morgan was looking at the floor. Wargo's glance flicked casually to the crumpled mountain of the dazed Ernie Crouch, and then his face hardened. He said in an acid voice, "I'm in a charitable mood, which is why I'm not gut-shooting you here and now. But remember this, Ranger. The next time you call me, I'm going to see you."

"You'll see me all of a sudden," Paradise replied grimly.

"I'll see you," Wargo answered, "in Boot Hill with dirt in your face. You've got till dawn tomorrow to ride out of here. After that you're fair game for me and Ernie."

Paradise massaged the soreness in his left hand. "I'll see you at sunup, then. If you're smart, you'll be on the run."

"From one man?"

"From the badge, Wargo."

"Get out of here," Wargo said softly.

His gun lifted.

Morgan came across the floor and touched Paradise on the arm. "Come on. You can't fight the drop."

They went outside and Paradise stood on the walk looking back at the saloon, half-expecting Wargo to explode out the door with a gun blazing. Morgan said, "He won't come after you. Not till morning. He's a skunk, maybe, but he keeps his word. You've got twelve hours. Get on your horse and use it."

Sweat rolled freely along the sheriff's flushed face. He spoke earnestly: "You don't have to finish the job, Paradise. Nobody cares."

"I care."

"You can't win it, man!"

Paradise said, "You can't always go by that. Doesn't that badge mean anything at all to you?"

Morgan looked away. Fear had robbed him of his dignity. Fear: it quivered in his eyes. Paradise said, "You don't want to hear this, and I don't particularly want to say it, but you'd better sort yourself out fast, Sheriff. Because if you don't back my play in the morning, you'll be out of a job and behind bars."

Morgan did not meet his eye. "I'm dead, Paradise. I just haven't got the guts to lie down." The one-armed sheriff turned, then, and walked away slowly.

His wife said, "Do you like my dress?"

"It looks good with your hair."

"John, you haven't even looked at it."

Sweat dripped from Morgan's scarlet face. He was staring vacantly out the window of the bedroom. Heat pressed down on the desert from the burning sky; the sun was about to go down.

She said, "Being frightened is a natural human reaction, like breathing."

"Will you please shut up?" he demanded. He turned in his chair; his voice dropped. "I'm sorry, Kit. You don't deserve that. You don't deserve any part of me."

"Come sit by me. Please, John."

He crossed to the loveseat and put his arm around her shoulders. She dropped her head against him. She said, "You're not cast in bronze. You can do anything you want."

"Sure."

"The Ranger," she said. "Does he have any chance at all?"

"I'm a sheriff, not an oracle. He handled himself pretty well against Ernie Crouch. Maybe he can do it. He doesn't look like the type to come out last in a gunfight. But then, neither does Doc Wargo."

He got up, restless. He passed the mirror and stopped in front of it. "I barely recognize that man," he said, looking at his image in the glass; he turned to face her: "Take a look at me, Kit. Take a good look."

His mouth twisted. "I lost a lot more than an arm in that fight last year." His face was sweat-drenched and greenish. "My guts spilled out with the arm." His voice climbed, pitched to a driving high recklessness: "Let the fool get himself killed. Let him die, to prove some stupid pride. Let him—"

"John! Pull yourself together. You've got to get hold of yourself!"

"Why?" he asked miserably. "Why?" He looked at her, and curbed his tongue.

At eight o'clock, in the residue of the day's torpid heat, Matt Paradise presented himself at the door of the sheriff's house. He was wearing a clean shirt and string tie, and a black, dusty coat that had become shiny with long use.

The sheriff's daughter answered the door. For a moment their eyes locked. Paradise regarded her gravely, saying nothing. She said, "My father is in the back. I'll get him."

"I didn't come to see your father, Terry."

She wore a dovegray dress. Her dark hair was swept back, pinned with a bow. She said, "You came courting," and he could see that she was laughing quietly.

He smiled and put out his hand. She considered it for a little while before she put her slender hand into his big fingers. He said to her, "You are the promise I made to myself when I was a kid."

"That must have been a very long time ago." She was still laughing at him. He pulled her forward. She closed the door behind her, and they walked down the road, hand in hand. Her head was at his shoulder. They did not speak until they reached the turning in the road, where the wagon tracks swung into the head of the town's main street. Here a cluster of tall heavy cottonwood trees surrounded the bubbling of a spring, and there was grass on a precious half-acre of earth. With a finger Matt Paradise brushed back a stray lock of her hair. He watched for her quick, slanting smile.

She said, "You want to kiss me, don't you?"

"Yes."

"Why don't you stop looking at me and do it?"

Her arms were folded. She leaned against him, moved her face up; he kissed her. Her arms did not stir. He put his hands softly on the gloss of her hair, holding her without pressure. It was a gentle kiss; yet it rocked him.

She smiled and laid her head on his chest. She made him feel drunk. She whispered, "Does everyone feel like this, or are we very special?"

"Don't ask any questions."

"Then I won't."

He said, "I'm crazy in love with you."

"I know." She was smiling: "A woman knows when she's loved." Abruptly, she walked away from him. She said, "I can't breathe when I'm with you."

He was going to leave her at the door, but her mother came from the parlor into the doorway. "Won't you come in?"

"No, thank you," Paradise said.

"Do you mind terribly if I insist?" The woman stepped aside to make room. She was handsome; she had not begun to thicken up.

John Morgan was striding back and forth in the parlor. He became still when they entered. "Well, then," he said.

Terry said, "I'm going to marry him."

Morgan said, "Then you'd better do it fast, because he's likely to be dead in the morning."

"I can live a lifetime in one night," she said, looking at Paradise.

Morgan uttered a monosyllabic curse. Trembling in anger, he raised his one arm. His hand was formed into a fist. His wife stepped in front of him. "She's a woman, John."

"I know that. She's grown."

"Yes. And she needs what every woman needs."

His wife turned to Paradise. He had not spoken. Now he said, "You have a wonderful daughter."

"Yes, I think so."

"That doesn't just happen," Paradise said.

"Thank you," said Mrs. Morgan.

"For Pete's sake," Morgan exploded. "Terry! Do you have any notion what it's like to marry a Ranger? He spends his life from town to town, from fight to fight—"

"I know," she said calmly.

"How long have you thought about this? How long did take you to make this decision? Two hours? Ten minutes?" He was roaring.

She said, "I've had all the time I need. And all the advice." She stood her ground and met her father's glance. She cried joyously, "Do you know what it feels like to love?"

"I knew your mother for years before I married her."

"That's not what I asked you."

"How do you know he's any better than the fly-by-night cowhands around here? One night's fling and then gone? How do you—"

She said, "Maybe he is just toying with my affections. All right. Maybe I'm just in a mood to have my affections toyed with!"

Morgan's sight was blurring. "I don't believe any of this," he muttered. "It's all a bad dream. It can't be happening. It's a nightmare." He swung his arm up in a gesture of frustrated anger, toward Paradise. He said bitterly, "Just the kind of moth-eaten son-in-law I've always wanted. What kind of a coffin do you want, Paradise?"

Mrs. Morgan pulled her husband's arm down. She said to him. "You've lost your nerve, John, and that's no crime. But you can't stand to see another man face up to the things you're afraid of."

She turned to her daughter and begged: "I made him into what he is, Terry. It's my fault. I washed him up because I wouldn't stop harping at him, trying to get him to hang up his guns. I kept trying to talk him into turning his back and running away."

She bowed, beaten. "I succeeded all too well. Don't make the same mistake, Terry. Follow your man to the ends of the earth, but never tell him to turn back."

The sun would be up in a little while. Matt Paradise stood within the darkened, empty sheriff's office. Waiting laid a frost on his nerves. For the tenth time he took out his guns and checked their loads.

Someone came down the street, tramping on heavy feet. Paradise moved close to the door.

Morgan came in, weaving slightly. He carried a whisky bottle by the neck. His eyes were stained with a bleak darkness. He put the bottle down and hitched his gun around. "You need help."

Paradise looked him in the eye. "And where am I going to get it?" He turned away. "You're drunk."

"Not really. I haven't done the bottle much damage yet."

"I didn't think you'd have the guts to come."

"I didn't either," Morgan admitted. "But I didn't have the guts not to."

After a moment he added, "You don't start a life over again, I guess. You just try to do the best you can with what's left of it. But maybe that's enough. *Whatsoever thy hand findeth to do, do it with thy might.*" He moved back into the office, an amorphous shape in the poor light. "If you survive this, you really mean to marry her?"

"I do."

"She's a wildcat."

"I know."

"Just thought I'd better warn you," Morgan muttered absently. "It's getting to be time."

"Yeah." Paradise pulled the door open and stepped out onto the walk. His eyes were ominous. Morgan came out beside him, and they stood there watching the dawn pink up. Morgan said, "Going to be another hot one today. Hot as blazes."

"There they are," Paradise said. "Spread out a little."

Morgan shifted three paces to his left. On the porch of the Occidental, half a block away to the southwest, the little shape of Wargo and the big shape of Crouch came out off the boardwalk onto the street, cuffing up dust.

Wargo's bass voice rolled across the hundred feet separating them. "You're all through, Ranger. Last chance—get on your horse and ride."

"I guess the cards are dealt," Paradise said. "Play your hand, Doc, or throw it in."

Crouch looked like a granite block set to motion. He waddled, lumbering, out to a point in the exact center of the street. The pink dawn caught him on one cheek and threw that side of his face into blood-colored relief. He was carrying so much armament that it was possible he might get confused as to which gun to reach for.

Wargo's nickel-plated revolver hung at his right hip, and his right hand was inches from it. He said, "You in this, Sheriff?"

"I'm in it."

"Too bad," Wargo murmured. "All right, then—"

He didn't finish the sentence; his gun came curling up.

Paradise whipped his Colt forward; as it settled in his grasp he heard the sharp crack of Wargo's revolver: The little gunman was fast, amazingly fast. The fist-sized blow of the bullet smashed Paradise half around in his tracks. He didn't know exactly where he was hit, didn't have time to care; he was still on his feet and as he turned his gun back toward target, he heard a mushroom roar of sound from his left.

The old sheriff was fast, too: That was his gun roaring. Morgan's bullet punched a hole in the front of Ernie Crouch's shirt. Dust puffed up. Crouch hardly stirred. He had guns in both hands, rising, but Paradise had no time for that; all in the space of this tiny split second, Wargo was cocking his gun for another shot, taking his deliberate time about it.

Paradise fired.

In slack-jawed disbelief, Doc Wargo shuddered back. His body went loose, and he fell down and began to curl up like a piece of bacon in a hot frying pan.

Morgan's gun was booming methodically, and every shot found a place in his ample target: but none of it seemed to trouble Ernie Crouch. Both guns lifted irrevocably in his ham fists and both guns went off, once each, before Crouch finally tilted like an axed redwood tree and crashed to the earth with a blow that seemed to shake the town.

The stink of powder smoke was acrid in Paradise's nostrils. He had only fired one shot; the wind drifted Morgan's smoke past his face. He looked down at himself and saw the long ugly bleeding slice, curving around his ribs, and he thought, *If the damn fool had used something bigger than that .38, he'd have killed me with that bullet.* The slug had been deflected by his rib.

Wargo was dead and Crouch was down, evidently dying, coughing blood into the street. Five bullets in his chest, Crouch still found the energy to yank back his trigger and pour lead into the street. Then, finally, the guns were stilled.

Paradise turned to look for Morgan.

The sheriff was walking backward with slow little steps. He swayed back against the wall and came away, leaving behind a red smear; he eyed Paradise petulantly and sat down, clumsy.

Paradise ran to him. Morgan looked up and said, "I guess that's all."

"You'll be all right, Sheriff."

"Not with two slugs in my lungs. So long, Paradise. Like I said," he grinned weakly, "the kind of son-in-law I always wanted." He passed out, and Paradise knew he would never awaken.

The crowd was gathering, gingerly coming closer, gathering boldness. When he looked up the street he saw the two slim women there, and he knew they had seen the whole thing. They walked forward now, breaking into a skirt-flying run.

Paradise put his gun away in the holster and waited for them. They knelt over Morgan, and Paradise said, "I tolled him into this. It was my fault. If it didn't sound hollow, I'd say I'm sorry."

"Don't be sorry," Mrs. Morgan told him. "Don't ever be sorry. He's all right now. Nothing can hurt him any more."

Terry's tears were glistening in the dawn light. Paradise lifted her by the shoulders and walked away with his arm around her. There was nothing that needed saying. She pulled his arm down off her shoulders and grasped him by the hand, and turned against him; he held her close and said, "Cry it out."

She said, "He died well?"

"Yes."

She reached up and pulled his shaggy red head down. Her cheeks were wet. He held her silently while the sun came up.

A TALL MAN HANGS FROM A SHORT ROPE

—

Robert J. Randisi

Part 1

Lancaster's only intention when he rode into the small town of Bedford, Arizona, was to have a drink. One beer to cut the dust, and then he was going to move on. He was anxious to get home to San Francisco, his base of operations.

Lancaster traveled all over the country for his business, but by the time his business was complete he always found himself longing for the hotels, restaurants and gambling palaces of Portsmouth Square—not to mention the women.

Bedford had a bazaar atmosphere, Lancaster noticed. Not strange, but like a circus, or a fair. The street was filled with people, and as he tied his horse off in front of the Black Horse Saloon he couldn't see what was causing all the commotion. A more curious man might have walked over to check it out for himself, but Lancaster craved that one beer.

As he entered the saloon he saw that the interior was a shambles. There were three men, one behind the bar, and two in front of it. There were chairs all over the place, standing at angles, some overturned, but the tables had been pushed back against the walls. There wasn't a bottle or glass in sight, and there were no saloon girls. It was getting on toward late afternoon, when saloons in most towns started filling up, but this one had only three men in it.

161

Or four, counting him.

Bizarre—the strange kind, this time.

"Can I get a beer?" Lancaster asked. He took off his hat and tried to wipe the sweat from his face with his sleeve, but there was too much of it.

"Sure, why not?" the bartender said. "We're open again."

He was a big, heavyset man in his forties, whose face was blazing red, probably because it was almost as hot inside as it was outside—or maybe it was a result of the extra weight he was carrying around his middle.

"Again?" Lancaster asked, as the man set a cold beer in front of him.

"Yeah," the bartender said, "we *were* closed for the trial."

Lancaster took two swallows of cold beer and shuddered. It was blazing hot out and the cold seemed to go right through him. He put the beer down, determined not to make himself sick by guzzling it.

"Trial? What trial?"

"Murder trial."

"Really? I thought, from the commotion, that there was a circus in town, or something like that."

"There is, sort of," one of the other men said. He was smaller than the bartender, thin, about the same age, not suffering from the heat as much, but still sweating. In his case it was no help that he was wearing a three-piece suit. His attire told Lancaster that he probably held some high position in the town hierarchy.

"A circus, *and* a trial?"

"Well," the man said, "not so much a circus as a hanging, with a circus atmosphere."

A chill went through Lancaster that had nothing to do with the beer.

"A hanging?" he asked. "So soon after the trial?"

"Guilty's guilty," the third man said, attracting Lancaster's attention.

He was younger than the other two, in his early thirties, maybe a few years younger than Lancaster. He had large half circles of sweat beneath his armpits. He was chewing on a toothpick and took it out when he spoke, then put it back in.

The gun on his hip wasn't fancy, but it was clean and the man wore it like he knew how to use it. That was something Lancaster had trained himself to notice, and it had saved his life many times.

"The town's real excited about it," the bartender said. "There hasn't been a hanging here in years."

"Why aren't you three out there, then?" Lancaster asked.

"I ain't interested in seein' a hangin'," the bartender said.

"And it won't start without us." The second man's tone was regretful, as if he *wanted* to miss the hanging, but knew he could not.

"Why not?"

"I'm the hangman," the younger man said, toothpick out, toothpick in. He smiled, as if the announcement had pleased him.

"And you?" Lancaster asked the second man.

"I'm the mayor of the town," he said, "and I was the judge at the trial."

"Who was the jury?"

"Six good and honest men," the hangman said.

"And they found him guilty, and sentenced him to hang . . . today?"

"That's right," the mayor said, looking away, not meeting Lancaster's eyes.

"And where's the sheriff during all of this?" Lancaster asked.

The hangman took out the toothpick and said, "Oh, he's the one bein' hanged."

Part 2

"In other words," Lancaster said, putting all the facts together, "it's a lynching."

"All legal and on the up and up," the hangman said, shaking his head.

Lancaster looked at the Mayor.

"What's your name, sir?"

"Hansen," the man said, "Mayor Fred Hansen."

"Mayor Hansen, are you a duly elected judge?"

"He's the closest thing we got to it in this town," the hangman said.

"And what's your name?"

"Quitman," the man said, "Sam Quitman."

"And Mr. Quitman, what qualifies you to be a hangman?" Lancaster asked.

Quitman took the toothpick out of his mouth, smiled and said, "I volunteered."

Lancaster wondered why anyone *would* volunteer for such a job?

Quitman replaced the toothpick and said to Mayor Hansen, "Come on, we got to get it done."

Lancaster noticed that Hansen didn't seem happy about it. He also noticed that of the three men, only Quitman was armed.

" 'scuse me," Hansen said to Lancaster, and moved past him.

"You got somethin' to say about this, Mister?" Quitman came up alongside Lancaster and had to look up, as Lancaster was a good four inches taller than Quitman's own six feet.

Lancaster picked up his mug and said, "I only came in for a beer."

"Well then take my advice, finish your beer and be on your way." With that Quitman moved past Lancaster and out of the saloon.

"Okay," Lancaster said to the bartender, putting the beer down, "why don't you tell me what's going on, and make it quick?"

"It's Quitman and his men, Mister," the bartender said, looking more agitated now that the other men had left. "They forced Mayor Hansen into this."

"And the townspeople?"

"They just went crazy," the bartender said. "It's hot, and Quitman incited them to have the trial and find Sheriff Lockheart guilty."

"Of what?"

The barkeep shrugged.

"Nobody knows."

"They're hanging a man—a lawman—and they don't know why?"

"Quitman said he knows why, and that's enough. Once the jury came back with a guilty verdict they took the sheriff down the street to get the rope ready, but it's Quitman who's gonna do the hangin'. Once that's done, him and his men will take over the town."

"And nobody'll stop them?"

"Sheriff Lockheart was the only one with enough gumption to stand up to Quitman and his men when they came to town."

"He has no deputies?"

"He did, but they quit when things got rough."

"And what about the jury?" Lancaster asked. "What's their part?"

"Quitman handpicked them, and they were all too scared to find him not guilty."

"How many men does Quitman have?"

"Two—three, countin' him."

"And a whole town is knuckling under to three men?"

"Three *killers*," the bartender said, as if correcting Lancaster.

"Have they killed anyone else since they got here?"

"No, but they would have."

"But nobody gave them cause, right?"

"Right."

"Because nobody stood up to them?"

"Right."

"Except the sheriff."

The bartender nodded.

"I don't know why they didn't just shoot the sheriff down, or run him out of town," the bartender said. "I don't know why they have to do this."

"Once it's done," Lancaster said, "they'll have a lock on this town, that's why. Once it's done everyone in town will be too sick and too scared to stand up to them, and every one of them will be as guilty as the other."

"You got that right, Mister," the bartender said. "Look, you got to do somethin'."

"Me?" Lancaster said. "Why me? I just came into town for a beer."

"Somebody's got to do somethin'," the bartender said. "You can use that gun on your hip, friend. I can tell by lookin' at you."

"Is that right?"

"Yeah, it is."

"You ever been a lawman?"

"No," Lancaster said. A bounty hunter at one time, yeah, and now a man with certain expertise that he hired out, but never a lawman, and not a gunman.

The bartender took something out from under the bar and set on the bartop. It was a sheriff's star, pitted, tarnished, dented but serviceable.

"You can be one now."

"Where'd you get that?"

"Quitman tore it off of Lockheart's shirt when they started the trial. I picked it up."

"I can't just put that on and be the sheriff. That's not the way it's done." There was also the fact that he simply didn't *want* to put it on.

"Yes, you can," the bartender said. "My name's Ted Ransom, and I'm head of the town council. Since I'm the only member of the council here that makes me a majority, and I can appoint you temporary sheriff."

"Temporary until when?" Lancaster asked, scowling.

"Until you save the life of the real sheriff."

Lancaster stared at the badge, then longingly at the remainder of the beer in his mug. He wanted nothing more than to simply finish it, turn, mount his horse and ride out of town.

"You know what gets me?" the bartender said.

"No, what?" Lancaster was still staring at the badge when he replied.

"The people."

"What about them?"

"Well, after a while they really—well, they *wanted* it, you know? They wanted the lynching. They got a taste for it. I don't get it, I just don't get it. I mean, they *know* Ben Lockheart, but when they dragged him out of here there was . . . hunger in their eyes, ya know?''

''Jesus,'' Lancaster swore, ''I only came in for a cold beer . . .''

He picked up the badge, put it on and left the saloon.

Part 3

Lancaster was a man who did very little he wasn't paid to do . . . normally. True, he wasn't being paid to face down a lynch mob. There was no profit going into his pocket for this, and he was taking his life into his hands trying to stop a mob that had the taste for it, but damn it . . . damn it all, *lynching* went against his grain. And this was a case of neighbors lynching a lawman, a man they knew—and they weren't doing it at gunpoint, not the way he'd been told the story. They were doing it now because they *wanted* it, and that just wasn't right.

Lancaster was a man who worked for profit, but for himself he did what was right. He just wouldn't be able to live with himself if he got up on his horse, rode out and let this happen.

And then there was Sam Quitman. He didn't know the other two men who were in on this with him, but he knew he didn't like Quitman.

Not one bit.

He stopped at his horse to grab his rifle, then pinned on the dented star and started off toward the mob scene down the street, hoping he'd be in time.

Part 4

As he approached the crowd he saw beyond them that the sheriff had been stood up on a buckboard, with a rope dangling down from a fancy new gaslight pole. The man's hands had been tied behind his back and the rope was already around his neck.

Lancaster was *just* in time.

He fired one shot in the air from his rifle, ejected the spent shell and pushed through the crowd, rifle in one hand, pistol in the other, until he was standing near the buckboard. A man was holding the head of the single horse hitched to the buckboard, else the horse would have bolted at the sound of the shot. Great. Lancaster had almost lynched the sheriff himself.

"Listen to me!" he shouted. "People, look at what you're doing. This man is your sheriff."

"Not anymore, he isn't," Sam Quitman said.

Quitman was standing alongside the buckboard, staring at Lancaster with his thumbs hooked into his gunbelt. Lancaster assumed that the man holding the horses was one of Quitman's men. He carried the same look.

"Who says?" Lancaster asked.

"The mayor," Quitman said. "Just ask him."

"Mayor Hansen!"

Hansen stepped forward from the crowd.

"Mayor," Lancaster said, challenging the man, "you look up at that man on the buckboard and tell him to his face that he's not your sheriff, anymore."

Together, Lancaster and the Mayor looked up at Sheriff Ben Lockheart. Lancaster saw that the man was in his thirties, tall—almost as tall as he was—and fit. His eyes were strong, boring into the mayor's until the man was forced to turn away. Lancaster knew instinctively that this man would go to his death with dignity—even at the end of a rope, the most undignified death of all.

"He's guilty!" someone shouted.

"Of what?" Lancaster demanded. "Does anybody here know?" He picked out a man and asked, "You, friend. Do you know what he's guilty of?"

The man looked dumbfounded.

Lancaster picked out a respectable looking woman to attack next.

"How about you, Ma'am? Do you know what he's guilty of?"

"I wasn't even in the saloo—I mean, the courtroom." She blushed.

"But you're here, aren't you?" he asked. "You're here to watch him dance at the end of a rope? Why?"

The woman averted her eyes.

Lancaster chose a boy of about ten, next.

"You, boy. Do you know what he's guilty of?"

"No, sir."

"Then why are you here?"

The boy shrugged. "I just wanna see a hangin'."

"Look at all of you," Lancaster said. "Look at what you're teaching your children."

"Mister," Quitman said, "you're pokin' your nose where it don't belong. Pinnin' on that badge don't give you the right to do that."

"This man," Lancaster said, ignoring Quitman, "and his men, want to take over your town, and this is their way of doing it. They incite a lynching, forcing you—no, *letting* you—lynch your own sheriff, your neighbor. Once you've done that you're under their thumb forever."

"This man is holdin' up a hangin'," Quitman shouted. "Are you gonna let him get away with that?"

"That's what I'm asking, too," Lancaster said, just as loudly. "Are you going to let him and his men turn you into mindless lunch mob?"

"Mister—" Quitman started, but Lancaster cut him off abruptly.

"Let them decide, Quitman."

"Hennessy?" Quitman called.

Foolishly, Quitman had himself identified his third man for Lancaster. The man stepped forward now, broad-shouldered, well-muscled, also in his thirties, his face covered by black stubble. The man stepped out and moved alongside the buckboard. Quitman stepped a few feet away, so that Hennessy wasn't between him and Lancaster.

"Yeah, Sam?"

"You got another rope?"

"Sure do."

"Get it."

Hennessy took a moment to look Lancaster up and down appraisingly.

"He's a tall one, Sam."

"That's okay," Quitman said. "A tall man hangs from a short rope."

"Don't move, Hennessy," Lancaster said.

Hennessy froze.

"These people haven't quite made up their minds yet, Quitman."

"I'm makin' it up for them, friend," Quitman said. He spread his legs, taking a belligerent stance. "You want to put your guns down and walk away now? Take that badge off and toss it in the dirt where it belongs? Or do you want to hang alongside the ex-sheriff, here."

"I'm not walking away," Lancaster said firmly, "and I'm not hanging, so I guess you better come up with another choice."

"You called it," Quitman said, then shouted, "Take him!"

Part 5

Lancaster had already decided that he'd have to take Quitman first, and then Hennessy. The third man was behind him, holding the horse. Maybe he'd have time to turn and fire, or maybe a bullet would rip into his back. There was only time to make is move and see.

He lowered his pistol and fired at Quitman once. The bullet struck the man in the chest as he was drawing his gun. He staggered back, his feet got tangled, and he fell onto his back, dead.

Hennessy's muscles had fooled Lancaster into thinking the man would be slow. He wasn't. He already had his gun out as Lancaster turned his rifle on him, and he knew he was going to be too late.

Whoever had hoisted the sheriff up onto the buckboard and tied his hands, however, had not taken the time to bind the man's feet. Lockheart took one step and kicked Hennessy in the side of the head. It was an awkward move, but effective. It gave Lancaster the time he needed to fire his rifle. The slug tore into Hennessy's torso, knocking him into the buckboard. The man fired his gun into the ground, then sprawled face first in the dirt.

Lancaster turned now to face the man behind him, knowing that this time he *was* out of luck. There was a shotgun blast but as he completed his turn he saw the man stagger back, his chest a mass of blood. Lancaster didn't have time to see who had helped him. He dropped his rifle, sprang forward and grabbed the horse's head, steadying it and keeping it from running off. Only then did he look around. He saw Ted Ransom, the bartender, and head of the town council, holding a Greener shotgun.

"Much obliged," Lancaster said.

"I think that's my line," Ransom said.

"Son?" Lancaster said to the boy who said he wanted to see a hanging. "Come here and hold this horse."

"Yessir."

The boy dutifully took control of the horse.

Lancaster holstered his handgun, picked up his rifle from the street and climbed onto the buckboard. The crowd had been stunned into silence, and no one had moved. The action had taken place so quickly that they didn't have time to.

"Quitman told me he volunteered to be the hangman," Lancaster announced. "Well, the hangman's dead, ladies and gents. Who wants to take his place?"

No one answered, as men and women in the crowd exchanged puzzled glances.

"Come on, come on," Lancaster said, "you all wanted to see a hanging a few minutes ago. Who's got the nerve to step up here and do it?"

"Your pushin' *my* luck, friend," Ben Lockheart said to Lancaster in a low voice.

"They're followers," Lancaster said, "not leaders." To the crowd he said, "No one volunteers? Well then, maybe you people should go home and think about what you almost did here today. Go on! Move!"

The crowd began to disperse as Lancaster slipped the rope

off the sheriff's neck, and then untied his hands.

"Mister," Lockheart said, rubbing his wrists, "I don't know who you are, but I owe you my life."

"Here," Lancaster said removing the badge from his shirt, "this is yours—and all you owe me is a beer. That's all I came into this town for, in the first place."

PULL YOUR FREIGHT!

Luke Short

It was close to the supper hour when Johnny Bishop wheeled his six teams and heavily loaded lumber wagon through the wagon-yard gate of the Primrose Freighting Company. At the moment the yard had a leisurely end-of-the-day tempo, with a half dozen returned wagons and teams filling its dusty expanse. Johnny pulled in his teams, tossed the reins down to the stock-tender and then climbed down from the high stack of pale, raw lumber.

Drawing off his gloves, he started for the office, calling over his shoulder to the hunchbacked stocktender, "That goes to Jessup's tomorrow, Humpy."

Johnny Bishop was a tall young man, perhaps in his middle twenties. Fine dust powdered his long jaw and clean shaven face, blurring its sharp planes. His pale gray eyes were red-rimmed from the dust. He halted before the door of the office for a moment, beating his dusty clothes with his gloves, then went inside.

He tramped up to the railing that separated the reception area from a pair of paper-littered desks. At the closest desk Herb Loftus, older than Johnny, sober-faced and harried, his Stetson shoved back from his forehead, was scowling down at a bill of lading before him.

Johnny took his battered Stetson from his head, reached inside the crown, extracted a bill of lading and laid it before Herb.

173

Herb looked up and his scowl disappeared. "Howdy, Johnny! Didn't think you'd make it before dark."

"It's downhill all the way, Herb," he said grinning, "too downhill in some places."

Herb smiled and picked up the bill of lading but did not look at it. Johnny started to turn away, waving a parting salute, when Herb said, "Got a minute, Johnny?"

Johnny halted, turned, and then looked carefully at Herb. "Sure." He came back to the desk.

"How long you been working for us, Johnny?" Herb asked idly. "About a year?"

"Closer to a year and a half," Johnny said. "Any kicks?"

Herb shook his head and smiled slightly, then picked up a pencil, held it between his two thumbs, leaned back in his swivel chair, and regarded Johnny. "Nary a kick," he said slowly. He hesitated. "I had a caller this morning, Johnny— a fellow by the name of Bill Minifee. You know him?"

Johnny shook his head in negation. "Should I?"

Herb shrugged. "He's a special agent for Wells Fargo. Seems he's tracking down the tag end of a big holdup job that happened a couple of years ago down in Wyoming." Herb studied his pencil thoughtfully. "He didn't say who sent him to Primrose, and he didn't say why he came to me, except he was interested in our teamsters."

"Any particular teamster?" Johnny asked slowly.

Herb pitched the pencil on the desk. "Well, I wouldn't blame him for being curious about Big Murph or Harry Tatum. If they thought of it, they'd likely try to hold up an Army payroll that was guarded by two companies of infantry."

Johnny smiled faintly and Herb continued, "He was looking for somebody younger." Now he looked at Johnny. "He described him as a little over six feet tall, maybe twenty-five, blond hair, gray eyes, handy with stock, and with a tattoo on his left upper arm. His name," Herb added, "was Jim Byers."

There was a long moment of silence.

"I don't recall any Jim Byers who worked here, do you?" Johnny asked. He and Herb were regarding each other levelly.

"Yes," Herb said. "I remember him very well. He quit us about a year ago. Don't you remember?"

Puzzled, Johnny shook his head.

"Think, man, think," Herb said softly. "He quit us about a year ago. Jim Byers."

The light dawned on Johnny. "You told him that?"

Herb nodded. "He didn't believe me either, but that's the story. Jim Byers quit us a year ago. You got it?"

Johnny smiled wryly. "I've got it, Herb."

Johnny turned toward the yard door, tramped across the room, and when his hand was on the knob he halted, then slowly turned and regarded Herb. "Was this Byers married, did he say?"

"Single," Herb said.

Johnny nodded. "Good night, Herb."

"See you in the morning, Johnny." Herb looked up. "Or will I?"

"You will," Johnny said quietly.

He stepped out into the busy wagon yard, his lean face grave and reflective. Herb knew, of course. This was Herb's way of warning a friend, of protecting him and of rewarding him for a year's faithful work.

For brief, bitter seconds Johnny weighed the situation. This Minifee hadn't believed Herb. That meant trouble. A year ago he would have cut through the alley to Jessup's Livery, rented a horse and under cover of darkness left the country. At one time, for months on end, that had worked, but it was a way that was closed to him now.

Out in the dusty yard the stocktenders were unhooking the teams and manhandling the big freight wagons under the open-faced shed. Across the way Al Cruse, another teamster and Johnny's best friend, was examining the front shoe of one of his mules.

Johnny cut across the yard to his lumber-loaded wagon, and drew out his battered round lunch bucket from the tool chest ironed to its side. At the same time, he heard the voice of Big Murph raised in sudden anger.

Looking over his shoulder, he saw the big teamster in heated argument with the crippled stocktender they all called Humpy. Humpy was a middle-aged, cheerful man, whose deformed and twisted back prevented him from doing a working man's heavy labor. His way with animals however, had won and kept him a job here, where he was a favorite among the rough teamsters.

Johnny could hear nothing of the argument, but he saw Big Murph suddenly belt Humpy across the face with the back of his hand. Humpy staggered back and fell in the slime at the base of the water trough.

Instantly, Johnny was in motion but Al Cruse was even quicker. So was Ed Ganton. The three of them, from different parts of the yard, converged on Big Murph. When Big Murph wheeled to face Ganton, Cruse took a flying leap and landed astride Murph's back. Brushing off Murph's hat, Cruse sank a hand in his coarse hair and steadying himself with this grip proceeded to drive his fist into Big Murph's face.

Big Murph was a mountain of a man, bull-strong and pig-dirty. He paid no attention to Al Cruse on his back, but concentrated on trying to grab Ganton, who was slashing at his arms with a lunch bucket.

Johnny, his left shoulder forward, dove solidly at Big Murph's knees. The impact drove the breath from Johnny, but he felt Murph's thick legs fold. Murph crashed to the ground with all three of them, Johnny, Ganton, and Al Cruse, piled atop him and slugging savagely at his broad bearded face.

When Big Murph's body relaxed, Johnny put a hand on Al's shoulder and said, "That's enough, Al."

Al Cruse rose. He was a lean, slight man in his thirties, with a tough, likable face. He was dressed in the dusty, ragged calico shirt and corduroy pants that were almost the teamsters' uniform. He looked briefly at Johnny, his eyes still hot, then he said, "You see him hit Humpy?"

Johnny nodded.

"He must be looking for something real safe," Al said bitterly.

Now Al glanced from Big Murph to the watering trough, and anger drained from his face. "Come on, Johnny," he said softly. "Let's wake him up real good." He gestured with his thumb toward the trough.

The three of them lifted Big Murph by the arms and legs, stumbled with him over to the watering trough, and pitched him in.

As Big Murph came up sputtering, Al Cruse shoved his head under the water again, then backed off. "You lard-legged jackass," Al said. "I thought we told you to leave Humpy alone."

"This's the third day he sawed off that crippled roan jack on my wagon!"

"If you can't skin mules, why don't you quit?" Johnny said derisively.

With a growl Big Murph lunged for the side of the tank. Johnny, who had been watching for this, took a step backward, reached out and picked up a pitchfork. Bringing it up, he moved slowly toward Big Murph until the tines gently nudged Big Murph's belly. One leg over the side of the tank, Big Murph halted. He looked down at the pitch-fork, then at Johnny.

"Better change your mind, Murph," Johnny said softly. "None of us are hunchbacks."

Al Cruse reached out. "Give me that, Johnny. I'll let some of the air out of this big wind."

Big Murph backed up and then straightened, eyeing the three of them. He was beaten, and his expression showed it.

"Next time you beat up on a cripple," Al said softly, "you'll get throwed back in there with an anvil tied around your neck. Now get out."

Dripping rivers of water, Big Murph stepped over the side of the tank, swearing bitterly. Then he picked up his hat and tramped out the alley entrance of the yard.

Cruse, watching him, observed, "That's the first bath he's had since the last rain." He eyed Johnny soberly. "He'll remember this, Johnny. He's an Injun. Better carry a rock in your pocket."

"He'll forget it," Johnny said carelessly.

Laughing, the three of them broke up. Johnny picked up his lunch bucket where he had dropped it and then headed for the street gate, the old depression again upon him.

As he passed through the gate, he glanced idly at a tall, middle-aged man leaning against the gatepost, a tooth-pick in his mouth. The man wore cattlemen's boots, and a worn shell belt and holster sagged below his open buttonless vest.

Johnny was already in the street when he heard him call, "Jimmy?"

For the briefest instant alarm came to Johnny Bishop, but he did not break step and did not falter.

"You, out there! Bishop!" the voice called sharply.

Now Johnny halted and slowly turned to regard the man. This was Minifee, of course, and Johnny felt a cold hatred for the man that he was careful to keep out of his eyes.

Minifee walked slowly out into the road and hauled up before Johnny, regarding him carefully. "Your name Bishop?" he demanded.

"That's right. Johnny Bishop," Johnny said with a forced mildness.

"You work for this outfit?" Minifee asked, nodding toward the freight yard.

Johnny nodded.

"Know a young fellow named Jimmy Byers—about your height, twenty-five maybe, looks something like you?"

"A teamster?" Johnny asked. At Minifee's nod, Johnny, remembering Herb's admonition, lied glibly. "Sure. He worked here awhile. Quit about a year ago."

"Sure about that?"

"Why shouldn't I be?"

"Funny that you and Herb Loftus are the only two who remember Jimmy Byers."

Johnny shrugged. "Why should anybody remember him especially? I just happened to. Maybe Herb did too."

Minifee smiled faintly. "Where'd you come from?" he asked.

Johnny's eyes grew cold. "Would that be any of your business?"

Minifee only smiled. "Just curiosity," he murmured.

"Get curious somewhere else," Johnny said. He turned then and headed for the far sidewalk. He could almost feel Minifee's glance boring into his back.

Johnny turned left at the corner where the plankwalk ended into a street of small stores, plain frame buildings, and an occasional modest frame house, unpainted and weathering. He turned in alongside a log cabin, traversed the narrow passageway between it and the next building, and came out into a small yard back against the alley shacks. The front portion of the cabin was occupied by old man Pritchard, who owned the harness shop. The two rear rooms were home for Johnny and Lillie Bishop.

Hand on the door latch, Johnny halted, composing his face. What was he going to tell Lillie? *The truth, of course,* he thought grimly. Then he opened the door.

The room he stepped into was a plain one, the combination kitchen and living room of a working man. There were gay curtains at the two small windows; and the small iron range, cracked but shining, threw a pleasant warmth into the room. A curtain divided this room from the one next, their sleeping quarters.

As Johnny closed the door, the curtain parted and Lillie came into the room. She was small, not quite pretty, with dark thick hair pinned atop her head. There was a measuring tape around her shoulders and her dress front held a cluster of pins. Crossing the room, she threw her arms around Johnny and kissed him.

"You're early, Johnny. I haven't even started supper yet."

"I got an early start from the mill," Johnny said cheerfully. He gave her an affectionate hug, then set his lunch bucket on the table and stripped off his shirt. Crossing the room to the washstand, he poured out a basin of water and began to soap his arms and upper body.

Lillie, meanwhile, was chatting about the dress she was making as she stirred the fire and put a kettle of water on the stove.

Johnny, drying himself, listened idly, looking into the mirror. Suddenly, his hands halted and he stared at his own somber face.

Lillie, watching him, ceased her chatter. "What's the matter, Johnny?" she asked, and started across the room to him.

Slowly Johnny balled up the towel in his fist, a kind of suppressed anger in his movements, and dropped it gently on the washstand. Then he turned to her.

"I told you once, Lillie, I'd never hide anything from you." He paused. "Well, they're after me again."

Lillie halted momentarily and then came into his arms. He held her awhile in silence and then, pressing her to him and speaking over her head, he said, "Herb warned me tonight. A Wells Fargo special agent, name of Minifee, stopped by the yard today. He had my description, even down to my tattoo." He paused. "I saw him. He tried to trip me up by calling me Jimmy."

Lillie looked up at him. "Did you give yourself away?"

"Not any," Johnny said. "He knows though."

"But he can't prove it!" Lillie said passionately. She stroked his upper arm, running her fingers over a rough triangular scar. "You've got no tattoo, Johnny. Anybody can have a scar there."

"Sure, sure," Johnny said softly, almost absently.

Lillie looked up at him, tears beginning to come into her eyes. "Oh, why can't they let us alone? Do you keep paying all your life for just one mistake?"

"All my life," Johnny echoed, bitterly. "All yours too."

Now Lillie seized him by both arms and shook him. "Johnny, we've got to clear you of this! Couldn't you go with this man? Couldn't you tell the judge all you did was bring four fresh horses to a certain spot and take four tired horses back? What's the crime in that?"

"I helped in a big express robbery," Johnny said tonelessly. "That's all the law wants to know."

"But you didn't even know what the horses would be used for!" Lillie protested.

Johnny looked down at her. "I knew," he said. "Nobody would have paid me what they did if they hadn't been breaking the law."

"But you didn't have a gun," Lillie protested. "You can tell them you were just out of the Army—sick, broke, and a stranger. You did it to live."

"Other people live and don't break the law," Johnny said grimly. "That's what the judge will say. That's what he'll tell me when he sentences me."

Lillie put her cheek against Johnny's shoulder, holding him tight. "What are we going to do, Johnny?" she asked softly.

"Bluff it out," Johnny said grimly. "They can't prove anything. I don't have to answer his questions."

"If he goes to the sheriff you will." Lillie looked up at him. "Won't you?"

Johnny sighed. "I reckon so."

Bill Minifee, watched Johnny Bishop until he turned the corner, then glanced back into the wagon yard. The big man whom Johnny Bishop and the other two had ducked in the trough was gone, but Minifee guessed he would not be hard to find. During the few hours he had been in Primrose, Minifee had quietly reconnoitered the town. There were two saloons, one at the Primrose House and one next to the livery stable. The teamster was unlikely to patronize the quiet and orderly hotel bar. Chances were, then, that now or later he would be at the other saloon.

Minifee turned and headed up the plankwalk toward Main Street, his pace unhurried. He knew, in spite of Loftus's attempt to cover up, that Johnny Bishop was Jim Byers. Trouble was he lacked final proof of the identifying tattoo. But he thought he knew now how to get it.

Minifee mounted the steps of the Bella Union and shouldered through the head-high batwing doors. The babble of voices filled the big high-ceilinged saloon, and the bar on the left was packed with customers. The gambling tables on the right were also filled down to the very last chair and onlookers circulated among the tables idly watching the games.

Minifee cruised down the bar and presently spotted his man. Big Murph had changed from his filthy wet clothes into equally filthy dry ones. He was engaged in desultory conversation with the man on his right while he drank great gulps of whisky from a water glass.

Minifee edged up to the bar alongside him, and Big Murph turned now to see who his neighbor was.

Minifee sized him up immediately as a born bully-boy, uneducated, simple-minded, surly, and truculent.

Minifee gestured with his thumb to the glass of whisky. "A little of that stuff in the water tank would have helped," he observed amiably.

Big Murph gave him a surly glance, and then regarded his glass of whisky.

"That was an Injun trick," Minifee observed. "It took three of them to do it though."

"It'll take six next time," Murph growled. "If they hadn't got me down, I'd of taken 'em."

"Know who threw you?"

Murph scowled. "Cruse, wasn't it?"

"Bishop," Minifee said, and added, "Why don't he stand up and fight like a man?"

Big Murph grinned. "He ain't one, that's why." He took another swig from his glass of whisky. "Just you wait, I'll get him."

"How?" Minifee challenged.

Big Murph looked at him, a kind of surprise in his broad face. "There's lots of ways," he said slyly. "Suppose I lock wheels with him next time we pass on the mill road? I'll dump him off a couple hundred feet into the canyon."

"That sounds kind of trifling," Minifee observed. "Still, he's a hard case to tangle with."

Big Murph looked scornfully at him. "If I could catch him alone, I'd stomp him flat. Trouble is, Cruse or somebody always buys into the fight."

"Then catch him alone."

Big Murph shook his head. "He won't even come out after dark. His woman won't let him."

"What's the matter with daylight?"

Big Murph looked sharply at him. "What do you care, Mister?"

Minifee shrugged. "I don't. I just watched that pile-up, and I wondered why a big man like you would take it. Especially," he added softly, "if you can make a double eagle by not taking it."

Big Murph gently set his glass down on the bar and turned his head to regard Minifee. "Say that again."

"A double eagle." He reached in his pocket, put a coin on the bar, and covered it with his hand. "There's ten—and ten more when you lay him out." Then he added softly, "And I mean laid out."

Big Murph scowled. "Why laid out?"

Minifee smiled as if to himself. "I want a close, careful look at him when his eyes are shut."

"When?"

"Tomorrow morning, say?"

Big Murph looked first at Minifee, then at Minifee's hand covering the coin. Slowly Minifee withdrew his hand, and now Murph regarded the coin with a kind of crafty disbelief.

Suddenly Big Murph held up his right hand, fisted it, and laughed. He brought his hand crashing down on the bar alongside the coin. The impact sent the coin six inches in the air. Big Murph opened his palms under it when it dropped. He pocketed the coin, nodded to Minifee, and winked.

On weekdays the Primrose Freighting Company was astir before daylight. The big wagons heading for the railroad sixty miles away, for the sawmill, and for distant mines were on the road at earliest light. From the gate Minifee watched the stocktenders, who were working by lantern light, maneuver the teams into place and harness them almost by touch. There was a steady background chorus of profanity.

Teamsters passed him on their way to the office to receive orders, and Minifee, standing in the shadows, observed that Johnny Bishop was among them. Big Murph, noisy and cheerful, arrived at last and stepped into the office to pick up his orders.

Minifee, watching him, began to doubt the wisdom of his investment. Certainly Big Murph didn't appear to be a man who was carrying a grudge.

Already the first wagon had pulled out past Minifee, its empty box rumbling, its wheels jolting against the axles and the driver cursing his somnolent mules. As the wagon rolled into the street, Minifee heard a shout, and he moved a few tentative steps deeper into the dark yard. He saw teamsters and stocktenders looking toward the open-faced wagon shed.

Then Johnny Bishop came into his line of vision. Backing slowly, Johnny was slugging viciously at Big Murph. The big teamster's shoulders were hunched, his beard buried in his neck, and he was making little effort to parry Johnny's blows.

Then, with an astonishing agility Murph lunged forward, and a big hand fell on either of Johnny Bishop's shoulders. The big man lowered his head and, yanking Johnny toward him, butted him savagely in the face. Minifee could hear the thud from where he stood, and he winced.

For a second Johnny stood motionless, and then his knees buckled and he fell. Instantly the yard boiled with activity. From all directions teamsters and stocktenders dropped their work and headed for Big Murph. Minifee saw the office door open and Herb Loftus, shouting angrily, jumped down the steps and headed for the fight.

Minifee was already in motion. He ran directly to where Johnny Bishop lay in the cool dust. The fight now centered at the rear of the wagon shed where Big Murph, his back to the wall, was taking on all comers.

Kneeling, Minifee took Johnny's left arm and, holding it out, grasped Johnny's shirt. With a savage yank he ripped the cloth and exposed Johnny's upper arm. Quickly Minifee examined the scar where Johnny's tattoo had been, and a faint elation touched him.

Then he moved down to Johnny's feet, lifted Johnny's left leg, and grasped his boot in both hands. With a tremendous tug he yanked at the boot and it slipped from Johnny's foot. Quickly Minifee pushed up the leg of Johnny's trousers until his lower leg was exposed. There on the shin was a long, deep scar.

Minifee was aware now that the shouting had subsided and he glanced over to the shed. Big Murph lay in the dirt against the shed wall, and now Herb Loftus's angry voice could be heard.

"—back to work or I'll fire the whole lot of you! This is a business place, not a saloon!"

The group broke up now, laughing, apparently unconcerned at Loftus's threats. Loftus, seeing Minifee kneeling beside Johnny, tramped over to him. Al Cruse, nursing a bloody nose, saw Minifee at the same time. Both he and Loftus arrived together.

Al, seeing that this stranger had removed Johnny's boot, asked Loftus, "What's he doing here?"

Minifee rose now, ignoring Al. He looked at Herb, nodded toward Johnny, and said, "That's my man, Loftus. You knew it all the time too."

Loftus knelt, lifted the cloth on Johnny's sleeve, and saw the scar. Glancing up at Minifee, he said, "That's no tattoo."

"That's where a tattoo used to be," Minifee said, dryly. "If you don't mind a little pain, it's easy enough to cut out the tattooed skin. It all depends on whether you figure it's worth it."

"You figure that'll hold up in court?" Herb asked skeptically.

"Together with the other it will."

Herb scowled. "What other?"

"Look at his left shin. I didn't tell you about that." Minifee smiled faintly. "An old ax scar went along with the tattoo as identification marks."

Herb pushed Johnny's trouser leg up until he saw the scar.

Al Cruse, who had been watching this in silence, said, "Who are you?"

"Wells Fargo special agent," Minifee said.

"What's Johnny done?"

"Helped in a big holdup a couple of years ago."

"I don't believe it," Al said flatly.

"I don't care if you believe it or not. You aren't the jury, friend."

Herb Loftus rose. Other teamsters had drifted up to them and were listening in silence. Herb said, "You're dead sure this is your man?"

"Dead sure. So are you."

"There's nothing we can do about it?"

"You can go get the sheriff," Minifee said.

"Get him yourself," Cruse cut in angrily. He looked around at his fellow teamsters. "I feel like another workout," Al observed. "How about you, boys?"

"Quit it, Al," Herb cut in. He looked around at the assembled teamsters and stocktenders. "That's the way the cards fall, boys." He looked now at Minifee. "He's married, you know. Got a pretty young wife."

"He won't be the first married man ever to go to jail,''
Minifee said dryly.

"He's a good man, the best. Steady, sober, and a hard
worker. I don't suppose that means anything to you.''

"Not a thing,'' Minifee agreed.

Al Cruse said softly, "Just give the word, Herb.'' He was
looking at Minifee with pure hatred.

Herb glanced over at Al and then at the other teamsters. He
took a deep breath then and sighed, "No, Al, I can't do it. I
did all I could, but I can't stop him now. It's up to a jury to
decide about Johnny.'' He inclined his head toward Minifee.
"After all, this man's paid to do a job. He's only doing it.''

Al Cruse took a step forward. "Herb,'' he said softly,
"don't it strike you that this fight between Murph and Johnny
come in awful handy for this gent?''

Herb scowled. "How's that?''

"He couldn't go up to Johnny and say, 'Listen, friend, I'd
like to see if you got a scar on your leg. I'd like to see if you
got a tattoo on your arm.' '' Al looked at Minifee now, and
then returned his glance to Herb. "Johnny wouldn't have
showed him and he ain't man enough to take a look himself.
I figure he put Murph up to it.''

"You're exactly right,'' Minifee said calmly. "I did.''

"Just give the word, Herb,'' Al said.

"I never like to put a gun on a man if I can help it,'' Minifee
said slowly, suggestively. "But that doesn't mean I can't.''

Al looked at him a long moment. "You ain't out of town
yet.''

"Quit it, Al!'' Herb said sharply. "Now break it up. Let's
get to work.''

Al gave Minifee a lingering look that held something of
promise in it before he turned away.

It fell to Al Cruse to tell Johnny's wife, and it took him the
best part of an hour to steel himself for the job. First, he had
to let his anger settle a little and then he had to dredge among
the bitter facts for some consoling word with which to comfort
Lillie. The trouble was there was nothing he could tell her that
would offer any consolation. Wells Fargo, he knew, were im-

placable; they never quit and when they nailed the man they usually made the charge stick.

Al had taken down deliveries that morning and after his first load, he drove his team around to Pritchard's house and swung down. He was thinking then of how Johnny Bishop, a little less than a year ago had pulled him, drunk and sick, out of the barrooms, of how Lillie had fed him, and of how Johnny had talked Herb Loftus into giving him a probationary job. Everything he was today—*Which isn't very damn much*, he thought—he owed to Johnny Bishop. A lot of other people in Primrose—humble, insignificant people like himself—were in debt to Johnny, too. Why, even Herb Loftus, with his crew of tough, irascible teamsters, was in debt to Johnny; somehow, with persuasion, logic, and sometimes fists, Johnny kept harmony and brought a sense of order to Herb's outfit.

At the Bishops' door, Al took a deep breath and knocked. Lillie appeared immediately and when she saw Al she smiled warmly. Slowly then, as she caught Al's mood reflected in his face, her smile faded.

"I got bad news, Lillie," Al began.

"They got him?" Lillie demanded swiftly.

Al nodded miserably.

Lillie sank into the nearest chair, folded her hands in her lap, and stared at the floor. "How did it happen?" she asked presently.

Al told her of Minifee's ruse. He finished by saying, "Weston's got him locked up for Minifee."

It was as if someone had kicked her, Al thought, and his anger returned. *Damn any law that could do this to a person.* Then he knew that was wrong, but he still thought it.

Lillie took a deep, shuddering breath and rose. There was a kind of determination in her small face as she said, "They can't do this, Al. I'm going to see Weston."

Sheriff Burt Weston was seated at his desk, writing, when Lillie and Al stepped into his office. When Weston saw them he rose slowly and indicated the barrel chair against the wall beside his desk.

"I don't reckon I have to guess why you're here," he said

wearily. He was an old man, white-haired, with heavy roan mustaches bisecting his lean face.

Lillie crossed the room to the chair and sat down, and Al took up his station beside her. "Why have you arrested Johnny?" Lillie asked quietly.

Sheriff Weston slacked into his swivel chair and eyed her patiently. "There's a warrant out for him down in Wyoming. He's charged with being an accessory in the murder of a stage driver and a Wells Fargo shotgun messenger. His real name," Weston added wearily, "is Jim Byers."

"Who said that?" Lillie demanded.

"Minifee. He's a Wells Fargo special agent. He's identified him."

"I grew up with Johnny Bishop," Lillie said flatly. "If he's named Jim Byers, why was his father's name Jim Bishop?"

"Quit it, Lillie," Weston said gently. "You grew up on a ranch in Kern County. There's not a Bishop in Kern County."

Lillie's face flushed, but she held the sheriff's gaze. "Have you checked all the gravestones in Kern County, too?" she asked bitterly.

"I don't have to." Weston's voice was gentle and held a quiet despair, and Al knew that the sheriff was hating this too.

"Why is this Minifee so certain Johnny's guilty?"

Weston made a wry face and said, "A tattoo and a scar that Minifee got from his army record identified him."

"He's not got a tattoo," Lillie said hotly.

"He's got a spot where one was."

"How can you prove that?"

"It's no use, Lillie," Weston said gently. "Johnny is Jim Byers. He's been identified by an old army man who was in Johnny's regiment."

"I don't believe it. Who?"

Lillie was fighting every inch of the way, Al knew, and he ached to help her.

"It's just plain bad luck, Lillie," Weston explained. "Johnny had just served out a cavalry enlistment. His regiment had been chasing Sioux all summer on half rations. He was sick and he couldn't work. His pay was gone. He figured to make a quick stake and get out of the country. That's what he did, just in case he never told you."

"I asked who identified him, not for a fairy story from Minifee."

"I'm coming to that," Weston said patiently. "This Minifee is a stubborn man. He's paid to be stubborn. As soon as he found out Johnny was in the holdup he went down to Fort Union where Johnny's regiment was stationed and asked around about Johnny. Sure as you're born, he ran into a trooper who talked. Remember that government survey party that was through here last summer?"

Lillie nodded.

"Well, they cut across the Raft Range with their cavalry escort. They just happened to take the logging road as far as the mill, and who do you guess they met bringing down a load of lumber?"

Lillie was motionless, waiting.

"It was Johnny," Weston said glumly. "This trooper that recognized Johnny had transferred out of Johnny's old regiment to a new one. The escort was picked out of that regiment." Weston spread his hands. "That's how things happen, Lillie."

"That's no proof," Lillie said stubbornly.

Weston looked at her a long moment. "Lillie, give up. Minifee will take him away. He'll be identified. There's nothing you can do to stop it."

Al Cruse said bluntly, "There's something you can do, Burt."

"What's that, Al?"

"You could forget to lock the cell, for one thing."

Weston only shook his head. "You know better than that."

"What's this Wells Fargo man to you?" Al demanded hotly.

"Nothing. I'll never see him again."

"Then just leave the key in the cell door. If Mr. Wells Fargo gets tough, let us know. We'll run his luck out and mighty sudden."

Weston shook his head. "I took an oath, Al. Sometimes I wonder why, but I did. That oath was to uphold the law against

lawbreakers. Johnny's a lawbreaker.'' He spread his hands.
''It's that simple, Lillie. You might as well face it.''

"Can I see him?" Lillie asked.

"Of course." Weston pointed to the door on the alley side
of the office, and Lillie rose, crossed the room, and entered
the cell block.

Al was silent for a long bitter minute, his mind refusing to
accept this. He looked at Weston then and said, "Why don't
you quit?"

"I'd like to, Al," Weston answered.

"You know what kind of a man Johnny is. How can you
do it?"

"How can I not do it?"

"But, damn it, you don't understand!" Al said hotly.
"Johnny's going to be something. He's not like the rest of us.
He's going somewhere. He's going somewhere big and he
ain't going to step on nobody's neck getting there."

"I know that, Al," Weston said gently. "He's a fine boy.
I wish he was my son, but even if he was, I'd have to do
this."

Al was licked and he knew it. "What happens now?" he
asked glumly.

"Minifee takes him out tomorrow morning as soon as the
papers are in order."

Lillie stepped out of the cell block then and Al pushed away
from the wall. "Take you home, Lillie?"

"I'd rather walk, Al, thanks." At the door she halted and
turned to regard Weston. "I'd hate to have this on my conscience, Sheriff," she said quietly.

Weston dipped his head. "I do hate it."

She left, and Al said, "Can I see him?"

"Sure. You got a gun on you?"

Al shook his head and Weston said, "Go ahead then."

Al tramped across the room and opened the door to the cell
block. There were two cells, and in the one on the right Johnny
was sitting on the cot, his back against the wall, looking out
the barred window. When he heard Al enter, he swiveled his
head. There was a bruise on his chin where Big Murph had
butted him.

Al came up to the cell, grasped the bars and he and Johnny looked at each other in sober silence. "Is that Wells Fargo story true, Johnny?" Al finally asked.

Johnny nodded.

"What can I do?" Al asked.

Slowly Johnny rose from the cot. He came over to face Al. "Lillie's going to have a baby, Al."

"Fine, fine," Al said bitterly.

Johnny smiled crookedly. "Old man Pritchard was in here this morning. He offered to forget about the rent."

"Don't you worry about grub and clothes," Al said. "As long as I eat, she does."

"Somebody'll have to take care of her. She's got no family and neither have I. After the baby comes, she can work."

"Don't worry about that," Al said. "How long will you be gone?"

Johnny shrugged. "Minifee says Wells Fargo'll ask for ten years."

"That's real fine," Al said bitterly. "What's ten years? Nothing! Why, by that time your kid'll only be punching cattle on the horse he earned the money to buy."

Johnny said nothing.

Al said slowly, "You ever thought of Canada, Johnny?"

"Canada? For what?"

"You can start over up there and the law will let you alone. They tell me it's not much different than here."

Johnny smiled crookedly. "When I get out of jail, the law won't be interested in me any more, Al."

"I mean now."

Johnny and Al looked at each other in silence. "If you're thinking what I'm thinking," Johnny said slowly, "don't do it."

"I'm old enough to vote," Al said dryly. "Just tell me how Canada sounds to you. As soon as you're settled, we can send Lillie up."

Johnny shook his head. "Don't do it, Al. Somebody'll get hurt. Even if they don't, who takes the blame?"

"There won't be any blame. Take my word for it. Now answer me about Canada."

"I won't even talk about it."

Al grinned. "You think real hard about it. There'll be a horse and grub tied behind the jail. Remember that, just in case it rains tonight and washes a hole in the roof."

Next morning before daybreak Al Cruse got his orders to pick up a load of concentrates at the Ajax Mine in the Raft Mountains. It meant a day each way on the road.

Al helped the stocktender load two days' rations for his teams, mounted to the seat and drove out of the yard, cheerfully cursing his mules. He swung left, crossed Main Street, headed north for the Raft Range.

When he had passed the county offices, however, he suddenly cut left into the alley and pulled through it as far as the corral behind Jessup's Stable. Here he swung down from the high wagon, walked into the livery and past the hostler who was sleeping in the hay. From a dozen saddles hanging on the wall in back of the office, he took one and went back with it to the corral. A score of horses, mostly rental mounts, were standing patiently in the quiet morning as he stepped inside the corral. It took him only a few minutes to catch and saddle a horse.

Al rode through the livery centerway, across Main Street, and turned in at the alley alongside the jail. Behind the sheriff's office Al dismounted and tied his pony to a ring at Packard's loading platform. It was full daylight now, and the town was beginning to come awake. Al left the alley, crossed the street, mounted the veranda of the Primrose House, selected a chair and slacked into it. *This beats freighting*, he thought wryly. *This is the life.*

He had smoked down five cigarettes and shifted to another chair before it happened. Soon after the breakfast bell rang in the Primrose House, Al saw Minifee, mounted and leading a second horse, turn off Main Street and rein in before the sheriff's office. The extra horse, Al knew, was for Johnny. Minifee dismounted and went into the sheriff's office.

Al rose. The time was here. Descending the veranda steps, he sauntered idly across to the two horses and stroked the nose of Minifee's mount, meanwhile looking first up the street and then down it. Al slipped his sheath knife out and quickly slashed the cinch of Minifee's saddle, leaving only the thinnest thread uncut so that the cinch would not fall and betray his act. Casually, unhurriedly, he did the same with the cinch on the saddle of the second horse.

Whistling, he headed back for the livery, tramped through it, mounted his high wagon and drove his teams through to Main Street. Turning left, he drove down a block, turned right, and was at the wagon yard.

He paid it no attention, however; he checked his leaders when they tried to turn in the wagon yard and held them straight until they were abreast the alley that ran behind the wagon yard, behind Packard's, and alongside the jail, where he reined in his teams and set the brake.

Still whistling cheerfully, Al dropped down in the bed of the wagon. Here was coiled a heavy length of logging chain which was used to lash loads. One end of the chain in his hand, Al swung up the steep side of the wagon box, which put his head level with the high barred window of the jail.

Putting one foot against the jail to brace himself, Al slipped the chain in back of the five iron bars of the window, then fitted the hook firmly into a link. He dropped to the ground, still whistling, and slowly pulled out the length of chain.

Taking the other end of the chain, he knelt and secured it around the rear axle and stringer beam of the wagonframe. Coming erect, he glanced over at Packard's loading platform. The pony he had left earlier was standing hipshot in the warm morning sunlight.

Al swung up on the wagon seat and uncoiled his whip, secured the brake even more firmly, and then started to swear at his lead mules. They danced back and forth, lunging into their collars as Al's whip cracked out and his curses poured forth. The other teams now caught the panic, lunging into their collars and inching the braked wagon forward.

With a fine sense of timing, Al knew when his teams were all pulling. Then with a tug of the brake strap, he let the brake off. At the same moment he vaulted from his high seat to the ground.

The wagon shot into the street, the lead team turning left at a dead run.

Hunkered against the wall of the jail, Al saw the chain play out, then rise horizontally into the air, taut as a fiddle-string. There was a rending crash, and the rear wheels of the big freight wagon rose two feet in the air, but the mules never halted, and the hitch did not break. The wagon careened into the middle of the street, turning on its two outside wheels, and then Al, watching it, smiled. Trailing at the end of the logging chain were the five jail window bars still set in the heavy oak window frame.

Al set his shoulders against the wall waiting, listening. He heard a sound in the alley as if a weight had fallen. Then he heard the pounding of footsteps, followed by the sound of a horse working into a dead gallop.

The noise on his right swiveled Al's head. The door of the sheriff's office crashed open and Minifee came out at a dead run. His horse, ground-haltered close to the jail steps, turned his head. Minifee didn't bother to mount. He simply vaulted into the saddle.

When his heavy body hit the saddle, the cinch broke. Minifee kept going. The saddle slipped, and with Minifee legs locked to it, it tore off, and Minifee crashed into the street on the far side of his horse.

Al knew now it was time to act. He ran out into the street, his whip trailing him, in apparent pursuit of his runaway team. He could see them a block down the street, still running.

Al was sure that Minifee had seen him, and he halted and turned. He was just in time to see Minifee swing into the saddle of the second horse. The horse, excited by all the commotion, reared, and Minifee began to saw the reins. Suddenly the cut cinch gave way entirely and Minifee, still in the saddle, slid down his mount's back and sat heavily on the ground.

By this time Sheriff Weston was on the steps of his office. Al, panting heavily as if he had run a great distance, came up to the sheriff and halted. He looked closely at Weston. The sheriff was regarding him with a quiet benevolence which Al could not exactly read.

Minifee, swearing bitterly, was kicking his legs free of the saddle stirrups when Al spoke: "Them jacks spooked there in the alley, Burt. When the wagon hit the jail it throwed me a country mile."

"You boys keep taking that alleyway too fast," Weston said in gentle reproof.

Elation touched Al Cruse then. The sheriff was playing along. They both looked at Minifee. The Wells Fargo agent was bent over the saddle. He looked briefly at the cinch, then straightened. "Cut," he announced. He looked balefully at Al. "You wouldn't know who did that, would you?"

"How could I?" Al said in a tone of surprise and injury. "I was trying to hold in twelve jacks!"

Minifee looked angrily at the sheriff. "You believe that, Sheriff?"

"Shouldn't I?"

"You believe that wagon rammed the jail so it tore out the window?" Minifee demanded.

Weston looked at him in amazement. "Now what else could hit it so it would tear out the window?"

"Your prisoner is gone," Minifee said angrily. "What do you aim to do about that?"

"He's your prisoner," Weston said flatly. "I just finished signing him over to you."

Minifee looked at the two men with quiet hatred, then pointed to his saddle and said, "You aim to find out who did that?"

"If a man rides a horse," Weston observed mildly, "he ought to learn how to saddle him."

This was too much for Minifee. He stalked over to the sheriff and said, "Sheriff, I demand you call up a posse."

"Sure thing," Weston said amiably. "There'll be a dozen or so men at the freight yard around noon. Good men, too. I'll deputize them all."

Despairingly Minifee looked from Weston to Al.

Al said quietly, "You better get going. Johnny's got a head start on you."

For a bitter moment Minifee looked at Al, and Al wondered if the man would pull his gun. Then Minifee's glance shuttled to Weston.

"You going to let it ride this way, Sheriff?" he demanded.

"Why, man," Sheriff Weston said sharply, and there was an edge of anger in his voice, "he's your prisoner. You want him. If you want help, I've offered to help you. All you got to do is speak up. What is it you want me to do?"

Minifee looked at him a long moment, and then he said bitterly, "Just fall down dead."

Under the curiously serene gazes of Al and Sheriff Weston, Minifee picked up both saddles, turned, and tramped down the street toward Jessup's.

Sheriff Weston settled his glance on Al, who was grinning. They looked at each other in silence.

"One thing you forgot," Weston said slowly. "Johnny will be picked up for stealing a horse, sure as shooting."

Al shook his head, grinning. "It was my horse, Burt. My bill of sale to Johnny is in his saddlebag."

BOY IN THE ROCKS

—

Richard Matheson

Part 1

The hands of the Circle Seven were just finishing up the great
pot of black coffee when Frank Bollinger saw the far-off dust
cloud.

"Looks like visitors," he said slowly, chewing up the last
of his steak, then washing it down with coffee.

Most of the men glanced across the plain but were too weary
to take much interest. Only their foreman, Rail Tiner, stood
up, his eyes peering out across the darkening prairie.

"I told them damn fools to—" he started, then broke off
and pressed his mouth into a tight, angry line. Abruptly, he
glanced to the south where the beef herd was beginning to
mill, and they all heard, faintly, the voices of the men on
watch, trying to calm the restless cattle.

"Frank, ride out there and tell them damn fools I said not
to bring them cows in till the mornin'," Tiner said.

Bollinger grunted twice, once in acknowledgment of the order, the second time indicating his exhaustion as he pushed to
his feet, pulling his unbuckled gun belt up with him, and
headed for the scattered remuda which was grazing a short
distance from the camp.

Tiner stayed on his feet, looking tensely toward the scaling
dust on the horizon while the rest of the men settled back on
their elbows and backs, eyes shut, cigarette smoke curling in

lazy wreaths above them, the light from the chuck wagon fire casting a flicker of shadows across their bronzed, motionless features. They paid no attention to their foreman or to the muffled curses which began drifting back to the camp as Frank Bollinger tried to saddle one of his horses.

Bollinger was just drawing in the hind cinch, his right foot shoved against the side of his mount, when hoofbeats sounded on the earth and, looking up, he saw an unfamiliar boy ride into the camp area. He finished bridling his apron-faced roan, then started walking it toward the fire.

The boy was sixteen at the most, seated on a panting buckskin pony, dressed in dust-covered flannel and wool, his hat looking as if it had suffered the pummeling crush of a stampede, the gun belt almost slipping over his hips.

As Bollinger entered the firelit area, he heard the boy answering Tiner.

"Hell, mister," the boy said, "how'd I know you was roundin' up out here? I ain't never been around here before. I'm just drivin' a few cows up north."

"You're alone?" Tiner asked, surprised.

"Sure enough," the boy answered, sounding almost belligerent. "Gonna fatten 'em up north and sell 'em."

"Well, you damn well better circle my herd wide, boy," Tiner warned. "I don't want your cows startin' no stampede."

"Don't worry none, mister, I'll circle your outfit," the boy said.

Tiner nodded. "Okay, boy," he said. "Care to light and put down some grub?"

"Like to," the boy said, "but I gotta get back to my cows."

"Wait a minute," said Tiner. The boy drew his pony around again. "Seein' as you're new to these parts," Tiner went on, "and just a one-man deal to the bargain, it'll only cost you ten dollars."

The boy's face went blank as he stared down at Tiner from the back of his shifting mount.

"What'd you say, mister?" he asked, but there wasn't a man there who thought he was asking a question. Some of them sat up or propped themselves on elbows, looking up interestedly at the lean, freckled face of the boy.

The corners of Rail Tiner's lips edged up a little, but he didn't say anything. Instead, with a casual gesture, he held out his left hand, palm up, toward the boy.

"This is free range." The boy's voice had become flat, stripped of emotion, and, although it was barely noticeable, the grip on his right-hand rein grew a little looser.

"Wrong," said Tiner, sounding amused. "This is Circle Seven range. Strangers pay. Or they don't cross." And he moved the outstretched fingers of his left hand a little as if beckoning in the money.

The boy's face was stone now, his body was like stone in the dark saddle.

"This is free range," he said.

Now all the men in the camp area were sitting up, watching attentively in the dim, smoke-pungent air.

"You ain't meanin' to pay then?" Tiner asked, sounding more amused than irritated.

"That's right," the boy said. "I ain't."

Tiner shrugged. His left hand moved down slowly to his side like the folded-in wing of a bird watching carrion.

"Okay, boy," he said. "Cash money ain't required. One o' your cows'll do for the crossin' price."

Sudden heated color sprang up the boy's cheeks. "Listen, mister, I drove these cows more'n four hundred miles. I chased off two thievin' bands o' Kiowas and one o' Comanches. I tussled with three wolves, five rattlers, and a cloudburst. You think I'm gonna give ya one o' my cows, you're loco!"

The smile was gone from Tiner's face as if it had been made of smoke. Eyes like black stones, he glanced over to the edge of the camp where Frank Bollinger stood beside his horse. His head jerked once in the general direction of the approaching herd.

"Go cut out a good one," Tiner said to Frank Bollinger. Then, without waiting to hear what the boy would say, he turned on his heel and walked toward the chuck wagon, spurs clinking on the hard ground.

"You ain't gonna *do* it," the boy said tensely as Bollinger swung up quickly into the saddle. "Mister, I'm warnin' ya. Leave my cows alone."

Bollinger laid reins across the roan's left side and nudged it with his knees into a slow canter away from the camp.

"Mister, I'm *warnin'* ya!" the boy shouted after him. Suddenly he dug his spurs in, making the buckskin pony charge out of the camp toward Bollinger's mount.

Several of the hands stood up to watch, and at the chuck wagon, Tiner turned his head quickly to see what the boy intended to do.

Frank Bollinger heard the sharp drumming of hooves behind him but kept moving forward, the pace of his roan quickening into a gallop. The boy raked spur wheels across his pony's flanks, and it leapt forward with a new burst of strength, head lowered, its legs drawn high, and pistoned at the earth in a blur of motion. Straight for Bollinger the pony swept. In the failing light, the Circle Seven hands saw the pony gain distance rapidly until, abruptly, it had cut across the path of Bollinger's roan and the two horses were rearing wildly, their sharp-edged hooves hammering at the air.

"Get back!" the boy yelled, his face twisted taut with fury.

Bollinger's answer was to let his right hand drop to his pistol butt. The boy's hand fell alike. Two eight-inch Colt barrels cleared their holsters almost simultaneously; two sharp explosions rocked the air. The boy's shot was first. Frank Bollinger was torn from his saddle and thrown to the earth like a rag doll stuffed with rocks.

A snorting bellow went up from the Circle Seven beef herd, and two scimitar-horned bulls lunged forward, great eyes dumb with fright.

"Mount up!" yelled Tiner, dropping his coffee cup and racing through the milling of hastily rising cowboys.

Out on the plain, the boy shoved his pistol back into his holster and, seeing the activity in camp, jerked his pony around and galloped off. The outer rank of Circle Seven longhorns started after him, the sound of their increasing run like that of thunder rising.

Now all the hands, exhaustion ignored, were thudding across the plain toward the remuda with the ungainly motion of high-heeled runners, heavy saddles slung across their shoulders. The men on herd watch had spurred forward and turned back the first tide of stampede, but now another bunch of cattle started off, one following another in thoughtless imitation.

"Hurry, damn it!" shouted Tiner.

The darkening sky was lashed by whipping lariats which fell across the heads of the scattering horses, adding their out-raged whinnies to the lowing and earth-trembling hoofbeats of the stampeding herd. Saddles were thrown on and cinched, bridles adjusted with jerking motions; the hands mounted and rode off quickly to tighten up the herd.

It took all of them forty minutes to gather in and contain the frightened longhorns, and they were able to do that only because it was the first day of roundup and the beef herd was not too big.

Even more exhausted now, the men walked their ponies back toward the camp area. Tiner and two hands rode over to where the cook knelt beside Bollinger, who lay dying in the August heat, his blood-soaked chest laboring for breath.

A minute later, Tiner straightened up, and the three men looked at him without a word.

"Have 'im buried," Tiner said evenly to the cook, who nodded once. Then the copper-brown skin tightened across Tiner's cheekbones and he jerked his head toward the horses. "Let's go," was all he muttered, but the two hands understood perfectly. Hitching up their gun belts, they strode quickly for their mounts.

Part 2

Jody Flanagan was honest. Hothead he was, truculent to a fault, one to take sudden and fiery offense; yet absolutely honest. Credit for that belonged to the mixed rearing he'd got from his parents, both dead now—his father, a wild-tempered Irish horsebreaker who died with a bullet in his back because no man dared attempt to put one in his front; his mother, a staff of fibrous strength around which she had formed an outward flesh of patient, Christian gentleness.

From this brew had been poured the integrity and volatile courage of Jody Flanagan.

Integrity made him thrust aside the constant temptation to build his herd from the unbranded strays of other men. While numerous of his contemporaries rode the spring-thawed range gathering in newborn calves—sometimes with their mothers; sometimes alone and bawling, their mothers lying shot and marble-eyed in the mud—Jody Flanagan had been socking away his forty dollars a month. He had avoided, also, that all too present temptation at pay time to ride hell-for-leather to the nearest town for the solace of liquor and women. Instead, he had lived the monastic life of the range and planned ahead.

Finally, the day had come when he had saved enough for his own herd—fifty head of stringy-muscled cows, and bulls with horns that thrust from their skulls like grappling hooks.

That was, almost to the day, Jody Flanagan's sixteenth birthday.

He had spent that spring and summer deep in the open range, nursing his herd along like a solicitous father, sleeping on the hard-baked sod at night, riding all day, shifting his herd around so they would have the best of grass, the best of water. With the help of two hired drifters, he had branded the cattle with his own brand, the *Lazy J-F*—a *J* lying wearily on its side with the arms of the *F* pointing earthward from its body.

Sleeping little, the waist of his pants getting slacker by the month, the color of his face deepening to a sun-scorched brown, his muscles becoming more and more like wire, Jody Flanagan had acquired reflexes like the nervous reactive jumping of a cat.

And then, after all that, some sidewinder had tried to take one of his hard-earned cows. It was the only man Jody Flanagan had ever killed, but he felt no regrets as he spurred back to his herd. As well as possible in the nearly obscuring darkness, he gathered in its drifting fringes.

That done, the longhorns bedded down for the night—some grazing, some snorting in a rhythmic sleep. Jody sat quietly on the pony, his black-barreled Henry repeater drawn from its quiver-shaped scabbard and lying across his saddle.

Grazing near him was his weary packhorse, still loaded in the event a sudden break became necessary. Far to his left, Jody could hear the rapid, stone-whipping current of a narrow stream and the occasional snort of a drinking steer. On the other side of that stream, Jody had noticed before the fall of night, was a great pile of rocks which, by their massing, had formed a sort of barricaded cave.

The exhaustion of an all-day drive was deep in him. He was just starting to nod a little when the thud of approaching hooves caused his head to jerk up alertly. Two, three riders, he figured. The Henry rifle was drawn up tensely in his hands. He'd been expecting riders.

He held in the buckskin's nervous shifting with his knees and a gentle patting on its cool neck. "Easy girl," he whispered, his eyes straining to the impossible feat of penetrating the heavy blackness around him.

The hoofbeats were closer now; no more than a hundred yards away. Separated too, he judged. The riders must have split in order to thin out his potential target. Jody swallowed quickly and drew in a shaky breath. It wasn't fear, he knew, so much as not knowing exactly what he was up against.

Then Jody saw the shadowy bulk of the horse and its rider loom out of the night about fifteen yards from him.

With a rapid hand movement, he jerked the trigger-guard lever down and up, loading and cocking the rifle.

The horseman reined up instantly, a figure frozen to its saddle.

"Get out of—" was all Jody had time to say before the night exploded with pistol blasts and he heard the whistle of slugs passing his head.

The pony jerked out of control under him and his returned fire missed widely. His left hand clutched down at the horn-looped reins, his spur wheels dug into the flanks of the spooking buckskin. The other man had fired twice more before Jody jerked his mount around, aimed quickly at the barrel flashes, and squeezed the trigger. The Henry jolted in his grip, its explosion drowning out everything.

Then, in the sudden silence, he heard the strangled coughing of the hit rider and the telltale, rustling slide and thud of his body on the hard, night-shrouded earth.

There was no respite. Almost in that same moment, the other horsemen charged toward him, converging as they came. Heart thudding, Jody levered another shell into the Henry's chamber but held fire so as not to offer even a momentary flash of target. He heard the frightened bellow of his herd and worried for a second about them stampeding.

Then suddenly it occurred to him that the approaching riders might be decoys, that there might be Circle Seven men all around him, closing in slowly, unseen. Cautiously, he backed his pony toward the rushing sound of the stream, a dry swallow clicking in his throat. Thirsty, he thought, his canteen empty and no chance to fill it now.

His attackers moved closer, the muffled hoof thuds of their mounts indefinable in location. Jody clutched the rifle. His sharp eyes moved restlessly, trying to pick the riders out in the night.

He started as a sudden curse broke the silence, drowned in the very second of its utterance by a double blast of gunfire. In the fiery splashes of muzzle blast, Jody saw two men firing point-blank into something. Then, in the abruptly renewed darkness, Jody heard the agonized death screech of a horse as it stumbled heavily for a few yards, then went crashing to the earth.

"It's his damn *packhorse!*" someone growled.

Jody felt rage well up in him. Throwing the Henry to his shoulder, he rent the night with explosions, levering and firing in a paroxysm of fury until his trigger pull brought only the metallic click of the hammer.

Only then did he realize that some of the deafening gunfire was not his own, because the darkness was still alive with powder flashes, still torn by the roaring of gun blasts and the whistling of slugs around his head and body.

He shoved the Henry into its scabbard and was just drawing his Colt when scudding clouds unveiled the moon, and the broad prairie was bathed with a sudden chalky illumination.

In the hesitant moment before firing began again, Jody saw three dark figures; one man writhing on the ground, a second still seated on his horse, and on the fringes of his vision, the motionless bulk of his packhorse.

Then the night exploded again and a slug drove into Jody's left arm, almost knocking him from the saddle. In one synchronized movement, he clutched at the horn and spur-scraped his pony into a startled run. Upright then, he pulled up the reins and jerked the buckskin around as two more slugs burned past his head, one of them whipping through the brim of his hat.

Hastily, while his wounded arm was still numb, Jody shifted the reins and jerked out his Colt. He snapped off a shot at the lone rider and saw the hat go flying from his head like a dark bird suddenly rising.

He was about to reverse direction again in a sudden desire to end the battle when he heard the drumming of hoofbeats. Casting a glance to the side, he saw four more horsemen approaching at a dead gallop.

Bullets whizzing past him, he spurred his pony into a gallop toward the suddenly remembered pile of rocks. He fired once more over his shoulder. Then his pony was lurching and sliding down the gravel-strewn incline of the stream, its hooves striking white sparks from the stones.

Pain started in his left arm and Jody holstered his pistol, shifting the reins again as the pony plunged into the moonlit current. More shots rang out, sending up crystal columns around him, sparking off stones.

The horse gained the other side of the stream where, with a bellow, one of Jody's steers lurched away into the shadow of the cottonwoods. Jody ignored it, throwing his right leg over the horn and dropping rapidly to the ground, taking the Henry with him.

Looking toward the opposite bank, he saw two of the five men ride into outline against the sky. Dropping the rifle, he jerked out his Colt and fired once. His mouth tightened in grim satisfaction as one of the men lurched in the saddle.

Jody tried to grab the saddlebags with his left hand and his teeth grated together, blocking the hiss of pain as red-hot pokers drove into the nerves around his wound.

Holstering his pistol, he dragged the saddlebags off the buckskin and swung them hard against its flank, sending it off with a startled whinny into the safety of the night.

Grabbing his rifle, Jody raced across the ground between him and the rock pile, bootheels crunching on the gravel, weaving his path a little to spoil the aim of the four men now on the opposite shore.

With a final lunge he dove into the shelter of the rocks, hearing the ping and whine of ricocheting bullets surrounding him.

There was abrupt silence then. Jody twisted around, again sliding the Colt from its holster; but the men were no longer silhouetted against the skyline.

He let his arm down and sat there on the damp ground, breathing raggedly, feeling waves of pain oscillate through his arm and into his shoulder. He licked his dry lips and glanced up at the moon. If only clouds would cover it, he might slip away—but the moon hung like a great white eye.

Fifteen yards away, Jody heard the tantalizing gurgle of fresh, running water. He closed his eyes and let his head sink forward until his forehead rested on the cool surface of the boulder. His arm hurt badly. He knew that the riders were going to take his herd and pin him down until he finally made a desperate run for it and was shot.

Yet none of these things seemed to matter so much as the sound of water in his ears.

A drink of water, he thought, just a little drink of water.

Part 3

On the morning of August 22, 1895, crossing that portion of the Texas Panhandle which belonged, by the practical legality of power, to the Circle Seven ranch, three riders were driving a herd of seventy-five longhorns ahead of them.

Earlier that morning, the three men had combined their separate drives—twenty-five head apiece—and now were guiding the dust-raising herd toward the holding point of the Circle Seven's beef roundup.

The three were hands of the region's smaller ranches—Bob Service of the Flying O, Mack Thursday of the W Bench, and John Goodwill of the Walking Diamond. The longhorns moving calmly and evenly, the three men rode together into the hot, blunt, llano wind.

"I don't give a damn about that," young Bob Service was saying, "it's still robbery in my log."

Mack Thursday shrugged. He was the oldest of the three, forty-two, in the decline of his cowpunching career; a heavyset man with iron-gray hair and quiet eyes who sat his roan like a man who knew the seating of a horse better than the seating of a chair.

"Sure, it's robbery," Mack Thursday admitted, "but that don't change a thing."

"Open range," John Goodwill said in a disgusted voice, "what a pile o' chips that is." He was young, twenty-six, resentful.

"Open range," said Thursday, "only means it's open till some outfit with faster guns closes it." He raised his bandanna and wiped at the sweat on his forehead.

"And how long do we swallow it?" asked Bob Service, his face tight with anger. "How long do we bring cows to them to pay our way across a range that belongs to all of us?"

"Well—" Thursday started.

"What kind of range is it when three outfits take orders from one?" Service cut in. "What kind of range is it when you have to pay a bribe so you can drive your herds north? What kind of men are we to *take* it?"

"Yeah," agreed a vengeful John Goodwill. "Why the hell should we give away cows to them?"

"Take it easy," Thursday pacified. "Neither of you was here when the range war was on two years ago. Neither of you saw the good men that was killed for this godforsaken piece of earth. Well, I saw it."

He paused a moment, his mouth turning down at the ends.

"I saw my own boy torn to pieces by a scattergun," he said. "He looked so awful bad I couldn't even take him to his own mother. He's buried out here on the range he fought for— died for." His voice was husky and bitter. "Well, it didn't do no good. A lot of men died, but Circle Seven still owns the range. And, as for me, I'd rather see twenty-five cows paid up spring and fall than see good men blown to pieces for nothin'."

The men rode in silence a while, Service and Goodwill still looking angry, Thursday, tired and resigned.

"Well, I *wouldn't* rather see it," Service finally said. "No disrespect to you, Thursday; I know how you must feel losin' your boy and all but—hell, if things go on like this, what's to keep Tiner and his crew from askin' thirty head next spring, fifty in the fall, maybe a hundred the next spring?"

"Nothin' I guess," said Thursday. "Though I wouldn't go blamin' the Circle Seven men for this setup. It ain't their doin'. They're just cowhands like you and me. It's Tiner holds it together."

"What about old man Ralston?" Goodwill asked, referring to the owner of the powerful Circle Seven.

Thursday wiped at sweat again with his finger and shook it away. "As you said, Goodwill, he's an old man. He ain't got the powers of his mind no more. Tiner feeds him locoweed talk, puffs him up like a boy with his first hoss and pistol. That's all Ralston is, actually, a little boy who likes to feel strong. It's Tiner runs the show."

"Then why don't someone call him?" Service said, slapping once at the wood stock of his holstered Colt.

A grim smile edged up the lips of Thursday. "Always open season on him. Anyone's welcome to try and call Rail Tiner. Matter of fact, least a dozen men already have." The smile faded. "They're all buried," he said flatly, "and Tiner's still ridin'." He glanced at Service. "You figure on callin' him?" he asked. "I don't."

Bob Service was not the kind to spout loose talk. So, directly challenged, he shut up and rode in silence, thinking about what Thursday had said.

Thursday went on, "No, I believe my boss has the right idea. He herds a thousand, maybe fifteen hundred cows a year. He'd rather give up twenty-five of them than risk losin' everything."

"Ain't no gettin' ahead that way," grumbled Goodwill. "A man just holds hisself back thinkin' like that."

"Like I say," Thursday answered quietly, "you're welcome to try and end it."

"No lone-hand job'll end this setup," Service allowed himself to comment. "It'll take all of us."

"That's for sure," Thursday agreed somberly, "but all of us don't feel the same about it. Well," he said, shrugging wearily, "maybe somethin'll prod us to it. Let's hope for that."

"Hope ain't gonna end the setup either," Service growled as he nudged his pony into a trot toward the east fringe of the herd where several steers were drifting out toward a thick patch of grama grass.

Sensing that talk was ended, Goodwill moved away, too, and for the rest of the way, the three men remained apart, riding with their thoughts and sweating under the hot sun.

By eleven o'clock they were moving the herd along the low ridge which overlooked Double Fork River, only a narrow stream now after a virtually rainless summer. In the distance they could see the Circle Seven's beef herd and camp, minus the chuck wagon, which had been driven out onto the range to feed the hands.

They were almost to the holding spot when a single rider started out toward them. Service, riding lead, spurred forward to meet him. As the man drew closer, Service was surprised to see that it was Tiner. The foreman was usually on the range during the roundup.

Tiner reined up in front of him and, without any greeting, gestured toward the prairie with his left arm. "Get away from the riverbank," he ordered. "Edge 'em out and circle 'em into the rock corral."

"Why?" Service asked.

"You heard me!" Tiner snapped irritably, then turned away and galloped back toward his camp.

Thursday rode up to ask, "What's wrong?"

Service told him in a disgruntled voice. Thursday, after a mild shrug, rode back to the herd point with Service where they arranged themselves on both sides and, swerving slowly, guided the longhorns away from the riverbank.

"Who the hell's he think he *is*, bossin' us around?" Service asked above the sounds of the herd.

"Tiner," was Thursday's reply.

They were almost to the rock corral when a single rifle shot sounded near the river. The three men each threw a quick glance in that direction but were forced to concentrate on the startled cattle.

With the aid of one of the Circle Seven hands, they delivered the seventy-five longhorns to the natural rock corral where they would be culled for beef stock, the remainder set loose on the range, re-branded. When the herd was installed, John Goodwill rode over to Thursday and Service, looking excited.

"Ya know what that shot was?" he asked them.

"What?" Service asked.

"They got some young kid down there, no more'n sixteen, trapped in the rocks." He gestured toward the rock corral. "Them's his cows. Tiner took 'em."

For the first time that day, Thursday looked something more than taciturn. "*Took* 'em?"

Goodwill nodded. "That's what the fella told me."

"Why?" Thursday asked quickly, despite his practiced caution.

"Dunno," Goodwill answered, shaking his head. "I only talked to him half a minute. All I know is Tiner took the kid's cows after some shootin' and now the kid's holed up down in a bunch o' rocks."

A disturbed expression settled across Thursday's face. Even though he had struggled long to maintain a detached view of Circle Seven dominance, this new situation was too strong to ignore and reaction showed in the tenseness of his jaw, the fleeting pain in his eyes. Worried anger held him, anger he could not help experiencing even though he didn't want to.

But then it was submerged, pushed down by an anger of resolve equal to it, controlled before Service said in a low, thoughtful inciting voice:

"Maybe we're next."

Thursday glanced at him without a word, seeing on the young man's face the very tension he had repressed; and, sensing the ire which fanned across them, seeking to express itself in action, he cut it off—willfully, with jerked-in knees that stirred his mount away from them.

"Come on," he said bluntly, "let's get the receipts signed."

The circle of resentment snapped. Goodwill and Service rode after him, not speaking, in their eyes the look of men who were defeated not by battle but by the failure to enter battle.

As he rode toward the Circle Seven camp, Thursday's glance swept along the riverbank, settling, for a moment, on the man stretched out behind two rocks, a rifle poked into the opening between them. There was a bandage on the man's left arm that caught the sun's rays whitely. A boy in the rocks, he thought, and his eyes moved on hastily across the camp to the milling beef herd, to the mounted cowhand watching over them, his right arm in a bandanna sling.

The lines around Thursday's eyes deepened with worry, then grew still harsher as his glance settled on the two man-length mounds of freshly dug earth near the camp. Something restless plucked at his insides like a hand prodding him to something he had no desire to do. A word moved emptily inside him: coward. It made him sick and furious. He didn't believe it, but he couldn't avoid it.

Then, in the camp, he saw Tiner mount again and he veiled anger with attention to the tall man's approach.

"Paper, Thursday," Tiner said when he'd drawn up in front of the older man.

Thursday reached automatically for the pocket of his shirt as Goodwill and Service edged up beside him. Tiner jerked a stub of pencil from his vest pocket and scribbled initials on the receipt.

"Next," he said, and Goodwill handed across his slip of paper. "Pretty rotten lot of cows," Tiner added, initialing the second receipt.

Just in time, Thursday saw that Service was about to flare up and cut him off hastily.

"Who's the boy, Tiner?"

"Circle Seven business," Tiner answered, looking up irritably into the flinty eyes of Bob Service. "Come on, come on," he snapped, "I ain't got all day."

Flat insult hung in Service's voice. "If they're rotten cows," he said, "maybe you'd like us to take 'em back."

When the skin grew taut across Rail Tiner's face, it was as if someone were turning screws under the edges of it, tightening it quickly but evenly. It did something to his eyes; made them appear to start as if he were, for the first time, seeing the person that, till then, he had paid no attention to. "Your paper, cowboy," he said, lips hardly stirring, his left hand extended.

"Get it signed, man," Thursday said in abrupt urgency.

With a twisting of his mouth, Service jerked the receipt from his shirt pocket and held it out.

Tiner took it from him, his pale green eyes fixed to Service's face. "Thanks, cowboy," he said flatly. Without looking down once, he scrawled his initials largely across the receipt and handed it back, the smile he held from his lips showing in his eyes. It was a mocking smile.

"Who's the boy, Tiner?" Thursday asked again, anxious to get the foreman's attention off Service.

A moment longer, Tiner's static gaze clung to Service's face as if he were memorizing it. Then his eyes moved a little and settled on Thursday's broad, noncommittal face.

If either Service or Goodwill had asked the second time about something which Tiner had already announced as Circle Seven business, words would have ended in sudden movement, either fatal or near-fatal. But Thursday was one of the old ones. He and Tiner had known each other for ten years, they had fought each other in a bloody range war. Even opposed as they still were, there was something more between them than enmity. Grudge there was still, even hatred maybe, but, as enemies who had measured the values of each other in a time of violence, they respected more, allowed more.

"Some drifter," Tiner answered. "Wouldn't pay his way across the range. Killed a pair of my boys last night, shot up another pair. He even"—not without some grim amusement, he reached up an exploring finger—"put a hole in my new hat."

"Why'd you take his cows?" Thursday asked.

Tiner slid the short pencil into his vest pocket. "He ain't gonna need 'em where he's goin'," he said, one end of his mouth twitching slightly in what might have been the beginning of a smile.

"You're gonna *kill* him?" Thursday asked, wondering, almost nervously, what it was that made the blood pulse so heavily in his wrist and temple veins.

"Me or the heat," said Tiner, and from the tone of his voice, he might have been discussing dinner plans.

"Why? Because he wouldn't pay your damn price?" Service burst out, infuriated.

Studiedly, Tiner kept his eyes on Thursday's tense features. "Take your friends out of here," he said with that voice which grew less aroused the angrier he became. "Our deal is finished. Clear out."

"You think you can—" Service started, then was drowned out by Thursday's.

"That's enough! Let's go."

Both Goodwill and Service stared wordlessly at Thursday, despite their rising tempers, according him the respect due his unwritten rank as senior cowhand of the trio.

"See you in the spring," Tiner said casually, turning his horse and starting back for camp.

Thursday pulled his mount around. "Come on," he said, the anger in his voice more for himself than Service and Goodwill.

The three of them rode away at a slow trot, faces set in grim lines, eyes staring ahead bleakly into the endless oven blast of llano wind which buffeted their cheeks like scorching bird wings.

After a mile of tense silence, Thursday drew in a harsh breath. "All right, spit it out," he snapped. "Spit it out, damn it."

Service licked his upper lip slowly. "I was just thinkin' how hot it is. A man gets mighty thirsty in a sun like this."

Thursday pressed his lips together tightly, throat drawing in with a dry swallow. It wasn't the approach he'd expected or wanted. To be reminded of the boy, that he couldn't take. His Tom had been sixteen, too. A full-front scattergun blast had seen to it that Tom never saw seventeen.

Hastily, Thursday tried to lead Service to words he could

combat. "And what did you think you were gonna do?" he asked in a clipped, angry voice. "Draw on Tiner?" He didn't wait for the answer. "You'd be dead now."

"Better dead than stepped on!" Service flared, giving Thursday the opening he wanted.

"*Think* a second, why don't you?" Thursday said sternly. "Is that the way you really feel? You'd rather be dead than alive? Dead with nothin' proved but your own bad judgment? Use your head, Service! You're no gunslinger. Ya didn't have a chance, not a damn chance, and you know it. I said it before, and I'll say it again: *There's no point to dyin' for nothin'!* I seen too many men go that way. I don't support it."

"And what *do* you support?" Service asked. "Knucklin' under? Lettin' yourself get shoved around like an animal? Lettin' a sixteen-year-old kid die when he ain't done a thing but fight for what was his?

"That kid might have a slug in him, Thursday, he might be bleedin' to death. Sure as hell he's dyin' of thirst. And here we go ridin' away like there was nothin' happenin'. Here we go ridin' away, talkin' like a pair of old ladies while that boy dies in them rocks!" Impulsively, Service jerked in his reins and glared at Thursday. "I'm goin' back. I'm gonna get that kid or a slug, either one. But I'm goin'."

"Man, use your—"

"No!" Service cut him off. "Talkin' don't mean nothin'. Words don't weigh enough to move the scales!"

"Man, if there's a thing to do," Thursday said quickly, not wanting to but unable to stop, "there's a right way and a wrong way. Gettin' killed for nothin' ain't the right way."

"It ain't for nothin'," Service said. "It's more than *nothin'* in them rocks." His head snapped to the side, his eyes lanced into Goodwill's. "What about it?" he asked.

Goodwill's mouth tightened. "I'm with it," he said huskily.

"Men, for God's sake!" Thursday burst out. "D'ya want to start another range war?"

"Come on," Service said through clenched teeth, pulling his mount around.

Thursday was silent. He sat motionless on his fidgeting horse, watching the two men gallop off. That core of tension in his stomach was expanding now. He felt as if he were turning to stone. He kept on saying it in his mind: They're wrong—they're wrong.

If only he could believe it.

Part 4

Rail Tiner was checking over the seventy-five cattle when an air-bursting flurry of shots exploded from the river.

Jerking his head around, his startled gaze jumped down to where Jake Kettlebar was firing rapidly at something across the drought-thinned river.

With a muffled curse, Tiner jabbed in spurs, and his horse began shouldering its way through the shifting herd. Tiner looked angrily toward his beef herd. The cows hadn't had an hour's peace since that damned kid had shown up.

Reaching the end of the corral, Tiner jumped to the ground and took down the bar. Pulling his horse through the opening, he propped up the bar again. He mounted rapidly, started for the riverbank where the exchange of shots still raged. *I thought he'd be dead by now,* Tiner thought irritably. He'd have gone down to get the kid long before, except that the kid was too good with a gun. Two men buried, two wounded; that was enough loss to take for fifty scrawny cows and a worthless life.

When Tiner reached the bank, Jake Kettlebar was looked up toward him. "Well?" he said loudly to the hesitant cowhand.

"You want me to—"

"I said go get those pistols!" Tiner ordered the lopsided Kettlebar.

With a swallow, Kettlebar struggled down the incline like a man with a wooden leg, his eyes wide and anticipating on the silent mouth of the cave.

"Never mind lookin' in the rocks," Tiner called down.

A trembling breath emptied from Kettlebar. He hobbled quickly to the first pistol and picked it up.

"All right, get up here," Tiner commanded the two men.

They trudged up the bank. "So you wouldn't listen to Thursday," Tiner said disgustedly. "Had to be brave little boys."

"Ya ain't gonna get away with this!" Service snapped.

"Shut up," Tiner said, turning and seeing that Kettlebar was scrambling up the bank and glancing over his shoulder as if he expected, at any second, to get a bullet in the back of his head.

"Take those two over to the camp," Tiner told the limping Kettlebar when he was over the ridge, the two pistols under his waistband. "Put 'em in a lariat circle, and if they try to leave it, kill 'em. Understand?"

Kettlebar nodded.

Tiner turned toward the two men. "All right," he said, "march. Unless you'd rather be dead heroes."

He stood there motionless awhile watching the three men walk slowly toward the camp, Service and Goodwill in the lead, Kettlebar limping behind, his rifle pointed at them.

"Heroes," Tiner muttered.

Then his lips pressed together and, turning, he looked across the stream to the pile of rocks where the boy was. He slid the Colt into its holster and leaned his empty rifle against one of the boulders near him.

Then he started down the incline slowly, heading straight for the cave. He'd had enough.

Part 5

When the blast of shots first began, Jody's head faltered up sluggishly from the boulder and his heavy-lidded eyes fluttered open.

At first he was unable to focus on anything; the landscape blurred before him as if it were a layer of stony earth lying on the shifting surface of a lake. Heart pounding, Jody strained desperately to see. They were coming to get him; he knew it. He had to see so he could stop them.

The numb fingers of his left hand touched the rifle stock and tried to grip it. A frightened moan quavered in Jody's throat as the fingers failed to close. He reached across his body with his right hand and it threw him off balance; his left shoulder thudded against the hard ground.

A strangled gasp shook him. Agony was like the jab of a branding iron in his flesh, driving the dullness from his brain. He shoved up again, blinking away waves of dizziness, and looked across the boulder with wide, staring eyes.

Outside, the firing, after a momentary pause, had begun again, filling the sun-baked air with the whistle of slugs. After a moment of strained effort, Jody could see a flash of rifle fire between the two boulders where the Circle Seven man was.

Yet there were no bullets landing near the cave; Jody couldn't understand it. A dry rasping sounded in his throat as he swallowed. Who was the man firing at? Jody sat slumped against the boulder, staring dully across the way at the boulders with the blazing rifle poked between them.

Then a horseman galloped up on the other bank and, dropping down with his rifle, made a crouching run to the man behind the boulders. Jody shrank back unconsciously. It was the foreman of the Circle Seven.

A wave of pain from the wounded arm rushed across his brain, blacking him out for a moment. The landscape spun. Jody fell helplessly on his right side, gasping, struggling to remain conscious. The makeshift bandage around the arm had done little good. The wound plus his terrible thirst told Jody that he couldn't keep going much longer.

The shooting stopped. Jody lay panting in the silence, hearing again the torturing sound of the stream that was no more than ten strides away, the rushing current of cool, clear, fresh—

Someone yelled, "Get the hell out o' there!"

Then there was firing again; one shot, two, spaced apart by seconds. As quickly as possible, Jody pushed himself to a crouch and, blinking away the waves of darkness that rushed across him, he saw the foreman standing and firing a rifle— but still not at the cave.

Silence again; the foreman ordering, "Drop it!" to someone Jody couldn't see.

Then another jolt of pain in his arm. His head ached, felt as if it were expanding hotly, then contracting and clamping in his brain. Sight fled. A ragged sob broke in Jody's throat and he fought it off. Hand clutching at his wounded arm, he slumped forward against the boulder while, outside, the foreman ordered someone to cross the stream. Jody's eyes clouded.

He thought hours had passed when someone said, "Shut up," very loudly, and he struggled up again. He started, a bolt of breathless panic hitting him as he saw a strange man heading for the rocks.

Hand like lead, Jody reached into his holster and slid out the heavy Colt. He raised it unsteadily and tried to aim, but his target seemed to break apart and was obscured by fluttering curtains of darkness. Jody blinked hard, swallowed. The tense-faced man was closer now, approaching the cave with rifle extended in readiness.

Jody pulled the trigger, and the pistol jumped in his grip, the recoil knocking him on his back. Not a moment too soon, for in the next instant, the cave was a frenzy of ringing bullets. Jody heard them whining off rock and thudding into the earth around him. A streak of hot lead burned away skin on his right temple and made him twitch violently. Another slug scraped away boot leather.

Then the echoes of the rifle bursts had faded away across the prairie and the only sound was that of the stream and the distant bellow of startled cattle.

Until the man near the stream said, "You want me to—" and the foreman interrupted loudly: "I said go get those pistols!"

Jody pushed up again dizzily and squinted out at the sun-blazing area. He'd knocked off the man's bootheel, he saw. The man had trouble standing.

Nervously, Jody reached down for his pistol again, but then the foreman told the man to never mind about the rocks and Jody relaxed for a moment. He looked up at the two men being covered by the foreman's pistol. They were moving up the incline on the other side of the stream. One of them said something to the foreman, and the foreman told him to shut up.

Jody sat there breathing fitfully and watching the three men stand on the ridge waiting for the fourth to get back. He picked up his pistol and raised it shakily. A perfect target. If only he could see clearly. But no matter how he squinted or strained his eyes, the view was blurred and without substance. I have to try, he thought, dazed. He didn't know who the men were, but they were against the Circle Seven foreman. That was enough. He aimed as carefully as he could.

The hammer clicked loudly on an empty chamber.

Jody shuddered with alarm and thumbed back the hammer again, pulled the trigger. Another click.

Automatically, he tried to raise his left hand to break open the chamber, but it wouldn't come. Hot pain flooded his arm and shoulder, and the pistol barrel fell. It's empty, he thought—and there's no more.

When he could see again, he put down the pistol and broke open the chamber with his right hand. Empty. He reached for his Henry quickly, eyes searching up toward the ridge.

The foreman stood there alone, looking the other way. Jody felt his heartbeat grow heavy again, the increased flow of blood making his head pound.

The Henry was empty, too. Jody's mouth fell open and he jerked up his eyes again.

The foreman was starting down the bank toward him, his pistol holstered but with a look of expressionless menace on his face.

With a gasp, Jody threw himself on the saddlebags, ignoring the jolt of pain and tore them open. He felt himself go limp with terror.

There was no more ammunition. Without realizing it, he'd fired it all.

His nostrils flared a moment, his teeth jammed together with a click. Jody Flanagan scuttled back into the shadows until his back was pressed against rock. The trembling fingers of his right hand dug into a pocket of his wool pants and closed over his jackknife. He didn't know what he meant to do with it, but he had to have something to fight with.

He opened the long blade with his teeth.

Breath shook his chest as he kept himself erect against the boulder despite pain and thirst and the welling threat of unconsciousness. The irregular opening to the cave seemed to waver before him. It fled away, then leapt back like a swallowing mouth. Jody wiped away sweat with the back of his right hand. The movement of his chest grew more agitated and his fingers became so tight on the knife that the blood was pressed from them.

The figure of the foreman appeared at the mouth of the cave.

Jody saw him crouch down, pistol in hand. Jody tried to hold his breath, tried to figure out what to do. Lunge toward the man? He'd be shot before he'd gone a step—even if he *could* lunge. Wait for the man to enter the cave? He knew the foreman wouldn't, and his throat drew taut.

Half-conscious rage blazed through him, and he braced himself against the wall for a fast start. At least he wouldn't die cringed against a wall like a frightened woman.

Outside, the foreman raised his pistol. ''I'm countin' to three,'' he said.

Part 6

After the two men had dwindled to specks in the distance, a grim-faced Mack Thursday eased his mount around and headed for his ranch.

He rode slowly, gazing straight ahead, his features molded to an expression of forced indifference. All right, if they wanted to kill themselves, that was their business. They didn't know, they just didn't *know*; not what a range war was like. Before they'd even come to the area, buffalo grass had overgrown the dozens of bleak, revealing mounds across the prairie—one of them belonging to the torn remnants of what had been his son.

Thursday's hands tightened on the reins. He wasn't going back and that was all there was to it. He wouldn't think about it anymore.

And why should they save this kid? he thought after a few moments. The kid had killed Circle Seven men. Tiner had a right to want his scalp. An eye for an eye. Through Thursday's mind filtered memories of the Bible stories his mother used to read when he was a boy. Daniel in the lion's den. Joseph and his brethren.

Jacob wrestling with an angel.

The angel represented doubt, his mother had told him. Thursday tried to push away the thought. It was something he didn't want to remember.

Tiner had a right to trap the boy. But the boy was only fighting for what was his. Men called this a free range; they expected it to be that way. A man had a right to refuse to pay crossing money. Tiner had no right to—

Tiner had a right—Tiner had no right. Was there a thing in life that wasn't mixed-up and twisted? What did a man decide? What was right and what was wrong?

If only it hadn't been a boy, a sixteen-year-old boy. Every time he thought of that boy, he saw his own son in those rocks, helpless. Tiner closing in.

Thursday pressed his lips into a bloodless line as though the effort would force back indecision. It wasn't his son; his son was dead and buried. He wasn't going to have a bloody range war on his conscience.

His chest rose and fell with heavy erratic breaths and the core of tension in him kept growing worse—like a watch spring being wound and wound.

Until the shots rang out in the distance and made him pull his mount around.

For a last uncertain moment, he held back the restless horse. Then with a jerk of his knees, he nudged it into a canter, then a gallop back toward the Circle Seven camp. He didn't know if he was doing wrong or right; he only knew he could not do otherwise. The loosening of tension in him told him so.

Decision made, his thoughts flew ahead to where the shots were being fired. What was happening? It sounded as if those two young fools had ridden straight into it without a plan in their hot heads. Thursday's lips twitched in a momentary grimace. I should have gone with them, he thought. There might have been a way.

Well, it was too late for that now. He spurred the horse into a faster gallop yet. Its hooves thundered across the hard-baked earth, and the wind was like an oven blast in Thursday's face. Far off, the shooting stopped, then started again.

Before he rode near enough to the rocks to be heard, Thursday reined his mount to the left and felt its jolting, sliding descent down the graveled incline beneath. The horse splashed across the river in a stride, over the cracked mud, and lunged up the opposite bank. There was a fringe of cottonwoods along that side, and the sound-carrying wind would be in his favor, too. He guided his mount along the ridge, eyes straining beneath the shadowing brim of his hat.

Far up the stream, he saw the small figures of two men walking across the water toward another man who had his rifle leveled at them. Thursday figured that the man with the rifle was probably Tiner. A fourth man was going past them, headed in the opposite direction.

Another shot rang out, this time from the rocks, and the Circle Seven man went down. The next second Tiner emptied his rifle into the rocks. Thursday wondered how well the boy was protected. He saw the man who had fallen down get up.

Then he saw Service's and Goodwill's horses grazing and, fearing that the hoofbeats of his mount might be heard despite the veiling of wind, he slowed the horse to a walk, then, after another sixty yards, dismounted and grounded the reins.

As he half ran, half walked across the hard ground, he could feel waves of heat billowing around him. He reached the end of the ridge and paused there a moment under the shade of a cottonwood, slipping a cartridge into the empty chamber of his Colt. Across the way only Tiner was left now, watching the three men move toward the Circle Seven camp.

Then Tiner turned around and started down the bank, headed for the rocks. Thursday's heartbeat jolted, and he skidded down the incline, losing balance and pushing himself up with his left hand on the burning hot stones. Shaking his hand, he hurried across the dusty dried mud and down along the stream edge so the sound of the current would cover his bootfalls.

Just as Tiner reached the mouth of what looked to Thursday like a natural cave, Thursday drew his pistol and stopped. He saw the foreman crouch before the cave, pistol in hand. Then Tiner stood up, raising his pistol.

"Tiner!"

The foreman's head snapped around, and his startled gaze

jumped over to where the older man stood pointing a pistol at him. Then the surprised look was gone from Tiner's face and it was a death mask again. "You want your friends," he said, "they're in my camp."

Thursday shook his head.

"I said they're in my camp."

"I didn't come for them," Thursday told him.

"What then?"

"You know. Put down your pistol."

Only the tightening of skin across Tiner's cheeks indicated his rising temper. "You better go, Thursday."

"Tiner, I want that boy."

"You're not gettin' him," the foreman answered slowly.

Silence a moment, the two of them looking at each other cautiously.

Then Thursday spoke in a tired, regretful voice. "Then I guess that leaves us only one way."

The two shots came so close together that the three men in the camp thought it was one gun firing.

Bob Service's face twitched involuntarily as he stood there rigidly, ignoring the trickle of blood on his right arm, looking blankly toward the river.

Then, after a moment, breath emptied slowly from him. "There it is," he said, almost inaudibly.

John Goodwill, squatting beside him in the lariat circle, looked up, face still contorted from the pain of his wounded wrist. "We tried," he said without conviction.

"Sure," Service agreed bitterly, "we—"

Another shot exploded down by the river.

Service raged, "What the hell's he *doin'*? Cuttin' him to *pieces*?"

"Shut up," said Kettlebar, but there was no authority in his voice.

Suddenly very tired, Service hunkered down beside Goodwill. "One more notch for the Circle Seven," Service muttered in a tense, hating voice. Goodwill said nothing. Service went on, "While good old Mack Thursday rides away and saves the range."

"I said shut up," Kettlebar said.

Service ignored him.

Goodwill asked, "What d'ya think Tiner's gonna do with us?"

"I dunno," Service said in a lifeless voice. "I don't care." He felt like breaking something, fighting with his fists, anything to release the frustrated rage knifing through him.

"I guess he won't do nothin'," Goodwill said. "I guess he would've plugged us before if—" His voice broke off abruptly as he saw Service looking toward the river with an expression of amazement on his face. He turned his head suddenly and gasped.

"*God*," he heard Kettlebar say in an incredulous voice.

Hobbling across the plain were two figures, one of them Mack Thursday. He limped heavily, a tense look of repressed pain on his face, his left arm around the waist of a young man.

Without a word, Bob Service bolted out of the lariat circle toward them.

"Hey, you—" Kettlebar shouted, then didn't finish. The rifle he raised to fire, he now lowered after an indecisive moment.

"Thursday!" Service greeted the older man as he ran up to him.

"Help the boy," Thursday gasped. "I'm all right."

Service put his arm around Jody Flanagan's waist. Relieved of the load, Mack Thursday limped on, his face set willfully as he fought down the pain of the slug in him. As Thursday limped into the camp, Kettlebar put down his rifle with a cautious movement.

"Go get your foreman," Thursday said.

"My—" Kettlebar stared at the older man as if he couldn't believe what he'd heard.

"Go on, go on," Thursday said irritably. Kettlebar turned without another word. "Goodwill, help him," Thursday said.

Still looking amazed, Goodwill started toward the river after the Circle Seven hand.

"Man, what *happened*?" Service asked excitedly after he'd put the boy down.

"Give him some water," Thursday told him as he slumped

down on the ground with a wince. Service got Kettlebar's canteen and handed it to the boy who, although he'd had water from the stream, was still thirsty.

"Here, let me do that," Service said, moving quickly to where Thursday was trying to wrap his bandanna around the bleeding wound in his upper right leg.

"Tiner's dead?" Service asked, bandaging.

"I don't think so," the older man replied. "He can't last long though."

Service nodded grimly. Then, aware of how he'd spoken to Thursday that day, he looked down at the ground awkwardly.

"Thursday, I . . ." Service began, and the older man opened his eyes.

"What?" he said, glancing toward the boy. Before Service could go on, Thursday asked the boy, "Feeling better?"

The boy nodded. "Yes, sir. Thanks a lot."

Thursday looked back to Service. "What is it?" he asked.

"I . . . I'm apologizin' for what I said to you before," Service told him.

Thursday shook it off. "Forget it." He closed his eyes. Then, thinking of something, he opened his eyes again. "Just remember one thing," he said, "there's more than one reason for not fightin'."

Part 7

They were all gone except for Thursday and Tiner. Service and Goodwill were taking the boy back to Thursday's ranch and, at the boy's insistence, the fifty cattle, too. Kettlebar had gone out to relieve the man on herd watch.

Tiner lay unconscious in the shade of an erected tarpaulin, his chest rising and falling in shallow, jerking movements. The dark red blotch on his chest bandage grew wider and wider.

Thursday sat near him, drinking a cup of water. He'd been thinking. All the time he'd ridden back, faced Tiner, fired on him, wounded him, gone to the boy, given him water, helped him over to the camp—all that time, he hadn't known why he was doing these things . . . not really, deeply.

Now he did. And he knew it wasn't because of his son. As a matter of fact, it was because of his son that he almost *hadn't* done it.

No, he'd done it because he'd realized, if not consciously, that a man had to settle each issue as it came up; he couldn't avoid the little battles without having to fight a bigger one later on when all the small, unsettled battles added themselves up. A man had to settle each conflict when it happened and at no other time; that was the way it had to go. Progress came in little steps.

While he was thinking that, he noticed that Tiner's eyes had opened.

"Drink?" he asked, and Tiner nodded once, weakly.

Thursday bent over him, but half the water ran from the edges of the foreman's mouth. Thursday patted away the heavy sweat on Tiner's immobile face.

"Th-thanks," Tiner muttered, a slow, rasping breath in his throat as he looked up at the older man.

There was no talk of the shooting; that was done with, accepted. Instead, Tiner said, "You'll be makin' some ... changes now." There was no angry regret or animosity in his voice. He spoke a simple fact.

"There'll be changes," Thursday said quietly. "I'm stayin' on here to see the start of it. To see your boys don't start up another war."

Tiner nodded. "Yeah," he gasped, "another war ... wouldn't be ... good." His head rolled to the side and he stared up at the bright, blue sky. He knew, as Thursday did, that when he was gone, the Circle Seven would lose its dominance. Ralston would capitulate, the range would open again.

Breath emptied from Tiner's lungs slowly until it seemed as if he were completely drained of it. "Well," he mumbled, swallowing, "I ... did my job." He drew in a whistling breath. "Can't ... nobody say ... different."

"You did your job," Thursday agreed.

Later, he pulled down the tarpaulin and drew it across the still face of Rail Tiner. As he did, he noticed how the foreman's hair ruffled slowly in the endless wind of the prairie.

Then, with a tired sigh, he sat down again and waited quietly for the men to come in from their day's work.

LITTLE PHIL AND THE
DAUGHTER OF JOY

John Lee Gray

"Whoa, that's new," Rolf Greencastle said. He couldn't help
sounding alarmed.

"Yes, it is," Jimmy said. She slid an old cloth along the
short squat barrel of the .44-caliber Deringer she'd taken from
the drawer of her writing desk. It was an old piece. Rolf always
thought of it as the Gold Rush gun because his talkative uncle
Wallace, one of the failed argonauts, had often mentioned the
large number of .44 Deringers carried by men in the diggings.
It was an outmoded weapon, but a murderous one.

Spring sunshine through the lace curtains ignited a little
white fire at one spot on the metal. Jimmy rubbed and rubbed
at the barrel, though it was spotless. Sunshine falling on her
flexing wrist illuminated the white scars there. Rolf was silent
and a little bug-eyed over the unexpected sight of the piece.

He considered the awkwardness of another remark. Her
three-word reply had shut the door on easy continuation of the
conversation. After several moments of combing his fingers
through his shoulder-length hair, he decided that this was serious enough for him to bull right ahead:

"What is it?"

Jimmy gazed at him with those wide eyes that reminded
him of a beautiful gray he'd ridden as a boy in Ohio. Jimmy's
eyes were her beautiful feature; she was otherwise a plain

young woman, with wrinkles already laid into her face by the ferocious Kansas weather and no doubt by her trade, which required her to deal with all sorts of rough types, from customers to her pimp (she had none at the moment). He had known her a little more than a year, both socially and in the biblical sense, and in that time he'd learned that she had a history of violent behavior, sometimes directed against herself.

"Why, it's a genuine Henry Deringer. I bought it in Dodge last Saturday."

"I mean what's it for, Jimmy? Is somebody bothering you or making threats?"

"Why no, I'm going to use it when General Phil Sheridan arrives next month to inspect the fort. I'm going to kill him with it."

Rolf Greencastle almost fell off his chair in the process of removing his bare feet from the edge of her table. He crashed them down on top of his fancy boots with the pointed toes and mule ears; Rolf was of the opinion that a cavalry scout had to project a special aura—one so strong and awe-inspiring that the officers who signed his pay authorization would think he knew exactly what he was doing even when he didn't.

"I beg your pardon?"

"You heard me," Jimmy said. She kept her eyes on him. It was a disconcerting habit. She kept them open even when she was bare naked on her back, taking care of him.

"That's a pretty damn strange thing to admit to me or anybody, Jemima Taylor."

"I wish you wouldn't use that name. My daddy gave it to me and it's the only thing he ever did that I hate."

"Let's get back to the subject of Little Phil Sheridan. I believe you said you figure on killing him."

"I do." Jimmy saw he wanted further explanation. She shrugged. "Once a Virginian, always a Virginian."

"What does that mean?"

"That foul-talking Yankee rooster and his murdering hordes of mounted shopkeepers and factory hands just completely tore up my daddy's farm in Shenandoah County in September of eighteen and sixty-four."

"You never told me that."

"Hadn't any occasion," she answered with another shrug. She polished some more.

"Jimmy, come on. What's the rest?"

"Simple enough. The day after Sheridan's brutes drove General Jubal Early off Fisher's Hill and sent him scooting down around Masanutten Mountain to hide and lick his wounds, the Yankees came south along the Valley Turnpike, where my daddy's farm was situated. They were chasing stragglers but they ripped up everything belonging to the local people. They trampled our vegetables and torched our fruit trees . . ." She closed her eyes briefly. Her voice grew much quieter. "Just terrible." A moment passed. "Next thing, Phil Sheridan himself showed up, with a lot of his officers. My daddy was mad and het up and he took a shot at Sheridan. Sheridan's men wrestled him down and carried him off and beat him. Then they sent him to prison in Detroit, Michigan. As if he was an enemy soldier. He was sixty-two years old! It ruined his health and gave him the glooms. Same ones that devil me sometimes. But his never left, and they ground him away to nothing. He died two years after they let him out."

"You saw your pa fire off a round at Phil Sheridan?"

Her eyes drifted to the windblown lace. A bugle pealed somewhere on the prairie. Out past the fence that neatly circumscribed her little house, called the Overton Place after a former owner, a troop of shiny-brown Negro cavalrymen cantered by.

"No, I never laid eyes on the little fiend. I was in the smokehouse with some of his men who ripped my dress and—took liberties."

Rolf Greencastle whistled. All of a sudden he was chilly in the spring air. He'd had a perfectly fine time with Jimmy, as per usual when he paid his weekly visit, but this new twist was disturbing; terrifying. Rolf reached for his fringed deerhide shirt. He pulled it on and smoothed it, then reached beneath to free the necklace of big bear claws he never removed. Rolf was a tall, skinny young man with eight knife and bullet scars at various points on his body.

"You absolutely sure it was Little Phil?"

"Yes, it was him. People described him later. Black horse . . ."

that funny flat black hat he always wore. It was him, and I'm going to kill him.''

"Jimmy, I don't think I'm making myself too clear. Don't you see that what you said is pretty—well—unusual? You don't just go tell somebody that you're going to do a murder.''

She didn't say a word; apparently she didn't agree.

"Why did you do that, Jimmy?''

She was tight-lipped and silent a while. Then it kind of erupted in a burst. "Because you're my friend. You're not just a customer. After I kill General Sheridan they're going to lock me up—hang me, probably. I'm going to need a friend to straighten things out. Sell this house and send the money to my sisters in Front Royal.''

"Well, I appreciate your confidence,'' Rolf admitted, touched by her unexpected words. "What I'd rather do, though, is talk you out of it.''

"You can't. Sheridan's villains raped and pillaged the whole Shenandoah, and they wrecked my daddy's health by throwing him in that Yankee prison, and a Virginian never forgets.''

"I think I ought to remind you that the war's been over for three years now.''

"Not mine, Mr. Greencastle. Mine isn't over by a damn sight. One more battle to go.''

And she snapped the cloth so that it popped. Then she wrapped it around the .44-caliber Deringer. He tried to undermine her determination with scorn:

"If you're going to kill Sheridan, you bought the wrong gun. That little toy only gives you one shot.''

She slid out the drawer. "That's why I bought a pair.'' The drawer clicked shut, hiding both Deringers.

She rose and smoothed her old black bombazine skirt. Rolf Greencastle fleetingly wished that he was just a customer again, not a friend, and didn't have to concern himself with Jimmy's mad pronouncement. Which he knew wasn't so mad. She was a determined thing. Whores had to be to survive.

"You'll have to excuse me, Rolf. Lieutenant Peebles is due any minute.''

"All right, but I wish you'd think it over.'' In the door he turned back to gaze at her in a pleading fashion. "Please."

She gave a little shake of her head.

"Once a Virginian, always a Virginian."

Rolf Greencastle put on his cream-colored Texas hat with its decorative star and red band and left. If General Phil Sheridan did arrive at Fort Dodge as part of his scheduled inspection of the Arkansas River posts now under his command, he was certainly a dead man unless the scout did something about it. But what?

Rolf lay in his bunk in his underwear with a copy of the *Police Gazette* in front of his nose. One of those inscrutable turns of fate seemingly designed to torment a man had brought this tattered copy of the paper into the barber shop in Dodge where he went for a semi-monthly trim of his luxuriant hair and mustachios. Who should be pictured in an heroic pose on the front page? None other than Jimmy's announced victim.

It was four days after his visit to the Overton Place, which Jimmy's husband and pimp, Nimrod Taylor, had bought and occupied for about three years before he up and disappeared. Jimmy once explained with a sad, resigned look that Nimrod had warned her on their wedding day that he was a restless man. He was also something else, because that day Jimmy had a large yellowing bruise around her left eye. She refused to talk about it. After Nimrod Taylor left, he never came back. At least Jimmy got the Overton Place.

In the bunk, Major General Philip Sheridan stared at Rolf from within the engraving as if he were infuriated with the scout. The man had a reputation for a temper, and for peppering almost every sentence he spoke with some kind of obscenity, plain or invented. To Rolf, the new commander of the Department of the Missouri looked like an Irish bartender from New York City (Rolf had never seen any of that species, but he had a fair imagination). With his fierce black eyes and squat, bull-like build, and the somehow sinister soap-lock hanging down in the center of his forehead, Phil Sheridan looked like one hard son of a bitch. Rolf Greencastle had seen a few other pictures of the general, and none was any friendlier.

He tossed the paper aside, hiding the face. "She'll never do it," he said.

Then he considered what he knew about Jimmy.

Suppose she really did murder Phil Sheridan; did she have much to lose thereby? No. Mrs. Jemima Sturdevant Taylor had apparently lived a pretty wretched life till now. She'd inherited the same dark moods, the glooms, that she said contributed to her father's death. Officers on the post had informed Rolf that on at least two occasions after her husband left, Jimmy had tried to commit suicide. Those scars on her left wrist were the evidence. When she was up, she was bright as a sunbeam, but at other times, there was no telling what dark, tormented thoughts roiled around in the depths of her soul.

In Dodge they said she had once grabbed a kitchen knife and mortally injured a teamster who had asked for more than he'd paid for and then began to abuse her when she refused. Evidently she thought a wife had to suffer beatings, but not an independent working girl. According to the story, the team-ster was not well liked; he died and Jimmy was released after one night in jail and no more was said.

The image of a gleaming knife sliding into some hairy back, with a consequent gout of blood, caused Rolf to cover his eyes there in the bunk, and change his tune.

"She'll do it."

He fidgeted for half an hour, trying to think of some scheme to forestall the assassination. He was not a bright fellow, and he knew it, so he didn't have much confidence in the scheme he finally concocted. But he could come up with no other right then. He found a tack and slipped it in the pocket of his buck-skin coat, together with the engraving of Sheridan ripped from the *Gazette*.

He saddled Kid, his swift-running little pie-bald, and set out from his cabin at the edge of town to ride the five miles along the Arkansas to the fort. It was a mean, gusty late-winter day, but you could smell April primping just around the corner. General Sheridan was scheduled to arrive at Fort Dodge the first week in April.

On the post, he nonchalantly tied Kid outside the adobe barracks that housed B Troop, waited until no one was paying attention, then stole inside. Luckily the dayroom was empty. He tacked Sheridan's picture to the notice board, slipped his sheath knife from under his jacket and proceeded to stab holes all over Little Phil's face.

"To what do I owe the pleasure of this visit?" asked Captain Tipton.

"Oh, I was just in the neighborhood," Rolf said.

Captain Tipton's face proclaimed his skepticism. "I never knew you to be so social, Rolf." The captain, whose behind-the-back nickname was Moon Face, was a pale, pudgy young man with a flaxen mustache and small oval spectacles. He'd once been a professor of geography at a young ladies' academy in Kentucky, a land of divided loyalties during the war. Rolf didn't know which flag Moon Face Tipton had followed, and Moon Face didn't say. That he was wearing Army blue meant nothing.

"Well, the fact is, Captain, I'm worried about this here visit of Phil Sheridan's next month."

"It's just a routine inspection of all the posts in the department. Hancock before him made the same tour. Every new commander does it."

"Yes, but it might be dangerous for him to stop at Fort Dodge."

Now he had Moon Face Tipton's full attention. "What the devil are you talking about?"

"Well, sir, I was just in the dayroom of B Troop, looking for a fellow that owes me a ten spot. On the notice board I saw this newspaper picture of Sheridan. Somebody cut it up pretty bad with a knife."

"You're jesting."

"Sir, I am not."

"But that's ridiculous. Why—?"

"Captain, there aren't more'n one or two other generals hated more than Phil Sheridan. Uncle Billy Sherman, for sure, and maybe that cavalry commander of his, Kil-what's-his-name."

"Patrick. Kilpatrick."

"Yes, sure. Sir, you know as well as I do, this Plains army

contains a lot of men who enlisted under different names than their real ones. A lot of former *Rebs*," he added with breathy melodrama, in case Tipton didn't get it the first time.

"I'll grant you that's true," Moon Face said. "What am I supposed to do about it?"

"Well, sir, I thought you might go up the line to your boss, the adjutant, and have him tell General Sheridan that he ought to stay away. Tell him that he ought to bypass this fort."

"*Tell* him not to visit a post he commands? *Tell* one of the toughest, most determined soldiers who ever served in the United States Army that he shouldn't come here because someone cut up his picture?" Rolf sank into his rickety chair. Of course he'd failed; he just wasn't a smart enough fellow. "I think you might as well try to stop one of Mr. Shakespeare's hurricanoes." It was all Tipton could do to keep from sounding supercilious. "Now, if you'll excuse me, I've been studying Pliny again, and I'd like to return to him."

"Yes, sir. Thank you, sir."

Rolf slouched out, humiliated.

Humiliated but not whipped.

He wasn't going to let the murder take place. He must use force on Jimmy. Restrain her physically from going anywhere near Fort Dodge while Sheridan was there inspecting it. He knew he wasn't glib enough to talk Jimmy out of her plan, so physical force was the only answer. He needn't hurt her—wouldn't ever do that—but he could lock her up and sit with her. For days, if necessary.

He stole into the B Troop dayroom again, to remove the picture of Phil Sheridan. Since his last visit, someone had penciled obscene words on the general's cheeks and forehead. It made him look all the madder.

During the next few days he blew around and around like a weathervane. "She'll never do it." "She'll do it." The two sentences became his litany.

He had never thought about Jimmy much when he wasn't with her, but now that she was endangered he thought about her a lot. He was surprised by the constancy and the urgency of these new feelings.

Riding past the Overton Place one showery afternoon, he saw her out in back, where the chicken yard sloped away toward the river. Three bottles of different size and color reposed on a log. Ten feet away, Jimmy extended her right hand. He saw a little squirt of smoke, then heard the crack as the amber bottle on the left exploded.

She heard Kid passing. Turned. Recognized him and raised her hand with the .44-caliber murder weapon over her head and waved. He snatched off his hat and waved back. "She'll do it," he said in a strangled voice. "By God she will."

Another blast from the other Deringer seemed to verify it.

On the night before General Sheridan's scheduled arrival, a dismal night of rain that made the Arkansas rush and roar, Rolf slanted his hat brim over his forehead to drip water and rode Kid to the Overton Place. He carried no weapons, but his saddlebags bulged with groceries bought in Dodge that afternoon. He was prepared for a long siege.

As he approached through the rain, opened the gate in front of the farmhouse, rode in, he heard a horse nicker. Then he saw the animal tied out in front. Regulation Army saddle. Did Jimmy have a customer from the fort?

He picketed Kid to the fence by the gate and walked to the porch. If she was entertaining someone, he'd just have to huddle out by the hen house till the man left. He'd just check to make sure; Jimmy never locked her front door even during business hours.

Sheltered by the porch roof, he eased the door open. Lamplight and the smell of dust drifted out. Beyond the closed door of the bedroom, bedsprings squeaked and groaned, and a bullish voice exclaimed, "Oh, that's mighty fucking good, oh my Lord yes . . ."

Rolf Greencastle would have lit out immediately for the hen house but for the intrusion of that obscenity into the unseen customer's declaration of pleasure. That word set his hair to crawling under his hat. An unbelievable premonition gripped him. Held him rigid on the porch a good five minutes, while similar professions of pleasure, similarly punctuated with all sorts of bad language, convinced him that his suspicion was

correct and that, somehow, he was caught in one of those
inexplicable apocalyptic disasters that left total carnage and
sorrow in their wake.

Blood rushed to his head. His eyes felt bulgy as he flung
the door wide and cannoned across the parlor, nearly knocking
over a flickering lamp with a pearly globe. He took a deep,
hurtful breath—this was worse than the time he'd ridden carelessly over a rise and come upon half a dozen young men of
the Southern Cheyenne tribe, each and every one in a bad
mood—and prayed for God and Jimmy to forgive him. But he
had to know.

He opened the bedroom door.

A fat-bottomed little man rolled over on his back and
shouted, "Who the profanity are you? What the obscenity is
going on here?"

"Rolf, oh Rolf," Jimmy said, trying to cover herself with
the bedding. She sounded more grief-stricken than angry. As
for Rolf, his aching eyeballs were fixed on the soap-lock of
the enraged chap leaping from the bed and seizing his yellow-
striped trousers while throwing all sorts of obscene invective
at the stunned intruder trembling in the doorway.

"Will you get the shit out of here, you bugeyed intrusive
little son of a bitch?" screamed General Philip Henry Sheridan; for it was the very same.

"General Sheridan, please calm down," Jimmy said. Rolf
could not see her just then, the general was in the way. But
he distinctly heard the cocking of the Deringer. Sheridan heard
it too, and it arrested his angry rush to dress and depart. His
little white corporation quivered above the waist of the regulation trousers he was hastily buttoning. Rolf reckoned him to
be in his middle thirties, with careworn lines around his black
eyes.

"I have a gun pointed at your back, General," Jimmy
added.

"You have what?"

The barefoot Sheridan spun around and his disbelief quickly
evaporated. Jimmy was sitting up in bed, one hand clasping
the sheet over her bosom, the other pointing the hideout pistol
at Sheridan's chest, which was white as a bottle of milk.

"General, how did this happen?" Rolf gasped.

"Who the double profanity wants to know? Who the repeated obscenity are you?"

"Just someone who wants to save your life if possible, General."

"Rolf," Jimmy said, "I don't want to shoot you too. My mind's made up. He's going to die. Don't make more bloodshed."

Water dripped from Rolf's chin. At first he thought it was rain but then he realized he was indoors, and it was sweat. The low-trimmed lamp at the bedside, the heavy draperies closed and securely tied that way, gave the room a confined, sultry air. The air of a tomb, he thought, wishing he hadn't.

Sheridan was struggling into his shirt, one moment looking miffed, the next letting his anxiety flicker through; the man was clearly no fool. "General, how the devil did you get over here?" Rolf exclaimed. "You're not supposed to arrive till tomorrow."

"Arrived early," Sheridan barked. "And I found this letter—this charming letter—" He indicated a paper sticking from the pocket of his blouse, which lay over the back of a chair half hidden by his rain-dampened caped overcoat. "From someone who signed herself Daughter of Joy. It was a very fetching missive." He sounded outraged. "It was a special invitation to one of our, ahem, country's heroes to enjoy an hour in the grove of Venus—free of charge." By now Rolf's mind had begun to edit out all of the simple and compound obscenities with which Sheridan filled these and all his other sentences.

"And you fell for it?" Rolf asked. In other circumstances, you might have heard the crash of an idol coming off its pedestal.

"Well, sir, God damn it, I am a bachelor—a man like any other. A man with appetites! A man with feelings!"

"You didn't have any feelings when you burned my daddy's farm on the Valley Pike in Shenandoah County, Virginia, and sent him off to Detroit, Michigan, to catch the glooms and die."

"Shenandoah County?" Sheridan muttered. He turned to

the bed. "I remember that place of course, but not your father. What was his name?"

Jimmy whipped her other hand onto the hideout pistol's grip, and the sheet fell, baring her breast. She took no notice. Her beautiful eyes burned. Rolf knew the end was at hand.

"Cosgrove Sturdevant was his name. He took a shot at you because your damned brute soldiers had ruined our farm and carried me off to rape me. For punishment you sent him to prison up north. A poor helpless middle-aged farmer!"

General Phil Sheridan gathered himself and hooked his thumbs in the waist of his trousers, further revealing his pot-belly, of which he took no notice. In a hard, strong voice, he said, "I do remember that incident. And you are wrong about it." He stepped toward the bed. "What happened was—"

"Stand back or I'll blow your head off," Jimmy whispered. Both hands, and the Deringer, trembled, and Sheridan's black eyes darted from the gun to Jimmy's face and back again. He clearly saw his death but a finger's twitch away. He didn't advance but he stood fast, and even a little taller. Rolf almost whistled; the man had testicles of steel.

"I ask you not to pull that trigger until I tell you what happened."

"Your men savaged me in the smokehouse, for one."

"I am deeply grieved," Sheridan said, without a single profanity. "I never intentionally made war on women. I do know such things happened."

Jimmy blinked and sat back, expecting, perhaps, something other than this soldier's calm and measured determination in the face of impending death. "I remember your father, and your farm, now that I put my mind to it, because it was there that we lost a young soldier named Birdage, the day after the battle at Fisher's Hill. A white-haired farmer came rushing from his house as we rode into his dooryard, and he fired a shot."

"Did you expect a man like Daddy wouldn't defend his property from filthy Yankee scum invaders?"

"No, I expect that would be any man's natural reaction," Sheridan said, his voice still level. Rolf swayed in the doorway, dizzy, hearing the beat of rain and what sounded in his ear like the rushing winds of black hell and judgment in the sky. Very soon, he expected to see fountains of blood all over the room's rose-pattern wallpaper. "I can understand why I was a target. Unfortunately your father's shot struck a soldier named Asa Birdage."

"Who cares, who cares?" Jimmy screamed. "He was sixty-two years old!"

"Asa Birdage was eleven years old. Asa Birdage was our headquarters drummer boy."

Jimmy's face was curtained by horror. She flung back against the headboard, wanting to deny Sheridan's statement. He simply stood there with his hands hanging easily at his sides—maybe he wasn't so easy inside, but you couldn't tell except for the rise and fall of his potbelly—and Jimmy began to shake her head from side to side. "No, no," she said, and then she burst out crying. "Liar. You're lying to save your hide."

"Young woman, I am an honorable man. I have been accused of many things, but never of deceit. Your father slew one of my soldiers. Who was scarcely more than a child. I felt prison was fair punishment. Perhaps I erred. Perhaps I was unjust. I acted to prevent another death. Others in my command that day wanted to shoot your father on the spot."

"No, oh no," Jimmy wept. Sheridan's eyes took on a pitying look. Rolf leaped by him, giving him a fist in the shoulder—how many times did you get to land a blow on a hero? on a legend?—and with one quick decisive grab, he removed the Deringer from Jimmy's hand.

"I am thankful that you believe me, miss," Phil Sheridan said in a voice oddly humbled.

"I'm not, I'm not," she cried, covering her tearful face. Rolf knelt beside the bed and with both hands delicately lifted the hem of the sheet so as to hide her breasts. His cheeks were scarlet.

General Sheridan quickly donned his singlet and then his blouse. He was once more sounding stern when he said, "If anyone mentions these events, I will deny my presence. I will lie till the throne of Hell freezes."

Rolf Greencastle was trembling inside. But he tried not to

let it show when he turned his eyes on the national hero and scorched him. "I think you'd better light out of here, Phil."

Phil lit out.

After about three hours, Jimmy's sobbing wore itself out and she fell asleep. Rolf pulled up a cane-bottomed chair and sat beside the bed, keeping a vigil. The rain fell harder. About four in the morning, Jimmy woke up.

She quickly covered her left breast, which had been peeping over the hem of the sheet as she slept; Rolf had been admiring it for the better part of twenty minutes. Although he knew her body intimately, his admiration was of a different nature than the simple lust he'd satisfied at the Overton Place before.

"Why did you do that?" she said. "Why did you stop me?" She sounded deathly sad. He feared the glooms were coming again. The terrible glooms.

"You tell me something first. How could you take him into your bed, hating him that way?"

"Oh—" A little sniffle. "Part of the trade, that's all. You learn to shut out everything. How bad the customer stinks. How mean he is. With him it was harder. For a while I thought it wouldn't work, I'd go to pieces. Then I remembered my daddy and I made it work. Got him right where I wanted him."

"It was a mighty good trick," he agreed. "You could have blown his head off any time you wanted to."

"Why did you stop me?"

"I didn't want anything to happen to you. I didn't want you to keep on having the glooms the rest of your life."

"Why, why?"

"I don't know, I guess because I love you."

They stared at each other. He was fully as surprised as she was.

The next day he helped her put the Overton Place up for sale and they rode away together and neither one ever saw General Phil Sheridan again.

GET OUT OF TOWN

—

Louis L'Amour

Ma said for me to ride into town and hire a man to help with the cows. More than likely she figured I'd hire Johnny Loftus or Ed Shifrin, but I had no liking for either of them. Johnny used to wink and call ma "that widder woman" and Ed, he worked no harder than he had to. Man I hired I'd never seen before.

He wasn't much to look at, first off. He was smaller than Johnny Loftus by twenty pound, and Johnny was only a mite more than half of Ed Shifrin, and this stranger was older than either. Fact is, he was pushing forty, but he had a hard, grainy look that made me figure he'd been up the creek and over the mountain.

He wouldn't weigh over a hundred and forty pounds soaking wet, which he wasn't likely to be in this country, and his face was narrow and dark with black eyes that sized you up careful-like before he spoke. He was a-settin' on the platform down to the depot with his saddle and a war bag that looked mighty empty like he was shy of clothes. He was not saying I, yes, or no to anybody when I rode up to town on that buckskin pa gave me before he was shot down in the street.

Pa let me have the pick of the horses for sale in the town corral, and I taken a fancy to a paint filly with a blaze face.

"Son"—Pa was hunkered down on his heels watching the horses—"that filly wouldn't carry you over the hill. She looks mighty pert, but what a man wants to find in horses or partners

241

is stayin' quality. He wants a horse he can ride all day and all night that will still be with him at sunup.

"Now you take that buckskin. He's tough and he's got savvy. Horse or men, son, pick 'em tough and with savvy. Don't pay no attention to the showy kind. Pick 'em to last. Pick 'em to go all the way."

Well, I taken the buckskin, and pa was right. Looking at that man setting on the edge of the platform I decided he was the man we wanted. I gave no further thought to Johnny or Ed.

"Mister," I said, "are you rustling work?"

He turned those black eyes on me and studied me right careful. I was pushing fourteen, but I'd been man of the house for nigh three years now. It didn't seem to make no difference to him that I was a wet-eared boy.

"Now I just might be. What work do you have?"

"Ma and me have a little outfit over against the foothills. We figured to roust our cattle out of the canyons and bring 'em down to sell. There's a month of work, maybe more. We'd pay thirty a month and found and if I do say so, ma is the best cook anywheres around."

He looked at me out of those black, careful eyes and he asked me, "You always hire strangers?"

"No, sir. We usually hire Johnny Loftus or Ed Shifrin or one of the loafers around town, but when I saw you I figured to hire you." The way he looked at me was beginning to worry me some.

"Why me?" he asked.

So I told him what Pa said when we bought the buckskin, and for the first time he smiled. His eyes warmed and his face crinkled up and laugh wrinkles showed at the corners of his eyes where they must have been sleeping all the time. "Your pa was a right smart man, son. I'd be proud to work for you."

We started for the livery stable to get him a horse to ride out to the ranch, and Ed Shifrin was in front of the saloon. He noticed me and then the man who walked beside me.

"Tom," Ed said, "about time your ma started the roundup. You want I should come out?"

Did me good to tell him, the way he'd loafed on the job

and come it high and mighty over me. "I done hired me a man, Ed."

Shifrin came down off the walk. You shouldn't have done that. The Coopers ain't goin' to like a stranger proddin' around among their cows." He turned to the man I hired. "Stranger, you just light a shuck. I'll do the roundin' up."

The man I'd hired didn't seem a mite bothered. "The boy hired me," he said. "If he don't want me he can fire me."

Ed wasn't inclined to be talked up to. "You're a stranger hereabouts or you'd know better. There's been range trouble and the Coopers don't take kindly to strangers among their stock."

"They'll get used to it," he said, and we walked away up the street.

About then I started worrying about what I'd done. We'd tried to avoid trouble. "The Coopers," I told him, "they're the biggest outfit around here. They sort of run things."

"Who runs your place?"

"Well. Me, sort of. Ma and me. Only she leaves it to me, because she says a boy without a father has to learn to manage for himself."

We walked on maybe twenty yards before he said anything, and then he just said, "Seems to me you've had uncommon smart folks, boy."

Old Man Taylor brought out the sorrel for us. While the stranger was saddling up and I sat there enjoying the warm sunshine and the barn smells of horses and hay and leather, Old Man Taylor came to where I sat the saddle and he asked me low-voiced, "Where'd you find him?"

"Down to the depot. He was rustling work and I was looking for a man."

Old Man Taylor was a man noted for staying out of trouble, yet he had been friendly to Pa. "Boy, you've hired yourself a man. Now you and your ma get set for fireworks."

What he meant I didn't know, nor did it make any kind of sense to me. My hired man came out with the sorrel and he swung into the saddle and we went back down the street. Only he was wearing chaps now and looked more the rider, but somehow he was different from any cowhand I could remember.

We were almost to the end of the street when the sheriff came out of the saloon, followed by Ed Shifrin. He walked into the street and stopped us.

"Tom"—he was abrupt like always—"your ma isn't going to like you hiring this stranger."

"Ma tells me to hire whom I've a mind to. I hired this man and I wouldn't fire any man without he gives me cause."

Sheriff Ben Russell was a hard old man with cold blue eyes and a brusque, unfriendly way about him, but I noticed he cottoned up to the Coopers. "Boy, this man is just out of prison. You get rid of him."

"I'll not hold it against him. I hired him and if he doesn't stack up, I'll fire him."

My hired hand had sat real quiet up to now. "Sheriff," he said, "you just back up and leave this boy alone. He sizes up like pretty much of a man and it begins to look like he really needs outside help. Seems to me there must be a reason folks want to keep a stranger out of the country."

Sheriff Ben Russell was mad as I'd ever seen him. "You can get yourself right back in jail," he said; "you're headed for it."

My hired man was slow to rile. He looked right back at the sheriff with those cold black eyes and he said, "Sheriff, you don't know who I am or why I was in prison. You recognized this prison-made suit. Before you start shaping up trouble for me, you go tell Pike Cooper to come see me first."

Nobody around our country knew a Cooper called Pike, but it was plain to see the sheriff knew who he meant and was surprised to hear him called so. He said, "Where'd you know Cooper?"

"You tell him. I figure he'll know me."

Seven miles out of town we forded the creek and I showed him with a sweep of the hand. "Our land begins here and runs back into the hills. Our stock has a way of getting into the canyons this time of year."

"Seems plenty of good grass down here."

"This here is deeded land," I told him. "Pa, he always said

the day of free range was over, so he bought homesteads from several folks who had proved up, and he filed on land himself. These are all grazing claims, but two of them have good water holes and the stock fattens up mighty well.''

When we rode into the ranch yard ma came to the door, wiping her hands on her apron. She looked at the new rider and I knew she was surprised not to see Ed or Johnny.

The hired man got down from his saddle and removed his hat. Neither Johnny or Ed had ever done that.

''The boy hired me, ma'am, but if you'd rather I'd not stay I'll ride back to town. You see, I've been in prison.''

Ma looked at him for a moment, but all she said was, ''Tom does the hiring. I feel he should have the responsibility.''

''And rightly so, ma'am.'' He hesitated ever so little. ''My name is Riley, ma'am.''

Ma said, ''Supper's ready. There's a kettle of hot water for washing.''

We washed our hands in the tin basin and while he was drying his hands on the towel, Riley said, ''You didn't tell me your ma was so pretty.''

''I didn't figure there was reason to,'' I said, kind of stiff.

He took a quick look at me and then he said, ''You're right, boy. It's none of my business.'' Then after a minute he said, ''Only it surprised me.''

''She was married when she was shy of sixteen,'' I said.

Supper was a quiet meal. With a stranger at table there were things we didn't feel up to talking about, and you don't ask questions of a man who has been in jail. We made some polite talk about the lack of rain, and how the water on the ranch was permanent, and when he'd finished eating he said, ''Mind if I smoke?''

Reckon that was the first time in a while anybody had asked ma a question like that. Pa, he just took it for granted and other men who came around just lit up and said nothing, but the way Ma acted you'd have thought it was every day. She said, ''Please do.'' It sounded right nice, come to think of it.

''You been getting good returns on your cattle?''

''The calf crop has been poor the last two, three years, but Ed and Johnny said it was because there were so many lions in the mountains. You have to expect to lose some to lions."

"Good range," Riley said, "and plenty of water. I'd say you should make out."

When he had gone to the bunkhouse ma started picking up the dishes. "How did you happen to hire him, Tom?"

So I told her about the buckskin and what I thought when I saw this man, and she smiled. "I think you learned your lesson well, Tom. I think he is a good man." And then she added, "He may have been in prison, but he had good upbringing."

Coming from Ma there was not much more she could have said. She set great store by proper upbringing.

Awhile after, I told her about the talk with Ed Shifrin and Sheriff Russell, and when I came to the part about Riley telling Russell to tell Cooper to come see him, I could see that worried her. Cooper had some tough hands working for him and we didn't want them around.

Year after Pa was killed, some of them tried to court Ma, but she put a stop to that right off.

Come daylight just as I was pulling on a boot I heard an ax, and when I looked from behind the curtain I saw it was Riley at the woodpile. Right off I could see he was a hand with an ax, but what surprised me was him doing it at all, because most cowhands resent any but riding work, even digging postholes.

The way it worked out we rode away from the place an hour earlier than I'd ever been able to with Ed or Johnny, and by noon we had hazed seventy head down on the flat, but we were mighty shy of young stuff. Whatever else he was, I'd hired a hand. He was up on Pa's bay gelding and he knew how to sit a cutting horse and handle a rope.

Next three days we worked like all getout. Riley was up early and working late, and I being boss couldn't let him best me, but working with him was like working with Pa, for we shared around and helped each other and I never did see a man learn country faster than he did. Time to time he'd top out on high ground and then he'd set a spell and study the country. Sometimes he'd ask questions. Mostly, he just looked.

Third day we had built us a hatful of fire for coffee and shucked the wrappings off the lunches ma fixed. "You said your pa was killed. How'd it happen?"

"Ma and me didn't see it. Pa had been to the Coopers' on business and when he got back to town he picked up some dress goods for ma and a few supplies. He was tying the sack on the saddle when he had a difficulty with a stranger. The stranger shot him."

"Was your pa wearing a gun?"

"Yes, sir. Pa always wore a gun, but not to use on no man. He carried it for varmints or to shoot the horse if he got thrown and his foot caught in the stirrup."

"You hear that stranger's name?"

"Yes, sir. His name was Cad Miller."

That afternoon we ran into Ed Shifrin and Johnny Loftus. First time I'd seen them up thataway except when working for us, but they were coming down the draw just as we put out our fire.

Riley heard them coming before I did, but he looked around at the mountainside like he was expecting somebody else. He looked most careful at the trees and rocks where a man might take cover.

Both of them were armed, but if Riley had a gun I had seen no sign of it. He wore that buckskin jacket that hung even with his belt, but there might have been a gun in his waistband under the jacket. But I didn't think of guns until later.

"You still around?" Shifrin sounded like he was building trouble. "I figured you'd be run out before this."

"I like it here." Riley talked pleasant-like. "Pretty country, nice folks. Not as many cows as a man would expect, but they're fat."

"What d' you mean by that? Not as many cows as you'd expect?"

"Maybe I should have said calves. Not as many calves as a man would expect, but by the time the roundup is over we'll find what happened to the others."

Shifrin looked over at Johnny. "What about the kid?"

Johnny shrugged. "To hell with the kid."

The way they talked back and forth made no sense to me,

but it made sense to Riley. "Was I you," Riley said, "I'd be mighty sure Cooper wants it this way. With the kid, and all."

"What d' you mean by that?"

"Why, it just won't work. There's no way you can make it look right. The kid doesn't carry a gun. You boys don't know your business like you should."

"Maybe you know it better?" Johnny sounded mean.

"Why, I do, at that. Did Sheriff Russell tell Pike what I said?"

"Who's Pike?" Shifrin asked suspiciously.

"Why, Pike Cooper. That's what they used to call him in the old days. He ever tell you how he happened to leave Pike County, Missouri? It's quite a story."

Something about the easy way Riley talked was bothering them. They weren't quite so sure of themselves now.

"And while you're at it," Riley added, "you get him to tell you why he left the Nation."

Neither of them seemed to know what to do next. The fact that Riley seemed to know Cooper bothered them, and Johnny was uneasy. He kept looking at me, and I kept looking right back at him, and that seemed to worry him too.

"You boys tell him that. You also tell him not to send boys to do a man's job."

"What's that mean?" Shifrin was sore and he shaped up like a mighty tough man. At least, he always had. Somehow when they came up against Riley they didn't seem either so big or so tough.

"That means you ride out of here now, and you don't stop riding until you get to Pike Cooper. You tell Pike if he wants a job done he'd better come and do it himself."

Well, they didn't know which way was up. They wanted to be tough and they had tried it, but it didn't seem to faze Riley in the least. They had come expecting trouble and now neither one of them wanted to start it and take a chance on being wrong. Or maybe it was the very fact that Riley was taking it so easy. Both of them figured he must have the difference.

"He'll do it!" Johnny replied angrily. "Cooper will want to do this himself. You'll see."

They rode out of there and when Riley had watched them

down the slope without comment he said, "We'd best get back to the ranch, Tom. It's early, but we'd better be in when Cooper comes."

"He won't come. Mr. Cooper never goes anywhere unless he feels like it himself."

"He'll come," Riley said, "although he may send Cad Miller first."

When he said that name I stared right at him. "That was the name of the man who killed my father."

"Riley, what I've seen today, I like. If this comes to a case in court I'd admire to be your lawyer."

"Thank you, but I doubt if it will come to that."

We had a quiet supper. We had come in early from the range, so Riley put in the last hour before sundown tightening a sagging gate. He was a man liked to keep busy.

At supper Riley said to ma, "Thank you, ma'am. I am proud to work for you."

Ma blushed.

Next morning Ma came to breakfast all prettied up for town. Only thing she said was, "Your father taught you to stand up for what you believe to be right, and to stand by your own people."

There was quite a crowd in town. Word has a way of getting around and folks had a way of being on the street or in the stores when it looked like excitement, and nobody figured to finish their business until it was over.

We left our rig with Old Man Taylor and he leaned over to whisper, "You tell that friend of yours Cad Miller's in town."

Ma heard it and she turned sharp around. "What does he look like, Mr. Taylor?"

Taylor hesitated, shifting his feet nervous-like, not wanting to say, or figuring why Ma wanted to know. But Ma wasn't a woman you could shake off. "I asked a question, Mr. Taylor. I believe you were a friend of my husband's."

"Well, ma'am, I figured so. I figured to be a friend of yours, too."

"And so you are. Now tell me."

So he told her.

It was a warm, still morning. We went down to the hotel, where I waited, and ma went out to buy some women fixin's like she won't buy with a man along.

All the chairs were taken in front of the hotel, so I leaned against the corner of the building next to the alley. Moment later I heard Riley speak from behind my right shoulder. He was right around the corner of the building in the alley.

"Don't turn around, boy. Is Cooper on the street?"

"Not yet, but Cad Miller is in town."

"Tom," he said, "just so you'll know. I was in prison for killing a man who'd killed my brother. Before that, I was a deputy United States marshal." He hesitated. "I just wanted you to know."

Nobody on the street was talking much. A rig clattered along the street and disappeared. The dust settled. A yellow hound ambled across the street headed toward shade. Ma went walking up the other side of the street and just when I was wondering what she was doing over there the Coopers turned into the upper end of the street. The boys were riding on his flanks and the old man was driving a shining new buckboard.

Cooper pulled up in front of the hotel and got down. His boys were swaggering it, like always, both of them grinning in appreciation of the fun.

Cooper stepped up on the walk and took a cigar from his vest pocket and bit off the end. His hard old eyes glinted at me. "Boy, where's that hired man of yours? I understand he was asking for me."

"He leaves town today," Andy Cooper said loudly, "or he'll be carried out."

Cooper put the cigar in his teeth. He struck a match and lifted it to light the cigar and I heard a boot grate on the walk beside me and knew Riley was there. Cooper dropped the match without lighting his cigar. He just stood there staring past me at Riley.

"Lark!" Cooper almost choked over the name. "I didn't know it was you."

"You remember what I told you when I ran you out of the Nation?"

Cooper wasn't seeing anybody but Riley, the man he had

called Lark. He wasn't even aware of anything else. And I was staring at him, because I had never seen a big man scared before.

"I told you if you ever crossed my trail again I'd kill you."

"Don't do it, Lark. I've got a family—two boys. I've got a ranch. I've done well."

"This boy had a father."

"Lark, don't do it."

"This boy's father has been dead three or four years. I figure you've been stealing his cows at least two years before that. Say five hundred head."

Cooper never took his eyes off him, and the two boys acted as if they couldn't believe what was happening.

"You write out a bill of sale for five hundred head and I'll sign it for the boy's mother. Then you write out a check for seven thousand dollars and we'll cross the street and cash it together."

"All right."

"And you'll testify that Cad Miller was told to kill this boy's pa."

"I can't do that. I won't do it."

"Pike," Riley said patiently, "you might beat a court trial, but you know mighty well you ain't going to beat me. Now my gun's around the corner on my saddle. Don't make me go get it."

Cooper looked like a man who was going to be sick. He looked like a school kid caught cheating. I figured whatever he knew about Riley scared him bad enough so he didn't want any argument. And that talk about a gun on the saddle—why, that might be just talk. A man couldn't see what Riley was packing in his waistband.

"All right," Cooper said. His voice was so low you could scarce hear it.

"Pa!" Andy grabbed his arm. "What are you sayin'?"

"Shut up, you young fool! Shut up, I say!"

"Cad Miller's in town," Riley continued; "you get him out here on the street."

"He won't have to." It was Ma's voice.

The crowd moved back and Cad Miller came through with

Ma right behind him, and trust Ma to have the difference. She had a double-barreled shotgun, and she wasn't holding that shotgun for fun. One time I'd seen her use it on a mountain lion right in the door yard. She near cut that lion in two.

Sheriff Ben Russell wasn't liking it very much, but there was nothing he could do but take his prisoner. Once Cooper showed yellow, those two boys of his weren't about to make anything of it, and any man who knew our town knew Cooper was through around here after this.

Back at home I said, "Cooper called you Lark."

"My name is Larkin Riley."

"And you didn't even have a gun!"

"A man has to learn to live without a gun, and against a coward you don't need a gun." He rolled a smoke. "Cooper knew I meant what I said."

"But you'd been in prison yourself."

He sat on the stoop and looked at the backs of his hands. "That was later. Ten or fifteen years ago, what I did would have been the only thing to do. There are laws to handle cases like that, and I had it to learn."

Ma came to the door. "Larkin . . . Tom . . . supper's ready."

We got up and Riley said, "Tom, I think tomorrow we'll work the south range."

"Yes, sir," I said.

WOLF MOON

—

Ed Gorman

The wolves lived on a perch high in the mountains so that the leader of the pack could see anything that threatened his mate or their pups. Behind the perch was a cave that served as a den. It was a shared responsibility to bring their pups food. It was not easy. The land was filled with two-legs and their guns. That was why they lived so high up, near where the jagged peaks touched the clouds.

Of course, the wolf knew that man was a devious foe. He did not always show himself when he meant to destroy the wolves.

The leader remembered last spring, when four of the pups had wandered off to hunt and had found for themselves a piece of buffalo meat that a rancher had poisoned with strychnine. The pups had died long and terrible deaths cuddled up against the belly of their mother, while she cried for hours into the dark and indifferent night.

Only one pup had lived, and about this last son the leader and his wife were protective to the point of mania. When the pup slept, the leader sat just outside the den, so that nobody could get inside without killing him first. When the pup accompanied the mother on a small hunt, she never once let him stray, despite the wolf ritual of letting the pups wander off and find their own food.

By the time he was six months, and by the time the white and bitter snows came, the pup stood thirty inches high at the

253

shoulder and measured six feet from the tip of his nose to the tip of his tail. An Indian boy with a white man's lasso managed to get the rope over the pup's neck one day but, incredibly, the pup's powerful jaws cleaved the rope with a single bite. The Indian boy ran off, convinced he had encountered a dire and supernatural being.

By the summer, leader and mate began giving their huge and eager pup a little more freedom.

Because of this, the pup was drinking from a winding mountain stream the day he heard the shots from up on the ledge where the den was.

In fear and rage the pup made his way quickly up the shifting rocks of the mountain.

He saw his mother lying dead, her head exploded from several bullets, her limp body hanging over the edge of a promontory.

At this same moment, his father was being held up by his rear paws and a shaggy and filthy man was gutting him with a bowie knife.

The shaggy man saw the pup. "Schroeder, look at that pup!"

For the first time, the pup set eyes on the sleek and handsome human named Schroeder. He was everything the other man was not—well-attired in fancy hunting clothes, well-spoken, composed and radiating a self-confidence that was almost oppressive.

Schroeder turned now and beheld the pup. His face showed true awe as he studied the imposing animal. He said, simply, "I don't care how long it takes you, Greenleaf. I want that pup. Do you understand me?"

And so the hunt began.

It took the wolfer known as Greenleaf four days, but finally, with the help of two Indian trackers, he captured the pup and turned him over to Schroeder. His reward was $1,000 cash and a night in a Denver whorehouse with a former slave girl named (by her madam) Esmerelda.

Schroeder never saw Greenleaf again and didn't care. He had the pup. And he had his very special plans for the pup.

Part 1

The first thing I did after leaving the saloon was find an alley and throw up. We'd been two hard days riding and I still hadn't gotten over the killing yet. I had never robbed a bank before, and I had certainly never seen a man die before, either, especially one of my own brothers. The man named Schroeder had killed him without hesitation or mercy.

So tonight I'd had too much to drink, trying to forget how I'd been changed from eighteen-year-old farm boy to bank robber in the course of forty-eight hours. And trying to forget how Glen had looked dying there by the side of the road when we were dividing the money with Schroeder.

After I finished in the alley, I went back to the dusty street. The water wagon had worked most of the afternoon, but by now, near midnight, the dust rose like ghosts from the grave. The eighty-degree temperature didn't make things any more pleasant, either.

The sleeping room Don and I rented was over the livery stable. The owner had built two small rooms up there and put in cots and a can to piss in and fancied himself in the hotel business. He wanted Yankee cash up front and he wanted a promise not to smoke in bed. All the hay in the stalls below would go up like tinder, he said. We wouldn't have put up with his rules, Don and I, but there were no other rooms to be had.

The livery was dark. You could hear the horses talking to themselves in their sleep. The windless air was sweet and suffocating with the aroma of their shit.

I took the outside stairs leading up to the sleeping rooms. Halfway up I heard the moan. I stopped, just standing there, feeling my stomach and bowels do terrible things. Despite the fact that I looked like a big, jovial, sun-baked farm boy, I was given to nerves and the stomach of an old man.

I eased my .45 from my holster.

I'd recognized the moan as belonging to my older brother, Don. You don't grow up with somebody and not know all the sounds he makes.

The night sky was black and starry. The animals below were still jibbering and snorting as they slept. The saloon music was distant now, and lonely in the hot night air.

I started climbing the stairs on tiptoes.

When I got to the landing, I found the door leading to the hall was ajar. I eased it open, gripping my gun tighter.

The shadows were so deep I had the momentary sense of going blind.

He moaned again, Don did, behind the door down the hall and to the right.

I tiptoed over, put my hand on the knob and gave it an inward push.

You could smell the dying on him. The blood and the seeping poisons.

In the pale light of the moon-facing window he lay on his cot as if the undertaker had already done him up. He lay unmoving with his hands folded primly on his belly and his raw, naked feet arranged precisely side by side, sticking straight up in a way that was almost funny.

Then I got foolish, because he was my brother and all, and because my other brother had passed on less than forty-eight hours ago.

I went straight into the room without considering that somebody might be behind the door.

Don moaned just as I reached his cot. I could see the wounds now, deep knife slashes across his neck and chest and arms. At least, I thought they were knife slashes.

The growl came up from the gravelike darkness behind the door. Hearing it, Don made a whimpering dying-animal noise that scared me because I knew he had only minutes to go.

I turned toward the growl and there they stood—a handsome, trim man in a dark suit much too hot for this kind of summer night, and a timber wolf so big and well-muscled he had to go at least 180 pounds. But size wasn't the only thing that made the lobo remarkable. His coat glowed silver—there was no other way to think of it except glowing—and his eyes glowed yellow, the color of a midnight moon.

The animal I'd never seen before. The man was plenty fa-

miliar. He was Schroeder, the man who'd hired us to rob the
bank he was part owner of. Afterward we were supposed to
split the money four ways—three for us brothers, one for
Schroeder. But he'd double-crossed us, killing Glen in the process. But we'd been suspicious of Schroeder and had stashed
the money under the foundation of a little white country
church. It had taken Schroeder a day and a half to figure out
that we'd double-crossed him right back.

Now he was here to get the rest of the money.

He used a few Indian words I didn't understand. And then
the lobo, growling again, sprang.

He went right for my gun hand, teeth tearing into my wrist,
knocking my gun to the floor before I could possibly fire a
shot.

The lobo then did to me what he'd done to my brother,
whose wounds I now knew had been caused by teeth, not a
knife.

He came for me then. He was so well-trained he didn't even
make much noise. He just worked his slashing teeth and ripping claws over my face and chest and belly.

I wasn't long awake, of course, not with all the pain, not
with all the blood.

There was just the lobo, that glowing lunging body, and
those haunted glowing eyes. . . .

For a time all I could hear was my own screaming. Then I
couldn't hear much of anything at all.

Part 2

Three months later, a judge named Emmanuel Byers sentenced
me to twelve years in territorial prison for my part in the bank
robbery.

You hear a lot of stories about prison, and most of them,
unfortunately, are true. I was put in a steel five-by-seven cell
on the south wing. There were two canvas hammocks for
sleeping and one chair for sitting. If you took instruction in
reading and writing, as I did, you were allowed to keep a book

in your cell. I learned to read and write so well that a lady reporter came out one time and wrote a piece about me. She was especially impressed with the fact that I could recite whole chunks of Shakespeare from memory.

Most of the time I did what most prisoners did. I worked at the quarry. The owner paid the warden eighty cents a day per man. The warden, it was said, paid forty cents to the territorial government and kept the rest for himself. This was in the summer. In the winter I worked on the river, cutting and storing ice for the Union Pacific Railroad. The warden had a cousin who was some kind of railroad vice-president, and the cousin was said to pay plenty for us men, with the warden and himself dividing the spoils.

The first man I bunked with was an Indian who had stabbed to death a man he insisted was a Negro. His lawyer eventually got an old Negro woman to swear that the dead man had been colored, which saved the Indian's life. The judge, learning that the victim was only one more shabby black man, called off the Indian's scheduled execution and let him go free after six months.

During all this time, I wrote letters to Gillian, a young woman I'd known my last two years on the farm. Her father had run the general store. She'd been my partner at harvest moon dances and on the sledding hills near Christmas. I loved her, though I'd never been able to quite say that out loud, and she loved me, a sentiment she expressed frequently. The first three or four times I'd written her, she hadn't responded. I imagined she was still upset over the fact that the man she loved was a bank robber, though as I pointed out in those letters, it was Don and Glen who'd been the robbers, I'd just sort of gone along this one time to see what it was like. Also to their credit, as I noted in those same letters, nobody had ever been killed or even shot during any of their robberies. Eventually she started writing back, though she admitted that she had to be careful her father didn't find out. He was a typical townsman in his belief that criminals of any stripe should be hanged and utterly forgotten.

About seven months into my sentence, I got a letter from Gillian with a new address. She said her father had found out about her writing me and had demanded that she stop. She'd refused. And so she was now living in the mountains in a gold-mining town where, after a few weeks, she'd met a dandy named Reeves, a man who reminded her an awful lot of Schroeder, at least as I'd described him. One day this Reeves got his photograph in the local paper. He'd just become co-owner of the town's largest bank. The other owner was a re-tiring Yankee major named Styles. This Reeves fellow would run everything from now on. The photograph showed that Gil-lian had good instincts. It was Schroeder himself, back in the banking business under a new name and in a new town. I wondered how long it would take him to arrange a robbery of his new bank.

One day at the quarry a fierce murderer named Maples, a man nobody troubled, not even the guards, started making fun of a fifteen-year-old boy who was serving time for killing his fa-ther. The boy was pretty and slender as a girl. It was whispered that Maples was sweet on the boy but that the boy wouldn't oblige him in any way. This day at the quarry Maples suddenly went crazy. For no reason that anybody could see, he grabbed the boy and hurled him into the water. Then Maples, still crazed and angrier than anybody had seen him, ran down into the water himself and grabbed the boy, who was just now getting up, and held the boy down under the water till he drowned. Several times the boy surfaced, screaming and puk-ing, but Maples just kept holding his head under until the deed was done. I started down into the water, but an old con who'd always looked out for me grabbed my arm and whispered, "Maples'll just kill you next, kid, if'n you go down there." And I knew he was right. And so I just stood there like all the other men in that hot dusty quarry and watched one man kill another.

My fourth year there tuberculosis walked up and down the cell blocks. More than two hundred men died in four months.

In all my time inside I had only one fight, when a new man, trying to impress everybody, made fun of my face, how it was all scarred up from the wolf that time. I don't know why it bothered me so much, but it did and I damned near killed him with my fists. For that I got what the guards called a "shower bath," which meant stripping me naked and directing a stream of high-pressure water from a hose to my face, chest, and crotch. When you fell down, they kept spraying away, till your balls were numb and your nose and mouth ran with blood. I was so sick with diarrhea afterward, I lost twenty pounds in the next week and a half.

In a way, even though I'd been angry when the warden told me I couldn't grow a beard, I was grateful for how scarred my face was. Sure, people looked away when they first saw me—I was a monster now, not a human being—but my appearance always reminded me of why, lying there in the doc's office right after the white wolf attacked me—why, despite the physical pain from the bites and slashes, and the mental pain of having seen both my brothers die—why I wanted to go on living.

I wanted to repay Schroeder for how he'd betrayed us. That was my one reason for existing.

Parole was not a major event. Early in the morning of a certain day, a guard took me forward to the warden's office, where I received ten dollars, a suggestion that I read every day the Bible the warden had just handed me, and a plea to stay away from bad people like myself. When you wait so many years for something, you expect to feel exuberant. I didn't feel much of anything at all. I just wanted to see Gillian and hear more about Schroeder.

A buggy took me to the train depot, where I sat for an hour on a hard little bench and let the locals gawk at me. It probably wasn't real hard to see that I'd just gotten out of prison.

By the time it was a year and a half old, the wolf was no longer a pup. Nor was it exactly a wolf. Its weight of 160 pounds marked its maturity, but the tasks it performed belonged not to the wolf family—which was essentially peaceful except for hunting—but to a predatory state that could only be man-made.

Schroeder, using methods a wolfer named Briney had shown him, built an enormous cage for the animal and let him out only when there was a task to be performed—or only when the wolf was being trained.

Schroeder believed that violence begat violence, and so he was remarkably cruel with the wolf. When the animal failed to perform properly, Schroeder beat the animal until it crawled and whimpered. Thus broken, it once again became malleable.

Schroeder trained the animal for eight months before testing it.

One chill March day, Schroeder took a husky about the same size as the wolf and put it in the cage, locked the door, and spoke aloud the Indian command for "kill," which was supposed to turn the wolf into a frenzied beast.

The wolf did not turn on the husky.

Schroeder spent an hour alternately calling out the command and threatening the animal.

When it was finally clear that the wolf would not attack the husky, Schroeder opened the cage, withdrew the dog, and then began beating the wolf until the animal seemed ready to turn on its master.

But Schroeder had been ready for that. He clubbed the animal across the skull with a ball bat. The animal collapsed into unconsciousness.

This training continued until the year that Schroeder met the Chase brothers and arranged for them to rob the bank of which he was part owner.

By then the wolf was obedient, as he proved when he murdered the one Chase brother and cruelly attacked the other.

The wolf no longer remembered the smell of smoky autumn winds and the taste of cool clear creek water and the beauty of sunflowers in the lazy yellow sunlight. He no longer even remembered his mother and father.

There was just the cage. There was just his master. There was just the whip. There was just the prey he was sometimes ordered to kill and rend.

He was still called a wolf, of course, by everyone who saw him.

But he was no longer a true wolf at all. He was something more. And something less.

On a fine sunny dawn, the roosters stirring, the wolf awoke to find that he had company in the large cage.

A raccoon had burrowed under the wire and was just now moving without any fear or inhibition toward the wolf.

Instinctively the wolf knew something was wrong with the raccoon. For one thing, such an animal was not very often brave, not around a wolf anyway.

And for another, there was the matter of the raccoon's mouth, and the curious foamy substance that bearded it. Something was very wrong with this raccoon.

It struck before the wolf had time to get to its feet.

It ripped into the wolf's forepaw and brought its jaws tight against the bone.

The wolf cried out in rage and pain, utterly surprised by the speed and savagery with which the raccoon had moved.

In moments the raccoon was dead, trapped in the teeth and jaws of the wolf as it slammed the chunky body of the raccoon again and again against the bars of the cage.

And then the wolf, still enraged, eviscerated it, much as the wolf had been taught to eviscerate humans.

Then it was done.

The wolf went back to his favorite end of the cage and lay down. His forepaw still hurt and he still cried some, but oddly, he was tired, exhausted, and knew he needed sleep.

When he woke, he stared down at the forepaw. A terrible burning had infected it.

He still wondered about the raccoon and where it had gotten all that nerve to come into his cage and attack him.

Soon enough the wolf went back to sleep, the inexplicable drowsiness claiming him once again.

Part 3

In the summer of '98 the folks in Rock Ridge were just starting
to sink the poles and string the wire for telephones. I knew
this because all three of the town's newspapers told me about
it right on the front page, in the kind of civic-pride tone most
mining-town papers use to prove that they really are, after all,
a bunch of law-abiding Christian people.

On a sunny June morning filled with bird song and silver
dew, I sat in a crowded restaurant located between a lumberyard and a saddlery. The place smelled of hot grease, tobacco
smoke, and the sweaty clothes of the laborers.

Near midnight I'd pitched from my dry and dusty mount
and taken a room down the street at the Excelsior Hotel. I
didn't know exactly what to expect from Gillian yet.

According to the *Gazeteer,* Rock Ridge was a town of four
thousand souls, five banks, twelve churches (I found it curious
that the *Gazeteer* folks would list banks before houses of the
Lord), two schools, ten manufacturing plants, and a police department of "eighteen able and trustworthy men, among the
finest in all the West." (On a following page was a small story
about how a prisoner had died of a "mysterious fall" in his
jail cell, and how his widowed mother was planning to sue the
town, which of course told me a hell of a lot more about the
police force than all of the newspaper's glowing adjectives.)

I was just about to ask for another cup of coffee when the
front door opened up and a man in a dark blue serge uniform
with shiny gold buttons on the coat came in, the coat resem-
bling a Union Army jacket that had been stripped of all insig-
nia. He wore a Navy Colt strapped around his considerable
belly and carried in his right hand a long club that had an
impressive number of knicks and knocks on it, not to mention
a few dark stains that were likely blood that soap hadn't been
able to cleanse. The contrast of his natty white gloves only
made the club look all the more brutal. He had a square and
massive blond head and intelligent blue eyes that were curi-

ously sorrowful. He was probably my age, on the lee side of thirty.

He made a circuit, the policeman, like a mayor up for re-election, ultimately offering a nod, a handshake, a smile or a soft greeting word to virtually everybody in the place. And they grinned instantly and maybe a little too heartily, like kids trying hard not to displease a mean parent. They were afraid of him, and some of them even despised him, and the more they grinned and the more they laughed at his little jokes, the more I sensed their fear.

When he was done, he walked over to a plump serving woman who had long been holding a lone cup of coffee for him. He thanked her, looked around, and then settled his eyes on me.

He came over, pulled out a chair, sat down and put forth a hand that looked big and strong enough to choke a full-grown bear.

"You'd be Mr. Chase?"

I nodded.

"Got your name at the hotel desk. Always like to know who's staying over in our little town."

I said nothing, just watched him. Hick law, I figured, trying to intimidate me into pushing on. He wouldn't know anything about my time in prison, but he wouldn't want me around town, either, not unless I had some reason for being here.

"Name's Ev Hollister. I'm the chief of police."

"Nice to meet you."

"This is a friendly place."

"Seems to be."

"And we're always happy to welcome strangers here."

"I appreciate that."

"Long as we know their business." When he finished with this line, he shot me one of his empty white smiles.

"May be looking for a place to settle."

"You have any special trade?"

Yeah, I wanted to say, bank robbing. Which bank would you suggest I hit first? "Nothing special. Little of this, little of that."

"Little of this, little of that, huh?"

"Uh-huh." I gave him one of my own empty white smiles.
"All strictly legal of course."

"Glad you said that."

"Oh?"

He took some of his coffee and wiped his mouth with the
back of his hand. He was proud of those hands the way a man
is proud of a certain gun. They were outsize, powerful hands.
"Cholera came through here three months ago."

"Bad stuff."

"Struck the Flannery family especially hard."

"They kin of yours?"

"No, but they gave this town two of the best officers I ever
had. Brothers. About your age and build. Damned good men."
He looked at me straight and hard. "You ever thought of being
a police officer?"

I could imagine the men back in territorial prison listening
in on this conversation. They'd be howling.

"Guess not, Chief."

"Well, if you stay around here, you should consider it. The
work is steady and the pay ain't bad, forty-eight dollars a
month. And folks have a lot of respect for a police officer."

My mind drifted back to the mother of the youngster who'd
died in a "mysterious fall" in his jail cell. I wondered how
much respect she had for police officers.

"Well, I sure do appreciate the interest, Chief. How about
I think it over for a couple days?"

"Lot of men would jump at the chance to be on my police
force." There was just a hint of anger in his tone. He wasn't
used to getting turned down.

I put forth my hand.

He stood up and made a big pretense of not seeing my hand
sticking out there.

"You think it over," he said, and left.

The smile was back on him as soon as he reached the front
of the place, where he flirted with a couple of ladies at a table
and told a bawdy joke to an old man with a hearing horn. I
knew it was bawdy by the way the old guy laughed, that burst
of harsh pleasure.

Through the window, I watched Chief Hollister make his

way down the street. The water wagon was out already, soaking down the dust as much as possible. A telephone pole was being planted on a corner half a block away. Ragged summertime kids stood watching, fascinated. Later they'd spin tales of how different a place Rock Ridge would be with telephones.

Up in the hills you could see the mines, watch the smoke rise and hear the hard rattling noise of the hoists and pumps and mills. In prison an ex-miner had told me what it was like to be 2,300 feet down when the temperature hit 120 and they had to lower ice down the shaft because that low your tools got so hot you sometimes couldn't hold them. And sometimes you got so dehydrated and sick down there that you started puking up blood—all so two or three already rich men in New York could get even richer.

And who would keep all those miners in line if they ever once started any kind of real protest?

None other than the dead-eyed man I'd just met, Rock Ridge's esteemed police chief, Ev Hollister. Over in Leadville they'd recently given a police chief and two of his officers $500 each for killing three miners who were trying to lead a strike. Law was the same in all mining towns.

I paid my money, went down to the livery and got my horse, and rode out to see Gillian.

Part 4

It was a hardscrabble ranch house with a few hardscrabble outbuildings on the edge of some jack pines in the foothills of the blue, aloof mountains. It was not quite half a mile out of town.

In the front yard a very pretty little girl of eight or so spoke with great intimacy to a dun pony no taller than she was. The little girl wore a blue gingham dress that set off her shining blond pigtails just fine. When she looked me full in the face, I saw the puzzlement in her eyes, the same puzzlement as in mine. She favored her mother, and that tumbled me into sorrow. I guess I hadn't any right to expect that Gillian would go without a man all these years. As for the little girl staring at me—I was long conditioned to people studying my scars, repelled and snake-charmed at the same time, but then I remembered my new blond beard that covered the scars. They couldn't be seen now except in the strongest sunlight. Yet the little girl still stared at me.

"I don't think I've ever seen eyes that blue," I said.

She smiled.

"Are you enjoying the summer?"

She nodded. "I'm Annie. I bet I know who you are. You're Chase. My mom talks about you all the time."

It was a day of orange butterflies and white fluffy dandelions and quick silken birds the color of blooded sunsets. And now fancy little conversations.

"I was going to write you a letter once," Annie said.

"You were?"

"Uh-huh, but Mom said I better not because of your major."

She smiled, sweet and shy and pure little girl there in the bright prairie morning.

"She said you were in the cavalry and that you had a real mean major named Thomkins who didn't want you to get letters."

I handled it best I could. "He was pretty mean all right."

"My mom's inside."

"You think it'd be all right if I went and saw her?"

"She's baking bread. She'll give you some if you ask."

I grinned. "Then I'll make sure to ask."

She put her tiny hand up in mine and led me up the earthen path to the slab front door of the ranch house. As we walked, I saw to the west a hillock where a well had been dug, probably an artesian that had failed because the water would not rise. Easier to walk to the distant creek and lug it back in buckets. Or make one of those homemade windmills you could now buy kits for.

I could smell bread baking. It reminded me of my own ma and our own kitchen, back before all the troubles came to us Chase boys, and for a moment I was Annie's age again, all big eyes and empty rumbling belly.

Annie pushed open the door and took me into the cool shadows of the house. The layout seemed to be big front room with a hallway leading to big kitchen in back. Between were two bedrooms set one on each side of the hallway. There wasn't much furniture, a tumbledown couch and chairs, a painting of an aggrieved Jesus, and a splendid vase lamp with an ornately painted globe. The flooring was hardwood shined slick and bright and covered occasionally with shaggy blue throw rugs.

In the kitchen, I found Gillian just taking a loaf of bread from the oven and setting it on the windowsill to cool. To clear room, she had to *shush* a cardinal away, and looked guilty doing it.

When she saw me there, led in by her little daughter, her face went blank and she paused, as if considering what to feel. I'd once promised Gillian I'd marry her, and never had; and when I was sent off to prison, she in turn promised she'd wait. But the birth of Annie had put the lie to that. I guess neither one of us knew what to feel, standing here and facing each other across a canyon of eight hard and lonely years.

She was still pretty—not beautiful, not cute, pretty—with a long fragile neck and fine shining golden hair, Annie's hair, and a frank blue gaze that was never quite without a hint of grief. She'd had one of those childhoods that not even a long life could outlive. She wore gingham, which she always had, and a white frilly apron, and even from here I could see how years of work had made her quick, slender hands raw. She was neither old nor young now, but that graceful in-between when a girl becomes full woman. She looked good as hell to me, and I felt tongue-lost as a boy, having no idea what to say.

"This is my mom," Annie said.

I laughed. "I'm glad you told me that, honey."

"He wants some bread."

"Oh, he does, does he?" Gillian said.

"And jam," Annie said definitively.

"Doesn't he know how to speak for himself?" Gillian said.

"He's so hungry, he can't talk."

I wondered, what had happened to that shy little girl who'd greeted me on the walk?

Gillian gaped at me a moment longer and said, "That sure is some beard you got there, Chase."

A few minutes later Gillian shooed Annie outside and set about fixing me up with that warm fresh bread and strawberry jam her daughter wanted me to have.

As she sliced the bread and poured us both coffee, she asked me how my first night here had gone, and I told her, with a laugh, all about how the chief of police had tried to recruit me.

"Maybe you should do it," she said.

"Huh?"

She set down my bread and coffee, slid the jam pot over to my side of the table, and then sat down across from me. "Maybe you should do it."

"Be a policeman?"

"There are worse ways to make a living."

"Seems you're forgetting where I've been the last few years."

"Hollister doesn't know where you've been. And he wouldn't have any reason to check unless you did something wrong."

We didn't speak for a time. She sat there and watched me eat. I tried not to smack my lips. I'd shared a cell with a man who snorted when he ate. I knew how aggravating noisy eaters could be.

When only my coffee was left, I looked up at her. "I'd appreciate it if you'd tell me about Schroeder."

"I was hoping you'd forget about Schroeder. Anyway, he calls himself Reeves now."

"What does he do?"

"Runs a bank. Has a partner who's very old, and lives in a big mansion by himself."

"The bank been robbed since 'Reeves' bought in?"

"No, but I imagine it's just a matter of time." She watched me the way Annie had when I'd first come into the yard. "Why don't you forget about him, Chase? That part of your life is gone now."

"He killed my brothers."

"They'd want you to go on with your life, Chase." She'd known both my brothers. While to the town they'd been bank robbers, to her they were never more than rambunctious boys who'd eventually settle down. "I knew them, Chase, and what they wanted for you. They didn't want you to be the way they were."

And then she was crying.

We were sitting in the kitchen with the scent of bread sweet on the air and a jay on the window ledge and the breeze soft and warm on the underside of the curtains.

And I didn't know what to do.

I just went over to her and knelt down beside her and took her tiny hand and held it gently as I could. I kept saying over and over, "Oh, Gillian, come on now; oh, Gillian, please," and things like that, but neither words nor touches helped, she just sat there and cried without sound, her frail body shaking with her grief.

And then Annie was in the doorway saying, "Did Chase hurt you, Mommy?"

Gillian got herself together quickly, brought apron to nose and eyes to daub tears, and cleared her throat sternly to speak. "No, hon, he didn't hurt me."

"I wouldn't like him if he hurt you, Mommy."

"It's fine, honey, really. You go on back outside now."

Annie looked at me for a time, confused and ready to hate me if Gillian said to, and then turned and slowly left the doorway.

We sat in silence again until she said, "I don't want you to come out here anymore."

"Oh, God, Gillian. You don't know how long I've waited to—"

"I was hoping prison would change you. Force you to grow up and forget about Reeves." She sounded as if she were about to start crying again. "But it hasn't. I was just fooling myself all those years while I waited."

I wanted to point out that she'd been doing more than "waiting," what with having a daughter during that time.

But the words died in my throat, and I felt guilty for making Gillian carry on this way.

She put her head down on the table and started crying again, her slender shoulders shaking miserably. I leaned over and kissed her on the back of the head and slipped out through the gathering blue shadows of the afternoon.

As I walked over to my horse, Annie looked up from combing her pony and said, "Is my mommy still sad?"

I swung up in the saddle and said, "Right now she is. But if you go in and see her, she won't be."

She nodded solemnly, put down the brush she was using and set off walking to the ranch house.

Part 5

"You got a name, son?"

"Chase."

"You got a first name?"

"Sorry. Guess people usually call me plain 'Chase.' First name's Robert."

"Well, son, I wish I could help you, but I can't. See that Indian out there on the loading dock?"

"Yessir."

"That sonofabitch does the work of three white men and he don't complain half as much as they do."

"Good worker, huh?"

"Good? Hell, great. That's why I don't need nobody right now. But I tell ya. If you're around town in three, four weeks, you try me again, 'cause you never can tell."

"That's right. You never can tell."

"Good luck, son, you shouldn't have no problem, big strong young man like you."

"Yessir. And thank you, sir."

That's how it went all afternoon. I went up and down the alleys, knocking on the back doors of every business I could find, and it was always the same story. Just hired me somebody last week; or business been a little slow lately; or why don't ya try down the street, son?

Near dusk, when I was walking into the lumberyard, I saw

Chief Hollister and he gave me a smirk as if he knew that I
wasn't getting anywhere and that I'd been damned foolish to
turn down his offer.

As I had been.

Part 6

That night, I sat in a chair next to Annie's bed reading aloud
a book called *Standard Fairy Tales*. Nearby a kerosene lantern
flickered light through the cottage.

"How tall was Jack's beanstalk?"

"Didn't you already ask me that?"

She giggled. "Uh-huh."

"It was eighty feet tall."

"Last time you said it was sixty feet tall."

"I lied."

She giggled again. "You don't lie. My mom says you're a
good man."

I looked up from my book to Gillian in the rocker in the
corner. She was knitting. The rocker squeaked pleasantly back
and forth, back and forth, as a slow summer rain pattered on
the full-grown leaves of the elm trees on either side of the
house.

"You said I was a good man?" I asked Gillian.

She smiled her easy smile. "I believe I said something like
that, yes."

"Well, I just want you to know that I'm mighty grateful.
It's nice to have somebody thinking nice thoughts about me."

"Did you really like my roast beef tonight?"

"I liked it very much."

"You didn't think it was tough?"

"I thought it was tender."

"You really mean that?"

"I really mean that."

Truth was, the meat had been tough as hell. Cooking had
never been one of Gillian's strengths. Great baker—breads and
rolls and pies—but terrible, terrible cook.

"I like to close my eyes and hear you read, Chase. I like it as much as Annie does."

"I'll read some more."

"I remember when you wrote and told me—when you were away, I mean—how that man taught you to read."

"When you were in the Army?" Annie said.

"Yes." I looked over at Gillian again. "When I was in the Army."

"Tell me about the Army. You promised."

"When we have a little more time, I'll tell you."

"Don't we have time now?"

"Nope."

"How come?"

"Because we've got to find out what the giant's going to do to Jack."

"Go on, Chase," Gillian said. "Annie and I'll close our eyes and you read."

So they closed their eyes and I read.

Later on that night, after Annie fell asleep, Gillian and I went down to the willow by the creek that ran in the back of her yard, and made love standing up, the way we used to sometimes in the old days.

When her dress was down and my pants were up, we walked along the creek listening to the frogs and the crickets and the owls. The rain had stopped and everything smelled minty and fresh in the midnight moon.

"You never did answer that one letter of mine, Chase."

"Which letter was that?"

"The one where I asked you if you'd ever say you loved me."

"I guess I figured you knew."

We walked a little more in silence. Stars filled the sky and everything smelled cool and fresh after the rain.

"Annie sure likes you."

"I sure like her."

"Says she hopes she sees you some more."

"Hope I see her some more."

We came to the small leg of river that ran below a railroad bridge. The water was silver in the moonlight.

I skipped rocks across the surface and she laughed and said it was good to see me acting so young; she'd been afraid that prison would make of me what prison had earlier made of an uncle of hers, a scared old man in a thirty-year-old's body.

About halfway back to the cabin I said, "Who's Annie's father, Gillian?"

"I was wondering when you'd ask me that."

"She's mine, isn't she?"

"Yes," Gillian said, "yes, she is."

Part 7

Just in case you think that a policeman's life is filled with the kind of derring-do you read about in yellow-backs or eastern newspapers, consider the fact that I spent my first two days walking all over town handing out circulars that came from Chief Hollister. They read:

> Cleanup notice is hereby given to property owners that all rubbish and disease breeding matter must be removed from their premises at once, or the work will be done by my officers at the owners' expense. The town board, sitting as a board of health, has ordered all pigsty and other nuisances to be abated. This order will be rigidly enforced.
>
> (Signed) Chief of Police, Ev. Hollister

As you might expect, humans being humans, very little in the town was cleaned up by the owners, so most of us men, fine and shiny in our blue serge uniform coats with the bright brass buttons and the snug white gloves—most of us had to do the cleaning up. The men called it the "pig shit detail," and you got on it by drawing the smallest straw. I got on it twice in three weeks, which meant that Gillian had to do some extra hard cleaning of my uniform. But I don't mean to sound as if I was unhappy. I wasn't. My second weekend as an of-

ficer, Gillian and I got married, and my third weekend we sat
Annie down and told her that I was her father and that we'd
all be living together now forever. Annie cried and Gillian
cried and I tried not to, but as I hugged them to me, I couldn't
help myself. I cried at least a little bit, too. The hell of it was,
I wasn't even sure why we were all crying. It was something
the two females understood, not me.

In my first three weeks as an officer, I did not get into a
gunfight, ward off an Indian attack, save a stagecoach from
plunging into a ravine, rush an infant from a burning building,
or even help an old lady across a busy street.

What I did do was spend from five in the afternoon till
midnight six nights a week walking around the town and making sure that everything was locked up tight. Because what
you had in a town like this, a mining town where bitter men
drank a lot, was robberies. So my job was to walk a six-block
area every night and rattle the doors on most of the businesses.
I had been given the right to shoot on sight any burglar who
offered me any resistance at all. I had also been given the key
to most businesses so that in case I had to get inside, sus-
pecting that a burglar might have hidden in there during business hours, I didn't have to bother Hollister or any of the
merchants who were all home, presumably sleeping. At first,
having the keys made me nervous—I'd never been one for
much responsibility—but then as Gillian said over Sunday dinner, "You should be proud the merchants have that kind of
trust in you, Chase."

Somewhere during those first few weeks, I gave up any
notion of getting back at Reeves. I had convinced myself that
Gillian was right, my brothers would have wanted me to pick
up my life after prison and do something decent with it. Every
once in a while I'd glimpse Reeves swaggering down the street
but I'd just turn my head and look the other way. I had a wife
and daughter now and they were all that mattered.

Summer became Indian summer and Indian summer became
autumn. By now most people in town knew me and seemed
to like me. I enjoyed the feeling.

"That uniform looks good on you."

"Thank you."

"I'm glad I spotted you in the restaurant that day." It was just afternoon, and you could smell the whiskey on him but you couldn't exactly say he was drunk as yet.

I nodded. "Me, too, Chief."

I'd been going to the back for a drink of water, passing Hollister's office on the way. He'd called me in and started talking, sitting behind his desk with his feet up and his hands folded on his stomach.

He smiled. "Merchants're always asking me how I think you're doing."

"The keys?"

He nodded. "Yup. They want to make sure you're the kind of man they can trust. They like you and they want to keep it that way."

"So do I."

"We had a fellow here—three, four years ago, I guess—good fellow, too, least he was when he started, but by the end he was breaking into the stores himself and then reporting all these burglaries."

"He might have been good but he doesn't sound too smart."

Hollister started to say something but then peeked out his window and saw a fancy black surrey pull up outside the two-story red-brick police station. The surrey belonged to his wife. She was always out and about in it. She had the kind of red-haired society-lady good looks that went just fine with a surrey like this one, and so naturally people resented her and whispered tales of her supposed infidelity. The police officers especially liked to tell such tales. It gave them a way to get back at Hollister, who always made it clear that he was at least one cut above us. He had been brought here by the merchants, and it was with the merchants he was friends. I'd even seen him eat lunch up to Casey's Restaurant with Reeves.

A minute later his eyes strayed from me and fixed on something over my shoulder. He smiled in a way that made him look ten years younger.

"Come on in and meet officer Chase," Hollister said in a smooth social voice.

I turned and saw her. She was a beauty all right, cat-green eyes to complement the silken red hair, nose and mouth and neck classical as a piece of sculpture. As she came into the room, she brought a scent of sweet cachet with her. In her crisp white blouse and full, dark green skirt, her hair caught up with a comb at the back of her head, she looked like a very beautiful schoolmarm.

"H-How are you d-doing?" she said to her husband.

That was the dirtiest part of the joke about Mrs. Hollister. Here you had all this beauty and grace and poise—she'd been schooled back East—and yet it was all marred by her very bad stutter, something she was clearly ashamed of. A lot of beautiful women like to flirt. They are saucy of eye and brazen of gait. But not Claire Hollister. She always walked with her eyes downcast, moving quickly, as if she wished she were invisible.

"Just a minute, hon," Hollister said, taking her hand and stroking it gently. "I'll finish with Chase here and you can tell me about your day."

Hollister was a hard man and a dangerous man and a proud man, yet right now, speaking so softly to his wife, I heard real tenderness in him and I was almost shocked by it. He had a locked room upstairs where he took prisoners at night after he'd been drinking awhile. There was no tenderness in him then. None at all.

"I just wanted to say you're doing a good job, Chase, and that I'm glad you got married. A man needs some responsibility. Otherwise he's not much better than a hobo."

It was like an awards ceremony, all the nice words, only there wasn't any plaque.

"Thanks," I said.

I turned toward the door. Claire Hollister nervously got out of my way. She was a skittish woman, which made no sense with that beautiful sad face of hers.

"N-Nice to m-meet y-you," she said, and dropped her eyes, ashamed of herself.

"Nice to meet you," I said, and left.

Part 8

With all the walking I did, I was pretty tired when I got home every night around one o'clock, the honky-tonk piano music still in my ears, the beery scent of the taverns I patrolled still on me. I'd eat the light meal Gillian had set out for me and then I'd go into Annie's room and kneel down by her bed and just look at her little face made silver by the moonlight, the stray damp wisp of blond hair making her look even younger than she was, and then I'd close my eyes and say the best prayer I knew how, a prayer that Annie and Gillian would always be safe in the invisible arms of the Lord, and a prayer that Hollister would never find out about my prison record and that I'd go on to be a good policeman who eventually got promoted. And then I'd lean over and kiss Annie on the forehead, her kid skin warm to my lips, and then I'd go into our bedroom and strip down to my underwear and climb in next to Gillian and hold her gently and think of how long she'd waited for me and how true she'd been and how her faith had given me this new life of mine, and all I could pray for then was that I would never give in to my worst self and go after Reeves.

The first time I ever saw Lundgren and Mars they were stepping off the train just about suppertime of an early November evening. Kids and dogs ran down the dark streets toward mothers calling them in for the night.

I don't suppose anybody else would have made anything special of them. They were just two middle-aged men in dark business suits, each carrying a carpetbag, each wearing a bowler, one tall and thin, the other short and heavyset. They stood on the depot platform looking around at the town. They tried very hard to give the impression that they were important men.

I was making my early rounds. After some months as a policeman, I'd already developed flat feet, bunions, and a suspicious eye for everybody and everything, and that included these two strangers.

I decided to follow them. They went down the boardwalk past the noise of player pianos and the smells of cigars and the laughter of whores, up past the livery where the Mex was rubbing down a horse that had just been brought in, and down past the gunsmith's.

I stayed half a block behind them, rattling doorknobs as I went, making sure the town was locked up tight. In the hills there was talk of a miner's strike. Socialism was just starting to get a grip on the miners. Hollister had told us to watch out for trouble.

This particular night, the two strangers ended their walk at the front door of the Whitney Hotel, the town's best hotel, and a place that always boasts of two presidents having slept in its hallowed beds.

When I'd given them sufficient time to find rooms for themselves, I walked up to the massive registration desk, turned the guest register around and stared at the names I'd been looking for.

"I don't remember inviting you to look at our registration book," said Hartley, the night man. Because he wears a cravat and attends all the musicales at the opera house, he seems to find himself superior to people like me.

But by now I didn't care what he'd said. I had their names and that was all I wanted.

"Next time I'd appreciate it if you'd ask me first," he said, petulant as ever.

"I'll be sure to do that," I said, being just sarcastic enough so he'd get the message but not so sarcastic that he could say anything.

Half an hour later I sat on the stoop of the police station, taking my dinner break.

In chill evening, the first stars showing, I heard the jingle of a bicycle bell and here came Gillian with Annie up on the handlebars, bringing me my dinner as they did every once in a while as sort of a special treat.

"It's getting nippy," Gillian said, handing me down a roast beef sandwich and an apple. "You can smell winter in the wind sometimes now."

Annie came over and sat down next to me. She couldn't get

used to the idea yet that I was really her father.

"Did you shoot anybody tonight, Daddy?"

"Nope. But I wrestled a bear."

She giggled. "You did not."

"And when I got done with the bear, I wrestled an alligator."

More giggling. "Huh-uh."

"What're we going to do with this kid, anyway?" I said to Gillian. "She doesn't believe anything her old pappy tells her."

"Mrs. Dirks sent a note home with Annie today. She said Annie's one of her best students."

I gave Annie a hug and she gave me a wet kiss. The temperature was dropping fast. Her little nose and cheeks were cold as creek stones.

"I'll have some stew hot when you get home."

"I'd appreciate that."

"I told Annie that maybe Sunday the three of us could go see the motor car over in Carleton County."

"That'd be fun."

"Goodie!" Annie said.

A minute later Annie was back up on the handlebars and Gillian was turning the bike in the direction of our cottage.

"Sleep tight," I said to Annie.

"I love you, Daddy."

"I love you, too, sweet potato."

And then they were gone, phantoms in the gray, starry gloom, the two most important people in my life.

Around ten I was finishing up with my second long patrol and just thinking of walking over to the bridge to roll myself a cigarette—I liked watching the river flow, and I couldn't even tell you why—when I looked down the street and saw two familiar shapes standing in the street in front of the Whitney Hotel. One tall, one short. Lundgren and Mars.

They stood for a time finishing off stogies, and then they flipped the butts into the street and walked on over to the livery. The Mex fixed them up with horses and saddles.

Five minutes later, seeming in no particular hurry, and

seeming easy and confident on their mounts, the two of them
rode out of town. I thought of going after them—they made
me damned curious—but I knew it would take too long to get
a horse saddled and follow them.

I stood there in the middle of the dark street, the bawdy
sounds of saloons behind me in the distance, the sounds of
their horses loud but fading into the night.

Where would they be going at this time of night?

Part 9

In the morning, after chores, I went into town earlier than
usual. I couldn't stop thinking about Lundgren and Mars and
what they might be doing in town.

The roan was fresh when I got him at the livery. A Mexican
rubbing down a palomino gave me directions to the Reeves
place.

An hour later, just as I rounded a copse of pines, I saw a
massive Victorian house, a tower soaring up the center and
seeming to touch the sky; a half-dozen spires; and three full
floors. The front porch was vast and shadowy; the eaves elab-
orately carved. The grounds, enclosed within a black iron
fence, looked relentlessly groomed. To the west was a large
stable, to the east a vivid red barn.

It would take a whole lot of bank robbing to buy a place
like this.

Just as I nudged the roan forward, I heard a rifle being
cocked behind me.

"Howdy," a man's voice said.

He knew I'd heard his Winchester.

I tugged the roan to a halt.

"I said howdy, mister. Ain't you gonna howdy me back?"

"I'll howdy you all over the place if you'll put the rifle
down."

"Just want to know your business out here."

"Far as I could tell, this is a public road."

"Yeah, but you ain't been on the road for ten minutes now.
You been on Mr. Reeves' property."

A horsefly, having partaken of the splash the roan had just emptied on the road, buzzed near my face, loud in the sunny silence.

"You gonna say anything, mister?"

"I'm gonna say that I'm an old friend of Mr. Reeves'."

"No offense, mister, in case you are and all, but a lot of people say that to get inside here. They're usually looking for handouts."

"With me it's the truth, though."

"You got any way of proving that?"

"You just go tell Mr. Reeves that the man who helped him with his bank in Dunkirk is here."

"Didn't know Mr. Reeves ever lived in Dunkirk."

"You do now."

Now it was the guard's turn for quiet.

The cry of jays and the screech of hawks played against the lazy baying of the cows.

His shod horse took a few steps forward and he came around so he could take his first good look at me.

"You don't look like no businessman, son. Don't take that personal."

"Didn't say I was a businessman. All I said was that I'd given Mr. Reeves a little help."

He was fat and fifty but quick for his size, and his dark eyes gave you the feeling that he was capable of just about anything. He held a Winchester in gloved hands and spat tobacco in sickening streams, chawing not a habit I'd ever taken to as either participant or spectator. His sweated white Stetson looked too big for him, as if his head was shrinking in the heat.

"Name's Hanratty. What's yours?"

I told him. He looked as if he thought it was a fake.

"You ride ahead of me," he said.

"Past the gate?"

He nodded.

We went inside, along a cinder path, to the right of which an old black man was now raking leaves.

We ground-tied the horses in front of the long, shadowy porch. He took me up and inside the house. Two feet inside, a tiny, white-haired man in white shirt, paisley vest, and dark trousers appeared. He had a tanned simian face with bright brown intelligent eyes. He reminded me of a smart monkey. He carried a dust cloth in his right hand and a small bottle of sweet-smelling furniture polish in the other.

"Fenton, this man would like to see Mr. Reeves."

Fenton looked at me as if Hanratty had just told him some kind of joke.

"I see," he said.

"He looks unlikely as hell, I got to admit that." Hanratty laughed.

"Very unlikely," Fenton said. "And the nature of your business, sir?"

"Mr. Reeves and I once did a little business with a bank in Dunkirk."

"Dunkirk, sir?"

"Yes, he'll know what I mean."

"I see."

"So I wish you'd tell him I'm out here."

Fenton glanced at Hanratty again, then disappeared down the hall.

"I got to get back to my post," Hanratty said. "Good luck." He grinned and leaned to my ear. "Reeves ain't any nicer than he was when you knew him before, believe me."

I grinned back. "Nice to know some things never change."

I stood alone in the shadowy vestibule. Directly ahead of me a large, carpeted staircase rose steeply to a landing that glowed in sunlight. On the wall of the landing was a huge painting of Reeves in an Edwardian suit, trying hard to look like the illegitimate son of J. P. Morgan or some other robber baron. To my right was a wall with three doors on it, each leading to hushed rooms. The floor was parquet; almost everything else was dark wood, mostly mahogany. The effect was of being in a very fancy library.

Far down the hall, to the left of the staircase, a door opened. Footsteps—and Fenton—approached.

"Mr. Reeves will see you now."

He stayed several feet away. He didn't know what I had but he sure didn't want to catch it.

I went down the hall, the rowels of my spurs musical in the silence. I knocked on the door Fenton had just left, but nobody responded.

The door was open an inch or so. I pushed it open a bit more and peeked through. The room was a den with expensive leather furniture, a mahogany desk big enough to have a hoe-down on, and enough leather-bound books to humble a scholar. There was a genuine Persian rug on the floor, and an imposing world globe sitting in its cradle on the wide ledge of a mullioned window.

I still didn't see anybody.

I took two steps inside, my feet finding the Persian rug. By the fourth step, hearing a human breath behind me, I'd figured it out, but by then it was too late. He did the same thing he'd done to me that night in my brother's room.

He came out from behind the door and brought something heavy down across the back of my skull.

My hat went flying and so did I.

"You sonofabitch. What the hell're you doing here?"

I was still on the floor, just now starting to pull myself up. I daubed the back of my head with careful fingers, finding a mean little lump and some blood.

Reeves sat behind his desk, a snifter of brandy near his hand. He was older and heavier, the hair gray-shot, and these days he looked like a successful politician in his dark suit and white shirt and black string tie.

"You're lucky I didn't kill you."

"I don't feel so lucky," I said, touching the back of my head again.

I got to my feet in sections and stood wobbling in front of his desk. Not until then did I realize that he'd slipped my .45 from its holster. I wondered how long I'd been out.

"As far as I'm concerned, our business is finished," he said. "You understand me?"

I reached down and picked up my dusty black hat and got it set just right on my head. I was taking everything slow and easy so as to not give him any warning.

I grabbed his snifter and splashed brandy in his face and

then I dove across his desk and hit him twice before he finally pitched over backward in his fancy leather chair.

I could hear Fenton running down the hall—then banging on the closed door.

"Sir? Sir? Are you all right?"

He knew better than to let Fenton in. Otherwise I'd tell Fenton a few things he just might not know about his boss man.

"I'm fine. I just knocked the globe over is all."

"You're sure, sir?"

"Of course I'm sure. Now you get back to your dusting. We're having company tonight, remember?"

"Yes, sir." Fenton didn't believe him, but what could he say?

We got to our feet and took our respective places—him in back of the desk, ever in command, and me, dusty and busted, in front—ever the supplicant.

"You killed my brothers," I said.

He smiled. "Does that mean you're going to kill me?" But before I could answer, he said, "I've got something for you."

He opened a drawer, pulled out my .45 and slid it across the polished surface of his desk.

"Pick it up."

I just stared at it.

"Go ahead. Pick it up."

I picked it up.

"Now ease the hammer back and point the gun right at me."

He was a smug sonofabitch, sitting there in a couple hundred dollars' worth of clothes and a lifetime's worth of arrogance.

I had the gun but he was giving the orders.

"You're right, Chase—if that's what you're calling yourself these days—I did kill your brothers, and you know why? Because they let me. Because they were just like you, a couple of goddamned farm boys who just couldn't wait to rob banks because it was going to be so easy and so much fun." He shook his head. "Prison's filled with farm boys, as you no doubt found out." He leaned forward. He was het up now, a blaze-eyed minister delivering the truth to the unwashed. "It's a rough goddamned business, Chase, and I ought to know. I've survived in it twenty years now and it's made me a rich man and I haven't spent one hour behind bars."

"What happened to your partner after we stuck up his bank?"

The smile again. "Well, for once my partner figured something out for himself—figured out that I helped set up the robbery to make things go easy. He was about to turn me in, so I killed him."

"You killed him?"

He shook his head, as if he were trying to explain a complicated formula to a chimp.

"I killed him, Chase. And that's the goddamned point which you never will understand. It's the nature of this business—of any business—to do what you need to when you need to." He sat back and made little church steeples of his well-tended fingers. "I'm able to do what I need to. How about you? Can you point that .45 of yours at me and pull the trigger?"

"You sonofabitch."

"Never forget I gave you this chance."

I cursed him again.

"Show me you're not a dumb goddamned farm boy like your brothers."

I wanted to kill him, I really did, but I also knew that I wouldn't. Not under these circumstances.

"Go ahead, Chase. Otherwise you're wasting my time and your own."

The gun felt good and right in my hand, and I could imagine the jerk of his body when the bullet struck his heart, and the red bloom of blood on the front of his lacy white shirt, and I could see my poor brother Don dying from the cuts and slashes the wolf had put on him, and I wanted so bad to pull that trigger, to empty the gun in his face.

"You sonofabitch."

"You said that before, Chase. Several times." He stared at me. "I want you to learn something from this."

I didn't say anything.

"I want you to learn that you should go somewhere and

buy yourself a little farm and find yourself a nice plump little farm girl and marry her and have yourself a bunch of kids and forget all about your dead brothers and forget all about me.'' He nodded to the .45 in my hand. ''Because you had your chance. And you chose not to take it. And so what's the point of wasting your life hating me or trying to pay me back?''

Before, he'd reached to a right-hand drawer. Now he reached to a left-hand one.

He drew out a pack of greenbacks bank-wrapped with a paper strip around the middle.

He threw the pack on the desk.

''There's five thousand dollars there. That's about what your cut of the job would have been, as I recall. Probably a bit more, in fact. Take it, Chase; take it and get on that horse of yours and get the hell out of this county—get the hell out of this state, in fact—and go start the kind of life I told you to. All right?''

I stared at the greenbacks. I just kept thinking of my brother Glen's eyes when I'd cradled him in my arms as he was dying off the side of the stagecoach road, after Reeves had double-crossed us and taken the money and killed Glen because Glen had said something smart to him.

I could still hear the sounds Glen had made, those terrible sounds in his throat, dying sounds, of course, the way I'd once heard a calf strangle on its own umbilical cord one snowy night in the barn.

I stood up and pushed the money back to him and settled my gun in my holster.

''Oh, shit,'' he said. ''You're still going to come after me, aren't you?''

''Two men came into town last night, name of Lundgren and Mars. And I'll bet I know why.''

''Lundgren and Mars. Don't know anything about them.''

But I could see the truth in his eyes. He knew damned well why they were here.

He tried to look relaxed, but mentioning the two men had infuriated him.

''You set foot on my property again, Chase, and I'll personally blow your fucking head off. Is that understood?''

I just stared at him a while, shook my head, and went back to the hallway.

When I got to the porch, Fenton was polishing some gold candelabras in the sunlight.

He said nothing, just watched me walk down the steps and start over to my horse.

It was then I heard the growl from somewhere on the other side of the house. I stopped, knowing right away the origin of the growl. The wolf that had killed my brother, the wolf of glowing coat and midnight-yellow eyes.

Fenton stopped his work and stared at me. "He's a killer, that one. The master would be just as well off shut of him, if you want my opinion. He's too dangerous."

I didn't say anything. I walked around the side of the house, and there, in a large cage made of galvanized wire, paced the wolf. In the sunlight his coat shone ivory; but his eyes, when his head swung up suddenly, were still the same odd yellow. An Indian was dumping raw meat through a small door in the cage. On the hot wind you could smell the wolf's shit and the high hard stink of the grass he'd pissed in.

I walked closer and he started growling again, that low rumble I'd first heard when my brother Don was dying in his bed that long ago night.

The Indian, still on his haunches, looked over his shoulder. "He don't like you, man." He had graying hair worn long and a faded denim shirt and work pants. His feet were brown and bare.

"So I gather."

"He's a bad one, this wolf."

"Yeah," I said. "I know."

The Indian pointed to a hole in the ground where a small animal had burrowed up into the cage. "Raccoon. Should've seen what the wolf did to that little bastard." The Indian grinned with teeth brown as his skin.

I knelt down next to the Indian, gripping the wire with two fingers for support.

The wolf, who had been growling and going into a crouch, lunged at me suddenly, hurling himself against the cage and ripping his teeth across the two fingers I had inside the cage.

The pain was instant and blinding.

I fell back off my haunches, grabbing my bloody fingers and gritting my teeth and trying not to look like a nancy in front of the Indian who stood above me grinning again with his bad teeth and saying, "I told you, man, that wolf just plain don't like you."

I got to my feet, still hurting, but I pretended that the pain was waning. "Maybe I'll come back here some night and kill that sonofabitch."

The wolf was still glaring at me, still in a crouch, and still growling.

"He'd like to fight you, man. He really would."

I glared back at the wolf and left.

Hanratty was still at his post behind the jack pines, Winchester laid across his saddle. He waved, friendly as always in his way, but he didn't fool me at all. If he had to, he'd kill me fast and sure and never pay me another thought.

That afternoon, Hollister held one of his weekly meetings for the entire eighteen-man police force.

We stood in the back of his office, at full attention the way he'd ordered, while he gnawed on our asses the way a military man would.

He had plenty of complaints. One officer, and he said the man would know who he was, was found sleeping down by the mill. The officer would be docked ten dollars from his next check—this was damned near a fourth of the man's pay.

Then he held up his whistle and showed it around as if we'd never seen anything like it before. "Some of you seem to think it's embarrassing to use this—but I want you to use it anyway. Any time there's a crime, any time you're pursuing somebody, I want that whistle blown so that the citizens and your fellow officers know that you're carrying out your duties. When your fellow officers hear the whistle, they're supposed to lend you a hand. And when the citizens hear it, they're supposed to get out of your way." He held the whistle up for us to see again, put it to his lips and filled the slow golden afternoon air with an ear-shattering blow. Then he said, "If I catch anybody forgetting to use his whistle, I'll fine him five dollars." There was the usual grumbling.

The final matter was drunks. "Our friends Hayes and Croizer have been getting overeager again. Last Monday night they arrested two miners who were walking home drunk. How many times do we have to go over this, boys? We're not here to make the lives of working men any harder. Those poor bastards catch plenty of hell during the day—they don't need us to add to it. The rule is—unless a drunkard is causing some kind of trouble, he's to be left alone. If he's having trouble walking, then walk him home if you've got the time, or find a citizen to go get the drunkard's wife or son to take him home. But I sure as hell don't want any more people arrested just because they've got a snootful. Understood?"

We nodded.

"Good," Hollister said. "Now get to work."

We were just turning to leave when Hollister said, "Chase, I need to speak with you."

I turned around and faced him. He sat himself down and took a pipe from a drawer and put the pipe in his mouth and his feet on the desk.

"I kind of got my ass chewed on because of you, Chase."

I couldn't figure out what he was talking about but I got a sick feeling in my stomach. Hollister was known to fire men almost on a whim—especially if he'd been drinking, and he had that look now—and I could feel that old prison fear in my chest. But instead of getting locked in . . . this time I was going to get locked out—of a good job and wages.

"Because of me?" I said.

"That fop of a night clerk at the Whitney Hotel."

"Oh."

"You sound as if you know what I'm talking about."

I shrugged. "Hell, all I did was look at the guest register."

He smiled. "Without asking that sweet little man's permission."

I laughed. "So he complained?"

"Oh, did he complain. He had a letter waiting for me on my desk this morning. He was filled with civic outrage."

He sucked on his unlit pipe. "Western towns like ours hate

police departments. Just about everything we do, the people consider infringing on their rights in some way.''

He wasn't exaggerating. Two towns over, a group of outraged citizens, angered that the police chief had imposed a curfew following three drunken murders, took two young policemen hostage and threatened to kill them unless the police chief packed up and left town. The outraged mob had been led by the mayor and a minister. Eastern papers liked to talk about how the ''Wild West'' had been tamed now that a new century was about to turn. But that didn't mean that police forces—too often crooked and violent—had found acceptance, because in most places they sure hadn't . . . not yet, anyway.

''Why were you looking in the register anyway?''

For the first time I noticed that he was watching me carefully. He seemed suspicious of me.

''I saw two men get off a train. They didn't look right to me. I just wanted to see what names they registered under.''

''Didn't look right to you?''

''Slickers, was how I had them pegged. Remember that confidence game that man named Rawlins was running on old folks a month ago? That's how they looked to me.''

I didn't tell him about them taking late-night horses from the livery and riding out of town.

''You ask them their business?'' Hollister said.

''No.''

''That would've been better than bothering that sonofabitch at the Whitney. He's very popular with the 'landed gentry,' as they like to be called, and the 'landed gentry' likes to see us as a group of barbarians. This only gives them something else to bitch about.''

''I won't bother him anymore.''

''I'd appreciate that, Chase. You're doing a good job. I don't want to see you get in any political trouble with one of the mighty.''

''I appreciate the advice.''

He looked at my bandaged fingers. I'd put some iodine on them. They still smarted from the wolf bite.

''What's wrong with your fingers?''

I didn't want to tell him about Reeves. "I cut them when I was sawing some logs."

He laughed. "You're about as handy as I am."

When he laughed, he pushed a little breath up on the air. Pure bourbon.

I said good-bye and left his office. Before I even reached the doorway, I heard him sliding a drawer open.

I glanced back over my shoulder just as he was turning his chair to the wall so he could lift up his silver flask and tip it to his lips.

Part 10

Before work next morning I took Annie up into the hills. She wanted to collect leaves.

I found some hazel thickets and showed her how to dig into the mice nests surrounding them. You could find near a quart of nuts that the mice had already shelled and put away for bitter winter. But we didn't take any, of course, because the food belonged to them.

Annie made a collection of the prettiest leaves she could find, taking care to pluck some extras for her mother, and then we stood on an old Indian bridge and watched clear creek water splash rocks and slap against a ragged dam some beavers had recently built. Annie counted eight frogs and six fish from up on the bridge.

We took the east trail back, watching sleek fast horses the color of saddle leather run up grassy slopes in the late morning sun.

When we got near the house, she stopped at the abandoned well. Four large ragged rocks formed a circle around the well, inside of which Gillian had placed a piece of metal to cover the hole.

Now, expertly, Annie bent down, lifted the piece of metal up, took one of her leaves and closed her eyes and said, "I have to be quiet now and keep my eyes closed."

"How come?"

"Because I'm making a wish."

"Oh."

"Mommy always says that's what you have to do for God to hear you."

"Be quiet and close your eyes?"

"Uh-huh. And drop something down the well that you really like."

And with that she let the pretty autumn leaf go from her hand. It floated gently down into the darkness.

Gillian had told me about the well, how it was pretty shallow, and how the folks who had the house before her got sick drinking from it.

"You glad you're my pop?" Annie said, opening her eyes. She'd heard a boy at school call his daddy his "pop" and had decided she liked it.

"I sure am."

"Well, I sure am, too." She smiled and put her hand in mine. "I always knew you were my pop."

"You did?"

"In my dreams I always had a pop. I couldn't exactly see him real good but he was always there. And then the day I saw you in front of our house—well, I knew you were my pop."

"Aw, honey," I said, feeling sad for all the years she hadn't had a pop, "honey, you don't have to worry about not having a pop anymore. I'll always be here."

"Always?" she said, squinting up at me in the sunshine.

"Always," I said, then reached down and swung her up in my arms and carried her home just that way, her blond hair flying and her laughter clear and pure. The only thing that spoiled it was the sore throat and aching muscles I had. I was apparently getting sick.

Around ten that night, I just happened to be standing half a block from the Whitney Hotel. And Lundgren and Mars just happened to be standing on the porch of that same hotel. They couldn't see me because I was in the shadows of an overhang.

Lundgren smoked a cigar. Mars just looked around. He seemed nervous. I wondered why.

Fifteen minutes after coming out onto the porch, Lundgren

flipped his cigar away exactly as he'd done the night before, and then, also as he'd done the night before, led his shorter friend down the street to the livery where the Mex gave them two horses already rubbed down and rested and saddled.

Lundgren and Mars rode out of town, taking the same moonlit road as last night.

I finished my rounds of the block then cut west over by the furrier, where the smell of pelts was sour on the cold night. Moving this fast didn't make me feel any better. The damned head cold I'd been getting was still with me.

The alley behind the Whitney was busy with the usual drunks. Henry, a half-breed, had pissed his pants and was sleeping, mouth open and slack, propped up against a garbage can. A hobo with but one finger on his left hand was having some kind of nightmare, his whole body shaking and cries of "Mother! Mother!" caught in his throat. And there was Jesse—Jesse as in female, Jesse as in mother of three, Jesse as in town drunk. Most nights her kids (the father having been killed four years earlier in the mines) kept tight rein on her, but every once in a while she escaped and wandered the town like a graveyard ghost, and usually fell over unconscious in an alley.

I debated waking them and making them leave. But that would only mean that one or two of them would possibly remember me.

I made sure as I could that they were all sleeping, and then I climbed onto the fire escape that ran at an angle down the back of the Whitney.

I moved fast. I could always say that I was following a suspicious character up here. But I wouldn't want to use that excuse unless I had to.

Lundgren and Mars were staying on the fourth floor. I pulled the screen door open and went in. The hallway was empty. I started toward 406. In one of the rooms I passed, an old man was coughing so hard I thought he'd puke. The corridor smelled of whiskey and tobacco and sweat and kerosene from the lamps.

I was two doors from 406 when 409 opened up and a man came out. He was so drunk he looked like a comic in an opera-house skit. He wore a messy black suit and a bowler that looked ready to slide off his bald head. He was weaving so hard, he nearly fell over backward.

I pressed flat to the wall and stayed that way while the drunk managed to get his door closed and locked.

He didn't once glance to his left. If he had, he would have seen me for sure.

He tottered off, still a clown in an opera-house turn.

Shaking, neither my stomach nor my bowels in good condition, I went to 406 and got it open quickly. You learn a lot of useful things in prison.

The room was dark. Some kind of jasmine-scented hair grease was on the air. I felt my way across the room, touching the end of the bed, a bureau, and a closet door. By now I was able to see.

I started in the bureau, working quickly. I found nothing special, the usual socks and underwear and shirts without their collars or buttons.

I then moved to the closet. Nothing there, either.

I was just starting to pick up one of the two carpet-bags sitting on a straight-backed chair when I heard footsteps in the corridor.

I paused, pulling my revolver.

In the street below there was a brief commotion as a few drunks made their way from one saloon to another. In the distance a surrey jingled and jangled its way out of town.

The footsteps in the hallway had stopped.

Where had the man gone? Was it Lundgren or Mars coming back?

My breathing was loud and nervous in the darkness. My uniform coat felt as if it weighed a hundred pounds. My whole chest was cold and greasy with sweat.

And then I heard him, whistling, or trying to—the drunk down the way, the one who'd barely been able to get his door locked. Easy enough to figure out what had happened. He had made his way down the stairs only to find that the people in the saloon wouldn't serve him. Too drunk. So he'd come back up here.

It took him several minutes to insert key into lock, to turn knob, to step across threshold, to walk across floor, to fall across bed, springs squeaking beneath his weight. Within thirty seconds he was snoring.

I went back to work.

I took the first carpetbag to the bed and dumped everything out. The contents included an unloaded .45, a few more shirts without celluloid collars, and a small framed picture of a large, handsome women I guessed was his wife. I took it over to the window and hiked back the curtain. A lone stripe of silver moonlight angled across the back of the picture: SHARON LUNDGREN, 1860–1889, BELOVED WIFE OF DUNCAN LUNDGREN. So he was a widower, Lundgren was. It made him human for me, and for some reason, I didn't want him to be human.

The second carpetbag didn't yield much more—not at first anyway. Mars was a collector of pills and salves and ointments. The bag had enough of these things to stock a small pharmacy. He seemed to be a worrier, Mars did.

I had almost given up on the bag when my fingers felt, way in the back, an edge of paper. I felt farther. An envelope. I pulled it out, winnowing it upward through tins of muscle ointment and small bottles of pills that rattled like an infant's toy.

I went back to the window and the moonlight.

I turned the envelope face up. In the left upper hand I saw the name and address of the letter writer. My old friend Schroeder, known hereabouts as Reeves.

The letter was brief, inviting Lundgren and Mars here to "increase their fortunes by assisting me in a most worthy endeavor."

I didn't have to wonder about what that "worthy endeavor" might be. Not when Reeves owned half a bank in town here.

I put the envelope back in the carpetbag and the carpetbag back on the chair.

I went to the door, eased it open, stuck my head out. The hallway was empty. In the hall I relocked the door, checked again to make sure that nobody was watching me, and then walked quickly to the screen door and the fire escape.

I knew now that I wasn't done with Reeves. Not at all, no matter how much I'd promised Gillian otherwise.

Part 11

"He's going to do it again."

"He?"

"Schroeder. Reeves. Whatever name he goes by."

"Do what?"

"Hire two people to rob his bank and then double-cross them. Take the money and kill them."

"You sure?"

"Positive. Those two men I saw in town?"

"They're the ones?"

"They're the ones. I got into their hotel room tonight. They had a letter from Reeves."

She didn't say anything for a long time. We were in bed. The window was soft silver with moonlight. Annie muttered in her sleep. The air smelled of dinner stew and tobacco from my pipe. Somewhere an owl sang lonely into the deep sweet night.

"You promised to stay clear of it, Chase."

"I was just telling you who they are."

"You'll get in trouble. I know it."

"I didn't mean to make you mad."

She was silent. "I thought we had a nice life," she said after a time.

"We do."

"Then why do you want to spoil it?"

"I won't spoil it, Gillian. I promise."

"You promise," she said. "Men are always promising, and it doesn't mean anything."

I tried to kiss her but she wouldn't let me. She rolled over on her side, facing the wall.

"You know I love you, Gillian."

She was silent.

"Gillian?"

Silent.

I rolled over. Thought. Felt naked and alone. My sore throat was getting worse, too, and every once in a while, I'd shiver from chills.

I couldn't stop thinking about Gillian. How she knew what was going to happen now, with Reeves and all. How betrayed she must feel.

I tried to make it better for her.

"I'm not your father, Gillian," I said. "I'm not going to hurt you and I'm not going to run out on you the way he did. Do you understand that?"

But she didn't speak then, either.

After an hour or so I slept.

Part 12

Next night, I made my rounds early. I had some business to do.

Lundgren and Mars put in their usual appearance at the usual time, strolling down the street to the livery, picking up their horses and riding out of town just as the moon rose directly over the river.

I rode a quarter mile behind them out the winding stage road.

They went just where I thought they would, straight to Reeves' fancy Victorian. But just before reaching the grounds, they angled eastward toward the foothills.

Half an hour's ride brought them to a cabin along a leg of the river. I ground-tied my horse a long ways back and slipped into the small woods to the west of the cabin. Everything smelled piney and was sticky to the touch.

When I got close enough to see through a window, I watched Lundgren and Mars talking with Reeves. He poured them bourbon. There was some quick rough laughter, as if a joke might have been told, and then quiet talk for twenty minutes I couldn't hear at all.

At one point I thought I heard a woman's voice, but I wasn't sure.

When they came out, Lundgren and Mars and Reeves, they were laughing again.

They stood making a few more jokes and dragging on their stogies and making their plans for the robbery.

"You don't forget about that side door," Reeves said.

"No, sir, I won't," Lundgren said.

Mars went over to his horse and hopped up. His small size made it look like a big effort.

"Talk to you boys soon," Reeves said, cheery as a state legislator on Flag Day.

Lundgren and Mars rode away, into dew-covered fields shimmering silver with moonlight.

Reeves stood there for a time watching them go, the chink of saddle and bridle, the heavy thud of horse hooves fading in the distance.

A woman joined him suddenly, as if from nowhere, slipping out of the door and into his arms. Silhouetted in the lantern light from inside, they stood there kissing for a very long time, until it was obvious that they now wanted to do a lot more than kiss. It took me a while to realize who she was.

A few minutes later Reeves slid his arm around her waist and escorted her back inside. They turned out the lights and walked back out and closed the door and got up in Reeves' black buggy.

Just before he whipped the horse, I heard her say, "K-Kinda ch-chilly out h-here t-tonight."

And then they were gone into the night.

There was a potbellied stove on the ground floor of the police station, and when I got back there, two men stood next to it, holding tin cups of steaming black coffee in wide peasant hands. Winter was on the air tonight.

Kozlovsky nodded upstairs. "Don't know where the hell you been, Chase, but the chief's been lookin' for you for the last hour and a half."

Benesh shook his head. "He's been drinkin' since late afternoon so I'd watch yourself, Chase. Plus he's got a prisoner up there in his little room. Some farmhand who got all liquored up because of some saloon whore. He made the mistake of making a dirty remark to the chief.''

In their blue uniforms, the flickering light from the stove laying a coat of bronze across their faces, they might have been posing for a photograph in the *Police Gazette*.

"I'd better go see him," I said, coughing. I was feeling worse.

The two men glanced at each other as I left.

The "room" they'd referred to was on the second floor, way in the back beyond the cells, which were dark now, men resting or sleeping on their cots, like zoo animals down for the night. Every time I came up here, I thought of prison, and every time I thought of prison, I thought of all those old men I'd known who'd spent most of their adult lives in there. Then I always got scared. I didn't want to die in some human cage smelling of feces and slow pitiful death.

Halfway to the room, I heard the kid moaning behind the door ten yards away. I also heard the sharp popping noise of an open hand making contact with a face. The closer I got, the louder the moaning got.

I knocked.

"Yeah?"

"Chief, it's me. Chase."

A silence. Then footsteps. The door yanked open, the chief, sweating, wearing only his uniform trousers and shirt, his jacket on a coat hook, stood there with his hands on his hips, scowling at me. For all that the police officers and some of the citizens talked about Hollister's "torture room," it was a pretty unspectacular place, just bare walls and a straight-back chair in the middle of an empty room. Right now, no more than half-conscious, thick hairy wrists handcuffed behind him in the chair, sat a beefy farm kid. His nose was broken and two of his front teeth were gone. His face gleamed with sweat and dark blood, and his eyes showed terror and confusion.

"I've been looking for you," Hollister said.

"That's what I heard. I had to go home. My daughter Annie's been sick."

"Nobody could find you for over an hour, Chase. Don't give me any horseshit about your poor little daughter. Now you go downstairs and wait for me in my office.''

He was drunk but you probably wouldn't have noticed it if you didn't know him. The voice was half a pitch higher and there was something wild and frightening in the blue eyes.

"You want me to put him in a cell?" I said, indicating the farm kid.

"I'll put him in a cell when I'm ready to put him in a cell."

"I wouldn't want to see you get in any trouble, Chief."

"I'll worry about that, Chase. You just go downstairs to my office and wait for me."

Just as the door closed, I glimpsed the kid in the straight-backed chair. His brown eyes looked right at me, pleading, pleading. I thought of the kid that day in the quarry, coming up and crying out for mercy. . . .

A moment later I heard a fist collide with a face. The kid screamed, and soon enough came another punch.

He was on the other side of a locked door now. There was nothing I could do.

I went back through the cells.

A man was lying awake on the cot, his eyes very white in the gloom. As I walked past his cell he said, "He gonna kill somebody someday, beatin' folks like that."

I just kept walking. Apparently the man was a drifter and hadn't heard that a prisoner had already died here in what the newspaper called a "mysterious fall."

Twenty minutes later Hollister walked into his office, sat down behind his desk, took a small round gold tin of salve from a drawer and proceeded to rub the salve onto the knuckles of his right hand. They looked pretty bad, swollen and bloody. He had his uniform jacket on now, and he once again appeared in control of himself.

"The sonofabitch tried to hit me," he said.

"That's a pretty neat trick when you're handcuffed."

He glared at me. "Are you accusing me of lying?"

I stared at my hands in my lap.

"Somebody in this town doesn't like you, Chase."

"Oh?" I raised my eyes and met his. He was sober now. Apparently, beating up people had a good effect on him.

He opened the center drawer of his desk, extracted a white business envelope and tossed it across his wide desk to me.

"This was waiting for me when I got to work this morning," he said.

"What is it?"

"You know how to read?"

I nodded.

"Then read it for yourself."

I opened the envelope, took out a folded sheet of white paper, and read what had been written on it in blue ink. The penmanship was disguised to look as if it was a child's.

The message was just one sentence long.

"It's a lie," I said.

"Is it?"

"Yes."

He took out his pipe, stuck it in his teeth and leaned back in his chair.

"It wouldn't be the first time, you know."

"The first time for what?" I said.

"The first time an ex-convict ended up as a police officer."

"I'm not an ex-convict."

"Whoever sent me that letter thinks you are."

"Somebody's just making trouble."

"How long were you in?"

"I wasn't in."

"Up to the territorial prison, were you? I hear it's not so bad there, at least not as bad as it used to be."

"I wouldn't know."

"The warden is a good friend of mine. I'm going to wire him and ask him a few things."

"Ask him anything you want."

He stared at me a long, silent moment. The clock on the west wall tocked. Out in front, around the potbellied stove, a man laughed.

"Your name really Chase?"

"Yes."

"Why were you in prison?"

"I wasn't in prison."

"Be a man, Chase. Tell me the truth."

"I robbed a bank."

"There. You said it. Now we can cut out the horseshit."
He stared at me some more, tilted back in his chair. "You
shoot anybody when you robbed this bank?"

"No."

"You ever shoot anybody?"

"No."

"So you're not a violent man?"

I shrugged. "Not so far, anyway."

He smiled around his pipe. "That's an honest way to put
it. 'Not so far, anyway.' " He sat up in the chair. "I'm going
to make some inquiries about you."

"Your friend the warden?"

"You can be a sarcastic sonofabitch, you know that?" He
shook his head. "What I was going to say, Chase, is that
except for your disappearance tonight, you've been a damned
good officer. Everybody likes you and trusts you, especially
the merchants, and that's very important to me. So believe it
or not, I'm not going to fire you just because you raised some
hell when you were younger. You've got a family now, and
that changes a man. Changes him a lot." Hard to believe this
was the same man who, half an hour ago, had been beating a
handcuffed prisoner. "I'm going to write the warden, like I
said, and if your story checks out—if you really didn't shoot
anybody and if you were a good prisoner—then I'm going to
forget all about that letter."

He put his hand out, palm up, and I laid the letter on it.

He checked the clock. "Hell, I'd better be going home. My
wife was visiting her cousin tonight and she'll probably be
getting home about now."

"You want me to keep working tonight?"

"Of course I do, Chase. If you've been honest with me
tonight, you don't have anything to worry about."

"I appreciate this, Chief."

"Get back to work, Chase, and forget about anything except
doing a good job."

I stood up, nodded good-bye, and left.

I had a cup of coffee out next to the stove and then I went
back to work.

Ev Hollister was one complicated sonofabitch, and those are
the men you always have to be extra careful of.

Part 13

The young man with the white shirt and the celluloid collar
and the fancy red arm garters peered at me from behind the
bars of his teller's cage and said, "Three other police officers
have their accounts here, too, Mr. Chase." He had a face like
a mischievous altar boy. He wore rimless glasses to make himself look older.

I smiled. "Then I must be doing the right thing."

I hadn't ever wanted to step inside any bank that Reeves
owned. But I wanted to see the place that Lundgren and Mars
were going to rob, because by now I knew what I was going
to do.

The layout was simple. For all its finery, the flocked wallpaper, the oak paneling, the elegant paintings, the massive
black safe built into the wall, which resembled a huge and
furious god—for all of that, the bank was really just one big
room divided up by partitions into four different areas. The
safe would be relatively easy to get to because, except for a
wide mahogany desk, nothing stood in the way. Women in
bustles and picture hats, and men in dark suits and high-top
shoes, walked around, conducting whispery business. The air
smelled of gardenia perfume and cigar smoke.

I looked over at the side door that Lundgren and Reeves
had talked about the other night. It used to open onto the alley,
I was told, before the bank had been remodeled. Now it was
never opened for any reason, though I had the key to it on my
ring.

"She's a beauty, isn't she?"

"Beg pardon?"

"The safe," the teller said. "Barely six months old. Straight
from Boston. I doubt even nitro could open it." He smiled.
"Saw you looking at her. Must make the police feel a lot
safer."

"A lot."

"But that's Mr. Reeves for you."

"Oh?"

"Sure. Always buying the best and the newest and the most reliable."

Yes, I thought, and probably spending his partner's money to do it.

I started hacking then, so much so that it got embarrassing. This morning my throat had been so sore, I could barely swallow, and the chills now came on with a sudden violence.

"Well, here's my first deposit," I said when I'd finished hacking.

I handed the teller ten dollars. He found a smart little blue bankbook and took an imposing rubber stamp and opened the book and stamped something bold and black on the first page. He then turned the page over and wrote $10.00 in the credit column. Then he wrote the date in the proper place and gave me the book.

"It's nice to have you as a customer, Mr. Chase."

"Thank you. I'm sure I'll like doing business here."

"I shouldn't say this, being so partial and all, but I think we're the best bank in the whole territory."

"I'm sure you are."

With that I turned and started back to the front of the bank. Then the front door opened and there stood Reeves, sleek and slick as always, staring right at me.

He was obviously angry to find me here, but he couldn't say anything with all the customers wandering around.

He came in, closing the door on the bright but chill afternoon.

He walked right up to me and said, "I'm glad to see you're still wearing that uniform."

"The chief is a more understanding man than you give him credit for."

"Maybe I'll just have to write him another little note about you." He frowned. "Why the hell don't you just get out of this town, Chase? I'd even be willing to give you some money if you just took that wife and daughter of yours and left."

"How much?"

"Maybe ten thousand."

"Maybe?"

"Ten thousand for sure."

I grinned at him. "No, thanks, I kind of like it here. Especially when I get a chance to ruin your day like this every once in a while." I started out the door and then said, quietly, "Be sure to give Lundgren and Mars my best wishes."

He looked around to see if anybody was watching. They weren't. "You don't know what you're getting into, farm boy."

"See you around," I said, and left.

I stood on the boardwalk for a while, enjoying the pale, slanting sunlight, enjoying the town, really, the clatter of wagons and horse-drawn trolleys, the spectacle of pretty town women going about their shopping, the way folks greeted me as they passed. They liked me, the town folks, and I enjoyed that feeling.

I was a happy man just then, and I walked down the street with my lips puckered into a whistle. I tried not to notice how bad my throat was hurting.

Part 14

That night, feeling even sicker, I dragged myself home and went right to bed . . .

In the darkness.

"Chase?"

"Huh?"

"I wanted to wake you up. You were having the nightmare again. About the kid, I think."

"Oh."

"I'm sorry you had to see that, Chase."

"Yeah."

"It must have been terrible to see."

I was sweating, but it was cold sweat and I wanted to vomit. There was just the darkness. And Gillian next to me in her flannel nightgown.

"I said a prayer tonight, Chase."

"How come?"

"That you wouldn't go through with it." Silence. "I know it's on your mind."

"It could work out for us. A lot of money. Going somewhere and buying a farm."

We were silent for a long time.

"Annie saw me praying—I mean, I was down on my knees with my hands folded, just like I was in church—and she asked me what I was praying for, and I told her that I was praying for Pop, that Pop would always do the right thing."

The miners got paid on Fridays. On Friday morning the bank always got extra cash for payroll. Today was Friday. Lundgren and Mars would hit the bank today sometime.

"You hear me, Chase? About my praying?"

"You know I love you and Annie."

"It'll come to no good, Chase. Men like Reeves just go on and on. I hate to say this, but sometimes evil is more powerful than good. I don't understand why God would let that be, but He does."

Just the darkness, and Gillian next to me . . .

I wanted to be content and peaceful. I really did. But I just kept thinking of how easy it would be to take that money from Lundgren and Mars.

I started coughing hard, the way I'd been doing lately. She held me tight, as if she could make my illness go away. Sometimes she was so sweet I didn't know what to do with myself. Because I wasn't sweet at all.

"Chase, I want you to go see the doc tomorrow. I mean it. No more excuses."

I didn't say anything.

I lay back.

The sweat was cold on me. I was shivering.

"Chase. There's something that needs saying."

I didn't say anything.

"You listening, Chase?"

"Uh-huh."

"Chase, if you go through with this, I'll take Annie and leave. I swear."

I wanted to cry—just plain goddamn bawl—and I wasn't even sure why.

"I love you, Gillian."

But then I went and ruined it all by coughing so hard I had
to throw my legs over the side of the bed and just sit there
hacking. Maybe Gillian was right. Maybe I needed to see the
doc.

When I finally laid back down again, Gillian had rolled over
to face the wall.

"Honey? Gillian?"

But she wasn't speaking anymore.

Both of us knew what was going to happen, and there
wasn't much to be said now.

"You're going to do it, Chase," she said after a time. And
I drew her to me and held her. And I could smell her warm
tears as I kissed her cheek. "I know you are, Chase. I know
you are."

Part 15

I got up early, before the ice on the creek had melted off, put
on street clothes and went into town. My bones ached but I
tried not to notice. The sounds of roosters and waking dogs
filled the chill air. The sky was a perfect blue and the fallen
leaves were bright as copper pennies at the bottom of a clear
stream. The fever had waned. I felt pretty good.

I went directly to the restaurant, ordered breakfast and took
up my place by the window. I wanted to keep a careful eye
on the street. I knew what was going to happen this morning.

Reeves arrived first, riding a big chestnut. In his black suit
and white Stetson he was trying, as usual, to impress everybody, including himself.

He dismounted at the livery, left his horse off and then came
back up the street to the bank. Ordinarily, like most of the
merchants, he stopped in here for coffee before the business
day started.

But today he took a key from his vest pocket and walked
around to the alley on the west side of the bank, and then
vanished inside.

I had more coffee and rolled a cigarette and listened reluc-

tantly as a waitress told me about a terrible incident next
county over where a two-year-old had crawled into a pig pen
where two boars promptly ripped him apart and then ate him.
She had a sure way of getting your day off to a happy start.

The stagecoach came in twenty minutes later, a dusty, creaking Concord with a bearded Jehu and two guards up top bearing Winchesters. If you hadn't already guessed that they were
transporting money, the two men with the rifles certainly gave
you a big hint.

The Concord stopped right in front of the bank.

The front door opened and Reeves came out. He looked
dramatic with a fancy silver pistol in his right hand and his
eyes scanning the tops of the buildings on the other side of
the street.

The two guards jumped down. One hefted a long canvas
bag and went inside. The Jehu had taken one of the Winchesters and was watching the street carefully. Reeves stood right
where he was, looking vigilant for all the townspeople to see.

It took three minutes and it was very slick. They'd all obviously done this many times. At this point, anybody who tried
to take the money sack would likely be outgunned.

Then the bank door closed, Reeves inside, and the two
guards jumped back up top and the Jehu took the reins and
snapped them against the backs of the animals, and the stagecoach pulled out.

The waitress with the dead baby story came back and gave
me more coffee. She was young and chubby but with a certain
insolent eroticism in the eyes, and a smile that made her seem
more complicated than she probably was.

"You ever see so much money?" she said and nodded
across the street. "They make that delivery every week, and
every time I see it, I think of what I could do with just one of
them bags of money."

"Buy yourself a house?"

"A house, hell. I'd take off for Chicago and New York and
I'd have me the best time a farm girl ever had herself."

There was a certain anger in her tone that told me at least
a little bit about how she'd been raised, and how she was
treated in a town like this. If she had the money, she was going

to tell a whole lot of people to kiss her ample ass. I understood her, but that didn't mean I liked her much. A hard woman is meaner any day than a hard man. Maybe I didn't like her because she was too much like me.

She drifted away to cheer up some other people. I kept on watching the street.

Around ten, Lundgren and Mars appeared on the steps of the Whitney Hotel. They wore their business suits and business hats and strode their important business strides as they made their way down the street amidst the clatter of wagons and the clop of horse hooves and the handful of lady shoppers on this beautiful autumn day.

They went straight to the livery.

A few minutes later they were back on this street, this time astride two big bays.

They rode straight out of town without speaking to each other or looking around.

I got up, paid my bill, went over to the livery stable, got myself a roan, and then walked it down the alleys to a place directly across from the bank.

Just after eleven, they came back into town riding two different horses. This time they were got up as dusty cowhands, not businessmen. They didn't look like their previous selves at all, which was just how they wanted it. Mars had what appeared to be a sawed-off shotgun in his scabbard.

I stood under the overhang as they rode down the street. Lundgren stayed up on his mount. Mars dropped off, grabbing the sawed-off shotgun. I wondered about the shotgun. I couldn't believe Reeves wanted anybody killed. A robbery would get you a jury trial and a prison stretch. A killing would get you hanged some frosty midnight while a lynch mob stood beneath you, grinning.

They pulled blue bandannas up over their faces.

Mars started moving quickly now, up on the boardwalk. But instead of going in the front door the way I figured he would, he ducked into the alley and went through the side door. He had a key and he used it quick and smart. He opened the door and went inside.

It sure didn't make any sense, him having a key.

Lundgren leaned over and put his hand on the Winchester in his scabbard. He was ready for trouble when Mars came boiling out of the door.

I rode my horse to the edge of town, ten feet away from the small roundhouse where an engine was being worked on. You could smell the hot oil on the cool fall air.

Five minutes went by before I heard the shotgun blast which was followed by a long, nervous silence and then horses running hard down the dusty main street out of town.

Six-shooter fire followed the horses. I imagined it was Reeves, emptying his chambers, making it look good for the townspeople.

Lundgren and Mars appeared a few minutes later, riding hard. At the fork they headed west, which was where I expected them to head. I gave them a five-minute lead and went after them, keeping to grass so I wouldn't raise any dust.

They'd had it all planned and planned well.

They rode straight to the river, where business clothes and fresh horses were waiting for them. In a couple of minutes they wouldn't look anything at all like the robbers. And they'd be riding very different horses.

They took care of the robbery horses first, leading them to the edge of the muddy rushing river where Mars took a Colt and shot both the animals in the head. The horses jerked only once, then collapsed to the ground without a sound. Lundgren and Mars pushed them into the river, where they made small splashes and then vanished. All I could think of was the hayseed kid the old con had drowned that day in the quarry. I cursed Mars. The sonofabitch could have just shooed the animals up into the foothills.

I also kept thinking of the shotgun blast back at the bank. Anybody who could kill an innocent animal the way they had would have no trouble killing a human.

They took the long sack of money, wrapped it in a red blanket, and cinched it across the back of Mars' mount.

They stripped down to their longjohns and then put on their business suits and climbed up on their business horses and took off riding again, though this time they went slow and leisurely, like easterners eager to gasp at the scenery. At the river they threw all their robbery clothes into the rushing, muddy water.

Fifteen minutes later they came to the crest of a hill and looked down on the cabin where they'd been meeting Reeves, and where Reeves had been meeting Ev Hollister's wife.

They rode straight down the dead brown autumn grass, coming into a patch of hard sunlight just as they reached the valley.

A few minutes later, Lundgren tied up the horses and Mars lugged the money sack into the big, fancy cabin.

I sat there for a while, rolling myself a cigarette and giving them a little time.

After a while I grabbed the rifle from my scabbard and started working my way down the hill.

Part 16

I went down the hill at an angle to the cabin and then along a line of scrub pines to the right of the place. There were no side windows, so that helped make my appearance a complete surprise.

I crawled low under the front window then stood up when I was directly in front of the door.

I raised my boot and placed it right above the doorknob, where it would do the most good. If my kick didn't open the door the first time, I was likely going to get a chest full of lead before I had a second chance.

The door slammed backward.

I put two bullets straight into a Rochester lamp hanging over a large mahogany table that looked just right for both a good meal and a poker game.

The Rochester lamp exploded into several large noisy chunks.

I went inside.

Lundgren and Mars were standing by the bunk beds, the money fanned out on the lower bunk.

They were just now going for their guns, but it was too late.

I crushed Lundgren's gun hand with a bullet. His cry filled the room.

"Throw the gun down," I said to Mars.

Lundgren had already dropped his when the bullet went smashing into his flesh and bone.

"Who the hell are you?" Mars said.

"Who the hell do I look like?" I said. "I'm a police officer from town."

"I'm impressed."

"You want me to shoot your hand up the way I did his?"

"Asshole," he said.

But he dropped his gun.

"Fill the sack."

"What?"

"Fill the sack."

"That's our money," Mars said. He was one of those belligerent little men whose inferiority about their size makes them dangerous.

"Do it," Lundgren said.

He had sat himself down on a chair and was holding his hand out away from him and staring at it. He was big and blond and Swedish. Tears of pain made his pale blue eyes shine. He was sweating a lot already and gritting tobacco-stained teeth.

"You heard what your partner said," I said to Mars.

"Maybe I don't care what my partner said."

I pointed the rifle directly at his chest. "I don't give a damn about killing you. After what you did to those horses, I'd even enjoy it."

"Do it," Lundgren said again. "Give him the goddamned money."

He was almost pathetic, Lundgren was, so big and swaggering before, and only whimpering and whining now. You just never know anything about a man till he faces adversity.

"He isn't going to turn this money in," Mars said, staring at me.

"What?" Lundgren said.

"You heard me. He isn't going to turn this money in. This is for himself."

"Bullshit. He's a police officer."

"So what he's a police officer? Half the goddamned cops

we know in Denver are crooked. Why shouldn't they have
crooked cops in a burg like this?''

"Fill the sack," I said.

Mars glared at me now, a tough little man in a brown business suit and a comic black bowler. He looked out of place
amidst the expensive appointments of a stone fireplace, a small
library filled with leather-bound classics, and leather furniture
good enough to go in the territorial governor's office. He
didn't belong in such a world.

"Fill it," I said.

"I'm going to find you, you piece of shit, and when I find
you, I'm going to cut your balls off and feed them to you, the
way the A-rabs do, you understand me?''

In two steps I stood right in front of him. As I brought the
rifle down, I thought of how he'd killed the horses, and so I
put some extra power into it.

I got him just once, but I got him square in the mouth, and
so the butt of my rifle took several teeth and cut his lip so
deep a piece of it just hung there like a flap.

He didn't give me the satisfaction of letting me hear his
pain. Unlike Lundgren, he was tough. He had tears in his eyes
and he kept making tight fists of his hands, but beyond his
initial cry, he wasn't going to give me anything.

"Now fill it," I said.

This time he filled it, all the while sucking on the blood
bubbling in his mouth.

When he was finished, I said, "Tie it shut."

"You tie it shut."

I hit him again, this time with the butt of the rifle right
against his ear.

The blow drove him to his knees and he fell over clutching
his head. This time he couldn't stop himself from moaning.

"Get up and tie the sack shut and hand it to me, you piece
of shit."

"You hurt him enough," Lundgren said.

"Not as bad as he hurt those horses."

Mars got to his feet slowly, in a daze, swearing and whimpering and showing me, for the first time, fear.

He tied the bag shut with cord and then raised it and dropped it at my feet.

I couldn't get the horses out of my mind. I hit him again, a good clean hit against his temple.

He went down quick and final, out for a long time. His head made a hollow sound when it crashed against the floor.

"You sonofabitch," Lundgren said. "He'll hunt you down, you wait and see."

He was still holding his hand. Blood had dripped on his nice black boots and all over the floor.

I hefted the bag, holding the rifle in my right hand.

"You'll want to know my name so you can tell Reeves," I said.

"How the hell do you know about Reeves?"

I didn't answer his question. "My name's Chase. He'll know who I am."

"You sonofabitch. You're fucking with the wrong people, you better believe that."

I backed up to the door.

"Remember the name," I said. "Chase."

"You don't worry. I won't forget it. And neither will Mars."

I went out the door and into the warming sunshine of late morning. I could smell the smoky hills and hear a jay nearby.

I walked around the cabin to where they'd ground-tied their horses. I shooed one away and then climbed up on the other.

I went up the hill fast. When I got to my own horse, I jumped down, put the money sack across his back, and then shooed the other horse away. He went straight across the hill and disappeared behind some scrub pines.

I got up on the roan and rode away.

Part 17

An hour later, I dismounted, eased the money sack down from the horse and then carried it, along with a good length of rope, over to the abandoned well near our house.

I knelt down, lifted up the metal cover and peered down

inside. Sometimes you could go down a couple of hundred feet and still hit shale. But Gillian had said this one had been easy, the water right there, just waiting. I took out my spike and the hammer I'd grabbed from my saddlebag and drove the spike deep into the shale on the side of the well. Then I took a piece of rope and tied one end to the top of the money bag and the other end to the spike. And then I fed the money bag, an inch of rope at a time, down into the well, stopping just short of the waterline. Nobody would think to look here. I pulled the cover over the well again and stood up.

Overhead, an arcing falcon soared against the autumn sky, swooping down when its prey was clearly in sight. I stood and watched until it carried a long black wriggling silhouette of a snake up into the air.

I stood there and thought about it all, what I'd done and what lay ahead, and what Gillian would say and how broken-hearted she'd be unless I could convince her that I'd done the right thing; and then I got on my horse and rode into town.

Part 18

Three hours after the robbery, people still stood in the street, staring at the bank and talking about everything that had happened.

On my way to the station, an old man carrying a hearing horn stopped me and said, "You catch those bastards, hang 'em right on the spot far as I'm concerned."

I nodded.

"That kid just died," he said, "a few minutes ago."

I rode another half block and saw Dr. Granville, a pleasant, chubby middle-aged man always dressed in a black three-piece suit to match his black bag. He was a real doctor, educated at a medical school back East, not just a prairie quack the way so many of them are.

He was crossing the dusty street, and when he saw me, he said, "Terrible business. I remember delivering that kid, the one that got killed. Hell, he wasn't twenty years old yet."

I went on down the street. I was stopped by half a dozen

citizens who wanted to express their anger over what had happened to the clerk.

I took my horse to the station and tied him up in back and went inside.

I was just passing Ev Hollister's office when I heard a familiar voice.

"I'm doing what I have to, Hollister, nothing more and nothing less."

He spoke, as usual, with a small degree of anger and a great degree of pomposity.

He sounded riled and he sounded rattled, and I wanted to get a look at him this way, so I leaned in the door frame and watched him as he bent over the chief's desk.

"Something I can do for you?" Hollister said when he saw me.

"I just rode in from town and heard that the bank was robbed."

As I said this, Reeves turned around and faced me. His look of displeasure was deep and pure.

"Yeah, and one of the tellers was killed. Had a gun in his cash drawer. Just a kid, too. Briney."

Briney was the youngster who'd opened my account. The one with the rimless glasses and the altar boy smile.

"Specifically against my orders," Reeves said. "I specifically forbid my tellers to keep guns in their drawers. I didn't want anything like this to happen."

Reeves wasn't angry only at me. He was also angry at Lundgren and Mars. A robbery would get a town riled. But the murder of a young man would put them in the same mind as that old man I'd just seen on the street. They'd want a hanging.

Reeves scowled at me. "What I want to know is how the robber got the key to the side door of the bank."

That had troubled me, too.

Hollister shifted forward in the chair behind his desk and started cleaning his pipe bowl with a pocketknife.

"Reeves here thinks the robbers got the key from somebody who had access to the bank."

"One of the employees?" I said.

Hollister shook his head. "Huh-uh. Bank employees aren'
given keys."

"Could one of the employees have stolen it?" I said.

"Reeves says no." Hollister spoke as if Reeves weren'
here. "Says the only person with a key is himself."

"And one other man," Reeves said, his eyes fixed on my
face. "You."

I looked at Hollister. His face was drawn and serious. "You
know where the keys are, Chase?"

"In the drawer in the back room. Where I always leave
them when I finish my shift at night."

"You never take them home?"

"Never. You said not to."

Hollister nodded somberly toward the back. "Why don'
you go get that ring of keys and bring it up here?"

I looked at Reeves. He was still scowling. "All right," I
said.

My bones were still aching and I was starting to cough
some, but those problems were nothing compared to what I
was beginning to suspect.

In the back room, where Hollister posts the bulletins and
directives for the men, I got into the desk where all the junior
officers sit when they have to write out reports.

Left side, second drawer down, I found the keys. Usually
there were seventeen in all. Today there were sixteen. I
counted them again, just to make sure that my nerves hadn'
misled me. Sixteen. The bank key was missing.

I sat there for a long time and thought about it. It was pure
Reeves and it was pure beautiful, the way he was about to tie
me in with Lundgren and Mars.

I went back up front. I set the keys on Hollister's desk.

He looked down at them and said, "Well, Chase?"

"There's one missing."

"You know which one that is?"

"Yes, sir."

"The bank key?"

"Yes, sir," I said.

"I knew it," Reeves said. "I goddamn knew it."

"I didn't take that key, Chief."

Hollister nodded. "I believe you, Chase, but I'm afraid Reeves here doesn't."

I met Reeves' gaze now. There was a faint smile on his eyes and mouth. He was starting to enjoy himself. If only one person had the key to the bank other than himself, then who else could the guilty party be?

I stood there feeling like the farm boy I was. I'd never been gifted with a devious mind. Reeves had not only robbed his own bank, he had also managed to set me up in the process— set me up and implicate me in the robbery.

"A little later," Hollister said quietly, "you and I should talk, Chase."

I nodded.

"Why don't you go ahead and start your shift now?" Hollister said.

"Yes, Chase, you do that," Reeves said. "But you can skip the bank. Thanks to you, there isn't any money left in there."

It was a long afternoon. The sun was a bloody red ball for a time and then vanished behind the piney hills, leaving a frosty dusk. Dinner bells clanged in the shadows and you could hear the *pock-pock-pock* of small feet running down the dirt streets for home. The only warmth in the night were the voices of mothers calling in their young ones. If there was concern and a vague alarm in the voices—after all, you could never be quite sure that your child really was safe—there was also love, so much so that I wanted to be seven or eight again and heading in to the dinner table myself, for muttered Praise the Lords and some giggly talk with my giggly little sister and some of my mother's muffins and hot buttery sweet corn.

There were a lot of fights early that night. The miners, learning that they would have no money tomorrow, demanded credit and got it and drank up a lot of the money they would eventually get. In all, I broke up four fights. One man got a bloody eye with the neck of a bottle shoved in his face, and another man got two broken ribs when he was lifted up and thrown into the bar. The miners had to take their anger out on somebody, and who was more deserving than a friend? Like most drunkards, they saw no irony in this.

Just at seven Gillian and Annie brought my dinner, cooked beef and wheat bread. It was too cold for them to stay, so they started back right away—but not before Gillian said, "Annie, would you wait outside a minute?"

She studied both of us. Obviously, just as I did, Annie sensed something wrong. She looked hurt and scared, and I wanted to say something to her, but when Gillian was in this kind of mood, I knew better.

Annie went out the back door of the station, leaving Gillian and me next to the potbellied stove in the empty room.

"There was a robbery this morning, Chase," she said.

"So I heard."

"Reeves' bank."

"Right."

"He did it again, didn't he?"

"Did what?"

"Did what? God, Chase, don't play dumb. You know how mad that makes me."

"There was a robbery, yes, and it was Reeves' bank, yes, but other than that, I don't know what you're talking about."

She studied me just as Annie had. "Chase."

"Yeah?"

"I made up my mind about something."

"Oh?"

"If you take that bank robbery money, I'm going through with what I said. About leaving you. I'm going to pack Annie and I up and go and that's a promise. I don't want our daughter raised that way."

"He killed my two brothers."

"Don't give me that kind of whiskey talk, Chase. Your brothers are dead and I'm sorry about that, but no matter what you do, you can't bring them back. But you can give Annie a good life, and I'm going to see that you do or I'm taking her away."

"I love you, Gillian."

"This isn't the right time for that kind of talk, Chase, and you know it."

She walked to the door and turned around and looked at me. "If you break her heart, Chase, or let her down, I'm never going to forgive you."

She went right straight out without saying another word, or giving me a chance to speak my own piece.

The fights went on all night. A Mex took a knife to a miner who kept calling him a Mex, and two miners who should have known better got into a drunken game of Russian roulette. They both managed to miss their own heads, but they shot the hell out of the big display mirror behind the bar.

Just at eleven, when I was finishing my second sweep of the businesses, making sure all the doors were locked, making sure that no drunken miners had sailed rocks through any of the windows, I was walking past an alley and that was when they got me.

They didn't make any noise and they surprised me completely.

Mars hit me on the side of the head with the butt of a .45, and Lundgren dragged me into the shadows of the alley.

"Where's our money?" Lundgren said.

I didn't answer. Wouldn't. Because no matter what he did to me, it wasn't going to be his money ever again.

Mars took the first three minutes. He worked my stomach and my ribs and my chest.

At one point I started throwing up, but that didn't slow him down any. He had a rhythm going, and why let a little vomit spoil everything?

By the time Mars finished, I was on my knees and trying to pitch forward.

Lundgren had better ideas.

He grabbed me by the hair and jerked me to my feet and then started using his right knee expertly on my groin.

He must have used it six, seven times before I couldn't scream anymore, before I let the darkness overwhelm me there in the dust that was moist with my own blood and sweat and piss . . .

Just the darkness . . .

Part 19

Six years ago, two Maryknoll nuns on their way to California
stopped through here. They stayed just long enough, I'm told,
to set up an eight-bed hospital. It's nothing fancy, you understand, but there's a small surgery room in addition to the beds
and everything is white and very clean and smells of antiseptic.

Doc Granville got me into his examination room but then
had to go out to get a man some pills. Apparently, people felt
comfortable stopping by at any hour. While I was in the room
alone, I looked through his medical encyclopedia. There was
something I needed to look up.

When I was finished, I went back to the table and laid down
and Doc Granville came in and got to work.

He daubed some iodine on the cut across my forehead. I
winched. "Hell, son, that don't hurt at all."

"If you say so."

"Miners do this to you? I know they're raising hell because
their paychecks are going to be late."

"I didn't get a real good look at them. But I think it was
Mexes."

"You must be at least a little bit tough."

"Why's that?" •

"That beating you took. And you're up and around."

I thought of mentioning what I'd just read. I decided not to.
Things were complicated enough. "I'm not up and around
yet."

He laughed. "I don't hand out that many compliments, son.
Just accept it with some grace and keep your mouth shut."

I smiled at him. For all his grumpiness, he was a funny
bastard, and a pretty decent man at that.

The pain was considerable. He had me on the table with my
head propped up. He'd fixed the cuts on my face and then
carefully examined my ribs. They were sore. Not broken, he
said, but probably bruised. I tried not to think about it.

He was about to say something else when knuckles rapped
on the white door behind him.

"I told you I'd be out in five minutes, nurse. Now you just hold on to your britches."

"It's not the nurse."

And it wasn't.

"Your boss," Granville said in a soft voice.

I nodded.

"They're going to hurt like a bitch when you get up, those ribs of yours."

"I imagine."

"Nothing I can do for it except tape it up the way I did."

"I appreciate it."

He went to the door and opened it.

Hollister, in his blue serge, walked into the room with the kind of military precision and stiffness he always used when he was trying to hide the fact that he'd been drinking.

He nodded to Granville and came straight over to me. He scowled when he saw my face.

"What the hell happened?"

So I told him the Mex story, the same one I'd told Granville. It was better the second time around, the way a tall tale usually is, but as I watched him, I could see he didn't believe a word of it.

"Mexes, huh?"

"Uh-huh."

"Two of them."

"Uh-huh."

"I'm told you didn't sound your whistle," he said.

"I didn't have time."

"Or use your weapon."

"I didn't have time for that, either."

"They just grabbed you . . ."

"Grabbed me as I was walking past an open alley."

"And dragged you . . ."

"Dragged me into the alley and—"

"Why did they drag you into the alley?"

"Because I saw them in the alley, fighting—one of them even had a knife—and I told them to stop, and they turned on me."

"Just like that?"

"Just like that."

"Before you could do anything?"

"Before I could do anything."

Granville was watching me, too. He was pretending to be sterilizing some of his silver instruments, but he was really watching Hollister try to break my story.

Hollister suddenly became aware of the doc. "You do me a favor, Doc?"

"Sure, Ev."

"Wait outside."

"If you want."

"I'd appreciate it."

"Sure."

Doc looked like a kid disappointed because he had to stay home while all his friends went off and did something fun.

Doc went out and closed the door.

Hollister didn't talk at first. He went over and picked up a straight-backed chair and set it down next to the table I was lying on. Then he took out his pipe and filled it and took out a stick match and struck it on the bottom of his boot. The room smelled briefly of phosphorous from the match head and then of sweet pipe tobacco.

He still didn't say anything for a long time, but when he did speak, it sure was something I paid attention to.

"Only one way those two boys that stuck up the bank could've gotten that key."

I didn't say anything.

He said, "How much did they promise you, Chase?"

I still didn't say anything. I just lay there with my ribs hurting every other time I inhaled. I had never felt more alone.

"Reeves estimates that they got away with fifty thousand. If they didn't give you at least a third of it, you're not a very good businessman."

"I didn't have anything to do with the robbery, Chief. I honestly didn't."

"I took a chance on you, being an ex-convict and all."

"I know that and I appreciate it."

"And now here I am kicking myself in the ass for doing it."

"I'm sorry, Chief."

"Every single merchant in this town knows what happened, how you threw in with those robbers."

"I didn't, Chief. I really didn't."

I closed my eyes. There was nothing else to say.

"They didn't hesitate to kill that clerk at the bank this morning, and they sure won't hesitate to kill you." He puffed on his pipe. "That beating they gave you was just a down payment, Chase."

He was trying to scare me. I thought of scaring him right back by telling him about that wife of his and Reeves.

He stood up and walked over to the table and faced me.

He jabbed a hard finger into my taped-up ribs.

I let out a cry.

"They worked you over pretty good. Maybe you should take a few days off."

"Is that an order?"

He sighed. "I can't prove you actually gave them that key, so I'm not going to fire you, even though every merchant in town wants me to."

"That's white of you."

He shook his head. "Chase, I thought you were smarter than all this."

"I didn't throw in with them, no matter what you say."

"Then where did they get the key?"

I stayed quiet. I didn't want to drag Reeves into this. That would only complicate things.

"You got any answer for that, Chase?"

"I don't know where they got the key."

"But not from you?"

"Not from me."

He took the last noisy drags of his pipe. "You've got a nice wife and a nice little girl. You don't want to spoil things for them."

"I sure don't."

"Then I'm going to ask you once more, and I want you to tell me the truth."

"You don't even have to ask. I didn't give them the key."

He walked over to the door. His boots walked heavy on the boards of the floor.

"You going to tell me why they came after you?"

"I told you. It was two Mexes."

"Right. Two Mexes."

"And they were drunk."

"Real drunk, I suppose."

"Right," I said. "Real drunk."

He looked sickened by me. "You're wasting your goddamned life, Chase. You've gotten yourself involved in something that's going to bring down your whole family. And you're going to wind up in prison again. Or worse."

He didn't even look at me anymore. He just walked through the doorway, slamming the door hard behind him.

I lay there, quiet, still hurting from where he'd jammed his finger into my rib.

Part 20

Gillian put a match to the kerosene lamp and then held the light close to my face and looked over what they'd done to me.

I watched her closely in the flickering lamplight, older-looking tonight than usual, her eyes moving swiftly up and down my face, showing no emotion at all when she got to the black and blue places. She didn't touch me. I knew she was angry.

I'd been home ten minutes, sitting at the kitchen table, rolling a cigarette in the dark, trying to wake neither Gillian nor Annie, but then I'd dropped my cigarette, and when I went to get it, my rib hurt so bad I made a noise, and that had awakened Gillian.

Now she finished with her examination and set the lamp down in the middle of the table and went around and sat across the table from me.

She just kept biting her lip and frowning.

"Two Mexes," I said, keeping my voice low with Annie asleep in the other room.

"Don't say anything, Chase."

"I'm just trying to explain—"

"You're not trying to explain anything. You're lying, that's what you're doing."

"But Gillian, listen—"

"You got yourself involved in that robbery somehow, and it all went wrong just the way I knew it would, and now Reeves is after you."

She started crying. No warning at all.

I sat there in the lamp-flick dark with the woman I'd loved so long, knowing how much I'd let her down. To get Reeves the way I wanted to get Reeves meant destroying her in the process.

"I'm sorry, Gillian."

"No, you're not."

"Well, I wish I was sorry, at any rate. I just wish I didn't hate him so much."

"And I just wish Annie didn't love you so much."

She went to bed. I sat there a long time. After a while I blew out the lamp and just sat in the moonlight. I had some whiskey and I rolled two cigarettes and I sort of talked to my dead brothers the way you sort of talk to dead folks, and I thought of Annie in her white dress in the sunshine and I thought of sad Gillian, who'd been done nothing but wrong by men all her life.

It was near dawn when I went to bed and slid in beside her.

Part 21

The next day, I fell back into my routine as husband and father and policeman.

Before work I went up the hill and knelt down by the deserted well. The day was gray and overcast. The wind, as I pulled the well cover back, was cold and biting. I could smell snow on the air.

Last night I'd dreamt that I'd run up the hill to the well only to find it empty. Behind me stood Lundgren and Mars. When I found that they'd taken the money, they'd started laughing, and then Lundgren had leaned over and pushed me down the well.

The rope still dangled from the spike. I reached down and gripped it and pulled the canvas money sack up the long dark hole.

I put the sack on the ground and greedily tore it open and reached inside.

I pulled up a handful of greenbacks and just stared at them momentarily. I gripped the money tight, as if I had my hands around Reeves' neck.

"You're destroying this family, Chase. That's what you're doing."

In the wind, I hadn't heard Gillian come up the hill. She stood no more than two feet behind me. She wore a shawl over her faded gingham dress. She looked old again, and scared and weary, and I tried hard not to hate myself for what I was doing.

"This money is going to save us, Gillian," I said, packing it all back up again, leaning to the well and feeding the rope down the long dark tunnel. I didn't let go until I'd tested the rope. Snug and firm. The spike held. The money was back in a safe place. I pulled the cover over the well and dusted my hands off and stood up.

I took her by the arms and tried to kiss her. She wouldn't let me. She just stood stiff. Her skin was covered with goose bumps from the icy wind.

She wouldn't look at me. I spoke to her profile, to her sweet little nose and her freckles and her tiny chin.

"All we need to do is wait a few months, and then we can leave town with all this money. Tell Hollister that one of your relatives died and left you a farm in Missouri or somewhere. Even if he suspects, he can't prove it. I'll wrap the money in bundles and put it in a trunk and send the trunk on ahead to wherever we decide to go."

When she finally turned and looked at me, she seemed sadder than I'd ever seen her.

"And won't that be a nice life for Annie, Chase? Watching her father scared all the time because somebody might find the money he stole?"

"I won't be scared, Gillian, because nobody will know except you and me. And it's not stolen money, anyway, not really—it's just what Reeves rightfully owes me."

"Listen to yourself, Chase," she said. "You've convinced yourself that what you're doing is right. But all you're doing is destroying this family. You wait and see. You wait and see."

She started crying, and then she was running down the hill, pulling her shawl tighter around her.

I started after her but decided there was no point. Not right now, anyway.

All I could do was stand there in the bitter wind, feeling like a kid who'd just been scolded. I wanted to speak up on my own behalf, but I knew better, knew that no matter what I said or how long I talked, straight and true Gillian would remain straight and true.

After a while I walked back down the hill to the house. Gillian was fixing stew at the stove. She didn't once turn around and look at me as I got into my police uniform, or say good-bye as I stood in the doorway and said, "I love you, Gillian. You and Annie are my life. And this is all going to work out. We're going to have the money and have a good life away from here. I promise you that, Gillian. I promise you that."

But there was just her back, her tired beaten shoulders, and her arm stirring the ladle through the stew.

Part 22

When I got to town, the funeral procession was just winding its way up the hill to the graveyard. A lone man in a Union uniform walked behind the shiny black horse-drawn hearse, beating out a dirge on a drum.

I went to the police station, checked over the sheet listing the arrests thus far that day, checked to see if the new and more comfortable shoes I'd ordered had come in yet, and then started out the front door. There was still time for a cup of coffee at the restaurant before my rounds began.

As I walked to the front of the station, I felt various eyes
on me.

A cop named Docey said, "Some of us were talkin' last
night, Chase."

"Oh?"

"There were six of us talkin', and five of us voted that you
should quit." He was leaning against the front door, a pudgy
red-bearded man with red freckles on his white bald head.
"We got enough problems without people thinkin' we're
crooked."

"I didn't slip that key to the robbers, in case that's what
you're talking about."

He grabbed me then. He pushed away from the door and
took his big Irish hands and grabbed the front of my uniform
coat. I heard the two other cops grunt in approval.

I couldn't afford any more physical pain. I used my knee
and I went right up straight and he went down fast and sure.

He rolled around on the floor clutching his groin and swearing. The other two started toward me but then realized that if
Docey couldn't handle me—Docey being a mean mick ex-
railroad man—they couldn't either.

I opened the front door, about to step out on the boardwalk
into the bitter blustering day, and I saw her shiny black surrey
pull up.

In her dark cape and royal-blue organdy dress, red hair
caught beneath a small hat, Claire Hollister was not only beautiful, she was also exotic, like a frightened forest creature you
see only once or twice a year for mere moments.

As she stepped down from the surrey, she nodded good day
to me.

"Afternoon, ma'am."

"Afternoon." She smiled. "D-Did y-you h-happen t-to see
that h-husband of m-mine in there?" As always, her sad eyes
reflected her humiliation.

"I think he's still at the funeral, ma'am."

"Oh. W-Would y-you l-leave a n-note telling h-him I was
h-here?"

"Sure."

She turned back to her surrey. As she seated herself and

lifted the reins, I saw how sad her face was even in profile. I couldn't imagine why a woman like this—a woman I sensed was decent and honorable—would give herself to a man like Reeves. Sometimes I suspected I didn't know anything about women at all.

After she was gone, I went back inside. I had to pass Docey and the other two cops, but they just scowled at me and let me go.

I wrote the chief a note and took it into his office. I started to set the note on his desk but then I noticed an envelope addressed to him. It bore the same handwriting as the note that had told him I was a jailbird.

I stood very still, staring at the envelope, making sure I was alone in the office, listening hard for any footsteps in the hallway.

I had to be quick. And I certainly couldn't risk reading it in here.

I snapped the envelope up, stuffed it inside my serge uniform coat, and walked straight out of the office and straight down the hallway and straight to the door, where Docey was still standing up and grimacing.

"You'll get yours, Chase, just you wait and goddamn see," he said.

Snow was still on the wind. The people on the street didn't dawdle now, they scurried like all other animals, trying to prepare themselves for the bitter winter soon to come. I imagined the general store, with its bacon and hams and coffee and cheeses and pickled fish and candy and tobacco and blankets and toys, was going to be doing a very good business the next few days as people set things in for the fury of winter.

I went over to the restaurant and ordered a cup of coffee. By the time the waitress came back with my steaming cup, I had already read the letter twice, and I sure didn't like what Reeves had written.

Part 23

Dear Chief Hollister,

As an upright citizen of this town, I've warned you

before about your man Chase. While everybody suspects
he gave the robber the key that let him in the bank, nobody can prove it. Till now . . .

Ask Hartley, the night clerk at the Whitney, about the
robbers and Chase meeting behind the hotel two nights
before the robbery.

If he tells the truth, you'll see that Chase was in on
this meeting all along.

So Reeves had got to Hartley, the night clerk at the hotel
where Lundgren and Mars had been staying. Wouldn't take
much to bribe a man like Hartley. Just as it wouldn't take
much to convince Hollister of Hartley's story, that I had met
with Lundgren and Mars to plan the robbery.

Even if I burned this particular letter, Reeves would send
Hollister another one. And keep sending him letters until Hollister decided to put me behind bars . . . a perfect target for the
lynch mob Reeves would quickly stir up.

I wanted to run. I thought about Mexico and warm blue
waters and sandy yellow beaches and Gillian and Annie and
I living in a fine stucco house. . . .

But if I ran now, it would be like signing a confession,
admitting that I'd been part of the robbery.

I sipped coffee. I smoked a cigarette. I thought things
through.

I had only one hope. I had to strike a bargain with Reeves.

"Yes?"

"Wondered if I could talk to you a minute, Chief."

"About what?"

"I might be a little late getting to today."

Hollister waved me into his office.

"By the way, your wife was here. I just wanted to make
sure you got my note."

"I got it. Now what's this about being late?"

"Couple hours is all."

"For what?"

"Some personal things."

"Personal things, huh?"

"Not anything to do with the robbery, if that's what you're thinking."

He picked up his pipe. He'd been cleaning it with his pocketknife. Now he went back to it.

"You're not telling me the truth yet, Chase."

"I am. You just don't happen to believe the truth."

"You've got those jailhouse eyes, Chase. You think you look like every other man in this town, but you don't. Prison does something to people, and it sure as hell did something to you."

"I didn't help anybody rob that bank."

He put the pipe in his mouth and drew on it. There was a sucking sound in the empty bowl. "You could always turn them over."

"The robbers?"

"Lundgren and Mars are their names, in case you need help remembering."

"I don't know where they are."

"Uh-huh."

"I don't."

"Take the two hours." He sounded disgusted. "I don't know why you'd want to waste a fine wife and daughter the way you are."

"I'll be back by four-thirty."

"Don't hurry on my account. I'm getting damned tired of seeing your face, in fact."

Part 24

Even on a cold drab day like this one, Reeves' Victorian house was impressive and sightly. I sat on my horse staring at it, trying not to notice that I was working up another fever and that my stomach was getting sick again.

Hanratty, the guard, appeared just when I expected him to, and leveled his carbine at me just when I was sure he would. He came out from behind the scrub pines, seated on a big bay.

"Nice uniform you got there, Chase. Maybe I could get Reeves to get me one like it."

"Maybe if you did an extra-good job, he just might do that."

Hanratty was bundled up inside a sheep-lined jacket, with his hat pulled down near his ears. He spat a stream of juice right near my horse's foreleg. "He'd be real happy to hear you went for your gun and I was forced to kill you. That's one way I could get me a uniform like that." He grinned. "Every time he works that wolf of his these days, he's always callin' out your name. And that goddamned wolf goes crazy, believe me. Crazy as all hell." He frowned. "Except the past couple days. Animal ain't hisself."

"All right if I go see Reeves?"

"It's your ass, son. He might put a couple holes in you."

I smiled. "I'm a policeman."

"Where you're concerned, I don't reckon that would make a whole lot of difference to him."

I rode up to the mansion and ground-tied my horse. Before going up the steps, I walked over to the side of the house and looked at the wolf in his cage.

The wolf, crouched on the ground, watching me carefully, wailed out something that resembled a song, a wolf song, I guessed. I'd never heard anything like it. It was angry for sure, but even more, it was sad.

I walked a few feet closer to the large, oblong cage that stank of feces and raw decaying meat, and I saw that Hanratty hadn't been exaggerating about the wolf's anger, either.

He got up on all fours, let out another terrible piercing sound, and then flung himself at the cage. His eyes burned with the same yellow glow I'd seen that night he'd killed my brother.

His bared teeth dripped with drool, and his entire body trembled as he slammed again and again and again into the wire trying to tear through the wall to get to me. The reverberating wire made a tinny kind of music.

I had my gun in hand and ready, just in case.

"Maybe I'll put you in there with him," said a voice behind me, the words accompanied by the nudge of cold metal against the back of my neck. "What the hell're you doing here, anyway, Chase?"

"Talk a deal."

"Deal?" Reeves laughed. "What the hell's that supposed to mean?"

"Let's go inside and I'll tell you."

He wore a riding costume, a fancy eastern riding costume, one of those things with jodhpurs and knee-length riding boots. He was real pretty.

"You're really serious, aren't you?" he said.

"Yes."

He laughed again. "Then you're a crazy bastard, Chase. A crazy, crazy bastard. Men like me don't make deals with men like you."

"If you ever want to see any of that bank money again, Reeves, you'd better invite me inside."

The wolf was exhausted. He'd spent himself and lay now panting, his entire body heaving with hot breath, and making those funny sounds again.

"Something's wrong with your wolf," I said.

"You and that goddamned Hanratty. The wolf's just got some kind of bug is all. Wolves get bugs just the same as humans. If he was really sick, he wouldn't be able to throw himself against the cage that way."

"Be sure to wipe that mud off your boots before you go inside," Reeves said. "I don't want some hayseed tracking up my good hardwood floors."

"I take it you're inviting me inside," I said, but when I turned around, Reeves was already up near the front porch, as if he didn't ever want to be seen with me, not even on his own land.

I turned back to the keening wolf and listened to his terrible sounds echo off the surrounding hills, like a distress call of some kind that nobody was answering.

"You have two minutes, and then I want you the hell off my property."

We were in his office, the same one where he'd cold-cocked me that day.

"I have your money," I said. He was behind his desk. He hadn't invited me to sit down.

"I'm well aware of the fact that you have my money."

"But I'm willing to make a deal."

"You heard what I said about deals, Chase."

"You get half and I get half."

"I get half of my own money and you get the other half? That sounds like a hell of a deal, all right."

"Otherwise you get nothing."

"We'll see who gets nothing, Chase. This isn't over yet."

I sat down. He didn't look especially happy about it. "You want to hear about it?"

I could tell he did but he didn't want to say he did—he didn't want to give any sign that I was in control here—so I went on anyway.

"You get ahold of Ev Hollister and tell him you made a mistake about me. Tell him that you forgot that one day you hung your coat up over at the Whitney while you were having lunch, and when you got back, you found your wallet missing. The bank key was in there. But while you went to the manager to complain, somebody slipped your wallet back into your coat."

"In other words, somebody had a duplicate key made?"

"Exactly."

"And why would he believe this?"

"Because it's you talking. Because you're a prominent citizen and he'd have no reason to suspect you're lying."

"And for this I get half my money back?"

"Right."

"And what do you get, Chase?"

"I get half the money and I get a chance to ease me and my family out of this town without this cloud hanging over me. I'll buy a farm in Missouri and disappear for the rest of my life with Gillian and Annie."

"Every jailbird's dream."

"I'm tired of your sarcasm, Reeves."

He smirked. "A jailbird sits in his cell and dreams up all these sweet little stories about how good life will be after he pulls just one more job." He leaned forward in his seat. "I should put a bullet in your face right here and right now." His anger was overtaking him now. He started spitting when he

oke. "You've got my money, you stupid hayseed asshole,
d I'm going to take it back and you're going to regret ever
ving anything to do with me."

He waved his hand, spitting and glaring, blood spreading
cross his cheeks. "Now get the hell out of here."

"I figured out a peaceful way to end all this," I said. "I
ought you'd want to listen."

He said nothing. Just glared.

I stood and picked up my hat and walked out of his den
d down the hall, my bootheels loud in the silence, and out
e front door.

I put my hat on and watched the wolf a moment. He was
ll crying, still that high mournful call, and still crouching,
if exhausted—until he saw me . . . and then he was up on
fours and leaping into the air and hurtling himself against
e cage.

"He sure don't like you," an old Indian cleaning woman
id, as she beat a rug against the porch railing.

"I guess he doesn't," I said.

On the way out, Hanratty waved to me and called, "Good
see you're still alive." I waved and rode on.

I just kept thinking of what Reeves had said, how every
ilbird sits in his cell and thinks of how pretty things will be
ter he pulls that final job. Not till the very moment he'd said
at had I ever thought of myself as a jailbird—just as a kid
ho'd gotten himself in some trouble, was all—but in his hard,
tter words I'd recognized myself. And now I felt every bit
e hayseed he'd said I was. Trying to make a deal with him
d been very foolish.

After a few more days, I'd gather up Gillian and Annie and
e money, and in the middle of the night we'd light out and
ver be seen by any of these folks again. . . .

art 25

e rain started just after dinner time. Except for the light in
e saloon windows, the stores and streets were dark as I made

my rounds, trying doors, checking alleys, peering into stora
shacks.

I was starting down Main, past three of the rowdier saloo
when I saw the two drunken miners weaving down the str
toward me. They were laughing and stumbling their way hor
to warm houses and irritated wives and disappointed childr

Then they saw who I was and stopped and one of them sa
"There's that sonofabitch."

"Who?"

"Goddamn cop who was in on that goddamn bank ro
bery."

"No shit?"

"Where they killed the poor goddamned clerk with a go
damned double-barreled shotgun."

"Poor sumbitch."

By now I was abreast of them, making my way through
cold and the night and the lashing rain. They were too dru
to notice the downpour, or care about it, anyway.

There wasn't much I could do about them not liking
the two drunks. I'd planned on taking their abuse and walki
on by. I'd feel sorry for myself a few minutes and then
whole thing would be over.

Then the first drunk hit me.

I hadn't been expecting it and I didn't have time to do ar
thing about it.

His punch came out of the gloom and struck me right
the jaw.

He'd hit me hard enough to daze me. There was pain a
there was an even deeper darkness, and then I felt a seco
punch slam into my stomach.

It should have brought me down, that punch. It drove de
into my belly right below the ribs and it was expert enou
and vicious enough to wind me for the moment.

But then rage and frustration took over. Suddenly this dru
became the whole town, everybody who smirked about r
everybody who whispered.

I threw down my nightstick, not wanting to make this
official act in any way, and without even being able to see y
connected with a strong right to the drunk's face.

"Hey!" yelled the second drunk, as if defending myself was against some unwritten code.

But I didn't even slow down. I just kept punching. I even got a knee straight up between the first drunk's legs, and when he started to buckle, I grabbed him by the hair and started hitting him at will with my right fist.

By now I could see. The guy was bloody, though the rain did a good job of washing him up. He hadn't been intimidated by my uniform, but his friend was. He stood three feet away and called me names.

At first I wasn't aware of the crowd surrounding us, not until there were twenty people or so. They'd drifted down from the taverns, animals who could smell blood on the wind, animals whose taste for violence was never sated, miners, merchants, cowboys, drifters—it was a taste and thrill that cut across all lines of class and intelligence and color. Most men, and a sad number of women, loved watching other men hurt each other.

And I was hurting him, hurting him bad, and I couldn't stop. If anything, I was piling more and more punches into his body. The crowd was with me now, frenzied, caught up in my rhythms as I slammed punches first to the head then to the chest then to the belly, the same pattern again and again. He was bleeding so badly, his blood was flying across my own face.

"That's enough, Chase!"

At first the voice seemed far away and not quite recognizable. Familiar, yet . . .

And so I kept on swinging and slugging and—

And then, too late, I recognized the voice and I saw him, peripherally, step up next to me and raise his own nightstick and bring it down and—

And then there was just the eternal cosmic night, cold and dark, not life yet not quite death, either. Just pain and—blankness.

The crowd noise grew distant—and then faded entirely. . . .

didn't get my eyes open right away. Couldn't. The pain across the back of my head was too considerable.

I became aware that my arms were stretched out behind m
and my wrists were bound together. I became aware that m
ankles were also bound. I became aware of some other pres
ence near me. I had to open my eyes. Had to.

I almost smiled. He was treating me as a respected gues
and he didn't even know it. None of his men ever got to se
the inside of the room where Ev Hollister worked over hi
prisoners. But now Ev Hollister was letting me see it for my
self.

"You were out a long time," he said.

He sat in a straight-backed chair directly across from th
one I was sitting in.

"Afraid I tapped you a little harder than I meant to," h
said.

There were dark brown splatters all over the wall the drie
blood of the prisoners he'd worked over in his time. Ther
were also dents and nicks and small holes in the wall. Whe
he got done punching the prisoners, he sometimes liked t
throw them around the room. Everybody likes a little variet
in his life.

I brought my eyes back to Hollister.

"You look pissed, Chase. Real pissed."

"Why'd you bring me into this room? I'm not a prisoner.

He smiled. It was a drunken smile, pleasing but crooked an
not quite coordinated properly. "You're not a prisoner ye
you mean, Chase. This whole town's just like that miner wh
swung on you. They hate you, Chase, and they hold you re
sponsible for the clerk's death and they're putting a lot c
pressure on me to arrest you whether I've got evidence or no
These are simple folks, Chase, they're not like you and m
with our fine respect for the written law." He tried to smil
about empty, high-minded words, but what came out was
smirk.

I decided I might as well tell him. Maybe it was what he'
been wanting all along, anyway. "I'm planning to clear out i
the next few days. Gillian and Annie and me. Gone for good.

"Well," he said, "now that's a damned sensible idea."

"So all your troubles will be over."

"The next few days?"

"So how about untying me?"

"You and your wife and daughter?"

"Right."

"As far away as you can get with no plans to ever come back?"

"That's the plan."

He stood up. The crooked smile was back. So was the drunken glaze of the eyes. He walked the four steps between my chair and his, and then he backhanded me so hard I went over backward, cracking my head on the floor.

I tried to struggle back up but it was no use. Lying on my back and tied up made me vulnerable to anything he wanted to do. But the fall had loosened the rope on my wrists.

He kicked me hard in the ribs.

The pain hadn't even had time to register properly before he walked around the chair and kicked me hard in the other rib, the one that I'd bruised a while back.

I closed my eyes and coasted on the blackness and the physical grief spreading across my rib cage and up into my chest and arms. Every few minutes, I'd become aware of my sore throat again. . . .

"Where are those two peckers?" he said.

I didn't want to give him another excuse to kick me. I answered right away. "I don't know."

"Like hell you don't, Chase. You stick up a bank with two men and you don't know where they are?"

"I don't. I'm telling you the truth."

"Then you've got the money, don't you?"

"No."

"Bullshit."

"Honest, Chief, I—"

He kicked me again. This was enough to shrivel my scrotum into the size of a walnut and to send tears streaming down my cheeks. The toe of his boot had found the exact spot where the doc had bandaged my rib.

"Where's the money?"

"Don't . . . know."

"You sonofabitch."

And I could sense it, the frenzy, the way I was sure all his other prisoners had been able to sense it. When he was sober, he was a decent, humane man who ran an honest police department and had a genuine regard for the people he served.

But when he drank . . .

This time he walked around in front of me and looked straight down.

"You know where I'm going to kick you this time?"

"Please don't. Please." I didn't care how I sounded. I just didn't want any more pain.

"Then you tell me, Chase. You tell me where those men are and where that money is or I swear you won't get out of this room alive."

"I don't know. I really don't."

My groin wasn't all that easy a target, what with my ankles bound and all, but his boot toe was unerring and he found the spot with very little trouble.

I screamed. I tried praying, but all that came out was curses, and I tried biting my lip, but I bit down so hard I filled my mouth with blood.

And he kicked me again.

Almost instinctively, I kept working my hands free from the ropes behind me. But even if my hands were free, he had a gun and a nightstick and—

"You tell me, Chase, you tell me where those men are and that money is."

My body was cold with sweat. My face was swollen from the punches of the miner. My ribs and groin hurt so much I was starting to drift into unconsciousness. . . .

"I'm giving you five seconds, Chase."

He was raising his boot. He was picking his spot.

"Five seconds, Chase."

"Please, Chief," I said again, and it wasn't even me speaking now, it was the scared little boy I'd been all the time I was growing up. "Please don't, Chief."

"Three seconds."

His foot came up even higher.

"Two seconds, Chase."

Oh and he was enjoying it, seeing me writhe on the floor, hearing me whimper.

"You sonofabitch," he said.

And was just starting to lift his leg when—

Somebody hanged on the door.

"Chief, Chief, you'd better get out here."

He was angry, Ev Hollister was. It was as if somebody had interrupted him having sex at the crucial moment.

"What the hell is it, Fenady?"

"Those two men we been looking for? Lundgren and Mars?"

Hollister's face changed. Anger gone, replaced with curiosity.

"What about them?"

"Somebody found them in a field the other side of Chase's cabin. And brought them in."

"They're dead?"

"Yeah. Back-shot."

Hollister smiled down at me. "Didn't know where they were, eh, Chase?"

This time he didn't give any warning. He just took two steps to the right, where he could get a better angle, and then brought his toe down swiftly and surely into my rib cage.

Fenady probably winced when he heard me scream. Even the cops who hate prisoners hate to hear human beings worked over the way Hollister works them over.

Hollister looked down at me. "I'm going out there and check those men over. When I come back, I want you to tell me what you did with the money after you killed those two men."

"But I—"

I'd started to say that I hadn't back-shot anybody, that Reeves had done it and made it look as if I had, the way he made it look as if my key had been used in the robbery.

But what was the point of talking now? Hollister wouldn't believe me no matter how many times I told him the truth.

He went over to the door, unlocked it and went out.

Part 26

The ropes slid off my wrists with no trouble. But bending down to uncinch my ankles, I felt nauseous and dizzy. Because of the beating, the sickness was getting worse.

Through the door I could hear the commotion far down the hall, in the front office.

As I started unwrapping the rope again, I thought of how long I'd suffered at Reeves' hands. Most of my adult life he'd ruled me in one way or another. I'd been a kid when I helped pull the robbery he set me up for. And now he'd convinced Hollister that I'd back-shot the two men who had allegedly been my partners.

I reached the door, eased it open, peered down the hall and started on tiptoes down the stairs and toward the back door. I reached the ground floor and continued to tiptoe down the hall and—

I got two steps away from the doorknob when somebody shouted, "Hey!"

I turned and saw Krause, a big red-faced German cop, lunging for me with his nightstick.

He swung but I ducked. His stick hit the door above my head so hard that it snapped in two.

I knew I had no chance other than to grab the knob, throw the door open and dive into the night outside.

Krause swore and lumbered toward me, but his jaw intersected with the edge of the door just as it was opening. He was knocked to his knees. I turned around, kicked him in the throat, and then pushed him over backward. As I hit the alley, he was swearing at me in German.

All I could do was run. I had no idea where I was going.

I came to the head of an alley and stopped, leaning out from the shadows to get a look at the street. Mrs. Hollister had pulled her fancy black surrey over by the general store and was watching all the men running in the street. Apparently all the shouting over the death of Lundgren and Mars had brought her out of the house. They lived near the downtown area.

I ducked back into the alley, pausing to catch my breath, then I started running again.

I went two blocks and then collapsed against a building, my breath coming in hot raw gasps.

There was moonlight and the deep shadows of the alley and the sweet smell of newly sawn lumber from a nearby store that had recently gone up.

And behind me I could hear the shouts. "He escaped! Chase escaped!"

They would come looking for me now, the human equivalents of bloodhounds, and there wouldn't be just policemen, but eager private citizens, too, eager for some sport.

I pushed away from the wall and started staggering down the alley. When I reached the last building, I pressed myself against it and peeked around the corner.

They already had torches lit, and they were coming toward me three abreast. They hadn't seen me yet but it would be only moments before they did.

I heard noise at the far end of the alley and turned to find three men with torches approaching. They would see me any time now.

I looked frantically around the alley. All I could find was a large barrel in which the general store threw food that had spoiled. Even on a cold night like this one, the contents of the barrel reeked. In the summer it had been noisy with flies twenty-four hours a day.

I had no choice. I jerked open the lid and crawled inside, hoping that the shadows would hide me sufficiently from the oncoming men.

I sank deep into a fetid, swampy mixture of rotted produce. For a long time I had to hold my breath. I was afraid I'd vomit and the men would certainly hear me.

Their voices and their footsteps came closer.

The two groups met in the alley, near where I crouched in the barrel.

"I never did like that bastard," one man said. "Just something about him."

"Strange is what he is," another said. "You ever get a good look in sunlight at how scarred up his face is underneath that beard? Very strange how a man would come to get scars like that. Kind've gives me the willies.''

"Enough talk," a third man said, sounding important. "You three take the Fourth Street alleys and we'll take Third Street. No way he could've gotten out of town yet."

"Oh, he's here somewhere all right," said another man.

As one of them turned around, he nudged the barrel. I froze. I had the sense that they could all hear my heartbeat like an Indian drum deep in the forest late at night.

"He could be hidin' right here," the man said. "In this alley. Maybe we should check it out before we go over to Third Street."

"Hell, Hawkins, look around. Where the hell would he hide?"

"Right over there in that privy, for one thing."

Another man laughed. "Yep, he's sittin' in there takin' a crap and readin' a Sears catalog."

More laughter.

"Well, it sure wouldn't hurt to check it out," Hawkins said, sounding petulant.

"Be my guest."

Hawkins walked away. Ten, maybe fifteen paces. The privy was right behind the back door of the restaurant halfway down the alley.

"Stick your head down that hole in there and see if he's hidin' down there!" one of the men said, laughing.

There was no response from Hawkins, none I could hear anyway.

Bugs and mites were crawling on me, species that apparently didn't relent in November weather. I wanted to scratch myself but there was no room, and anyway doing so would probably make too much noise.

And then the lid was lifted.

This time my heart didn't start pounding. It stopped.

I sank as far down into the garbage as I could go and watched as a plump white hand dangled over the rim of the barrel.

One of the men was dropping his cigar in here.

"What a goddamn smell," he said. "All that produce."

"Had a little girl in South Dakota who smelled just like it."
The other man laughed.

The lid was still off. The man's hand was still dangling, his
cigar butt looking like a red-eyed snake.

And then he tossed it.

The lighted end of the butt struck me right in the forehead.

The pain was instant and considerable. I gritted my teeth. I
made fists. I wanted to curse. But no way I could indulge
myself.

The lid closed.

Hawkins returned. "Nobody there."

"Gee, what a surprise."

"Well, he coulda been there," Hawkins said.

"Yeah, and so coulda Jesus H. Christ himself."

"C'mon," said the third man. "Let's get moving. I'd like
to find that sonofabitch myself. Show him that without that
fancy blue uniform to protect him, he ain't jack shit."

I waited five minutes, during which time I had a pretty crazy
thought. What if they actually knew I was in the barrel and
had just snuck away a few feet and waited while I climbed
out?

I would climb out of the barrel and they would open fire
and I'd be dead. A nice, legal execution, something to talk
about in saloons and taverns for the next twenty years.

I slid the lid open.

I reached up and grabbed the rim of the deep barrel.

Above me I saw the cold starry sky.

I pushed myself up, tatters of garbage clinging to me, and
started to climb out of the barrel.

So far, so good, but I knew that my biggest problem was
ahead of me.

How was I going to escape a town filled with torch-bearing
posse members?

I scrambled from the barrel and immediately hid myself in
the shadows again.

What was I going to do now?

And then I saw the buggy, the shiny black buggy, and without any thought at all I started running toward it.

Part 27

The Hollister woman wasn't expecting me.

I ran from the mouth of the alley straight at her surrey, my toe landing on the vehicle's metal step while I dove down beside her feet.

She started to scream, but all I had to say was one thing. "If you don't help me, Mrs. Hollister, I'll tell your husband about you and Reeves."

She'd been all set to cry out, her mouth forming an O, but at mention of Reeves the scream died in her throat.

"I want to go out Orely Road, and fast," I said.

She seemed confused, as if she hadn't quite recovered from the shock of seeing me jump into her surrey. But then intelligence returned to her eyes and she gathered the reins tighter, made a wide turn with horse and surrey, and started us on our way out of town. The animal was running at a good steady clip.

I kept watching her face to see if she was trying to signal the men who were running past, sounding excited as hayseeds at a county fair.

The ride, with me all curled up at her feet, was bumpy. Every time we hit a rut, she kicked me in my rib with the pointed toe of her high-button shoe. I could smell horseshit and axle grease. I wanted Gillian and Annie in my arms.

The flickering street lamps fell away after a time, as did the sound of running feet slapping the hard dirt road. Even the high, charged shouts of the eager posse.

After a while I raised myself up enough to look out at the rutted road. Moonlight showed a narrow stage road with ice shining in the potholes, and all around an autumnal mountainous land touched with glowing frost. Bears would be sleeping deep in winter caves by now, and kids would be asking for extra blankets.

I swung up from the floor and sat down next to her.

"H-How did you know about R-Reeves?" she said, and

when she stuttered, I felt ashamed of myself. I had no right to judge this woman the way I had.

"Forget I said anything. I'm not fit to pass judgment on you, Mrs. Hollister."

We didn't say anything for a time. The only sound was the crack of hooves against icy road.

I sat and watched the frozen night go by, the jet silhouettes of mountains against the darker jet of the sky, the hoarfrost quarter moon, the silver-blue underbellies of clouds . . .

"Y-You d-don't know what my h-husband's l-like when he d-drinks."

She sounded miserable and I had to stop her. "I shouldn't have said that, Mrs. Hollister. Really. I don't have any right to judge you."

She started shaking her head from side to side, reliving an old grief. "I'm a s-sinful w-woman, M-Mr. Chase. I'm a h-harlot."

We fell into silence again.

Then, "I t-told him t-today that I d-don't p-plan on s-seeing him a-anymore."

I reached over and touched her shoulder. "You should have respect for yourself, Mrs. Hollister. You could do a lot better than Reeves, believe me."

And Gillian could do a lot better than me.

She didn't say anything the rest of the way.

When the road turned westward, I took the reins from her and brought the horse to a halt.

"I hope things go right for you, Mrs. Hollister. You seem like a decent woman."

She smiled and leaned over. I thought she was going to kiss me. Instead she just touched my cheek with long fingers. Tenderly.

I jumped down and started walking to the edge of the hill, from which I could look down into the valley and see our house.

What I saw was the old farm wagon that Gillian kept in back. It was loaded down with clothes and furnishings. Gillian and Annie sat up on the seat. They'd hitched up the horse and were just now pulling out of the yard.

The sickness was getting worse all the time, but I ran anyway, ran faster than I ever had in my life.

"Gillian!" I cried into the night. "Gillian!"

Part 28

By the time I got near the wagon, it had climbed the hill and was just starting down the road.

As I came close, out of breath, my legs threatening to crumple at any moment, I heard the clang of pots and pans as the wagon bounced along the road.

I fell.

I was twenty feet at most from the wagon, and I went straight down, my toe having stumbled over a pothole.

I stayed on my hands and knees for two or three minutes like a dog trying to regain his strength. The vast night was starry and cold; the clang of pots and pans faded in the distance; and all I could smell was the hot sweat of my sickness.

After a time I got to my feet. But I promptly sank back down. Too weak.

I stayed down till I lost sight of the wagon in the moonlight far ahead. It had rounded a curve and was now behind a screen of jack pines. By this time the clank of kitchen implements was almost endearing, like a memory of Annie's smile.

All of a sudden I was having trouble swallowing, taking saliva down in gulps. Part of the sickness, I knew.

I started off walking and slowly began running. I had to catch the wagon. Had to.

By the time I caught up with them, the fever was so bad I was partially blind, a darkness falling across my vision every minute or so.

This time Annie heard me. She stood up in the wagon and turned around and saw me.

The last thing I heard, just before I pitched forward in the sandy road, was Annie's scream.

Darkness.

Squeak of wagon; clop of horse on hard-packed road; faint scent of perfume in the bed of the wagon.

Gillian.

"You're going to see that doctor in the morning, and I'm going to personally take you."

"I can't see anything."

"You just rest."

"My eyes—"

"Rest."

"Where are we?"

"Annie's taking us back home. She convinced me to give you another chance."

"Gillian—"

"And you're going to turn that money over and you're going to face whatever punishment you've got coming, and then we're going to be a real family for the first time in our lives."

She leaned down. All I could smell in the darkness was her soft sweet scent. She kissed me on the forehead, a mother's kiss.

"Sleep, now. We'll be home soon."

And so the old farm wagon tossed and squeaked down the road, the horse plodding but true, Annie talking to him most of the time, imitating the way adults talked to their wagon horses.

After a time the darkness was gone and I could see the stars again, and I wondered what it would be like to live on one of them, so far away from human grief. But they probably had their own griefs, the people on those stars, ones just as bad as ours.

Part 29

She got me out of my sweat-soaked clothes and put on water for hot tea. She put me in bed and had Annie come in and stand over me while she gathered up more blankets. By now the chills were pretty bad.

"Mommy said that in a little while things will be all right again and you won't be in trouble anymore."

The bedroom was lit by moonlight, and Annie, one half of her face silver, the other half shadow, looked like a painting.

"That's right, honey."

"She said some men would probably come after you. Chief Hollister, she said. "Doesn't he like you anymore?"

Gillian was back with more blankets. Annie helped her spread them over me.

Annie started talking again. I held her small hand in mine and tried to say something in return but I didn't have the strength. My throat was raw, my head hurt, every bone in my body ached, and I was having a hard time making sense of words.

I slept.

At first I thought it was part of a dream, the way the horses thundered toward me from the distant hill. I often had dreams where I was being pursued by fierce men on fiercer horses.

But then I heard Gillian saying, "They're coming down the hill, Chase. The posse."

Instinct took over. In moments I was out of bed, grabbing dry clothes and a jacket and throwing them on, picking up my .45 and a fancy bone-handled bowie knife I'd bought on a lark before going to prison.

Gillian watched me. "I thought maybe you'd turn yourself in, instead of running away."

As I buttoned the fleece-lined jacket, I said "I don't want them to take me into town tonight, Gillian. Not with everybody worked up the way they are. I've seen two lynchings in my life and they were both real scary."

"Where are you going?"

"I'm going to get the money and then wait till the posse leaves."

"But they'll find you."

"Not where I'm going to hide."

The horses were closer, closer.

She came into my arms and we held each other. And then

I took off, moving quickly to the back door. In moments I was out in the cold night again.

I peeked around the corner of the cabin and saw them—
Six horses coming down the dark November wind—
Six riders on the hill, three bearing torches with flames that crackled and flapped like pennants in the wind, and three with carbines already drawn from leather scabbards.

Ready to make the descent, encircle the cabin, and drag me out to meet their justice.

Part 30

The wind was raw as I dropped to my knees up there where the deserted well lay. A dark cloud passed across the moon, and for a brief time all color was blanched from the land, and the rocks and plains and mountains did not seem to be of earth at all, but some strange land from my prison nightmares.

I jerked the lid from the well and plunged my hand down into the chilly darkness below. All I could feel was the cold, empty blackness of the grave.

They would be coming up here looking for me, the posse would. There was only one place I could hide.

I wound the top of the rope tight around one of the large rocks at the mouth of the well. I tugged it several times, making sure that it was strong enough to hold me. The rock must have weighed two hundred pounds. It would be fine. But the rope was frayed . . .

I didn't have any choice.

I grabbed the rope end, climbed up over the rocks around the opening of the well and started my descent, feeding myself rope as I went.

Dirt and small rocks from the sides of the well fell to the water below, making a hollow splashing sound when they hit.

If I fell, nobody would ever find me. I'd hit my head or drown or I'd be trapped down there and freeze to death.

I kept on moving down, inch by inch. I kept thinking of sad Gillian there at the last moment . . . wanting only the one thing

I couldn't give her . . . wanting to be safe from my hatred of Reeves.

There was a sour smell just as I got so low that darkness took me entirely. Gases . . .

Far up above me I saw a portion of the well opening and a piece of cold midnight sky.

I was tightening my grip on the rope when another wave of blindness overwhelmed me. All I could do was hold on and hope it would pass.

And it was there, blind, suspended halfway down a well, that I whispered the word to myself, the word I'd been avoiding the past few days. . . .

Then the voices, harsh male voices on the witch's wind down from the mountains.

Coming up the hill—

Looking for me.

"Here's a well!" somebody shouted.

They would find the cover off and put a torch down into the darkness and find me.

"The hell with the well! Look over there in that stand of jack pines."

This was Ev Hollister's voice. He was leading his own posse.

I went lower and lower in case they came back and looked down the well. They wouldn't have much trouble finding me, if they wanted to look. It was a very shallow well.

The heels of my boots touched water.

I stopped my descent, just hung there listening to the voices of the posse fade in and out on the wind.

Obviously they'd given up; the voices were moving back down the hill, in the direction of the house.

I just kept thinking of that word I'd been so afraid to say the past couple of days. . . .

I felt the top of the money sack.

I grasped it and began to pull it up and—

The rope started to give at the very top.

Even as I hung there, I could feel it begin to fray and weaken.

In a moment I would be dropped into the water and entombed forever . . . terrible fever pictures came to me. I would be prisoner down here forever, till I was only white bones for greasy black snakes to wind in and out of, and for the rats to perch on as, crimson-eyed, they surveyed the well. . . . I felt as if I was suffocating.

Distant starlight in the midnight sky was my only guide now.

I stabbed my heels against the shale walls of the well. Propped up this way, I could at least keep from being pitched into the water.

With one hand dredging up the money sack, and my boot heels digging into the wall . . .

I started to climb.

All I could hope was that Hollister and his men would be gone by the time I reached the top.

I just kept looking straight up at the bright indifferent stars above. In prison I'd read about how many worlds our stars shine on, so many that our little world hardly matters at all.

Even with everybody on our planet screaming, nobody in the universe could hear us anyway. . . .

I knew I was getting sicker all the while, my mind fixing on things like astronomy, my bones and joints aching so bad I could hardly keep a grip on the rope or the sack.

And every few feet the rope would fray a little more and I would feel the tug and jerk as it threatened to tear apart completely . . .

But I kept on climbing.

I have no idea how long it took me.

By the time I reached the top, I was gasping for breath.

I threw the bag over the top of the well first. It landed on the frosty earth with a satisfying thump.

And then I wrapped both hands in the rope and climbed the rest of the way up, cutting my hands on hemp and jagged rock alike, till hot blood flowed from my palms.

But I didn't care. . . .

I lay for long minutes on the hard cold earth. The chill air felt cool and cleansing on my fevered skin.

I got to my feet, grabbed the money sack, and started walking back up the hill.

Beyond the hill were Gillian and Annie. . . .

When I reached the other side, I swung wide eastward, so
I could come up behind a copse of jack pines. From here I
could see the front of the cabin clearly . . . yet I was so well-
hidden that nobody could see me.

Five riders with torches sat horses. The wind-whipped
flames made the faces of the men look like burnished masks.

There was a sixth horse, its saddle empty, standing ground-
tied. Where was its rider?

Gillian stood in the doorway—Annie clinging to her like a
very small child—talking to the men.

Suddenly a man came from the cabin. He was toting a Winchester. He'd obviously been searching the place, seeing if I
was hiding there.

It was Hollister. He got back up on his horse.

There was more talk between the men and Gillian, the words
lost in the midnight wind.

And then they left. Abruptly. Just turned their horses and
headed westward, the light from their torches diminishing as
they reached the edge of the great forest, where they likely
thought I'd gone.

Gillian and Annie stood outside the cabin for long moments
watching the men disappear into the great pines.

And then, just as I was about to call out for Gillian, I felt
the darkness overwhelm me again, felt all my strength go and
my body begin to sink to the ground.

Once again I slept. . . .

Part 31

The prison dreams came again . . . watching the teenager
drown as the old con held him under . . . listening to the
screams of the men as whips lashed their backs . . . seeing a
wolf silhouetted against the full golden moon as he stood on
the hill overlooking the prison. . . .

Even in sleep my teeth chattered from the cold of my skin
and baked in the heat of my insides.

I wanted Gillian . . . I wanted Annie. . . .

And then the scream.

At first I counted it as part of my nightmares. Only when its intensity and pitch were sustained did I realize that it was Annie screaming.

I crawled to my feet, covered with pine, so dry I could barely part my lips. I felt at my side for my .45. Still there.

Annie kept on screaming.

I staggered across the clearing.

The cabin was dark but the front door was flung wide, and there in the doorway I saw him crouching—

The wolf.

His yellow eyes gleamed and across his face were dark damp streaks of—blood.

I tried to understand what had gone on here. . . .

Reeves had come here to get the money and had brought his wolf along with him.

He growled but moved cautiously away so I could go inside.

I went into the cabin.

And saw Annie at the entrance to our bedroom door.

Her flannel gown had been shredded by wolf claws, and she lay bloody and unconscious, half propped up against the door frame, her golden hair darkened by splashes of her own blood.

I stumbled toward her, paying no attention to the snarl and growl of the wolf behind me. I reached the door and looked in on the bed and there—

Gillian had not been so lucky. She had been eviscerated.

The wolf had ripped most of her clothes off and had then torn open her throat and stomach.

I struggled toward her, fell next to her on the bed, felt for a pulse I knew my fingers would never feel.

Gillian—

She looked like a fawn that had been attacked by a ravenous predator, and when I put my fingers to her lips . . . she was already getting cold. I must have been out longer than I realized.

I took out my .45 and went over to Annie.

Beneath her bloody flesh I felt a pulse in both neck and

wrist, and I snatched her up like an infant and carried her in the crook of my left arm.

I kept my right hand free to use the gun.

The gray lobo still crouched in the front doorway. A growl rumbling up its chest and throat. Waiting for me.

I raised my .45, sighted, began to squeeze the trigger, and— He sprang.

He was so heavy yet so fast that he knocked my gun away before I could shoot accurately.

Two, three shots went wild in the darkness, the flame red-yellow in the shadows.

And then the wolf was on top of me, Annie having rolled out of my grasp as I was knocked to the floor.

He was all muscle beneath the blood-soaked gray fur, all madness in yellow eyes and blood-dripping mouth.

All I knew was to protect my throat. Once his teeth or claws reached it . . .

I rolled left and right, right and left, trying to keep him off balance until I could roll away from him completely.

By now I was beyond pain, he had ripped and bitten me so often, first across the forehead and then across the chest, and then across the belly, heat and saliva and urgent, pounding body slamming into me again and again.

And finally I started to feel myself give up. No more strength; maybe not even any more determination. Too much pain and weakness. Overwhelming . . .

And then I heard, as if I were unconscious and dreaming again, a terrified but very angry voice saying, "Leave my daddy alone! Leave my daddy alone!" She was awake now, and had found my .45, which she held up with surprising confidence.

And then there were two huge booming shots in the gloom, and the sudden cry of a wolf seriously wounded, and then the cry of a young child as she collapsed again to the floor.

The wolf, shocked, bleeding badly already from the bullets in his chest and stomach—the wolf began to crawl out the front door, crying so sadly even I felt a moment of sorrow for it.

I slowly got to my feet and crawled over to Annie.

I took her to me and held her, and at first I couldn't tell if the crying was hers or mine.

"I'm sorry I brought all this on, Annie," I said. "Your mother was right. I shouldn't have tried to get Reeves."

But she was unconscious in my arms, and my words were wasted.

And then I heard the wet snort of a horse near the front door.

I lay Annie down carefully, grabbed my .45 and ran to the doorway.

In the moonlit grass before the door, Reeves knelt next to the wounded wolf, stroking the animal as it crouched, growling, at the sight of me.

To Reeves' left his horse stood waiting for him. And then—

Reeves brought his right hand up—

I barely had time to duck back inside before the bullet tore away an inch of wood from the door frame.

Two more shots, quickly. And then silence.

Before I could crawl back to the door frame, I heard Reeves swing up on his horse—saddle leather creaking—and start to ride away.

By the time I reached the door frame and steadied my hand enough to squeeze off some shots, Reeves was fast becoming a silhouette on the hill—fast-retreating horse and rider with the gray lobo running alongside.

I fired twice but only to sate my rage. From this distance, I had no hope of hitting him.

I forced myself to ladle up some water for Annie. The mere smell of it still nauseated me.

I got her on the floor in the kitchen, dragged out a blanket, and propped her head up on a pillow I'd taken from the back of the rocking chair.

Every few moments I felt her wrist for a pulse. I had to keep reassuring myself that she was alive.

I raised her head and gave her water. Her eyes fluttered open but remained so only briefly.

I was just starting to examine her wounds when I heard, on

the distant hill, the sound of a rider coming fast.

Reeves. Come back for the fight that was inevitable.

I kissed Annie on the forehead and then grabbed my gun and moved to the doorway, keeping to the shadows so he couldn't see me.

As I leaned against the wall, waiting for him, I heard Annie moan. She needed a doctor, and quickly. After I finished Reeves . . .

The rider stopped short a few hundred feet from the cabin. Eased off his saddle. Ground-tied his beast. Grabbed his carbine from the scabbard. Crouched and started moving toward the cabin. All this in black silhouette against the silver moonlight.

Pain and my sickness were taking their toll on my eyesight again.

Not until the rider was very close to the door, just now getting his carbine ready, did I realize it was not Reeves at all, but Hollister, who must have doubled back and let the rest of the posse continue on. Good lawman that he was, he'd known that I couldn't leave without seeing Gillian and Annie one more time.

Now I knew how I'd get Annie taken care of.

I pressed back against the wall and let Hollister come through the door. Soft jingle of spur, faint creak of holster leather, hard quick rasp of tobacco lungs, scent of cold wind on his dark uniform.

He got four steps in and saw Annie where I'd rested her on the floor and then said, "My God!"

And set his carbine down on the kitchen table.

And rushed to little Annie. And knelt beside her. And lifted her head gently and tenderly upward so that he could see her face better. He no longer cared about his own safety—he knew I could be hiding anywhere in the cabin, but he didn't care. His overwhelming concern was Annie.

It's a funny thing about a man, how he can be crooked the way Hollister was with his prisoners when he was drunk, but be absolutely straight otherwise. Despite the animal he sometimes became in that little locked room of his in the police station, he held in his heart love and pity and duty, and I was watching all three at work now.

He rested Annie's head again and then started to stand up. I stepped from the shadows, put my .45 on him.

"I want you to take her to the doc. Reeves brought his wolf out here. The wolf has rabies." I paused, wondering if I could actually say it out loud. "And so do I."

"Rabies!" he said. "You sure about that?"

"Yeah, I'm sure. That's why I've been so sick the last few days. One day I went out to Reeves' and the wolf bit me. There's a shot the doc can give her. You need to get her there now, and fast."

"But what about you? Won't you need the shot?"

"It's too late for me. All I'm worried about is Annie here."

We stood in the shifting darkness of the big front room, wind like ghosts whistling through the front door, fire guttering in the far grate.

"That posse'll find some way to kill you, Chase, if they ever catch up with you."

"I know."

"Why don't you come in with me?"

"I want to finish my business with Reeves."

"You keep mentioning Reeves. What the hell's he got to do with this?"

So I gave him a quick history.

"I'll be damned," he said.

"I just want you to get Annie to the doc."

"All right." Then he looked around. "Where's your wife?"

"Bedroom. You don't want to see her."

"The wolf?"

"Yeah."

"I'm sorry, Chase."

"Help me with Annie."

We bundled her in blankets and carried her out in the moonlight to Hollister's horse. He got up first and got himself ready, and then I handed her up. He cradled her across his saddle.

"She's a sweet little girl, Chase."

"She sure is."

"I'll get her to the doc right away."

"Wait here."

I went to the pines where I'd been hiding and got the money and brought it back and then tied the cord to Hollister's saddle horn.

"There's the bank money," I said.

"You're a pretty hard guy to figure out, Chase."

"Look who's talking."

He smiled. "I guess you're right."

I reached up and touched Annie's leg and stood there for a long moment with tears in my throat and a silent prayer on my lips.

And then Hollister was riding off, a dark shape against the moon-silver top of the hill, and then just receding hoofbeats in the night.

Part 32

I took Gillian's horse.

In an hour I slid off the animal and started working my way to the poplars on the west side of Reeves' mansion. There would be an armed guard in those poplars.

The fever was getting worse. Every few minutes my vision would black out again and I'd feel a spasm of ice travel down my back and into my buttocks and legs. Then the dehydration would fix my tongue to the roof of my mouth.

The frost gave the land a fuzzy look, as if a silver moss had suddenly grown over everything. The stuff was cold on the palms of my hands, and when the fever got especially bad, I'd stop and put a cooling hand to my cheek.

From the size of him, I knew the man on duty had to be Hanratty. Reeves probably knew I was coming, so he put his best man on the job. Hanratty had likely been sleeping down in the bunkhouse when Reeves had roused him. Hanratty was day guard, not night guard.

He didn't hear me till I was close, too close, and just as he turned, I brought the butt of the carbine down against the side of his head.

He managed to swear and to glare at me, but then he sank

in sections to the ground. I had nothing against Hanratty, but I wanted to make sure he didn't wake up and follow me into the house. I kicked him in the side of the head. He'd be out a long time but eventually he'd wake up. He was luckier than Gillian had been.

The first thing I wanted a look at was the wolf's cage.

I crept around the edge of the sweet-smelling jack pines for a good look. The cage was empty, its door flung wide.

The wolf was inside with Reeves.

I slipped through the shadows to the Victorian estate house. In the moonlight the cupolas and captain's walk had an exotic aspect, troubling the plain line of prairie and the jagged, barren stretch of mountains beyond, too fancy by half for such a landscape.

I was two steps from the front porch when I saw the man step from the shadows around the doorway.

The tip of his .45 glinted in the moonlight.

I put two bullets into him with my pistol before he could fire even once.

The noise was raucous in the vast prairie silence. The smell of gun smoke filled my nostrils.

Inside, in addition to the wolf, Reeves would have one, maybe two more men. And because of the gunfire, they now knew I was here.

I went around back, dropping to my knees halfway when blackness rushed up and knocked me down. The chills kept getting worse. I threw up, scared halfway through that I was going to choke on my own vomit. Panic . . .

When I was on my feet again, I reached the wide porch that ran the entire length of the rear.

The guard posted there wasn't very good. He was smoking a cigarette and the fire end made an easy target.

I put two shots into his face.

He made a grunting sound and fell facedown on to the porch.

I crouched, moving over to the porch door, got it open and then half crawled up the three steps.

Ahead of me lay the darkened kitchen door. Beyond that waited Reeves. . . .

On my way across the porch, I nudged a chair. The scraping noise could be heard clearly in the silence. The men inside would be able to chart every step of my progress.

I eased the kitchen door open. The scent of beef and spices filled the air.

Three more steps up and I stood in the kitchen. It was long and wide, with a fancy new ice box that stood out even in the gloom.

I got four steps across the linoleum floor when the gunny appeared in the archway leading to the dining room and shot me dead-on in the shoulder.

Pain joined my sickness and spun me around entirely. But as I was spinning I knew enough to put a shot of my own into him. I got him in the stomach.

I beat him with my fists until I knew he was dead. I'd actually done him a favor. Dying gut-shot was an experience nobody should have to go through.

Only as I started walking again did I realize how badly I was bleeding from my shoulder. I almost had to smile. There was so little left of me. The sickness had taken most of me; the gunshot claimed what remained.

I had just enough life left to finish what I needed to finish. . . .

When I got to the bottom of the staircase, my footsteps hollow on the parquet floor, I heard the wolf.

He was crying, and his cry was very much like my own. But that wasn't surprising. We were both dying of the same disease.

I started up the sweeping staircase, grasping my weapon tight in my hand. With the shoulder in such sudden pain, I had to hold my gun very tight.

I reached the landing and stopped, staring up into the gloom above me. No lights shone; not even moonlight lent highlights to the darkness. Reeves had drawn all the heavy curtains.

I started up the remaining six steps. . . .

One, two, three steps, each one an agony for a man in my condition, my legs feeling as if they were weighted down by massive invisible boulders . . .

The gunshot flared against the shadows, there was even a certain beauty to it.

I threw myself on the stairs. The bullet ripped into the wainscoting behind me.

Four, five, six rifle shots cracked and roared and echoed down the sweeping stairway.

All I could do was lie there and listen to them, and listen to the wolf crying all the time.

I tried to remember how much I hated the beast for what he'd done to my brother and to my wife and daughter. And yet no matter how much I hated him, I hated Reeves even more, for what he'd trained the wolf to become.

I started crawling on my belly up the stairs. I didn't have much strength left. I needed to spend it while there was still time.

When I reached the top step, still lying flat, I raised my head an inch and stared deep into the gloom.

Reeves was crouched beneath a large gilt-framed painting of himself. A very aristocratic pose, that one.

Next to him crouched the wolf, eyes yellow in the darkness, the cry still in its throat, forlorn as the cry of a wolf lost in a blizzard some prairie midnight.

Reeves saw me peeking up over the stairs and squeezed off several more shots. Apparently he had two or three rifles with him. He wouldn't need to reload for a while.

A silence, then, as I lay on the stairs, my body trembling from the chill, my throat constricted for want of water.

And then a whisper, a word of Indian I did not understand, the same word used that night when the wolf attacked me in my brother's room.

And then I heard the wolf, his paws scratching the floor as he began to pad over to the top of the stairs, a deep, chesty sound coming from him.

I raised my eyes and looked up directly into his as he lowered his blood-spattered head and prepared to lunge at me. He was still bleeding from the bullets Annie had put in him.

I slowly raised myself to my feet, sighting the .45 on his chest.

And he dove at me, all slashing teeth and furious noise.

He knocked me backward down the steps. My gun had fallen from my hands. I could defend my throat only by keeping my arms folded over my face.

Meanwhile we tumbled over and over down the stairs.

When we reached the landing, he renewed his attack, ripping flesh from my forearms so he could weaken me further and reach my throat. His teeth cut so deep that soon he was gnawing on raw bone. . . .

I was in the kind of delirium—fever, pain, fear, rage—a kind of dream state in which I functioned automatically.

Perhaps this was hell . . . a battle with the beast lasting for all eternity.

And then I remembered the knife I'd taken from our cottage. The bone-handled bowie . . .

Reaching it would mean that I would have to take one of my arms from my face . . . but there was little choice.

I started rolling across the landing, trying to confuse the wolf, trying to keep him from my throat. He kept crying and biting and hurling himself at me—

And as I rolled, I found the bone handle of the knife and yanked the blade free, and as I rolled over once again and saw the beast ready to spring—

I held the blade of the bowie knife up so that when he lunged—

He came in with his head down, teeth bared, spittle and blood flying from his mouth—came in so that he impaled himself on the blade.

It went straight and deep into his chest, and for a moment in his fury he did not allow himself to feel the wound—

He just kept trying to get at my throat, to rend and rip open so that I would look like poor Gillian there on the bed.

But then the pain of the knife I kept pushing deeper and deeper into his chest finally registered—

And he stood on top of me, hot splashing blood beginning to flow from his wound, and he began to cry so loud and sad in the gloom that I had no choice but to pity him. He cried his wolf song of cold icy waters and long lonely hunts; seeing brothers and sisters die in bitter winter; of finding moonlit pond in a midnight forest and sleeping peaceful there; of finding a mate strong enough to follow him into the mountains and bear the offspring who would make them both so proud—sadness and grief and joy and pride, all that and much more in wolf song as the beast stood upon me and I in my pain and sickness and weakness and curious final strength watched as Reeves descended the stairs, wanting to finish me off since his trained wolf could no longer do the job himself.

But when he was halfway down the stairs, Reeves in his fancy ruffled shirt and expensive dark suit, his rifle aimed directly at my heart—when he was about to kill me, the wolf turned abruptly and sprang on him and proceeded to tear and rend in a frenzy so loud and vicious I wanted to cover my eyes.

All I could hear was Reeves screaming and screaming and screaming there in the moonlight of the stair landing. . . .

And when the wolf was finished, he came back and lay next to me, and took up his crying once more.

In some way we are brothers, this wolf and I, lying here dying as the cold dark winds of November whip through this now-useless mansion. . . .

His cry is even louder now, and I wish I could comfort him, but there is no comfort for either of . . .

. . . not for a few minutes yet . . .

. . . not until the darkness.

It is a sunny afternoon and Gillian and Annie are coming toward me on the bicycle, Annie on the handle-bars, golden hair glowing.

And then it is dark and I am looking down at my dead brother in the bed that night and I am wanting to cry.

And then there is a barn dance and Gillian looks so beautiful in the autumn night and—

And then my mother is there, plain prairie woman, plain prairie wisdom evident in her kind gaze, and she puts out her hand so I will not be afraid in these last moments.

Dreams, phantasms, memory . . . all memory dying with me now . . .

Gillian—
Annie—

   And finally the darkness
   the wolf and I
   and the   darkness.

Credits

—

"Trains Not Taken" by Joe R. Lansdale. Copyright © 1986 by Joe R. Lansdale. Reprinted by permission of the author.

"The Alchemist" by Loren D. Estleman. Copyright © 1996 by Loren D. Estleman. Reprinted by permission of the author.

"Sisters" by Marcia Muller. Copyright © 1989 by the Pronzini-Muller Family Trust. Reprinted by permission of the author.

"McIntosh's Chute" by Bill Pronzini. Copyright © 1989 by the Pronzini-Muller Family Trust. Reprinted by permission of the author.

"Between the Mountains and the Sky" by L. J. Washburn. Copyright © 1996 by L. J. Washburn. Reprinted by permission of the author.

"The Wish Book" by James Reasoner. Copyright © 1996 by James Reasoner. Reprinted by permission of the author.

"Red Feather's Daughter" by W. W. Lee. Copyright © 1996 by W. W. Lee. Reprinted by permission of the author.

"The Death(s) of Billy the Kid" by Arthur Winfield Knight.